## About the Author

G J Lewis grew up in Redhill, Surrey. The only child of a war widow, his upbringing was unorthodox and isolating for much of his youth. The house did have an extensive library, but with no books for children, and so he learned to read quite advanced literature at a very early age. His love of history and literature stems from that grounding. He was sent to Balham Grammar School and then attended Gidea Park College. He won a scholarship to art school, but it wasn't possible to take it up. For the most part, he is self-educated.

He was awarded a mental nursing scholarship, but that was ended for him less than a year after it had properly begun, and he left home to join the Navy. After leaving the services, there were many adventures in employment and self-employment and he has now retired; which is the busiest phase of his life! He now lives in Europe.

He has travelled around forty-five countries, at the last count, and sailed five of the seven oceans.

Being a quite private individual, he has only ever written for his own leisure and enjoyment. Much encouragement from those close to him has finally seen his work in print.

# Orestes

# G. J. Lewis

## Orestes

Olympia Publishers
*London*

www.olympiapublishers.com
OLYMPIA PAPERBACK EDITION

Copyright © G. J. Lewis 2024

The right of G. J. Lewis to be identified as author of
this work has been asserted in accordance with sections 77 and 78 of the
Copyright, Designs and Patents Act 1988.

**All Rights Reserved**

No reproduction, copy or transmission of this publication
may be made without written permission.
No paragraph of this publication may be reproduced,
copied or transmitted save with the written permission of the publisher, or in
accordance with the provisions
of the Copyright Act 1956 (as amended).

Any person who commits any unauthorised act in relation to
this publication may be liable to criminal
prosecution and civil claims for damage.

A CIP catalogue record for this title is
available from the British Library.

ISBN: 978-1-80439-772-5

This is a work of fiction.
Names, characters, places and incidents originate from the writer's imagination.
Any resemblance to actual persons, living or dead, is purely coincidental.

First Published in 2024

Olympia Publishers
Tallis House
2 Tallis Street
London
EC4Y 0AB

Printed in Great Britain

# Orestes Crew Featured

| | | |
|---|---|---|
| Bates | Ginger | Seaman. |
| Bob Tideway | Tiddles | Radio or Radar Operator. |
| Brown | Jock | Able Seaman. |
| Charlie | | Torpedo Instructor. |
| Conrad Blinveld | Binny | Able Seaman (Pinger). |
| Curtis | Curly | Cook. |
| Ernie Crouch | | Cook. |
| Graves | Digger | First Lieutenant. |
| Harman | | Radio or Radar Operator. |
| Jay Sudswell | Bubbles | Leading Seaman (Weapons). |
| Jeff Hawkes | | Captain. |
| Joel Skilly | Silky | Engine Room Artificer. |
| John Bishop | | Leading Seaman (Pinger Ace). |

| | | |
|---|---|---|
| Owen Hogarth | Big Garth, Taff | Leading Mechanical Engineer. |
| Peters | Scouse | Able Seaman. |
| Petters | Pet Hulk | Seaman. |
| Phil Green | Shane | Torpedo Officer. |
| Randolph Sanderson | Randy Sandy | Steward. |
| Reginald Grimes | Raging Reggie | First Lieutenant. |
| Simeon | Simmo/Simple Simon | Asdic Operator. |
| Swingle | Creeper | Leading Radio or Radar Operator. |
| Webb | Spider | Battery King. Electrician. |
| Theodore Brooks | Theo | Navigator. |

# Key Submarine Crew

| | |
|---|---|
| Artificer | 'Tiffy'. Chief Petty Officer. Essentially, an engineer without a degree. |
| Battery King | Electrician or Leading Electrician. Looks after the boat's batteries. |
| Captain | 'Skipper'. Commander of the ship. Lieutenant (very senior). |
| C in C | Commander-in-Chief. |
| CME | Chief Mechanical Engineer. Engineer Chief. Chief Petty Officer. |
| Control Room PO | Petty Officer. Any Seaman branch Petty Officer on Control Room watch could be the Scratcher also. |
| Coxswain | 'Swain', 'Regulator'. 'Grocer' or 'Butcher' if dealing with stores. Chief Petty Officer. Leave Supervisor dealing with pay books and travel warrants. The only crew member trained in medical first aid. Butcher might be an Able Seaman assistant for stores. |
| Engineer Officer | Engineer. All mechanical equipment, unusually watch officer if no executive officer. |

| | |
|---|---|
| ERA | Engine Room Artificer. Chief Petty Officer. Five years of specialist engineer training. |
| First Lieutenant | 'Jimmy', from Jimmy-the-One, 'the Jimmy' or 'Number One'. Lieutenant. |
| Hydroplane Operator | Petty Officer Seaman. |
| Leading Seaman | 'Killick', 'Leading Hand' or 'Hookey'. Small circular anchor badge on left sleeve. Any branch. |
| LME | Leading Mechanical Engineer. Leading Stoker. |
| LRO | Leading Radio or Radar Operator. Usually only one on a submarine. |
| LTO | Leading Telegraph Operator. Interchangeable with LRO. |
| ME | Mechanical Engineer. 'Stoker'. |
| Mechanician | Artificer with less training. |
| Navigating Officer | 'Navvy', 'Pilot'. (Plots course). |
| Officer of the Watch | Any of the executive branch (First Lieutenant, Navigator, Torpedo Officer). |
| Petty Officer of the Watch | Seaman, any branch. Usually only two on a conventional submarine. |

| | |
|---|---|
| RO | Radio or Radar Operator. Two on a submarine. |
| RS | Radio Supervisor. Chief or Petty Officer. Responsible for radar and radio transmissions. If necessary, could be an LRO, in which case there would be two of them. |
| Second Coxswain | 'Scratcher'. Usually, Petty Officer Seaman branch. |
| Sonar | 'Pinger'. Specialist Sonar/Asdic Operator. Able Seaman. |
| Sonar Operator | 'Pinger'. Sonar Operator. Two on a submarine. |
| Steward | Only one, serving the Captain meals and drinks. The other officers pay him to look after them, too. |
| Telegraph Operator/ Helmsman | Able Seaman. Could be a Leading Seaman. |
| TI | Torpedo Instructor. Petty Officer Seaman. Weapons branch. |
| TO | Torpedo Officer. Weapons specialist responsible for all weapons, sonar and radar communications. |
| Trot Sentry | Casing Sentry. One duty watchman. Seaman. |

# SUBMARINE

| | |
|---|---|
| Casing | Walkway above the hull. |
| Conning Tower | 'Fin', 'Tower'. |
| Conning Tower Hatch | Possible escape hatch. |
| Escape Hatch | In torpedo tube space or fore-ends. |
| Flag at Aft | Ensign. Mast is Ensign Staff. |
| Flag at the Bow | Jack (Union). Mast is Jackstaff. |
| Fore-ends Hatch | Loading torpedoes. |
| Rear Hatch | Stokers' Mess space. Possible escape hatch. |
| Submarine | 'Boat'. A ship less than sixty tons is a boat. A submarine is much more than that but 'our boat' is a term of affection used by the crew. |
| Torpedo Tubes | Six at the front, two at the rear. |
| Trot | Several submarines berthed alongside each other. |

# Terminology

| | |
|---|---|
| Buzz | Information. Usually, to do with ship's movements or schedule. |
| Closed up | On station. Ready. |
| Drafted | New tour of duty. |
| Drips | Complaints. |
| ETA | Estimated time of arrival. |
| HE | Hydrophone Echo. |
| Heads | Toilets. |
| Homer | Homing device. |
| Inboard | Off the submarine. |
| Jolly | Pleasure trip. |
| Make and mend | Few hours of down time. |
| Motto | The motto of Submarine Service, dating from WW2, was "We come unseen". General Service corrupts this motto to "We come unclean". |
| MFV | Motor Fishing Vessel owned by the Admiralty. Used for ferry duty between Naval vessels. |
| Navigation | Fixings. Points of landmarks. Waypoints on ship's charts. |

| | |
|---|---|
| No. 1's, No. 8's | Uniform, from best to working. |
| Parties | Girls in general. |
| Rabbit | Gift. |
| Read horoscope | To tell what is wrong or what is going to happen. |
| Sneaky Peeky | Undetected patrol. |
| Snorting | Inducting air into boat through snorkel tube raised to surface while dived at snorting depth. Unseen but when at snorting duties, only the top of tube can be seen from above. |
| Tilly | Utility van. |
| Tin fish | Torpedo |
| Tot | Issue of rum. |
| Trap | Pick up. |
| TS | Transmitting Station. |
| Up homer | Visiting someone's home. |

# Prologue

There were thirteen of these Oberon-class submarines built for the Royal Navy. In later years, some were sold to Commonwealth navies and other friendly navies. Of the British ones, two are preserved and on show in naval dockyards.

One was lost.

Nothing official was released about it. The rest were broken up and destroyed. The Oberon-class submarines no longer exist.

All of these Oberon-class submarines were given names beginning with 'O'. Most of the early ones were named after Greek or Egyptian deities or classical characters.

Orestes, from Homer, was the son of Odysseus and Penelope. When Odysseus returned from the Trojan wars and his wandering travels after ten years, he was slain by his wife's lover. Orestes, on becoming a man, avenged him by killing the usurper of his father's kingdom and his own mother.

A classical source says that Orestes was either bitten by a sea snake or was killed by the furies. The furies were classical monsters of the sea.

# Chapter 1

"Land Ho! Port beam," the voice was that of a young man, twenty or so, who just happened to feel in a flippant mood this cold November evening.

"On the beam, a submarine," the same voice continued. Eyeing the dark, slender promontory of land move slowly past them in the night.

The silence was broken by a chorus from three others of the Casing party. "Up the mast, another bast-id," they chortled, emphasising the broken parts of the last word. No one else on the submarine's deck took any notice of the working party's remarks.

The Captain and officer of the watch peered down from the conning tower at the white-topped figures moving around the foredeck casing. The white nylon ropes glistened in the moonlight, the water draining from them in pools upon the deck. The men worked hurriedly to stow them on the hull. Everyone knew exactly what their task was, but the rope was bitingly cold to the hands.

"Passed Rhu narrows, nineteen ten." The pilot heard his breath funnel down the voice pipe, to be distantly echoed back up the tube by the faceless helmsman.

"Permission for Able Seaman Peters to take the wheel, sir," the distant voice came, insistent and clear up the tube. A fleeting picture of the man's face flitted before the Navigating Officer's eyes as he stood there, his own face leaning so close to the voice pipe.

He craned his neck to glance up at the Captain, who nodded. "All right, Coxswain, let him take over, but stand by for an alteration of course."

As usual, the Coxswain was being quick off the mark and eager to relinquish the steering to one of the able seamen. He pulled the white silk scarf a little closer around his neck, tucking it into the anorak. He wished he had worn a nice thick towel like the skipper was just pulling on. He stood there looking at the Captain, wondering just what thoughts occupied that silent figure. He seemed so relaxed and yet an underlying tension was there. It came as a slight shock to hear the rising pitch of the intercom yowl. He had missed the skipper's hand movement.

"Diving stations. Open up for diving," the deep voice trailed away, and the microphone yowl with it.

Two figures with slim white torsos balanced gingerly against the guardrails. The ensign staff was stuck; the long flag post was always difficult to lift out of its socket. From the Bridge, two pairs of eyes watched the struggle. One of the men darted down, lifted something heavy and gave the base of the mast a resounding thump with the object. They both nearly lost their balance as the staff pole lifted suddenly, tottering against a background of streaming white sea foam. A third figure, only just aware of the problem, went racing up the narrow deck ledge to catch hold. The mast was safely held and brought down, leaning inboard.

"As quick as you can, Aft Casing party," the voice carried from the Bridge and was swept past them in the wind. The slender, dark silhouette purred its way down the loch, alone in the rippling, moon-reflecting waters. The bows cleft neatly through them, creating a plumed white crest which arched in a continuous motion around the hull, cascading and dropping smoothly along the curvature of the craft's ballast tanks.

Three very cold figures stood looking down, feet wide apart, hands thrust deep into pockets, clustered around the gaping dark patch of open metal hatch coaming. A white-hatted head danced into view and ducked again in the act of securing all moveable parts for the sea trip. The petty officer who was Second Coxswain, traditionally known as 'The Scratcher', moved a little closer and called down to Leading Seaman Sudswell. "You about finished down there, Bubbles?" he asked.

"Yes, Scratcher, come on down, I'm just securing the masts." The man rubbed his hands together, feeling the water turn to ice on his fingers. The draughts were creeping all around his back and up the bell bottoms of his uniform, blowing like Dante's fury through the casing holes. He crouched down upon the hull, leaning up against the torpedo hatch. Momentarily, the light was blotted out from above as a pair of booted legs dangled and then dropped down beside him.

"Evening, Scratcher," Bubbles greeted the arrival. The Second Coxswain nodded and then tucked his head down, performing the curious shuffling motions necessary to crawl along the hull.

"Clear below," a plummy voice called, and immediately another figure dropped, to quickly disappear, bent double, waddling past the steel bottle group cylinders that braced the hull from its outer casing. The officer and petty officer crawled the whole length of the fore deck, checking that everything was securely lashed and that nothing would rattle when the boat was dived. They worked their way for'ard and, when satisfied, climbed out through the anchor hatch.

The conning tower door yawned wide. The interior void was briefly illuminated by two inhaling red dots. Two men sat huddled among the girded structure, waiting, trying to bring their hands alive, cupping them around the warmth of a cigarette. The brief comforts diminished, hurried away by the wind that fanned up the tower from those white-flecked rushing holes which lay gaping to the sea along the tower base.

More heads leaned in, teeth chattering. The remainder of the Casing party climbed in, spacing themselves around the open conning hatch.

"Casing secure, permission for the Casing party below." The rich tones of the officer were hurled upward at the Bridge, the tones high-pitched to overcome the stinging elements.

"Yes, please," a distant voice replied from high above. One by one, they lowered themselves into the funnel of ripping wind. Feet were feeling out the rungs in haste so as to shift the icy hand grip from one to another on the steel ladder before a foot could find it. Instant relief, to step from that wind tunnel into the bristling Control Room lights and the relative warmth of still air.

On the Bridge, the night closed in around the men. The channel widened, casting the bright clustered lights of shore in sprinkling bands. The business of noting each arrival of rotating flickers of light went on. The azimuth points were recorded and voiced to the chart table, thereby fixing the submarine's position on the sprawling contours of the spread white chart.

Peters, the helmsman, was discussing his adventures the night before in town, with Jennings the log keeper. "Anyway, she took me back to her place, see, and—" He was interrupted by the officer of the watch.

"Captain coming down." The conning tower had someone in it. The noise of the disturbed, uplifted wind increased as a pair of ruffling trousers appeared. All voices stopped.

"Red lighting, Control Room," the Captain, Jeff Hawks, spoke to no one in particular and strode to the Radar. Lights flickered on throughout the room and the white ones went out. A dim red haze pervaded all. Low voices were hard in discussion. The Captain leaned in, peering at the slowly rotating wiper of the radar screen.

"Ron, stick that bloody thing away, will yer; it keeps clouting me round the ear." Peters was talking to Jennings, who eyed the dangling wedge of metal which swung gently on its chain from above.

"No, last time I tucked it away, Jimmy couldn't see it and gave me a right roasting 'cos he thought the main vent was still cottered." He remembered now the fury of the first lieutenant on that occasion of opening up for diving. Curious thing, him getting so nasty about it. Everyone reckoned his wife was giving him the run around at home, so he got back by having a go at them.

The First Lieutenant, Reginald Grimes, appeared at that moment from the Wardroom passage. Following closely was a chief in a red pullover covering filthy overalls. "Stow that cotter pin somewhere safe behind the pipe." The officer smiled and turned to inspect the other main vents.

The voice from the Bridge engaged the plotting table petty officer on watch. He transferred the figures to the chart, plotting another visual fix. "Hey, Jenny." He turned to the steering console. "Go and make some coffee." He grinned at Jennings, who, only too glad to go to the Mess, dumped the logbook in the helmsman's lap and went for'ard.

Submarine *Orestes* slipped through the night, negotiating the channels and keeping careful watch amongst the shipping lanes. *S12* was alive again; her twin diesel engines thundered the length of her Engine Room, reverberating along the narrow passage of deck plates between them. A group of figures in blue overalls stood around the engine platforms, their ears obscured by the bulbous blue ear defenders.

"Engine Room ready for diving," the chief stoker shrieked at the immaculate uniformed figure of the first lieutenant, who had bobbed through the round hatch.

The officer grimaced at him. "Thank you, Chief." He then clattered off down the deck plates to look for himself.

The officer in the red pullover laughed broadly. "You forgot he hasn't got earplugs in," he said, pulled his own pair out of the desk and fitted them in. Now he disappeared under the plates amongst the auxiliary machinery down in the bilges. After some minutes, he appeared and conferred with the officer. Engine Room completed, they continued through the familiar checklist and on to the Motor Room. The whole well-known process, nevertheless, had to be scrupulously followed. No detail could afford to be overlooked. Just one oversight could possibly have repercussions of tremendous importance to them all. The checklist became increasingly covered in blue Chinagraph pencil crosses and ticks, notations and comments.

The white overalled figure of the Engineer Officer stood at the Captain's cabin. He knocked lightly on the door, waited a fraction of a second for the signal, which didn't come, and slid the door open. "The fuel consumption report, sir." He entered the tiny cubicle, barely large enough for two men. He was just as senior in rank, but like all the rest, he gave due deference to the skipper.

The crew were settling once more into the familiar routine of going to sea. The business of all the initial preparations and the coordinated bustle of getting under weigh was over. The first brooding period caused by having to leave relaxed home comforts behind was dissipating.

Leading Seaman Sudswell sat uncomfortably in the curve of the torpedo room hatchway. He shouldn't really have been facing into the Seamens' Mess, and due to the restricting circular space, he needed to lean forward and tuck his head inside as well. Nevertheless, he could hear anything that happened behind him and, if necessary, still reach the intercom microphone by ducking his head back inside and reaching a long right arm upward. The cup of coffee warmed his hands; they were only just beginning to stop that painful tingle from working up top with sodden ropes in the bitter cold. Momentarily, he cursed Ginger Bates, the other killick who was normally the leading seaman of the Casing party. Still, he didn't really think Ginger had fallen under the bus in Helensburgh, presumably dead drunk, just so that he would have to do it. It would be some months, maybe, before they would see him again. There were only a couple of new faces in the for'ard Mess this trip, he noticed. As new submariners just finished basic training always were on their first boat; they didn't quite know what to do with themselves.

Just then, one of the radio operators appeared in the narrow passage doorway. Leaving the door open and sticking his head round, he was greeted with the usual abuse. "Shut the bloody door," three voices chorused.

"It's cold enough to freeze a monkey's nuts," one of them ended the taunt. There was no response.

"Come on, the leading RO wants you in the Transmitting Station," he said to one of the new men, who was in the process of yawning hugely. He looked a bit startled but got up and made to comply. Bubbles decided he had better get it over with.

"Just a minute," he said, looking at the man's name tape sewn neatly above the shirt pocket. "RO Harman, isn't it?"

The man stopped. "Yes, Hookey." The man was eyeing Bubbles' left shirt sleeve, where the anchor badge of authority lay.

"No need for that down here; my name's Bubbles. No need for 'Hookey'. 'Leading Seaman' or 'Killick', okay, but..." He paused and looked at the vacated table. "Don't leave your cup lying there. It only means someone else has got to clear up after you've gone. There's a washing-up bucket over by that battery board; put it in there, okay?"

At last, the door was shut, and the five men seemed pleased about it. It was a fact that the cold air did funnel through the passageways. Some of the men were searching under a bunk or lifting the seat lids to retrieve a favourite shaggy sweater from home, definitely not Navy issue, from a small kit locker.

"What's with the young lad? He seems exhausted," someone asked, tipping his mug and head towards the door after Harman had left. The other newcomer stood apart, concentrating very hard on the sheet of typewritten paper that had been sellotaped to the battery board. He turned and made a gesture that could have been a ring being placed on a finger.

"Ah, newlywed, eh? That explains it," commented the enquirer, grinning widely.

The newcomer turned back to the battery board and continued his study of the submarine's intended programme. No one took much notice of him but Bubbles watched him, noting the almost imperceptible nervous twitch at the corner of the one eye he could see. "You'll find that programme is out of date." He looked hard at the new able seaman. "The rumour is that the Denmark jolly is cancelled, and the torpedo trials have been brought forward," he finished speaking. They were all looking at him now.

"That's a new buzz," somebody said. The Torpedo Instructor had told him since they both needed to know in order to prepare for it, but officially, he wasn't supposed to know yet. He knew damn well it wasn't a rumour.

Bubbles stared back at them. "We wouldn't be opening up for diving if we were going to Denmark, would we?" he asked.

The burly, jovial Torpedo Instructor leaned round the door. "Can I come through, lads?" he asked. With only the slightest hesitation, he opened the door wide and shut it firmly behind him. At least they appreciated the formality. A lot of the petty officers didn't bother.

"This is the Captain speaking." The whole boat was filled with the metallic voice from the loudspeakers. "I'm sorry to have to tell you, but Captain Submarines has told me that the flag showing pleasure trip to Odense will have to be deferred." The master intercom switch was still held down and during the pause, the frequency oscillated higher, picking up the engine's vibration. "We are proceeding to Arrochar to commence torpedo trials. This, as you know, was scheduled for after Christmas, but the Calibration Team are much in demand. There are other technical difficulties, but the crux of the matter is that we must fit into their schedule. I would like to take this opportunity of welcoming the new members of the crew. You will, however, need to fit in quickly, since we have an extensive programme. That is all."

The mood in the for'ard Mess was sombre after this announcement. They were back, brought crashing back, to the realities of being at sea. Events would fall quickly into routine.

The doorway suddenly seemed darker, and the small pane of glass at the top allowed little light through from the passageway. A very light drumming tap heralded the arrival of Big Garth. The monstrous figure squeezed through and stood hesitantly, blocking the passage. "Can I borrow a quarter of tea, lads?" the big voice in muted Welsh tones matched his frame.

"Yes, 'course you can," Bubbles replied.

"Won't Coxswain give your Mess any?"

"Well, Grocer says he gave us a quarter last month between the sixteen of us, and that ought to do. Wanted to know what we did with it, he did."

Hogarth stood there grinning genially; the tea packet dwarfed in his hand. "Told him we got two new stokers, and like you got to welcome them with a cup of tea." He stood looking a little abashed.

"Thought you only drank whisky," one of them said, and they all laughed. Hogarth was known for his capacity to put away the amber fluid.

"Sit down, you chump. Have one with us." That was Spider, the battery king. Bubbles watched warily to see just what would happen. Instead of the expected hostility, the electrician poured a cup from the big metal teapot.

The main intercom clicked on. "First Lieutenant speaking. We will be diving in one hour. At that time, we will go to diving stations again. From now watch diving, Red Watch close up. The immediate amended programme is as follows…"

Everyone listened to the dull-voiced monologue just long enough to know what would be happening of short-term importance. They knew that a new typewritten sheet would appear shortly to replace the old one, which now lay crumpled in the 'gash' bag; they would learn the rest when it was pinned up. Soon, they were animatedly talking above the droning voice, kidding each other or recounting recent achievements ashore.

Theo Brooks, 'Navvy' to everyone outside the Wardroom, was glad to get back into the Control Room. His cheeks felt suddenly flushed, coming into that red, warm glow. It was bitterly cold up on the exposed conning tower; he knew that if he clasped his hands together, they would probably stay locked. The radio supervisor was grinning at him from the chart table. He was holding out a steaming cup.

"That's very kind. Er, thank you. No." The Navigator hesitated. He didn't want to offend the man, and he would dearly have loved to clasp it between his frozen hands but he hadn't been able to overcome the immediate repulsion at the thought of drinking from another man's cup. The thought crossed his mind that his upbringing hadn't equipped him to deal with others at this human, personal level. Would he ever get used to it? But really, he knew he didn't want to. The Control Room petty officer had turned away, poised over the charts. He was sipping from the steaming froth.

"I'll be going to the Wardroom soon. I just want to check our position." The Navigator's remark seemed to have worsened the insult.

"I've already worked out the ETA, sir, and that was your last fix." The man had tucked his bristly chin into the clinging roller neck of his submarine jersey. He wasn't looking at him.

Lieutenant Phillip Green sat as far away from the Wardroom door as it was possible to get. The chintzy curtain draped across it prevented the worst of the draught, but this was going to be a busy night. It kept opening and closing.

"Steward!" He voiced the word in rising tones, not quite shouting. "Two cups of coffee!" Brooks looked like death warmed up except for the two bright red cheek patches. They looked so alien in the rest of his face. Still, he would avoid that thumbnail character evaluation of the man for this evening anyway.

He considered why they were going to do night fixings. It was most unusual, but the skipper hadn't deigned to inform them yet. Well, he would have to soon; after all, he, the Torpedo Officer, had to know, didn't he? The steward stumbled in, finding it awkward to manoeuvre around the sliding door, over its sill and through the curtain whilst both hands were holding something. He was muttering under his breath. He deposited the two cups on the table, none too gently, and went to retreat.

"Sanderson." The Captain blocked the Wardroom passage. "If you have any left, I'd like a cup, please, and ask the engineer to join us, will you?"

He brushed aside the curtain and held it back for the steward to exit as he stepped in. Sanderson turned, heard the curtain drop behind him and disappeared.

"Now, gentlemen, the plans for this evening." The officers slid further around the table to make room for him. Lieutenant Hawks glanced at them. "The Electrical Officer is on the Bridge," It was a statement.

"Torpedo trials, gentlemen." The Captain drew a sheaf of papers from the much-battered briefcase and, with arms resting on the single table, glanced at each of the officers in turn around it. He returned his scrutiny to the papers, waiting for the engineer. The curtain rustled and a figure in a red pullover squeezed himself onto the remaining bunk space and replaced the curtain.

"Our trials have been brought forward for planning reasons which need not concern us." Jeff Hawks glanced once, quickly, at the curtain. It remained still. He knew well that no one would dare to loiter in the tiny passageway outside, and even then, the cold air rushing through from the Control Room hatch and down that passageway would make it virtually impossible to eavesdrop. Nevertheless, the Captain had a cautious nature.

"Something rather special here. A new box of tricks for us to practice with." The head looked up from the papers and directed its glance at Phil Green, the Torpedo Officer. "Your department, Phil."

The cool eyes were sizing him up, noting for a brief moment the thin, sleek yellow hair. A thought flashed across the Captain's mind. The crew called his Torpedo Officer by the nickname 'Shane'. He conjured up the film character played by Alan Ladd and hoped indeed that they hadn't sent him a cowboy. The Captain continued, "As I understand it, this new box of tricks is to be the latest line in guidance devices, presumably for the torpedoes."

The Captain hesitated, thinking that he really knew little more than that, but it lay upon his shoulders to stress the importance of it here. "Naturally, we are the only ones to know anything about this. Strictly no information to the crew. Discourage any questions. This is to be considered a normal torpedo trials training session, preliminary to our full work-up to squadron strength."

All five heads were alert, upright and now gazing intently at Lieutenant Hawks. He glanced at his watch. "We will rendezvous soon. Again, gentlemen, it is significant I think that we carry out this exercise in the dark, reduces the possibility of prying eyes. I am informed that the direction sonar for this device will be given to us later. I don't know why but apparently, it is known as 'Penguin'."

A packet of cigarettes appeared with its distinctive blue band and the initials 'R. N.' emblazoned on its surface. The red flame of a match flickered, and the Captain inhaled; the chin jutted slightly to force the issuing smoke upward. "We will be given a full brief by a gentleman from the Portsmouth weapons establishment. His name is Gray, and hopefully, he will be with the trial party. We will be carrying out a firing run before picking them up."

Once more, the wristwatch was consulted. The coffee cup vapour rose in a swirling mist, briefly encircling the watch, to drift on upward.

# Chapter 2

The crew were at diving stations. They each had a designated station, except for the new men. The Coxswain hadn't yet found time to fit them into the Watch Bill. They just sat in the Mess watching, listening, feeling out the unfamiliar, and waiting for the new sensation of a first dive.

Bubbles sat perched on the arm of a torpedo loading beam. It was a comfortable position with his feet jammed against the fin of another tin 'fish' in the lower rack. From here, he was high enough to see everything that went on inside the torpedo compartment, still be able to reach the microphone if necessary, and at the same time, see through the round patch of light into the Mess. It was at eye level now and he could clearly see in. The other torpedomen were sitting on the lower tier, except for Jock, who was polishing a copper pipe in the corner. Everyone reckoned that Jock Brown hadn't done the submarine course. He was just sent off somewhere for six weeks with a duster and can of 'Brasso'.

Bubbles watched him for a moment, seeing the shoulders heave with the effort and apparent dedication he was putting into the simple task. No one ever told him to do it; he just did. One of those blokes who didn't want to be idle, not even for a second. He didn't want to think, that was the real reason. If he had time to think, then it would be about Glasgow, the slums and his childhood, and about his wife.

Once or twice a year, the lads would get together and throw a dance or maybe just a booze-up in some Helensburgh Hotel. The whole crew would turn up, or at least forty to fifty of them. How many others, he wondered, had noticed that Jock never brought his wife? Everyone brought a girlfriend or the wife. One or two had been known to bring both. Nobody mentioned it to Jock if they had noticed. He was a handy bloke with his fists, and you got the feeling that the inevitable wheel spanner tucked into his jeans might make a good weapon if he was roused. Everyone was a bit careful around Jock.

The Klaxon sounded twice, signifying they were about to go down. It startled them in the fore-ends. Jock actually stopped polishing for an instant.

The sound which affected them was the rush of air from the tank deep under the deck plates. The Kingston valve would open, hissing, creating a fine misty spray and Q tank would flood.

*The main vent chief was a bit quick off the mark today,* Bubbles thought.

The two new faces, perched on the edge of the locker seats, were wide-eyed at the gurgle of rushing water in the pipes along the hull interior. Bubbles had sat just like that himself the first time and maybe the second as well. The angle wasn't very steep but with all the accompanying sounds and the vibration, it seemed like it was. The torpedo fin started to rattle under his feet and he could feel the tension in the metal.

It was funny, he thought, how much you took for granted being on a level plane until you weren't. He supposed it was quite natural to sit there wondering if it would come up again. He looked down the front end towards the tubes and saw the Torpedo Instructor standing and watching the clinometer. Really, he was just being efficient, doing what they were all there for and ready to spring into action if things went wrong. If the hydroplanes failed, he would have that changeover control as quick as you like.

The boat started to even up. It was quiet now the flooding had stopped and the air was no longer escaping along confining pipes. It was warmer, too, but not in the huge area of the compartment for'ard. The torpedoes held a shroud of beaded water, like sweat.

The steward barged through the accommodation door, still mumbling. Now he was inside the Mess, the door closed, he could articulate his frustrations.

"Bloody Shane, I'll screw his bleeding little neck for him one of these days," the voice trailed away.

There was no real venom in the statement; Bubbles knew that. It was just Randy Sandy's way. He wondered why a man like him should have chosen to take up that way of life. There was absolutely no servile fibre in his body. Funny-looking cove, too. A big hook nose, invariably red from drinking, once they had been in some port for a few days. Always a scruffy-looking type was Sandy, with a mop of hair placed across the top of his head as though it had just come off a pineapple. This display of agitation was the usual performance from him when he finally finished his work. Maybe he was entitled, being as he never got finished till around eleven or midnight. Still, he got more sleep than the skipper. Randy Sandy was the only one on board who could get a full night's sleep at sea.

Sandy was talking to the two new men, and since everything had begun to quieten down, they were thawing out. At least one of them was, he seemed quite unconcerned at the clicking noises which emanated from the hydraulic system. He was returning to normal, beginning to accept it all as a natural way of life. The other one, Simeon, the able seaman who had so meticulously studied the ship's programme, was hearing Sandy talk, but all the time, his eyes were roving as though searching out the noises. Bubbles watched him closely, unobserved from his lofty perch. That nervous tick was playing around the eye again, and he wondered if he had always had it. It didn't necessarily mean anything; after all, Bishop, who had arrived to take over Ginger Bates' job, always gave the impression of being a shell shock victim, permanently in the circus clowns' last act. Bishop was just highly strung and very intelligent with it. Just a natural-born court jester. Maybe it was the same with Simeon. He would need to talk with him when there was time.

"Action Stations, attack teams close up. Torpedo tube crews close up." The staccato broadcast was short. It was the voice of the First Lieutenant, 'Raging Reggie', as he was beginning to be called. It seemed as though Reggie was feeling the strain again. Where the hell did he think the torpedo crew had been for the last half hour? It didn't seem they were going to let anyone have time for a quick cigarette tonight.

The preliminary business of loading all six tubes was completed, made slightly easier by the fact that all the 'fish' preps had been done that afternoon. The tubes were being flooded up now, with Jock on one side and Peters on the other. He was a bit slow for somebody who was supposed to be a physical training instructor. That was how Peters thought of himself anyway. It was true; he had requested and been accepted for the physical education school, but he would need to move a bit faster when he got down there.

Lieutenant Green, or 'Shane' of the long yellow hair, had agreed to Sudswell's suggestion that it might be a good idea for the two recent arrivals to watch the proceedings. Bubbles waved to them that they could come up close behind the tubes once loaded. He warned them to stay on the hatch platform while the crew were actually loading or moving the monsters about.

Meanwhile, Shane and Charlie, the Torpedo Instructor, were in a huddle off to one side. Shane was trying to listen for instructions through the headset whilst Charlie was telling him about the disappointingly poor show of Brussels sprouts he had been able to grow this year.

The top row of red lights came up on the console between the two rows of tubes. It was time for someone to get up in the hot seat. "Do you want me to do it, or are you going to let someone else have a go?" Bubbles was talking to thin air. Charlie was enthusing about his carrots. Sudswell climbed up into position and sent his return sequence to display a set of red buttons in the Control Room. Almost immediately, the second row came up.

"Bow caps," he flung the words over his shoulder. Charlie had stopped talking.

The levers moved forward and the thrumming sound terminated in a final thud. He had lost count; were there five or six? A quick visual check, all six indicated open, levers forward. "Bow caps open."

"I feel like a test pilot up here," said Bubbles, watching the lights.

"Don't be silly; where are you going to get one this time of night?" Charlie was enjoying one of his chortling laughs at his own joke.

"Are we going on lights or verbal instructions?" Bubbles didn't want to be too flippant at this moment. It was all right laughing until something went wrong, and he didn't trust little Alan Ladd down there with the long hair and headset. He couldn't hear him anyway. He was too busy listening to the running dialogue of the attack team down at the other end of the line.

"Firing pins out, ready all tubes." Bubbles couldn't take his eyes off the panel now, or he would miss it. One, two and three came up. That wasn't normal, he hesitated. Usually, only two at a time went.

"Fire one, two, three!" He recognised the voice behind him; already, it was being drowned by the whoosh of air thumping behind the tons of steel. One and two went from the Control Room firing position, but number three solenoid stuck. The torpedo didn't go. He felt the first half inch of the lever travel in his right hand and pulled it through the rest of the way, all the way back. The tell-tale hiss of venting air gave him the necessary hint and he released.

"All pins in," he reported and in the same instant, the board went dead, all lights extinguished. Bubbles climbed down from the seat. There would be a long wait until the next run. Charlie was already closing the empty tubes' bow caps and still talking about his vegetable patch back home. Shane was listening in on the headset. At the same time, he was aware that the TI was still mouthing words at him in a continual flow, gesticulating and smiling, obviously warmed to the subject of his produce. The lieutenant would have liked to shut him up, which would have been easy enough to do. After all, he, Phil Green, was the officer here and, therefore, in charge of the loading arrangements. The truth was that he knew quite well that it would be a mistake.

Not many of the crew knew anything about Shane's background or that he was still a very new boy to submarines. He still smarted a bit at the memory of his first arrival on board and the long, long wait alone in the Wardroom. This Captain, such a taciturn sort of man, was sitting quietly in his cabin, reading Shane's naval record. When, finally, he had been summoned, it had come as something of a shock to be told in no uncertain terms that Lieutenant Hawks wanted only first-class submarine officers on his boat and that he had better shape up fast.

He remembered the incident well, that which had caused this dark cloud to hang so threateningly over his career. The Admiral's youngest daughter was, of course, quite well able to look after herself, and she had definitely fancied him. The whole mad-cap adventure had gone undetected for some months, and they had made a lot of fun together, getting drunk and haring off to some lonely beach. Normally, if things had run their natural course, it would have put an absolute seal of approval on his career. Admiral Samuel Thanet would have seen to that. The car crash had finished all that, and them both being drunk at the time had not helped. She was a pretty girl, and even if he hadn't been serious himself, she would have made a good wife to someone. Now, she was in a wheelchair for life and his career was blighted.

Since then, he had gone from one ship to another, and each time under the cloud of another dismal report. Irresponsible and undisciplined, the words followed him everywhere. No Captain would endure him on his ship for long. They didn't want his stain on their record, so they got rid of him. An adroit word in the right ear, a telephone call or two, and he would be packing his bags again. The last one, of course, had been really clever. 'Has all the potential qualities for Submarine Service.' Those bold black words on the paper had been like a hammer blow to him at the time.

He had taken the bull by the horns and requested to see the Admiral to discuss this final seeming backstab. So far as he could see, being sent to the Submarine Service was like being hidden in some murky backwater to stagnate for all time. The admiral would not see him, but at least Shane's very long and complaining letter had been passed on. Shane had thought long and hard about the resulting meeting. He had been summoned to a back room of a not-too-well-known hotel called the Astoria in the dingy west side of Glasgow. *Very unusual this,* he had thought at the time. There were certainly no naval installations, establishments or the expected normal functions of the service in this area.

The orders had been well authenticated and specific, so he had gone in civilian clothes to meet the two men. This, too, had come as a surprise to find one of them at more or less his own age and the other possibly only five years older. Reasonable enough this, but he could never face considering that ginger-haired and stubbly-chinned character to have had any connection even in a remote sense with the RN. It had been put to him at that meeting that Shane could consider himself on special liaison duty to submarine *Orestes*. He was left in no doubt that his career was under a cloud and that Admiral Thanet was quite prepared to shove him under. However, he did have specialised knowledge, which was needed. That is of sonar equipment, and this was his opportunity to work his way out of the mess he had got himself into. The lilting Welsh voice had seemed so out of place, both in the frame of a short, squat and quite untidy man and also with his, Shane's, and the other younger man's clipped and precise English accent.

After the meeting, Shane had given it some considerable thought, knowing that he had, by that chance of fate, been caught up in something larger than he was aware of. It troubled him, not knowing just how involved and in what. He was to become an intelligence stooge but would not know at what level for some time to come. It was obvious too that this new sub-commander, Hawks, regarded him merely as another recruit, a new torpedo officer albeit with a clouded past. Jeff Hawks had made it quite clear, though, that he did not intend to fob him off to some other commander. He would make or break and had just that simple option.

Shane came back to the present, realising the earphones had been dead for some time. The Torpedo Instructor was pointing upwards, a little darting motion of a big finger. Shane lifted the headphones.

"Going up," said Charlie. Shane hadn't heard the 'Surfacing' broadcast. He made his way along to the Control Room, fast. It was his turn of duty on the Bridge and there wasn't time to dress for it.

The submarine lay still in the torpid quiet at the centre of a lonely loch. The night was close around them. Only vague distant spots of light reached across the expanse of moody black water, spots of warmth emanating from far away hillside houses.

The scientists came onboard, scrambling from their ramshackle wooden jetty, up the slippery ballast tanks and trying to retain a firm hold of the briefcases and rolls of paper under their arms.

The conning tower door swung open to greet them. Their camel hair duffel coats did not protect them as well as they might, and proved something of a hindrance in climbing down the vertical steel rungs to the heart of the submarine. The figures in coats glanced around them, blinking at the subdued red glow of the Control Room. They shuffled in relaxation of cold tensed muscles. They were greeted and ushered into the close confines of the Wardroom, glad to be out of the blast of cold air sweeping along the passageway. The Wardroom table was a scrambled jumble of papers and trace records. All the seats were filled, and they were jammed together like sardines, the air thick with blue spiralling cigarette smoke.

Mr Gray, a short man with a distant, bemused expression constantly lurking about his face, was brought for'ard to the Torpedo Room. No introductions were made. The torpedomen knew that this was highly unusual. The boffin was setting up his monitoring equipment, looking like so many radio spares, and was now apparently going through some complicated procedures in a torpedo warhead. This had never happened before. Still, they had got used to the possibility of unusual occurrences in this service. It would have been pointless to ask questions; they knew it and kept quiet.

This was the first brief respite in which the non-duty crew could at last enjoy a cigarette. A third of the crew were still closed up at their stations, waiting for the orders to get under weigh and start again the whole long process, which would culminate in another mock attack and firing run.

The next single torpedo firing run was carried out. Most of the crew knew little of the details. They went about their duties, waiting for that final crucial shudder through this living steel cylinder, the signal to tell them that the fish had gone. Those who were close to the for'ard end could hear the tell-tale whoosh of air blast into the tubes forcing several tons of metal thundering out of their steel silos.

In the Control Room, the figures were still, monitoring the submarine's progress and watching the onboard computer assimilating details of the torpedo run. Soon, it would be time to surface and analyse the results. Stretched, worn faces glared at their instruments, the seconds ticking by endlessly between muffled yawns. It was three o'clock in the morning, but no one slept, not even the steward.

The pieces of the jigsaw fell into place. The boffins were reasonably happy with their results, but to be certain, they wanted to do another run. This would confirm the errors in the guidance system, which they had deduced, but they needed to be quite sure before their full written report went in.

It was regrettable, yes, but unfortunately, they must catch the nine o'clock train. Yes, they were expected in London tomorrow evening, and there was more work waiting in Portsmouth. Mr Gray, however, would be staying.

The scientists collected their long streams of paper rolls and their briefcases and went back to their recording shack on the wooden jetty, which jutted as though floating in the middle of the Loch.

By six o'clock, the third firing run had been completed. All for'ard tubes were empty, and now *S12* nudged her way on the surface towards the concrete jetty complex at the head of the loch.

The intercom crackled. "Do you hear there? First Lieutenant speaking. We have accomplished three splendid runs today. Well done, ship's company. It's a good start, but we have six weeks of hard work ahead of us," the voice droned on.

Some of the men who knew they would not be required in the next few hours began to unzip their sleeping bags, hoping to grab a few hours of rest before the next hectic day. Overhead, the voice continued, "We will remain opened up for diving, and in view of that, we shall go to Anchor Watch."

There were a few groans in the for'ard Mess since this meant that more of them would need to stay awake and would probably get only two or three hours of sleep. "The Tenders will be alongside at 0800, and we will take on some electric torpedoes, sailing on completion around mid-day. That is all."

"Could be worse," Bubbles stated to the Mess in general. They were tied up alongside the jetty now, and the Mess was starting to fill. Bishop had just come in from topsides, having gone up there directly from the Sonar Room, suffering with what he called 'Pinger's earhole'.

Bubbles continued, hoping to ease the tension, "We might have stayed at Watch Diving, you know." Nobody answered; they were all climbing into their bunks.

"Yes," said Bishop, "and we might all have been summoned to dance round the maypole in tee shirts and wooden clogs." Bishop, twitching at both eyes now, heaved himself into bed, fully clothed. "With bleeding dandelions in our teeth," he muttered and lit himself a last cigarette before sleep.

Bubbles had a discussion with Charlie in the fore-ends, pointing at the last few tin fish in their racks. Charlie went to see Shane. Shane went to see the First Lieutenant. He didn't know what type of torpedoes were coming on the tender. He went to see the skipper. Leading radio operator Swingle was sent for and told to send a signal. The skipper informed the 'Jimmy', the second in command. The Jimmy informed Shane. Shane went to see Charlie, and Charlie had a discussion with Bubbles.

"We'll leave it till they arrive," Charlie told him.

"Well, why don't we shove this lot up the spout, leaving the bottom two tubes? That way, we can save time tomorrow." Bubbles knew that this was going to be a continual repeat performance during the next six weeks and nobody was going to get much sleep. However, if they worked now and could get rid of the whole torpedo consignment early, they could get back into base earlier and load the next consignment. The end result being to get up to that hotel up the road for a few pints.

"Well, that's up to you; I'm easy," said Charlie, shrugging his shoulders. He then disappeared through the hatch on the way to his own Mess. Jock didn't mind working, and Peters didn't get asked if he minded. The three of them began rigging the loading wires, turning out the suspended steel beams and started the heavy work of dragging the long steel monsters out to the centre of the compartment. They had loaded two, clipped the tube rear doors behind them, and were sweating quite freely by now when Charlie reappeared. He had difficulty getting through the hatch, probably because he couldn't steady himself with his hands. Three frothy-headed glasses of lovely, cool brown fluid were grasped firmly by the handles in each hand.

"Here you are, lads," he said, placing them carefully down. It didn't take them very long to finish the beer, but it was enjoyed and provided a welcome rest. This was not a usual thing, but a good boss would let his men know that their efforts were appreciated in some manner such as this. Of course, nobody ever said so in so many words, but it was understood. They also knew that the fact of being given this one pint of beer each was a form of self-sacrifice. The chiefs and petty officers were allowed only two pints each on any day at sea, and of course, it had to be paid for. In a day that might well be crammed with activity, a pint or two in the evening was something to look forward to and not something that was given away lightly. They realised that this was two days without those comforts for Charlie.

"Bit of luck, we'll get a run ashore tomorrow," said Jock. It made a change to see him sitting still.

"Tonight, you mean," Peters had said something useful instead of the usual long stories about his conquests.

"Right, let's see if we can keep this effort up today, and we'll have a torpedomans' sods' opera at the Anchor Hotel later." Charlie seemed pleased with his idea.

"As long as you don't bore us with how long you can grow your rotten carrots." Bubbles was smiling, taking the sting out of the remark. They all laughed and got on with the task. They still had time for an hour's sleep. The torpedo tender was late.

Breakfast, as usual, was a noisy and hurried affair. There were only four tables and seats for as many at each. To do this, each kit locker with its padded top had to have its hinged flap erected. Once they were up, anyone still in the bottom tier of bunks had to stay in his 'coffin'. You couldn't force your way out with a few twelve to fifteen-stone men sitting six inches away from your face. Once a meal was over, the utensils would be cleared away and ironically, there was always someone waiting to sit down and have his own meal.

Bishop, who occupied one of the middle-tier bunks, decided it was time to get up and swung his feet out accordingly. Unfortunately, he wasn't quite awake yet and lowered himself gingerly into somebody's bacon and fried eggs. He sat there on the edge of the bunk, sleepily rubbing his eyes and waggling his toes in the sticky yellow stuff.

"Hey, that's my breakfast." The speaker had a very gravelly, deep voice, as you might expect from a very hairy-chested and muscle-bulging wrestler. Nobody knew if Petters, the huge hulking figure with a soggy breakfast, had ever been a wrestler. However, he did look the part, and as someone remarked, they were likely to find out soon.

John Bishop looked down nonchalantly at the square-headed Petters, knowing he wasn't dealing with a super intellect here. "Aw," he said quite casually, "what did you do that for? I'll have to change me socks next week now." Having completed the statement in a very relaxed drawl, he grabbed his boots and flashed across that and the next table like a bolt of lightning, disappearing completely from view.

The astounded Petters was still assimilating the words into his head. It was only just dawning that he had been insulted. "Give him mine," a sleepy, thick voice came out of Sudswell's bunk. He was still trapped in his coffin and wanted another two minutes prone rather than breakfast.

"Here you are, Pet." A hand appeared with a spare breakfast. This was definitely the best way to shut the 'Pet Hulk' up; he liked his food.

The tender arrived alongside. They heard the boat's single screw churning up the water as it approached and the clunk against the steel hull as it settled into position. This was the signal that Bubbles had been waiting for, and the time had come for him to force the tired body out onto the floor. On a normal day, he would be preparing the fore-ends to receive the arriving tender load of torpedoes but the work had been done the night before. Apparently, the Torpedo Officer did not know this.

Shane chose this moment to arrive, pushing the connecting door wide and admitting himself into the Mess. He stood there, still with his cap on. Everyone in the Mess stopped what they were doing and looked at him.

"Sudswell, I'd like a word with you. The rest of you, out." He glared round at the men, and especially at Brown and Peters, who only now were emerging from their bunks. Without another word spoken, all the others filed out.

The two stood facing each other, and the officer glanced at his watch. Bubbles decided to hold his peace until he knew what was coming, although it was pretty obvious. He debated in just a split second whether to forestall the recriminations and read Shane's horoscope for him instead.

"I expect you, as a leading seaman, to set an example to the men," Shane paused, waiting for the effect of his words to strike. The other face remained quite expressionless. "Furthermore, as Leading Hand of the Mess…"

Bubbles cut him short, "Look, sir." He stressed the 'sir' a little wearily and rather slower than he had intended. The fact was, he was finding it a little difficult to repress the anger. "I expect you to knock before you come in. Also, it is customary to remove one's cap when entering. Furthermore," it occurred to Bubbles that he was mimicking the other's form of words, but that couldn't be helped now. "Furthermore, I don't need to be told how to do my job. I'll be in the fore-ends doing just that when you send the Coxswain along to charge me." With that, he turned and stepped through the hatch. Already, he was thinking about the day's work.

Charlie was deep in conversation with Shane, who was getting redder in the face by the minute. Here was Shane being told off twice in one hour, and what was galling was that they were both junior to him. This would not have happened on a ship, and he wished he was back in General Service now. The trouble was that he knew that they were right, and he was accustomed to thinking that an officer was always right when dealing with 'inferior' (lower) ranks. The Captain didn't like him either, so in the face of the forces against him, there wasn't a great deal he could do.

Something inside Shane stirred, but he couldn't yet grasp what it was. He heard Charlie out, listening to him this time and noting that this man knew how to handle a delicate situation. Without meaning to, he admired the way he had been admonished, but it was cleverly done. The lecture had stopped.

"This time, I will accept what you say, but I will not be spoken to in that way again. Do I make myself clear?"

The imperious tones had crept in again. "Excuse me, I have work to do." It was like water off a duck's back to Charlie. Shane could go and boil his head for all he cared. Who needed him anyway?

The loading went slowly. There were some delays and the inevitable hitches, but one by one, the new aluminium torpedoes' slim shapes slid down the rails. None of the loading crew had seen this type of fish before. They were gingerly lifted on the hydraulic winch, expertly manhandled and eased into position on their assigned racks. Shane made his appearance later and stood non-committal, well to the back of the platform, watching all and saying nothing.

This was a slow, wearying business. Each torpedo, when touching the loading rails, had a tendency to lurch forward and down since it was extremely difficult for the winch aligner to calculate at exactly what point the weight would be taken off the winch wire. Once inside the compartment, the torpedomen completed each torpedo's transfer from rail to stowage in a well-practised manner. All the hold-ups and the most dangerous were in that vital stage at the top of the rails.

Shane decided to take himself up onto the casing in an attempt to expedite matters. He stood and watched. The three civilian seamen hauled on their ropes to persuade the metal load to settle in the correct attitude. It became obvious to Shane, before very long, that one of these men was not as well-versed in the procedure. His torpedo tail line would go slack at precisely the wrong moments. It occurred to Shane that the man was not unintelligent. He could tell that in the way he moved, avoiding the various jutting protrusions in the boat's hull, there was a light of knowledge in his eyes. He had not spoken at all during this process. Shane decided not to interfere. He knew that it would be a tricky business attempting to correct the man's lapses by talking to him about it. These civilian seamen would not take orders or instructions from the ship's crew. He had heard plenty of embarrassing stories in the past to confirm this. As Shane watched, he grew aware that this particular man, with a distinctive shock of blond curly hair, was also the one who seemed to have taken on the duty of uncovering each silver tube from its protective sheath whilst onboard the Lighter in preparation for its coming across. He seemed to be intensely interested in the mechanisms along the warhead, as well as the circular inset transducer heads. It was as if he was taking mental pictures and of course, all of this equipment was new and rather hush-hush.

A sudden flash of insight came to Shane at that moment, and he took a solid, involuntary step forward before he could stop himself. For one suspended moment, he remained poised there in mid-balance while his mind flashed back to the interview in that back room of the Astoria Hotel.

The Welsh-lilting voice had been specific. "Watch and report. Do nothing out of the ordinary." The image of the interviewer's stubbly face faded from Shane's mind. He bent forward and down and began to tie a shoe-lace that had not needed it; no one seemed to have noticed his peremptory moment of startled action. After a moment or two longer, he turned slowly and made his way to the conning tower door.

The Captain listened and sanctioned the signal to Box Ten. To Shane, of course, it was meaningless. 'Box Ten', he wondered what that was. For the moment, he would let the matter rest. Jeff Hawks made a mental note to get official clarification of the business from Captain SM3's office once they got back to the depot ship. Perhaps the security clearances for the civilian dockside loading party had not been as scrupulous as was necessary.

All the torpedoes were in and the procedure was completed by midday, just as the lads were beginning to drift into the Mess for the cook's speciality of the day. Irish stew with Irish rock dumplings, as someone was heard to observe. There was time to grab a half-hour's sleep, too, before the boat sailed once more for another onslaught into the torpedo range. The normal and expected broadcast was made, informing everyone of what they had already gathered, that they were going to sea and, as practically everyone chorused throughout the boat, "To fire electric torpedoes!"

Amongst the stokers in the after-ends of *Orestes*, there was a poker session in progress. This bunch of men were fortunate in that they had a close-knit community with pretty much the same tastes. They all enjoyed birds, baccy and booze, to a greater or lesser extent according to each man's needs, but not necessarily in that order.

They all reclined in diesel-covered overalls. All were originally blue but some faded almost to white, while the not-so-fortunate were clad in a more traditional dark blue. It had become rather a matter of prestige to own extremely faded, albeit artificially faded, monkey suits. It gave the casual onlooker a certain hint as to seniority amongst the engineering fraternity. The fact that the impression might well be false had nothing to do with it, as far as they were concerned. It did destroy the intended image of uniformity, after all, and nobody wanted to look like the bloke next to him. Also, possibly, the brightly coloured rags tied 'Tex Ritter' cowboy-style around the neck might also assuage this need for individuality. It was considered natural enough because they did have dirty jobs, and as everyone knew, a stoker needed to clean his hands on something before he rolled a fag or made yet another pot of tea for the 'syndicate' back aft, that is, the Stokers' Mess.

A few of these derring-do sorts who weren't due on watch for a while yet had shed the top half of their boiler suit; the sleeves needing to be tied around the waist to prevent the bottom half from falling down. There they sat, side by side, scrunched up alongside each other, waiting for the play to continue. Most of them sported the odd tattoo, or even three. A few had motifs on their arms, like 'Mavis loves Herbert'. A number had the traditional favourite of a sword and entwined serpent with the single word 'Mother' stencilled below. Others favoured the full torso spread of a ship under sail and the slogan, 'Rule Britannia'. Normally, the word had two tees and one enn. 'Pinky,' the tattoo artist in Portsmouth, was notorious for his lack of spelling skills.

At last, the tea was coming. The after-ends watch-keeper was getting very slow, as though he had better things to do. Never mind, they'd had a quite enjoyable afternoon cruise. It would have been pleasanter, perhaps, without all that banging up at the sharp end of the boat. Never mind, the stokers had seen them safely through another day and back into port. The broadcast system was switched on. Oh, yes! Their favourite executive officer was about to make another speech.

One or two managed bravely to stagger into their suits. There was going to be night leave. Some of the crew wanted to catch up on the lost night hours of sleep, but in that case, the long humdrum routine would continue without a break. This reasoning caused many to forego the needed rest and go in search of some pleasant diversion. After all, they could sleep when they were old.

For the torpedo crew, the day had not yet finished. The Tenders were coming alongside yet again. Not until they had been emptied and the contents neatly tucked away could they think about a good old booze-up.

# Chapter 3

The leading cook and his assistant cook were not so pleased that evening. They had not been able to use the proper heating equipment in their Galley. The day had been spent in messing about; what with diving, surfacing and going down again. It was definitely all done on purpose to make the cooks' lives more difficult, or so they persuaded themselves. The Galley's range took a lot of electrical juice, and that was okay while the diesels were churning the generators around. While dived, those monsters had to be silent, and then everything was powered by batteries. There were long banks of them stowed beneath the accommodation deck, running the whole length of the submarine with various manipulative connections. Rules were rules, however, and the Galley machinery took too much power. Like it or not, the crew would get a mostly cold supper.

Ernie Crouch, the head cook, liked to be thought of as a chef, and so did his sidekick 'Curly' Curtis. Everyone was always getting on to Curly about finding strands of his hair in the food. After many years of these repetitive taunts, Curly became quite sage since he was completely bald.

In order to make cold food more attractive, the cooks spent a lot of time over it, and for sixty-eight men, that meant most of the day. One thing you could say about Ernie and Curly, they did turn out an appetising product most of the time, given the right materials. Today, they weren't pleased. Nobody told them what time the boat was getting in or that there would be leave. Here, they were stuck with about forty suppers because that many had decided shore leave was of paramount importance.

"Right, Curly," said Ernie, "never mind the clearing up. Just nip down the fridge and get the bacon out for tomorrow, and then I'm off ashore." What was good enough for the boss was good enough for Curly.

Bubbles and his work crew had the Mess almost to themselves. There were only a couple of the duty watch sitting around now. It was a good opportunity to catch up on personal washing. Everyone seemed to keep a polythene bag in his locker, which would grow fatter and longer until, eventually, it took over all the space in there. Either that or some of it got washed at the end of a week, just the essential items. Everyone lived in the same top clothes nearly all the time if it was a short trip.

With the Mess so empty, the three fore-ends men had the luxury of taking their time with the food. It was tempting to have another. There were still four or five suppers tucked away in a table locker. The temptation was resisted. Some of the lads might fancy it when they got back, if any were still capable, that is. Ernie used to leave his Galley open at night during times like this, but the Coxswain didn't like it. He had to do the food accounting, and it was traditional for coxswains to get mean about it. Bubbles was thinking about just that, but as he said to the others when they were talking about it. "You've got to see the 'Grocer's' point of view. He can hardly go up to the Jimmy and say, 'We'll have to go back into port now 'cos the food's run out.'."

The torpedo loading crew were so relaxed now, especially after eating and they all felt too tired to really be bothered about going ashore. Still, they knew they had another hard day's work tomorrow, and then another, and again the day after that. John Bishop had put their tots of rum safely away where he had said he would. Sipping it now made all the difference. It was going down a treat, warming up the places that mattered and driving the tiredness out of the body.

"Right, that's it then," said Jock, "I'm off." They walked along the concrete, feeling the strange hardness of unmoving Terra firma. The boat, just lying there dark and quiet, long and sleek with its black tower jutting into the evening sky, looked lost and deserted. They were glad to turn their backs on it for a while. The dockside meshed cages and padlocked doors confined them to a narrow track, twisting around corners of red brick buildings. The dockyard copper stood by the open wire and steel gate. His hands were clasped firmly behind his back, waiting for the stragglers to saunter through.

"Anything on in town tonight?" one of them asked.

"You're about the fifteenth bloke to ask that," was the reply.

"No, it's pretty dead up there, except for Saturdays, of course. You want to go up there on Saturday. Some of the locals get their fiddles out and have a bit of a sing-song on Saturdays."

The dockyard policeman stood at his gate, teetering on his heels and watching them as they strolled out onto the road to disappear up the hill, remembering the old times. Well, he'd seen plenty of these young lads come and go through here. There was quite often a submarine up here, doing just what they were. *Did them good to get a bit of fresh air,* he thought. Of course, he had seen it all before. Used to be in them himself, he did. *Smaller than these boats,* he thought. Good days they were. Back in nineteen thirty-four, he had joined his first boat and remembered it well. They served in T-class or A-class boats then, of course. There was 'Chalky', 'Woody', not forgetting Sparky Parsons. Good days, in the memory, so it seemed to him.

It was cold out. The policeman stamped his feet and then turned to go back into his little wooden hut with no door. That was so he could see anyone who went past, but by God, it did let the cold in. Still, his cup of thick brewed tea stood atop the bulbous-bellied iron stove in the centre of its concrete floor. He nodded at the seaman chappie huddled close up to the fire, his hands thrust out over it. Glad of a bit of company he was. Shouldn't really allow anyone into his box, of course. He was on duty, making sure no unofficial persons came in. This bloke was all right, though. Had seen him himself earlier on. One of the civilian loading crew for the torpedo lighter. Pleasant enough bloke to talk to. Yes, he liked to have someone to talk to about the old days. These young submariners now didn't have it tough like it was in the old days. The two men sat on their wooden bench and raised the steaming tea cups to their lips.

Some of the new equipment had come in during the day and then, even in the dockyard copper's own shift of duty, well, it was interesting, to say the least. This young chap with the unruly shock of curly blond hair seemed to know quite a bit about it himself. Talking made the shift watch go faster, so it felt like. *Where's the harm in discussing it,* he thought. Bloke's got the right security tags, after all. Didn't know about any Box Ten, though. Well, he had counted in twice that number himself, from memory, like. Couldn't answer that one.

It really was quite cold, and already a light frost was forming on the grass. Bubbles knew it was going to be very cold later when they were on the way back. They wouldn't feel it, though and so it didn't matter that they hadn't bothered to bring jackets. This was a long, hard walk over the open gorse land, but it was good just to feel free in the open, wide spaces. The feeling palled after a while as the chill crept in, and the effects of the rum wore off. The village lights were in view now, and it wouldn't be long.

It was only a hamlet, really, although this was the main part, where the single road ran through it; all the same, one or two fabulous big houses stood up on the hills. Each one was architect-designed to an individual style that showed there was some money in this sleepy place. Further on up the hill, they came up onto the main road. It was much wider, and the buildings were definitely more functional and commerce-orientated.

The hotel stood alone and grand, adjoining another main road intersection. If the fine furnishings and full-length carpet, along with the crystal chandeliers, were ignored, it was possible to think they were back on board. They knew just about every face in the place since it was occupied mainly by their crew, this side of the mahogany bar anyway. The room was buzzing with conversation, including exuberant jokes. The mood of the crew had softened; they were determined to take life lightly and one step at a time, even if those steps were hurried. The room was so big that it accommodated them all and even left a space at the bar.

"What'll it be, Jock, Scouse?" Bubbles was ordering. Already, Scouse Peters was eyeing up the barmaid; his eyes were positively twinkling.

"How's about a short for starters." Jock was eyeing the long line of bottles behind the bar.

"A Scotsman, oh lovely!" The blowsy barmaid, her face shiny in the close atmosphere, was beaming at Brown.

"Thought the English had taken the loch over." She was smiling. "Got to be a whisky for you, love?" Jock nodded, looked at the others and ordered three doubles, smacking his cash down on the bar.

Bubbles looked at the beer dotted about in clusters of glasses along the counter. "And three chasers – pints." He was pointing at the best bitter tap with a painted picture of a little old man in tartan on the pump. "Youngers."

Already, they were beginning to feel light-headed. After a couple more, they wanted to sit down. Looking around, they could see that others had the same idea.

"What's the lounge like, darling?" Peters was still trying. She was moving fast behind the bar, filling one order after another. The crew was thirsty.

"Through there," she told them, pointing with her elbow. The hands were too busy pulling pints.

Strolling past the opened lounge door, the first thing they saw was Bishop slumped back in one of those awful tall-backed spindly chairs, which had an ornate curved finish at its top. His feet were stuck out under the big round table, its dark-hued top littered with bottles and half-empty glasses. He was holding what seemed to be an animated conversation with the only other figure at the table. Theodore Brooks, the Navigator, reclined in a very comfortable-looking armchair. The discussion stopped, and Bubbles could have sworn the jaw dropped a fraction at sight of them, but he had recovered quickly. John had merely lifted an arm in greeting, but the lieutenant made as if to stand up, thought better of it and acknowledged them with a "Good evening".

*Lieutenant Brooks certainly looks the country squire,* Bubbles thought, and smiled at him. "May we join you?" he asked, risking the expected peculiar look from his two companions. It was an attempt to observe the niceties which might let that poker back relent, and it worked. This man belonged to the fishing and hunting set, or more properly, the genteel pace of country farming for gentlemen. Bubbles wondered why he had chosen this life.

John was talking, "I'll have a Campari on the rocks, a twist of lemon and crushed cucumber, laced with brown sugar – just a dash of bitters."

"You'll have a brown ale, same as you got there." Jock was stumbling off to the bar and then remembered, turned and looked at the Navvy, quirking an eyebrow in enquiry.

"I'm quite happy with this, thank you." He had done it again. Theo looked at the man's frown and saw he had been antagonised. Jock went to the bar and stayed there. Peters hesitated and went with him. Bubbles sat in one of the hard-backed chairs. He hadn't bothered to dress up since he never did. John and himself wore old shirts and jeans with a pullover. His own jeans were pretty filthy and not normally acceptable wear for going out in, but then, this was an out-of-the-way little place. Still, he thought better of putting himself in one of those nice brocaded armchairs. John was cracking some subtle joke and the Navvy seemed to be getting the point quite nicely. He sat there as though to the manner born, in a tweed hacking jacket, striped shirt and tie.

Upon their arrival in the lounge, a middle-aged couple got up and sauntered out. He looked the retired Colonel type, and she must at least have been a Duchess by the looks of her. Her neck was smothered in tiers of jewels, and in her ears dangled matching glittering fobs. Her green taffeta evening dress rustled as she walked, and a lot of heads turned to look, although she looked straight ahead, ignoring everyone. The hotel had suddenly become rather uncouth. Bubbles watched them depart and could see them outside the bay window. They were obviously exchanging angry words. They disappeared, and a minute or two later, a bright green Mercedes purred off up the road.

John was talking about dogs and horses now. The Navvy seemed to know a lot about them and was actually relaxing. Bubbles went for the drinks: a pint of tartan, a brown ale and a double gin fizz. The tall blond barmaid was not rejecting the insinuating remarks whispered by the Liverpudlian. She giggled a lot, and Bubbles could see that Scouse Peters had spent quite a bit on whatever it was she was drinking. He was making a hard pitch anyway. Jock was bored and looked likely to depart for the other bar shortly.

The drinks were deposited on the table, and the seat resumed. The Navigator was far away in a distant land, sitting right there talking about Labradors and breeding them, how they had to be looked after. Out of the corner of his eye, Bubbles saw movement and realised it was Shane heading this way. He hadn't even known he was in the room.

"Lieutenant Brooks." Shane stood at the table. "I think we ought to be getting along. I think it was nine o'clock, wasn't it?" Shane was looking at his watch. John hadn't moved, still slumped in his chair.

"Going to a party?" he enquired.

"The Captain has asked the officers to join him at The Captain's Table." He referred to a little pub down in the village. When naming the place, the owners must have had a certain clientele in mind.

"That's ironic, isn't it?" John didn't like the look of Shane very much.

"That was very enjoyable, but do excuse me. See you tomorrow." Theo Brooks had made his excuses and was once more the figure who didn't quite seem to fit into any group. The two officers left immediately. The lounge door opened fractionally, and a deafening roar emerged from the saloon bar. The stokers were apparently in their cups and having a good sods' opera. The sound of singing was gradually becoming louder. More people were leaving the lounge bar, some to join in the merry-making, but a lot more to resume the quiet life beside their own fireplaces.

"Right, we'll have another one," John was slurring his words, and his eyes were not exactly glazed but somewhat glistening. All trace of the nervous twitch had long since departed. Peters was a little annoyed at their arrival beside him. He thought they were going to queer his pitch with the dolly blond barmaid. In fact, she was a bit bored with the 'Physical Training

Instructor Officer' and his last attempt to swim the English Channel. She eyed these two up speculatively and wondered if they were three of a kind.

"Are you two his lifeguards then?" she asked.

"No, I'm the helicopter pilot, and this is my boot-black." John wasn't really interested, but he thought he would play along. It wasn't long before she was a bit drunker still and confiding in them her secrets whilst on a working holiday in America the year before.

"No, seriously, I was driving a truck," she was telling them, and they had to believe her because she was a big girl. She had been down to Greenwich Village, and there were all sorts of funny types down there. She could hardly repress the giggles at all now. She knew a few racy stories as well.

Bubbles decided the night was still young, and he wanted to go down to the dance at Inveraray that she had told them about, even if it was twenty-seven-odd miles away. Bubbles just felt like dancing and having a bit of fun. Well, she wanted to go dancing as well, but she wasn't going to go without John. So, John, who wasn't much bothered one way or the other, had to go as well. She would be finished work in half an hour, and they would all go in her car.

It was such a difficult decision. She just couldn't make up her mind what to wear, so John had to come along to her room in the staff quarters to pick out a dress for her. Bubbles stood out in the car park; he had located the blue MG and found it unlocked. After five minutes, it got a bit chilly standing, so he got in and pressed the horn twice. Since there was only one light on overhead in all the similar room windows, he knew that was the one. It was a good thing he was watching the lighted window, or he might not have seen the keys come sailing down into the car park, the message clear.

Driving along the deserted road in the chilly night, he was surprised just how quickly he covered the distance he had walked earlier. He could see the still, silent submarine nestled up close to the jetty, dwarfed by the tall buildings. He was glad he didn't have to go back yet. It was nice just to be on his own, cruising along in a borrowed car and taking in the night air. The whole forbidding complex of brick, steel and wire fences was left far behind. He felt clear-headed and alive; all the old tiredness had vanished. There was a lot of road to roll over if he was going to make it to the dance, but she had said it wouldn't end until two or three in the morning. It was early yet and so very peaceful, just mooching along, getting the feel of the car, and seeing the road's twists and turns unfolding beneath the wheels. The night seemed endless. The road was empty; no cars passed him by, and he felt that the whole world was asleep. Only the tall trees flashing past beside the road and the sometimes-glimpsed loch reminded him that this moment was real. Every village and hamlet was so quiet and deserted; the sounds of the car reverberated from the buildings, and the only lights were from the headlamps.

After what seemed an eternity, the long, low shapes of buildings appeared, grouped together to form a suburb. He was nearing the town. The hall was alive with lights and moving people, creating a sudden and exuberant charge in the atmosphere. Bubbles parked the car and joined them, alive to the music which enticed him in. For such a sleepy town in the middle of nowhere, the place teemed with restless people who danced and mingled in search of some new excitement. For him, the feel of such a large room filled with strangers gave him the freedom to participate without involvement. A sense of belonging to the place and time without the need for responsibility. A moment for relaxing amongst people, and yet no demands could be made upon him.

There were plenty of pretty girls around and they brought brief tinges of jealousy to him because of their carefree happiness and the apparent loose-knit mood they were in. Some were free, and some were not. He danced with some and not with others, feeling no need to communicate, no need to pursue, only the fleeting pleasure of untangled, meaningless and momentary acceptance of their company.

Only one appealed to him at the deeper level, someone he might like and who attracted him at the same time. Partly, he enjoyed her company because he knew that she was married, that her husband was here, and that, therefore, there was no pretence and no effort required. They talked and sometimes laughed, but the laughter was lost, drowned in a sea of aimless laughing faces. It was late and there was hardly a sober one amongst them. Bubbles was intoxicated himself by the effects of the drink and the drain on his reserves of strength. The long-postponed tiredness crept up to overtake him.

The girl was talking, reassured by his presence, probably equally glad that the moment was transitory and pleased for a respite from domesticity.

"I have two children." She was smiling, looking pleased with herself, waiting for the expected reaction. She had the slim figure of a young girl not long left school. She knew that and waited for the compliment to follow. Bubbles looked at her, finding it difficult to know what she said. She misconstrued the meaning and wondered if she had made an invitation. Somehow, she had said it in an apologetic tone.

"I don't care," he said, and somehow, at this moment, the realisation came to him that he really cared about nothing. He could not really see any clear plan for any meaningful future. Perhaps because his past had been tainted already, therefore no clear insight for a happy future with anyone else. Her eyes were wide and blue, deep in vague surprise. She was trying to understand but couldn't see his reasoning. What had she said? She wondered what could have triggered such a response. Their lives were too different, and so they parted. The baffled, silent sadness of each went with them.

The automatic reactions of past experience and the minimum of awareness brought the car and occupant back down the winding road. The light of the morning spread with the promise of a new, bustling day. The car was placed a little unevenly back in its previous parking slot. The quiet of the morning became more apparent with the terminal sound of the closing door.

Bubbles walked back along the dew-laden grass, feeling the tiredness flow around him and the vital body heat diminishing. The cold was biting through him. As he neared the loch head, he saw a strange huddle of a dark patch embracing the wet grass. On nearing, it took a recognisable shape. Bubbles stood and looked down on the cramped and sleeping steward. Sanderson lay, his cheek pressed close to the earth, oblivious to all, the long, hooked nose red still from the effects of alcohol. The coarse bunched hair, which seemed to flop in all directions, was covered in a fine layer of glistening light. He must, then, have been here comatose for some many hours. The dew had saturated his clothes, and a fine spider's web tracked from the unmoving elbow to earth. Bubbles, tired though he was, stooped and began to drag the body upright. In vague complaint, the man protested but finally came awake enough to assist his staggering companion towards the submarine.

Many sad faces, slow-moving and pained, proceeded to cope with preparations for sea. The pressure of work made it necessary to ignore discomfort, and slowly, the faces began to adjust. John Bishop returned, practically the last to do so, and announced that he was engaged. This came as no great surprise to those who had known him for some time. John always seemed to be getting engaged.

The calibration team arrived onboard with barely time to spare before they sailed. Some of them had been travelling up by train overnight, but the equipment was already waiting by the jetty, brought there by the chosen civilian dockside workers brought in, especially for that purpose. They had the tags to prove necessary security clearance. The fore-ends torpedo crew gave a hand to bring it all in and assist with its setting up. Within the hour, the submarine was ready to sail, moving slowly at first with the cautious, low-powered thrum of her engines. The sleek, dark shape slid its way through the still waters out to the centre of the loch to commence another day's work.

# Chapter 4

The communications rating sat hunched at his desk. The stinging rapid succession of morse sound flashes penetrating deep into his ears. His gaze was intent on the transmitter/receiver before him, one hand ready to tap a response if necessary, the other feeling for the slightest movement in signal strength on his dials. Even as he rested lightly on his arms, he did not see the mass of dials and meters in the large cabinet to which he ministered. His mind's eye 'saw' only the message that came into the headphones. He did not even feel the fly which decided to explore his hand.

Another naval rating walked briskly by the table, a clutch of blue printed papers in his hand. The red-bordered word 'Secret' stood vividly out from the blue. His highly polished shoes momentarily scuffed in his haste upon the white marble textured expanse of floor. A frown crossed the face of the young lieutenant at another table further down the large hall as the noise momentarily disrupted his flow of thought. The messenger did not knock; merely pushed on the huge oak-panelled door and entered, walking briskly towards the double-tiered desk. He glanced briefly out on the panoramic sea through the high bay windows, their leaded panes seeming to enhance the blue empty expanse of sea behind them.

"Are those the reports from the Scottish sector?" The blond, close-cropped head did not look up as the staff officer glimpsed the blue sheaf of papers.

"No, sir, Home Command ship displacement assessment for next month." The messenger paused to straighten the blue denim sailor's collar, which somehow had ridden up on his shoulders.

"Scottish sector intelligence reports are being decoded now, sir." The sailor finished his report, laid the batch of papers down, waited for only the briefest of moments for a response, and then turned to retrace his steps.

Somewhere close by in that vault-like room, a telephone buzzed, barely perceptible, but its position was marked by a gently pulsating red light the size of a sixpence above it. Another uniform-clad figure moved to answer it, pencil poised above the pad, which always hung from a point close to any phone in this labyrinthine complex. Two senior ranking officers stood talking in the corner of the room; their eyes calmly fixed on a wall-drop map of the world's land masses. At present, they were interested in an area above Central Africa.

"How the devil did these arms get into Chad?" The tall, grey-haired figure pulled at his earlobe in an absent-minded, pensive movement. The heavily ridged brow thickened to a deeper frown.

"Siegfried reports from Ankara that the Soviet track mission to Ilmor has engaged several launches, ostensibly for a fishing trip." The second man was reading this information from the top sheet. He flicked through the others in a quick assessment of their relevance to the discussion at hand. The older Commander stopped playing with his earlobe for a moment. His face split into a grimace-like grin.

"Comrade Sobalatov may be fishing further afield, eh, perhaps Libya?" His face softened into a kinder resemblance of a smile.

"Very convenient for Chad, a landfall in Libya. It seems we need another frigate in that area. What have we got in the area at the moment?" Commander Ruskin took two steps nearer to the centre of the map.

"The displacement chart for the Ministry of Defence gives one goodwill visit to Greece for the destroyer *Ceroses*." The speaker consulted one of his papers; this one denoted 'CLASSIFIED' in large red letters.

"Right, better contact London. Divert *Ceroses* to whatever they can fix up for an exercise." The older man had realised immediately that any goodwill visit could be only between a few days and a week. Rustling through his papers, the younger man extracted another, this time green, classified document.

"The Americans have a carrier and escorts from the sixth fleet in aircraft exercises in that area for the next two weeks, sir."

"Good," came the retort, "better get in touch with Washington, give them a brief. Make sure those carrier-based fighters are carrying cameras. Tell the sixth fleet to keep the carrier…?" The Commander snapped his fingers, impatient at the delay. The papers rustled once more.

"Carrier *USS Indianapolis*, sir."

"Yes, tell the *Indianapolis* to stay away from the coast of Libya. We will supply *Ceroses* to plane guard." The Commander thought for a moment.

"Well, set that up; I will be seeing the director of Naval Intelligence shortly." The wristwatch was consulted before he spoke again.

"See if we can get someone in there." The long wooden pointer came up to the map and rested on the edge of Benghazi.

Elsewhere in the sprawling complex, a signal came in and was decoded and a messenger immediately delivered it to the Northern Hemisphere Submarine and Amphibious Operations section. Lieutenant Colonel Henry Gilchrist, nominally the head of this section, read the signal from *Orestes*. He, too, would soon be in conference with the Director. He glanced at his watch and turned to his second in command, Major of Marines Robin Drew. "This guidance system the 3rd Submarine Squadron have got," The Colonel's bushy eyebrows hoisted themselves a fraction of an inch in enquiry.

"Phosphor-Cobalt CV6, Colonel." The Major did not need to consult notes; he had been dealing with swathes of notes directly from the Portsmouth weapons establishment over the past month.

"Long-winded name, that." The colonel permitted himself a thin chuckle. "Hope it does what it's supposed to." He hissed his approval at his own remark.

"Well, actually that is the name for the complete system, but it is incomplete at present Colonel. It is being tested in several phases. Apparently this is intended, in different forms of course," the major's lean shoulders emphasised this with a shrug, "to be a long-range direction finder for both torpedoes and missiles. Once it is used on missiles the cat will be out of the bag. We don't believe the Soviets are onto it yet." Major Drew was well into his subject, warming to his work and enthusiastic about this particular aspect of it.

"So, for the moment, we are using it for submarine torpedoes only." This time, he permitted himself a glimpse of the inevitable sheaf of blue papers rolled casually in one hand.

"A Mr Simon Gray from the weapons establishment is the key to the successful completion. We have got him in Scotland at present, and…" The stream of one-sided information was abruptly curtailed by the Colonel.

"Yes, I have it here, but Mr Gray has an associate who has come up with something else. Very versatile this apparatus."

"Is this the Penguin system, do you know?"

"No, sir," the Major replied, "that is the submarine sonar guidance system that can range a hundred miles and allows for the Earth's curvature without affecting its accuracy. Something else the Soviets don't know about yet. However, they have a very sophisticated new radar situated here in the Arctic. You have the dossier about it. We need to know more, of course."

The Colonel chuckled to himself, this time almost soundlessly. "I want you to organise a commando exercise using canoes, launched from a submarine perhaps. We can arrange a raid on the Russki radar upon completion of that exercise, I think."

The Colonel and the Major began a slow walk in the direction of Northern Fleet Operations, a small unit in this very large granite house in its sheltered haven of rolling pastures and a sheer cliff perch.

This location was perfect for Box Ten's purpose, with little chance of surveillance or interception being able to take place. The conference room door was opened and held wide by a leading telegrapher, who immediately hid himself behind it as the portly, moustached Director made his ponderous way through. The telegrapher sailor waited for the assembled company of all the services uniforms to make their unhurried way through, and then briskly deposited himself on the other side of the door. So far, the large ink blot that he had so recently managed to mark his white front with had not been detected. It would not do, however, for it to be noticed. The top brass around here seemed to respect only absolutely one hundred per cent efficiency in everything.

The leading telegrapher permitted himself a quick lift of his eyebrows to heaven and then hastened to change his offending garment. Just as well they lived on the premises in the converted cells below. Fortunately for himself, he thought that he was exactly in the right place to get access to all submarine and ship movements and find out which were short on complement of crew. He was a qualified submariner and in a good position to slot himself into a suitable draft. Somewhere not so busy, not too hectic a schedule, somewhere likely to give a good sea-to-shore ratio. Looked like submarine *Orestes* was coming up to do a good few 'jolly' runs and plenty of time in harbour. Well, as good as could be predicted that is! LRO Swingle decided that he would send a signal getting himself inserted as replacement for that LRO who had just gone down sick onboard that sub.

The Director seated himself at the head of the gigantic mahogany table, managing to fit his vast frame into the former Laird's Jacobean chair.

"Pity about this deputy foreign minister, chappie." The director wheezed his comment, at the same time wiping the spittle from one side of his moustache. Many of the uniformed figures were seated now. Arranged so that their second in command would sit opposite, ready if need be to slide folders full of information across the polished table surface, open at any relevant page.

"Assid Mochbe was assassinated last night in Chad, poor blighter." The Director was receiving polite stares from his congregated staff.

"The Chad Government expects reassurances from Whitehall, and no doubt some foreign aid increase." The Director seemed to be having less difficulty now with his breathing.

"What's the latest on this rebel insurgence, Commander Ruskin? Soviet backing, eh?" The grey-haired commander cleared his throat and prepared to give his analysis. His heavy brow began to crease in thought.

# Chapter 5

Six weeks had passed by slowly, interminably long, but paradoxically almost without time for the crew of *Orestes* to think of other things. During the brief intervals of leisure, each man determined his own priorities according to his nature. For many, the pace was too hectic to consider anything but sleep in those pauses between. Each settled into a routine and adjusted to the vagaries of this hidden life at sea.

*Orestes* had completed her trials and was on her way to the next assignment. Life became a little less hectic with this easing of workload. Most had spontaneously adopted the essential cheerfulness needed to cope, especially now that thoughts were becoming centred once more on returning home.

The engine throb died away, and its Engine Room crew were idle momentarily, waiting for the order to come that could set them into action again. The submarine swayed gently in the disturbed eddies of green sea around her.

*S12* was conned from the Bridge by her Captain and Navigator, binoculars in hand, waiting for the first glimpse of the commandos' canoes. The Bridge lookout voiced his sighting of a low-lying white streak of foam that denoted paddling movement. The rocky headland towered out of the sea three miles distant.

"Ahead slow both engines. Port twenty," the Captain voiced his orders into the voice pipe to hear them promptly echoed. The engines purred, setting up pulsing vibrations through the flimsy steel tower on which the officers stood. The boat began to roll gently to starboard as the bows came around to head into the rocky land. The submarine nudged its way in towards the two canoes. The day was overcast and cold; a light wind whipped up the sea surface and sprayed it across the faces of the Royal Marines. Sunlight found a pocket through the clouds and attempted to warm them. From the Bridge, their low shapes were distinct now; two men in each could be seen dipping paddles in a long powering stroke, the two in unison. Dark-olive coloured camouflaged jackets leaned out from the low hulls.

Sunlight glinted sporadically on beret badges. The men were making a wide circuit, fighting the cross current in an attempt to bridge the gap between them and that intended black haven.

The Captain brought his craft closer into them, adjusting his power and steering to remain broadside on to their approach. It was a tricky business to align the boat's position with the current. More difficult still to prevent sideways drift. The submarine's manoeuvred position eased the commandos' task. They powered in with aching yet persistent arms. Now with the current, their tiny craft was scudding over the swell. They were close, coming in fast, one canoe behind the other. The strenuous task of braking water began. Tired arms thrust paddles deep into the sea, slowing the rush toward the hull. Skilfully, they rode the swell, reducing speed, removing paddles and with one quick gliding stroke, turned their craft alongside. Paddles were used as spars to fend off the resilient steel, and the current held them in.

First Lieutenant, Reginald Grimes, appeared on the casing, immaculate as ever and stood in readiness to greet them. Heaving lines were cast across both canoes by figures in white jerseys, and heavier lines were brought up to haul in the canoes. The commandos secured lines to their boats and quickly scrambled upward to the casing, out of reach of the licking waves which threatened to drag them back. Greetings were exchanged, and the commando captain was quickly led below to the Wardroom once the canoes were on deck.

"Morning Royal, just in time for lunch." Sudswell's head had appeared through the opened torpedo loading hatch.

"Pass the lines in, and we'll get your boats down." He had located the sergeant and was engaging him while the corporal and private started doing just that.

The first canoe wouldn't go in and had to be hauled back while the ladder was unbolted and removed from the hatch. Although the boats were lightly built, their bulk began to dwarf the interior once inside the hatch, and it took four of them to manhandle them down onto two torpedo securing racks.

The marines gathered their action kit, which consisted mainly of eating utensils, billy cans and a hard rubber mug which hung from their waist belt. Towels were lent to these two sodden figures while combat jackets were hung to dry. A hot drink was provided for them, and they became settled into the for'ard Mess.

The submarine dived, and immediately after, its crew started the normal procedure for collecting their meals. The next change of watch was, by established routine, the first to have theirs. It was decided unanimously, independently and without discussion that they would tell the strapping marine private that his lolling position at one of the tables took too much room. He was indeed a big lad and the way his elbows, although extending in line with his shoulders, managed to cover two-thirds of the table was quite impressive. It hadn't yet dawned on him that he was the reason, partly for those three men standing as best they could outside in the passageway, trying to eat with the absolute minimum of elbow room.

Bubbles and the corporal were busy in the fore-ends, making sure that the recently loaded craft were securely lashed into position. There would definitely be trouble if anything was damaged during changing speeds and dive angles. John Bishop had just been relieved from watch on the sonar and now stood in the Mess door entrance with his dinner plate in both hands. He stopped, eyed the big lounging marine and received a few glances from around the Mess, which told him the whole story.

"You won't be going out again for a few hours, Royal. You might as well get your head down over there." With this, John pointed to one of the 'coffins'. The lower bunk might well be a tight squeeze for him, but at least they would get him neatly stowed out of the way.

"Yeah, smashin'. Just the 'ammer. Fink I will." The marine was beaming a broad grin and mumbling away to himself in a deep, gravelly voice, and at the same time trying to push his body, boots as well, into the two-foot wide and two-foot high slot.

A few laughed nervously as John, having placed his meal on the table, proceeded to assist the marine by shoving behind him. Another pair of hands joined him and, between them, managed to ease him down and out of sight. Soon, the stertorous snores were heard clear into the accommodation passageway, and they wondered if perhaps they shouldn't have bothered. Meanwhile, John sat leisurely to enjoy his food in his uncramped surroundings.

The marine sergeant grinned and nodded to all he passed on his way through the Control Room. His tousled hair flopped forward across his wide, beetled brow. Stripped to the waist, he towelled his neck and back vigorously with a borrowed strip of navy-issue white cotton. His cheerful acceptance of this blasting wind and his ready smile, would not cause him any disagreeable encounters with *Orestes'* crew. He was perfectly at ease here, accepting whatever might come.

Unaccustomed to the sliding door, the sergeant fumbled the catch and swore softly at it, grinning all the while. Behind it, a chief nearby opened it for him.

"Bloody ripe down here, mate!" The big-shouldered one shuddered in mock concern for the cold and the heavy scent of confined bodies and stale beer.

"Got room for a little 'un?" The eternal smile still played around the corners of his mouth. Two of the petty officers made room for him on one of the bunks, and one grasped at the outstretched hunk of hand.

"Joe, Joe Bolton." The sergeant pumped hands quickly and sat as the tot of rum was passed around from hand to hand until it reached him.

"You're a clearance diver then, Sergeant?" The Coxswain was busy pouring careful measures of the pungent precious red liquid into tot glasses for the other senior rates.

"Call me Joe, yes I do some diving, among other things." Joe's hair flopped forward again in a dishevelled mop once he had drunk the fiery ration. Someone was passing the blue-lined cigarettes around. The men lit one up, inhaled deeply and held the match for the sergeant to take the taste of the new cigarette.

"What's this exercise, then, Joe? Just a daft game?" came the initiative in questioning.

"Oh! Er, yes." Joe was reluctant to divulge the purpose of their expedition but knew that he needed to give some reply.

"Yes, I'll be going for a little swim tonight. Our captain wants to try out some new equipment. Nothing clever, really." Joe hoped this explanation would be sufficient to satisfy these submariners.

"What's the food like onboard?" He felt there was a good chance of diverting attention away from himself with this ploy. He knew that in confined conditions with little real entertainment in a very monotonous routine, the highlight of any day was likely to be centred around food time.

"It's okay; they'll be along shortly with it," so, saying, the Coxswain opened the door and stuck his head out, just to make sure the 'Butcher', an able seaman who worked generally as a stores assistant to the Coxswain, was actually out of sight. This could well indicate that they would be queueing down at the Galley.

"Hey! I hope I haven't got one of those top bunks." Joe was chuckling to himself. Thinking about the incident, he was just going to tell. Something he had done once, making him feel a bit stupid. Falling out of a top bunk whilst asleep. Still, that's life for a marine! The event amused him still.

"Well, I've raked out as much as I can." Jock was lying down on the deck plates between the tubes and looking up to explain to Bubbles and the Torpedo Instructor, "The suction pipe must be blocked." Charlie was eyeing the bilge-well, noting how oily and black the foul-smelling water had become.

"You'll need to clear it, Jock," he continued.

Jock already had his sleeve rolled up, his right arm thrust deep into the mess, and the scum was all the way up to his upper arm.

"It must be blocked to overflow like that." Bubbles was talking.

"If we wait till surfacing to get it pumped out, the stokers won't go much on it if we cause a vacuum on their pump." He was looking at his petty officer to see what the reaction would be.

"We had better scoop out as much as we can and ditch it down one of the other bilges," Bubbles suggested.

"What with?" asked Jock.

They looked around for some suitable container, small enough to be manageable and yet still get the oily water out without taking too long. Just then, Bubbles saw the rubber mug by the hatchway into the for'ard Mess. Without being seen by the corporal and the other marine not being in sight, it was quickly retrieved and handed to Jock.

It took them an hour, taking it in turns to get the level down to the bottom of the well. The suction grill was now accessible, so they dismantled it and extracted all the choking debris from the pipe access. The commando's rubber mug had fulfilled a useful purpose and, having been wiped out with a rag was placed in its former position. There was no fresh water outlet to wash it in at this end of the boat, and it would be best not to be seen wandering along to the bathroom with it.

It was sometime later that they surfaced and later still that they would disembark the canoes onto the upper casing. The marines were waiting for the dark of night, which would soon fall. It was cold out there, and the chef had provided soup to warm them. There was just time to enjoy a cup.

A big hairy hand retrieved his mug from beside the hatch and dipped a huge mug full of the tasty steaming soup. It did seem a bit odd that no one else was having any, the marine private thought. Still, they were a funny lot these matelots laughed at anything; they did. Seemed to think it was funny, him having a good mug of soup.

"Very tasty," he said. "Wish I had time for another one." *Still,* he thought, *he had got on with one of them and talked quite a long time with Petters.* He couldn't understand why they called him 'Pet Hulk'. Seemed a nice bloke, came from the East End, same as himself.

The marine sergeant laid out the contents of his rucksack on the fore-ends deck plates, careful not to risk ripping his wet suit on the torpedoes which lay either side of the narrow gangway or on any of the seeming hundreds of traps for the unwary. He checked his gear methodically and re-packed the regulation clothing. The Tannoy crackled and then the thin metallic voice issued its announcement, "Prepare to launch canoes."

The background whine faded away. Joe looked up, momentarily caught in surprise at the sound of the torpedo hatch lifting off its seal and the slight hiss of air escaping as the pressure equalised from the compartment to outside pressure. Less reluctant now, the round metal hatch swung back, revealing a circular patch of star-studded sky. A dark smudge of crawling cloud began to clear from the stars. The canoes were thrust out, straining men sweating in sustained effort, painfully easing thin fabric past rough edges of metal. Joe was in his final preparations, dipping his hands now into a tin of grease and rubbing the dark brown glistening stuff around his neckband and wrists of his frogman's suit.

With a final wave, the commandos thrust their oars out, driving themselves hard away from the pressure hull, before commencing powering strokes away into the night. The burly commando private struggled to quickly pick up his scything stroke, testing the strength of the tide. The divers sat ready, waiting for the night to close around the black silhouette of *S12*. Out of sight, Joe switched on a small box, adjusted the straps to fit tight along his forearm and carefully described an arc with the loaded arm until a pinpoint of light flickered from the left lamp into the right. Reversing the swing of his arm, he noted the change with satisfaction. He had located the target with this new aid strapped to his arm. A good tactical piece of kit.

Joe gave the signal to move, a series of taps on the private's right shoulder. The canoe slowed to a halt. The spur of water stopped cascading past them. The tenseness of silence closed in. The commandos' shoulders heaved sideways. The canoe and both passengers rolled over, hesitated upside down, until it finally sprang upright again. Now, the private was alone. The diver had dropped free, his inertia still carrying him down. Joe fumbled in the coldness around him, followed the thin lifeline of silk rope attached to his wrist and felt the drag of the metal air cylinder which had rested so recently and precariously between the two of them. In earnest now, he rotated himself to wedge the cylinder up to his shoulders, found the mouthpiece and, in one deft movement, settled it between clenched teeth. He breathed the damp air, heard the reassuring suck of his own lungs, the roller diaphragm being forced out, the sound of exhaling air.

His slide into the deep had slowed to nothing. He was alone, had no sensation but cold, no feeling of direction, and was completely disorientated with no lifesaving rope line to follow. He knew that somewhere above him in the Atlantic swell, three comrades waited in their flimsy craft, powerless to assist him. He relied entirely now on the functioning of this device. His arm floated level with his head. Slowly, the red dot of light winked at him through his goggles. Joe felt a surge of reassurance. Cautiously, he began to swim a tight circle. The direction-finding carrier beam would guide him into the headland, he hoped.

Submarine *Orestes* lay quietly on the surface, the night closing in around her. Her radar was scanning all around, the operator changing channels to cover all ranges. They needed to be careful. As yet, they could not switch on their steaming lights. The canoe landing exercise required this, or the mock enemy might yet detect them. The radar scanned, giving continuous reports to the Captain via the officer of the watch on the Bridge. An hour passed, and the order was given to switch on steaming lights. The sub proceeded to Rothesay for the next assignment. The crew were informed that the programme had been altered but that it would not affect the coming weekend leave.

The First Lieutenant was not very popular at this announcement, especially amongst the men who lived close to their depot ship at Faslane. It now meant that since the submarine would anchor at Rothesay, those men able to take weekend leave would need to travel thirty-odd miles by ferryboat up the channel and into the Gare loch. For the benefit of those who needed to travel by train, it was decided that the same small vessel would drop them off at Gourock. Then, they would travel by train up to Glasgow and on to their separate destinations. A large chunk of the weekend would disappear as a result of this extra travel.

The Captain sat in his cabin considering the signal that the new onboard leading radio operator had just brought him. He pondered how to present this news to Brown about this domestic development. Jock returned to the Mess after hearing what the Captain had to tell him and was immediately plied with questions by the two or three who sat there, unable to see that this was a serious situation. Jock did not acknowledge them, merely getting changed into his clean going ashore clothes, even though it was far too early for any of them to consider doing so. Jock didn't want to talk, and this was his way of telling them so. The Mess fell silent, knowing by that single act that this must be bad news from home. Simeon made him a cup of coffee, but he wouldn't drink it. It sat there, growing cold, while the others tried to ignore the change in the atmosphere around them.

Cautiously, the submarine nosed its way into Rothesay Bay, preparing to anchor for this Friday night and the weekend. Leading Seaman Sudswell had taken over Ginger Bates' duties on the casing by arrangement with the Coxswain. John Bishop wanted to be off ashore early, which meant catching the first liberty boat and that would arrive soon after anchoring. Since Bubbles was duty anyway, it seemed the logical thing.

The Casing party were always busy upon arrival and invariably missed the first boat ashore. Bubbles was up on deck with a reduced anchoring party for entering. He only really needed two men, but he had the new submariner Able Seaman Simeon up this time; this was to form part of his post-course training.

The boat edged in, about two miles from the bright lights of town. The casing officer stood up close to the monstrous bubbled sonar dome on the bow peak. He stood straddling the open anchor casing doors, facing the Bridge, walkie-talkie in hand, waiting for the word. Already, they could see the faint red and green navigation light of the motor fishing vessel, their ferry, coming out from the long, low jetty, streaming white foam falling away from its bows as it crawled towards them.

Constantly repeated depth readings were voiced up to the Bridge from the Control Room. The pen strobe flicked across the echo sounder, leaving another dark trace on the paper, and the operator would voice up a new reading. Coxswain sat behind the wheel, alert and waiting for the expected order. He had done this many times before and knew the approach to Rothesay well. He knew almost by heart the sequence of engine and telegraph orders which would bring them safely in. His hands rested lightly on the horizontal steering bar, ready to dart upward to the engine order indicator controls.

"Slip," the single word emanated from the First Lieutenant on the Bridge. Even without the portable intercom, it was audible across the casing. The long-handled sledgehammer known to them as a 'Maul' arced its tangential curve inward, striking the anchor cable slip neatly along its steel ring. The follow-through of the impetus of the blow carried it backwards, free from the steel tongue.

"Stop both engines, half astern both." The order was carried out instantly, even before the repeated order had finished echoing up the tube. The boat throbbed with its reversing engines thunder, reverberating throughout the whole length. The deafening roar of the free-falling anchor chain rattled its way along the metal plates and gradually slowed to a halt.

"Stop both engines." The numbing sensation ceased. All sound was dying away. Coxswain waited. Five minutes passed while 'Jimmy' made certain that all was well.

"Revolutions zero. Finished with main engines." At last, they were in. Coxswain wound his revolutions down to zero and put the engine orders through the whole range to finally come back to a stop. This indicated to the Engine Room that they could close down. That was it now until next Monday morning.

The yellow superstructure and black sweeping hull of the liberty boat approached, narrowing its angle, slowing to bump gently just once to rest alongside the submarine's flared bows. The main broadcast buzzed its announcement of leave and expiration times for various parties. Already, men were streaming up through the tower, emerging out of the narrow hatch, tumbling out onto the upper deck for their first open view of this weekend. They looked about them, at the town lights and the long sweeping coast road, before stepping onto the MFV, the first stage in going their separate ways.

The only one oblivious to his surroundings was Brown, seemingly unconcerned by anything or anyone around him. He stood looking into the distance at something that no one else would see. Bubbles stood for a moment, watching the crew leaving the submarine, noting the different expressions. Every landfall held a different meaning for each of them.

"Good luck Jock." Bubbles knew he had been heard. It was a long time before the man turned to stare at him. The remark had registered but had no meaning to him. Bubbles thought it was as though the man looked through him, seeing something else. Eventually, he focussed and nodded, just the one taciturn acceptance of that intended comfort. Then, turning, he stepped hurriedly onto the MFV just as the lines were being slipped and found a place on deck away from the others, out in the bitter icy blast of cold air. No one else wanted to stand just there.

This was the first real opportunity Bubbles had to observe the young Simeon at work. He seemed competent enough, allowing that this was a new experience for him. He seemed keen enough to learn and watched everything that went on around him. Now that there was little left to do on deck, Bubbles had time to see his face clearly and time to converse alone.

Second Coxswain had gone below whilst the casing officer was reading the night order book. Bubbles sent the other two men to rig the anchor lights and stood on deck where he could watch the activity. There was no trace of twitching or nervous facial expressions on the newcomer's face.

"Don't you want to go ashore then, Simmo?" he said. Simeon looked at him.

"I've swapped with Harman and I'm doing his duty tonight." He stopped, not seeing that there was anything wrong with the statement.

"I'm duty killick and I didn't know anything about it." Bubbles didn't want to be hard on him, but he could see that the two new men had just decided amongst themselves without bothering to get the exchange accepted officially.

"Go down and get yourself an anorak. You'll be first on watch. Then get Harman and tell him to see me." Bubbles sent the man below and waited, thinking. There had to be a radio operator in the duty watch, and that was Harman tonight. He didn't yet know who the duty petty officer or chief would be, and it would depend on whether the swap was acceptable or not.

The two men came up on deck five minutes later. One of them was already in civilian clothes and obviously keen to be on his way ashore. Bubbles didn't like to lean on people; he reckoned only bumptious types threw their authority around, but still, he had to make the position quite clear to these two. He explained, in as easy a manner as he could, why it was necessary for the various people concerned to be informed and how it should be done. He also explained why each branch member was incorporated into each watch, enumerating the duties they had to perform. He knew that a lot of what he said, they already knew. Bubbles wanted to make sure that they would have no excuse in future to say they didn't know. The thing was that he was letting them get away with it this time instead of reporting it officially. He wanted to make sure they understood. Bubbles quite often found that it was better to sort things out himself than go through the nausea of making an official report with all the subsequent trouble it could cause. This was a minor infraction anyway, so best to let it go.

"Right, now go down and try to find another radio operator who isn't going ashore and ask him to stand in for you. If you can't find anyone, you'll have to stay on board. I want to know either way within half an hour, okay?" The two men appeared suitably impressed by the leading seaman's edict, though Harman's face couldn't help but show concern at the prospect of not being able to spend a few hours with Moira, his new wife.

Simeon remained on watch, standing in the accommodation hatch-well to at least prevent the cold wind from affecting his legs. Bubbles decided he would chat with him later, but now he had a lot to do; he still hadn't made out the watch list. There was still the cleaning up throughout the boat to be supervised, and things still needed to be done in the torpedo compartment. It looked like a busy time ahead, for a few hours anyway. The boat seemed deserted, without the normal melee of voices and usually crowded places. Bubbles sat alone in the for'ard Mess, working out the roster for sentry duty. All the others of the watch were spread through the boat on hands and knees, scrubbing out the passageways in preparation for the duty officer's rounds of inspection.

Harman was fortunate in finding that the radio supervisor, his own boss, was duty PO and was prepared to let him go ashore; he would handle any messages which might come in himself. The radio supervisor reminded himself, though, to give Swingle, the new onboard LRO, a hard time when he came back in the morning for allowing this to happen.

They were all lucky, too, in that the Navvy was duty officer. He was known to be a real gentleman and always made the right noises of appreciation for their efforts when conducting his inspection during the evening. Bubbles asked the other six members of his watch, and they agreed to ask Navvy to sit in on the movie. He duly asked permission to show a film and invited the officer to join them.

"Well, yes, he would like to see 'The Great Escape', but unfortunately he had letters to write." The refusal was not unexpected, but in any case, they always felt a bit uneasy having one of the Wardroom up front with them. It somehow restricted the natural exuberance they could show at the unfolding action. The film had been shown onboard a few times already, but their Watch had missed out on it so far. The others reckoned it was good, and it was accepted that they had been lucky to get it. The film had only just recently been released, and all the boats in the 3rd Submarine Squadron were trying to get it. At least Shane, who was also the film officer, had done something right.

The evening progressed smoothly, with only the brief interruptions caused by men taking their turn to relieve others on watch. Two hours at one stretch was enough time for someone to stand out in the unprotected spaces above. Occasionally, they heard the man above hail a passing boat, determining its presence there. An answer would be shouted back across the water, stating their business and sometimes destination as well.

The sentry paced the casing, hearing only the cold crunch of his shoes at each footfall along the thin ribbon of black steel which had become his beat. Big Garth huddled closer into the heavy serge greatcoat, its full rough collar turned up around his ears, protecting his neck from the biting sea breeze which swept in across the unprotected hull. The lateness of the day, the interrupted rhythm of the body's need for sleep, nudged him into a shell-like inclination to resist any encroachment from the outside world. Eyelashes felt the sting of the night air. The bright spots of light from all along the shore battered against his need to shut it all out.

It had seemed to Garth, whilst still inside the warm womb of the hull, not too rigid a burden to stand a double watch. The men had reasons to go ashore, and the big Welshman understood well enough the need to be with your own warm, caring woman rather than be adrift in a rigid steel coffin. Garth dismissed the regret from his mind as he paced. There would come a time when someone would do the same for him when his need was great and the opportunity near. Pacing the deck, circulating some warmth into his legs and driving the numbing sensation of isolation out of his bones, his thoughts were of home. The plump little woman with always a wisp or two of stray hair escaping its tie to lay across her face while she worked, and the laughing, if sometimes grubby, children playing noisily among the Welsh hills.

The wind stabbed at his wrist as he uncovered the watch and noted the time. Was it really only two o'clock? he thought. The night seemed endless. For a brief respite from the wind, he climbed with aching muscles into the hatch well, crouched and glared in the sudden lifting of that cold weight against his body. Protected for a while, he could feel the body heat flowing in its cocoon of rough serge. A stab of guilt made him half rise from the crouching stance on the open hatch rim. His eyes arced slowly to take in the towering submarine conning fin and then the empty expanse of the white-tipped sea until a black headland rose in a lumpy smudge out of it. His gaze swept in minute observation of the whole coastline. Nothing stirred but the taught scraping stretch of the anchor chain as the tide current washed against it. Eyes closed for a moment in anguish against the sting of those few remaining darts of light. The trembling morning air seemed to heighten the shafts of light from ashore.

Garth heard his own breathing; the sound synchronised to the puff of frosty air which streamed from his numb lips. The sound seemed to take hold of him, took over his whole attention. Vaguely he realised that the rasping flutter of sucking and blowing appeared to be outside himself. Suddenly, in a burst of guilty anguish, Garth was wide awake, and his adrenalin stirred. The sound of breathing was not his; he looked down at the dim circle of light through the open hatch beneath his feet. Nothing stirred. Carefully, he eased his feet onto the ladder, concerned that it might settle as he brought his weight onto it. Five steps more, and he was upright in the accommodation passageway. He looked into the open bunks at the sleeping figures. No sound came from any of them. It was still.

*That settles it,* thought Garth, *the disturbance is outside.* Quickly and in stealth, he climbed again and crawled out onto the flat surface. Ignoring the biting sting of steel against his hands, he crept pressed flat along the top.

The metallic click and stutter of measured breathing drifted along at hull level. Garth knew now, with the extra clue of a flipper clearing the water, that he had a frogman to contend with. Garth removed his white cap, placed it on the casing, and crawled past it. Hidden by the shadow of the conning tower, he raised onto haunches and leaned out. He saw them close-by now, two frogmen. One shallow and one deeper by several feet, the thin beam of the diver's torch stabbing about in the brine. Garth crept along the casing, slid back down to the hatch, and, reaching the bottom, ran through the passageway, shaking every sleeping figure he passed. Flinging the Wardroom curtain back, he tripped over the hidden shoes scattered along the carpet and fell heavily, crashing into the table. This disturbance of breaking cups startled the two officers awake.

Garth hurriedly gave his report and dashed immediately to the Control Room, reached up and triggered the emergency alarm. Figures emerged from the depths of their slumber, the resonating clamour of the alarm penetrating the deepest layers of sleep. Hurried shadows reassembled, crashed onto cold floors and lurched to their emergency stations.

"Engine Room, Engine Room," Navigator's voice was insistent into the Control Room microphone. He willed himself to calm the raging flutter in his chest. The First Lieutenant grimly wrestled with the padlock and key. His haste made the restraining chain rattle even louder against the key cabinet. Just as the lock sprung, LRO Swingle scrambled to a halt, seeing the bending figure.

"Radio ashore, get the police, coast guard, anyone with a launch. We want launches and arc lights out here immediately." Reggie dismissed Swingle, who now continued his flight towards the Radio Room.

"Engine Room," the Tannoy at last crackled in response. Navigator willed himself to stop sweating. His clammy fingers pushed down on the button.

"Engine Room, run up both diesels, turn both screws. We have two unidentified divers." The outburst over, for a full second, Theo Brooks forgot to release the microphone. He wondered why the metallic hiss drowned the reply.

"Roger, what revolutions?" Already, the thunder of the engines springing to life funnelled into the Control Room. The rush of scurrying figures was slowing.

"Helmsman closed up, sir." A figure had just flung itself into the seat in front of the huge steering console.

"Revolutions thirty. Full port wheel," the orders were repeated.

By now, the executive officer had got the keys free and had unlocked the rifle stowage outside the Galley.

"Ammunition, sir?" Bubbles was incredulous. He could not believe his ears. The First Lieutenant was telling him to load the rifle.

Up on the casing, in his mind's eye, Bubbles could see the rifle coming up in his own hands, raised to his shoulder, and the trigger being slowly squeezed. His fingers mechanically manipulated the bolt into the 303 muzzle. No thought is required for this! He finished the action on the run.

Nevertheless, he was reluctant to fire. His thoughts ran ahead: *How could there be any certainty about these frogmen? Surely, they could simply capture them.*

Hogarth was back on the casing. The incessant clamour of the alarm had been suddenly shut off. Its ringing persisted in his ears. A slim projection of what he knew to be a boat was furrowing a cream channel to either side of its bows away in the distance. It must be ten minutes before it could reach them, he calculated. Shifting his gaze downward, he saw one of the frogmen break the surface. He could just make out the eyes behind the glistening oval mask. The other was some hundred yards away, the flippered feet causing a dirty, foamed wash as the diver struggled to thrust himself down below the surface and away to the east. Almost without thinking, Garth grabbed the iron stanchion, wrestled it from its socket above the hatch and with all the power of his right arm, hurled it javelin-like at the nearest frogman. At that moment of impact, a cone of light from an arc lamp spread from the tower. Two electricians scurried in shirt sleeves across its top.

"Over here, to starboard!" Garth cupped his hands around his mouth as he shouted. The action was unnecessary as his voice carried clear across the short distance, and away from the approaching launch. The water close by erupted into a foam of agitation as the stanchion struck and the frogman thrashed about. He could feel the piercing ache and knew that fluid was oozing from the ripped black sheath of his suit. His misted eyes looked up through the water spray and restricted vision of his goggles to see two men. One huge, black coated and another scantily clad, legs well straddled, a rifle at his shoulder. The diver waited. A mass of figures were appearing on deck now. The thrum of the launch's engines came closer. The dark-coated figure was reaching out to him, fingers spread towards him, but the diver felt mists of pain, and he could not respond. The waiting seemed endless. Hardly aware of it, hands grasped him and pulled him inboard onto the submarine deck. His consciousness was fading. Mission failure loomed in his fading thoughts. They would now be aware of their attempt to learn the new sonar equipment's secrets.

# Chapter 6

Saturday morning brought the rest of the crew back on board, except for those few on their way home. Some were to be the day's duty watch, and others had simply no money to waste. The incident of the early morning brought a ripple of speculation through the boat. No information was forthcoming. The diver had been recovered and had now disappeared ashore. None of them knew what his fate would be. Interest slowly diminished. This was just yet another isolated incident, the end to which they would never know. The daily routine took over.

LRO Swingle had begun the day in a jovial mood. The excitement of the last few hours had done wonders for him. His mood waned once he heard what his boss had to say. It was made quite clear to him that he had failed to instruct the radio operators about the requirements for a duty. So Swingle strode into the Mess now in an ugly mood and proceeded to harass the men of his department.

No one liked him very much since he thought so much of himself and often abused the authority he held. He would have liked to be called by the nickname of 'Swinger' and often referred to himself as such. That is how he thought of himself, and he wanted others to do the same. Swingle was, however, the type who found it necessary to ingratiate himself with officers or anyone else he thought might be of use to him. Perversely, everyone called him 'Creeper' instead, since it more suited his activities. He thought he could advance his career by being in the company of the right people. Creeper was being his usual obnoxious self by passing the 'hard time' he had received on to Harman in front of everyone else in the Mess.

"You can conduct your inquisition somewhere else. Nobody wants to hear you ranting on." Bubbles glowered at the offending creature. Swingle began blustering, not taking kindly to this remark.

"Go on, bugger off back to your radio shack. Polish your golf clubs or something." Bubbles showed his temper very rarely, but this creep annoyed him.

"Harman, you stay here; I want you to help in the Mess." The final insult was quite dismissive of the LRO's presence, who now strode off in an even fouler mood. Bubbles was annoyed not only at the LRO but also with himself for such an open display of antagonism. It was, after all, everyone's job to get along with everyone else, even though there were inevitable dislikes amongst such a varied group of men. The general guiding rule was that if you couldn't stand a person, you just didn't talk to them, and if you had to, you kept a civil tongue. Friction must be kept to the absolute minimum, and he had broken the unwritten rule of conduct.

Swingle was later seen going ashore with Navigator to play golf. The social climber could be very charming when he chose to be and spent quite a lot of money on plying the right people with free drinks. After he had departed, the rest of the weekend onboard went by in a quiet, untroubled and fairly relaxed way.

Monday morning seemed to come early, particularly since the duty petty officer came around the Messdecks at 0600. The liberty boat had stopped running its shuttle service to the submarine at eleven o'clock on Sunday evening. The first boat out was at six in the morning. The weary, unshaven figures tumbled out onto the casing, intermingling with the rising duty watch. Monday had arrived.

The second and final MFV arrived alongside just a quarter of an hour before the scheduled seven o'clock sailing. Heads of department were busy finding out if all their members had returned from weekend leisure. There were some new faces on board: four officers, all of lieutenant rank. These were the men for whom this week's activities had been planned. All the week would be spent running out each day for manoeuvres to test the skill of each individual, returning each night to the same port.

The submarine commanders' training school was based nearby. It was known to all who ever became involved with it as 'The Attack Teacher'. The itinerary included a full week of practising surface and dived attack from a real submarine. Sooner or later, some of these officers would command their own boats. Before that could happen, they would need to pass the stringent and competitive tests in order to qualify. Only the best would make it, in direct competition with their comrades and after having served in an executive specialisation and as the first executive officer. Lieutenant Grimes waited to meet these four men, and the memories of his own Commanding Officers' Qualifying Course came back to him. In some embarrassment, he renewed acquaintance with two of them. He had already served with them in years gone by. They had been junior to him then. It was a galling experience to realise that he was being left behind. Even though they were all of the same rank and he had seniority due to his long experience as a first lieutenant, this was the test which could put them in the same position.

Looking at their faces, seeing how much younger they were, he saw his own dream of becoming a boat commander fade ever more into the distance. It wasn't just the fact of qualifying that mattered; there were the crucial captain's reports. He still couldn't understand why it was, but the reports had always been detrimental. Reggie believed that he was able and ready for command, but his superiors, for some reason, did not agree. Reggie had been passed over twice for promotion. He had only one more chance.

The First Lieutenant's mood that morning was sombre. He had been in closed session with the Captain early before sailing. The Captain, it seemed, was not impressed with his, Reggie's, handling of the incident with the frogmen, especially the ordering of loaded rifles. With all the resources available and faced with an absolutely unknown situation, the very last thing they wanted was to escalate the incident into a public witch-hunt. The Captain had made his displeasure felt.

The four officers were polite and even warm. They glowed with enthusiasm and vigour. This, after all, was their time of testing.

*Orestes* cruised into the channel and out to sea, distancing itself from the busy shipping lanes. The business of opening the boat up for diving proceeded. Lieutenant Grimes carried out his duties in his usual meticulous, if uninspired way and tried hard not to brood. He was a little sharper in his comments this morning, the men noticed, and yet there was no real need for complaint. *So, it was going to be one of those days, was it?* Some of them thought.

The crew busied themselves with their allotted and well-known tasks. Once out to sea, they made rendezvous with the Royal Fleet Auxiliary, which was to exercise with them for two days. She was to act as a target. Later, there would be faster ships capable of retaliation, but this must wait. Warships could not be spared for the moment. A frigate or a destroyer would be diverted for this exercise in a few days' time.

The RFA signalled. Her captain wanted to know when to commence his run. The submarine replied and proceeded to dive on schedule.

Bubbles sat in the torpedo compartment on his usual perch, waiting for the vibration to cease. The dive angle was not steep, but the hull always vibrated its agony at being thrust under the waves too sharply. He felt quite at ease this morning, knowing that his part in the week's events would be small. Now, it was the turn of the attack teams to be rushed off their feet. They would get little rest during the week. There would be one attack after another, and since the officers were reasonably new to the game, each approach would be a protracted affair, frustrating for all until the final close.

Charlie and Bubbles decided this would be a good time to catch up on some of the fore-ends maintenance. There was a full schedule of work to be carried out over the Christmas period, and it would be all to the good if some of it could be done now.

"Attack teams close up," the broadcast announcement was short. No time was being wasted today. The temporarily appointed first officer was ready to commence the boat's first run. The Control Room was packed. No one was allowed passage through it during an attack, but even if they had been, it would have been difficult to find a way around everyone. The Captain remained close to the chart table. From here, he could monitor all that happened and still see the plotting table near the helmsman and be in position within seconds at the search periscope. He would not interfere unless a vital mistake was made that endangered the ship.

Sonar was reporting. "Twin screw cavitation. RFA bearing Green three zero, fading. Range fourteen thousand," John Bishop was speaking in a loud, clear voice. He would hesitate only very slightly when voicing his thoughts as to the vessel's type. He knew he was right; he had a good ear for such things, and he spent a great deal of time listening to recorded tapes in order to increase his knowledge.

"One hundred feet," the qualifying officer ordered and glanced at the depth gauge to assess how long it would take to come up.

"Course," he hesitated, "one nine zero." He completed the order trying to get a visual picture in his mind of relative positions. "Full ahead together, revolutions three zero zero."

The helmsman was busy complying, his hands travelling as fast as they would go. "Watch your depth." There was still a nervous tinge in his voice. He knew how difficult it would be to keep the submarine at a constant depth at this speed and without breaking the surface.

The planesmen were skilled and paid rapt attention to the inclinometer positioned in front of each man. The hydraulic hiss was loud and constantly changing with the planesman's to-and-fro movements of the control bars.

The computer calculator dials were whizzing around in the glass-fronted display case. The PO Mechanician was giving read-outs of the closing gap and relative positions.

"RFA altering to starboard; increasing speed," John's voice came cool and clear.

"Range?" the officer demanded. John was still calculating and would not be hurried. At this speed, he could hardly hear anything but their own turbulence. Better to give no answer than the wrong one.

"Twelve thousand," he said, but already he knew that they were going to miss.

"Starboard thirty," the words were hardly out of the officer's mouth before the order was countermanded.

"Belay that. Suggest you reduce speed." The Captain was looking directly at the attack commander designate. The officer flushed and gave orders to reduce speed and then the alteration of course.

The Control Room crew realised that the rushed attack had given their position away. They had been detected. Therefore, it was now going to take a long, slow chase to intercept. The attack commander made a mental note not to repeat that particular mistake and amended his orders in an attempt to redress the balance. Now, he would use cat-and-mouse tactics. He would lie in wait once he had achieved enough distance.

Throughout the morning, the pitch of the motor shafts altered, sometimes fast and at other times slow. Depth kept changing, and at last, the submarine was lying in wait for the opposing vessel. *S12* remained quiet at a slow speed. Her attack periscope just protruding through the wash of foam.

"Mark." The lieutenant had aligned his cross wires on the approaching vessel and had adjusted to sharp focus. Two voices reacted to the single word, one from the other side of the periscope and one beside.

"Bearing Green ten."

"Range ten thousand." A sigh ran through the attacking team. They had a good position and set up for attack.

"Down periscope. Starboard twenty. Group up. Half ahead together. One hundred feet." The attacking officer was gaining confidence and was quite determined to make no error. They waited ten, fifteen minutes.

Converging courses and relative speeds were read out from the computer. Soon they would pass with a three-mile gap.

"Port twenty. Slow ahead starboard. Stop port." The seconds ticked by. Now, the attack depended almost entirely upon the vessel's beam angle. She was turning away.

"Full ahead together. Ready on one and two tubes." The vibration heaved along the submarine's flanks.

"Fire one! Fire two!" the officer's voice had risen to a strident pitch, and he noted it, correcting rapidly to a better modulated voice. The excitement had come close to overtaking him.

"Slow ahead together. Group down." His shoulders relaxed. He had scored a strike. Everyone was smiling.

"Stand down attack teams. White watch, watch diving. Hands to dinner," the broadcast announced.

Like actors waiting in the wings, a dozen sailors followed each other into the dispersing Control Room. In hurried sequence, men were relieved from watchkeeping and instructions given to the replacements. Others carried straight through to where Ernie and Curly waited to serve out meals. "What's the choice then, Chef?" a stoker stood outside the Galley, addressing Curly.

"Take it or leave it," Curly replied tersely. It was ruining his cooking, all this dashing about the ocean.

"Well, I'll take it then, in that case." The stoker was suitably abashed. He didn't want to tread on the cook's toes, and he could see that the little man wasn't too happy. The for'ard Mess was starting to fill as more of the men came off watch.

"Attack teams will close up in half an hour." The announcement was met by a series of groans.

"The sooner we get it over with, the sooner we get back in," stated Bubbles, but the feeling was growing in him that somebody down the Wardroom was due for a horoscope reading. 'The Jimmy' was obviously still feeling churlish, but taking it out like this wasn't going to solve anybody's problems. Bubbles sat in the fore-ends hatchway, having his meal from his lap. Better to let the attack team have what room there was at the tables. He had to remind a few of the seated figures about that, too, including Creeper Swingle. There was no doubt he was going to have to have a quiet talk with him before long. He should have known better.

"The skipper wants you in his cabin right away. Wants to send a signal." John stood in the doorway, talking to the LRO, who had only just sat down as a seat was vacated. John immediately set himself down at Swingle's seat as he hurried out. It wasn't until Swingle was at the cabin door that he realised they were still dived and, therefore, couldn't send a signal. He'd been had, but he wasn't going to go back now and lose face again. He saw Lieutenant Phil Green in the Control Room, put his best smiling face on, and began chatting with him about the yacht club.

The short meal interlude was over, and there had been no time at all for even a quick game of cards. That was the usual pastime after the meal, but not this week, not until they got back into harbour, at least.

During the afternoon, the Control Room was alive with the continuing dialogue of attacking tactics. The Captain would step in and point out the most glaring mistakes after each run. His assessment and guidance were listened to in awe. After all, this man held the coveted position that they all sought. They knew it was not easily gained and so the man who commanded, without a doubt, knew his job well.

The manoeuvres involved all the officers, most of the technical senior ratings and only others of the crew whose specialisation made their skills essential. Mainly, that was the sonar operators, with one exception and he was the new man, Simeon. Nevertheless, he was there in the sonar shack, too, listening, observing and learning.

The Asdic team, and in particular John, who was instructing the new crew members of his team whenever time allowed, noticed how ill at ease the man appeared whenever the speed picked up. The vibrating hull and sounds of rushing water had a peculiar effect on him. He seemed fascinated by the pumping noises of water and would sit with eyes closed, hearing the rush in his earphones. As a matter of course, everyone else removed their earphones to avoid the dulling of their hearing perception, saving that sensitivity until the boat slowed and they could use it again. Simeon, however, was at his most alert during this period. The eye-twitching spasms seemed to coincide with these intervals. John was careful not to mention it to anyone else, but he thought Simeon had a mild sort of water madness. He couldn't really define it better than that, but it was some strange affliction which, with luck, would pass in the coming months.

John didn't want to jeopardise the man's chances of becoming one of the team by spreading the word that he wasn't stable. No one would take a chance on keeping someone who could conceivably be thought of as a potential psycho. In that event, he would be sent away to the 'Funny Farm' at Netley. If that happened, he would be finished in submarines, and not only that, but a damaging report would hound him all his service life. Therefore, John was going to be very careful about this, but he would keep his eye on him.

The attacks continued, usually long, drawn-out affairs, and if a run was not successful, it would be started all over again with the same designated attack leader. There were very few moments of ease, and only after a successful completion did the magic words come.

"One all round," the Captain would say, and everyone who smoked could willingly light up, relax mentally and enjoy five and sometimes ten minutes of almost euphoria. Then, the cycle would begin again.

Down at the stern ends, the stokers off-watch were playing cards. There was more room at the long, narrow table today since several had turned in to grab two or three hours of shut-eye. They were storing up on sleep in advance. The stokers were going ashore en masse tonight.

'Big Garth' was making the tea, since the after-ends watchkeeper was too busy dipping tanks and taking readings at the moment. One of them had just played a card and was watching Hogarth spoon the tea in and fill the pot.

"Come on, Garth, put some tea in it. Looks like gnat's water," he taunted. The Welshman was indignant.

"Got to go easy, boys. Owes the sailors up front three pounds as it is."

"Ah, they don't expect to get that back, and anyway, it's about time we got another issue. What's Coxswain doing, saving it for Christmas?" The stoker smirked at his own witticism, and a few laughed.

"Fair do's. What you borrows, you pays back. Come on, you lot, put a couple of bob down. We'll have a whip round and I'll buy some ashore tonight." They looked up and saw Hogarth wasn't joking. It was well known that Big Garth had an unusual sense of fair play. That was probably why he was the only one among them who could go down forward on the bum and be lent anything. The smirking stoker winked at one of the others as he spoke.

"Better have a whip round to pay for the stanchion you chucked overboard. The Jimmy will make you pay for that, you know." The speaker was taking a risk by pushing his wit so far. He relied heavily on the fact that the big man would not actually resort to thumping him.

"Go and boil your head, boyo." Garth had already dismissed the jibe from his head. He wasn't about to get heated up by a twit like this young lad.

Reluctantly, a few hands went into pockets, and a few others rummaged about for loose change under the bunks amidst the books and clothes. The big Welshman took a note of who gave him what and duly put their names down in his little notebook. He would collect some more from the others who were sleeping or on watch later. He had enough to do for now, anyway. Hogarth started to get changed; he would have a wash tonight. At the moment, the boat was coming in. Leave would be piped soon. The watch-keeper was going around, shutting off from diving.

Lieutenant Hawks sat alone in his cabin, quietly studying the report. He thumbed through the thick buff papers to determine the full mass of content. He allowed himself the one brief moment of regret that his schedule of work was limitless. The day's activity was over now that the submarine was in once more and anchored safely. For himself, there was always more paperwork to do; just so many aspects to a command.

Jeff Hawks brightened. This, after all, was his life; it excited him, even though all this paperwork unfolded whole new aspects before him. He began to read and absorb the report brought by a special messenger. The frogmen, only one of whom had been caught apparently, had been sent to find out about the new sonar homing device. The Captain smiled to himself. It appeared the other side had made an error. Somewhere along the line, their communications had gone wrong. *Orestes* did not yet have the sought-after device. They did, however, have a lot of secret equipment which would undoubtedly have been of interest to the enemy. Enemy? Well, yes, the Russians needed to be regarded as such, even if hostilities were not open, yet. So his thoughts ran. Anyway, it was lucky that the Russians knew little about the new weaponry *Orestes* carried.

The Captain digested the report and all its implications. He would indeed need to be wary. He fancied that this thing was much bigger than he had thought. Foreign agents did not run these sorts of risks unless it was of the utmost importance. The pieces of the jigsaw were beginning to fall into place. Obviously, this was Intelligence Operations work. Jeff Hawks now began to understand the connection between Lieutenant Green and this Box Ten unit, whoever they were.

His mind turned now to the problem of his first officer. He had until recently considered Lieutenant Grimes to be a good officer, dedicated, efficient, if somewhat dull. Now, it seemed he suffered lapses of judgement. Not the type of officer one wanted for a second-in-command. Yes, the Captain reflected; he certainly had an assortment of problems. Well, for the moment, he had a lot of paperwork to catch up on. He settled to the task.

The next folder, sealed in red wax, was emblazoned in the familiar bold red letters, 'Secret'. He slit the seal with the ornate and dainty silver knife, which his beautiful wife had given him. With that thought, he glanced for a fleeting moment at the small framed photograph above his bunk before his attention was riveted on the words stark against the paper. 'Expedition to investigate the site of new radar installations', he read, and stopped as he encountered the place names which came next. 'Murmansk and Zemlya'. He read on, absorbing the details. It gave dates, locations, specific instructions, and the names of the submarines involved in the rotation. The thought crossed his mind that this document should be incinerated tonight. First, he must memorise the dates.

# Chapter 7

Bubbles and John Bishop, along with Charlie the TI and Scouse Peters the torpedoman, were all on the liberty boat going ashore. They sat on the weathered wooden slats, which served as seats, bolted down to the yellow coaming. Bubbles and John sat with their feet up on the wire guard rails, glad to feel the breeze whipping past, making them feel alive and glad to be going somewhere different. The MFV was slowing to drift in towards the long jetty at Rothesay. The four of them were sat outboard and could see the other submarine coming in past the breakwater and into the bay. They scrutinised the faces of the white-topped Casing party, looking for familiar faces.

"*Seawolf*," Charlie stated.

"Yes, *S07*, that's *Seawolf*!" Charlie turned to the others for confirmation.

"Hey, that's Jim Paine up by the anchor, isn't it?" Bubbles was pointing at the distant bending figure on the fore-casing.

"Yes, he was on the *Auriga* out in the far east with me about five years ago," John was saying. Apparently, they both knew several of the faces from service in many places. "I expect we'll see them all up the Harbour Lights later on."

Figures appeared from the cloistered hatches and leapt from the liberty boat deck onto the jetty as though it were a race to be first into a pub. The four of them took their time; they had all night and weren't in that much of a hurry to get blind drunk.

The streets looked cold and empty. The civilian population would be at home having their tea. For them, there was no reason to be out on the streets looking for some adventure.

"Whitecap! Whitecap!" some kids were shrieking from a street corner, voicing their disapproval of the few uniforms amidst the group of sauntering sailors. Apparently, there were some mothers in the town who didn't know where their children were tonight. None of the group took any notice; they were only bored thirteen or fourteen-year-olds who had already been taught to despise anything they didn't understand. They were to be seen in every port, but particularly in deprived areas.

They climbed the narrow, winding streets with the children left far behind, playing around the lamp posts, wondering what to do next. The centre of the town had a bit more life to it; there were lights on in the pubs, which were usually small but clean. There was a chance now to take over a few of them before the locals came out to find their favourite chairs and positions at the dartboard.

The Harbour Lights was more spacious in the back room, and in fact, most of the pubs didn't have a back room at all. They were well used to having a few ships in at a time, and the management of this pub had planned accordingly. In the summer, particularly, the place would be crowded if there were ships in.

A lot of the local girls, and quite a few more from outside, would come in for the excitement that new faces could afford. Now that it was winter, there was much less going on, but still, it appeared the submarine crews liked to congregate in one large room somewhere and sling insults at each other across the tables. It was all fairly light-hearted, and they knew each other well enough for no offence to be taken. Of course, it would be a different story if any other crew started the same thing. Some of these boys were known here from many previous trips, even though they might have been on different boats then. There would be a big show of welcome for these lads, from the local girls who made this their haunt.

Bubbles and Co. came into the back room and settled with their beer. What they liked about the wooden tables was that they had a trestle rail running along between the diverging legs that formed a very handy, comfortable foot rail. Nobody liked a place where the proprietor fussed if you put your boots on the furniture or spilt a drop of beer on his table. The proprietors knew what the lads liked, and it was a lot less likely that 'Jack Tar' would throw these long, heavy wooden tables about if trouble brewed later in the evening. There was always somebody who said the wrong thing to the wrong person once they were drunk, and it was much more likely if more than one crew was in.

Some of the *Seawolf* crew had begun to filter in but were not known to the occupants. The place was beginning to fill, and the air became thicker with the comforting smog of cigarette smoke. The room was getting warmer with the heat given off from many bodies. Already, the room smelt more like a submarine than a pub. Diesel fumes seemed to pervade everywhere. Even if none had worn uniform, and there were a few of those about, nobody would have needed to ask where they were from. It was a distinctive smell that every seafaring town knew. Almost none of the sailors noticed it, being so much a part of their lives that it would have seemed strange not to be surrounded by it. Apart from them, the girls liked it once they got used to the overpowering strength of it, that is. After all, it was a very masculine smell and appealing because of its connotation with sex appeal.

As usual, Scouse Peters was weighing up his chances and, deciding that they were quite favourable, strolled across to start chatting up one of the girls. The three men from *Orestes* were not in the slightest bit interested, and they didn't think much of Scouse's taste either. Still, that was his business.

The doors opened and in walked half a dozen crew members from *Seawolf*, the submarine whose arrival they had watched. The new arrivals looked around the room, not taking them long to find familiar faces. "How are you, Bubbles, John?" Jim Paine nodded at each in turn, including Charlie, in a smiled greeting simply because he was there with the two he knew of old.

"I'll be over here. Bring the drinks over; these are good mates of mine." Jim Paine was throwing instructions over his shoulder to the other five and quickly settled himself down at the table.

One of the girls was already eyeing him up but soon gave it up since he patently wasn't showing her any interest. She turned her attention to the other newcomers.

"Well, how's it been going, Jim? I see they haven't made you a PO yet," John was the first to speak.

"No, well, I didn't get on too well with our Jimmy, you see." Jim was smiling wryly, and they all laughed, knowing just what he meant.

If a man had ideas of promotion, then it was necessary to be on the right side of certain officers, among them the first lieutenant. "Who is it then? Maybe I know him." Charlie had been around submarines longer than any of them; in fact, he was a good five years older and consequently knew most of the changes that went on around the 3$^{rd}$ Squadron.

"By the way, this is Charlie, our TI," Bubbles made the introduction and then watched the two shake hands. It was the usual first meeting, shake of hands, warm enough because of mutual acquaintances, but short too. It would have been obvious to any onlooker that they were strangers.

"I'm doing 'Scratcher' now," Jim Paine told them. "Our second Coxswain went sick, and our Jimmy decided that, since I had qualified for PO, I would replace the scratcher. Only trouble is, he likes to tell me how to do the job. That's typical of 'Billy Butlin'."

Charlie was laughing, holding his sides, trying to keep control of his own mirth. "That explains a lot. I know Billy Butlin; he used to be the navigator on one of my old boats." Charlie was remembering the lieutenant in question.

"He refers to himself as 'Lieutenant Bootline', now, of course," Jim Paine was saying.

"I suppose he thinks it sounds more like a commanding officer's name. He gets a bit upset if you call him 'Billy Butlin'. I don't think he wants to be thought of as an entertainer." They were all enjoying the joke. It was well known that some people who were sensitive about that sort of thing did change the pronunciation of their names. They somehow thought it would cut a dash.

"And who's your skipper?" Bubbles was asking.

"Speedy Rawlinson," Paine said.

"Good skipper, too, except that he gives the Jimmy too much rope."

"Yes, well, they all do that." John Bishop was finishing his beer.

"Have another?" he asked. John went up to the bar, where Jim Paine's companions were stood.

"Plenty of seats over there; come and join us," John said. It looked as though this was going to be a good yarn-swapping night.

There was a great crowd of them now, both seated and standing, in a cluster around their corner of the room. Bubbles was talking. "So, he's not popular with the Greenies then?"

"No, well, the electricians reckon that Speedy does it on purpose, you see."

"What's that?" asked John, returning to the table and intrigued to know what the new topic of conversation was.

"Jim was just saying how their skipper is fond of using full speed on diving runs during exercise. So, the electrical branch stays up all night putting the batteries back together again." Charlie was giving John a recap.

"I suppose the electrical officer never tells him off for it, then?" Bubbles was saying but knew very well what the answer would be. It was just that he liked to know the personalities involved in case he ever ran across them.

"Have you ever yet met the officer who can smack the skipper's hand and tell him what a naughty boy he's been?" Somebody joined in. They were relaxed, having had a few beers and in good company. Bubbles and John were both thinking that they probably wouldn't stay all that long. It was pleasant enough, but as always happened in a big gathering, they always seemed to be talking shop. Probably because it was the only real link they had with each other, and besides that, it made them a fraternity against the world. That was important, the sense of belonging, even in a new place.

"Where are you going after this? The boat, I mean," John amended his spoken thoughts to direct the question at the *Seawolf* bunch.

"Sneaky Peeky," The voice which uttered this was loud. Many of the gathering turned their heads to see if the words had drawn any glances from unknown faces.

"Keep your voice down. You never know who's listening," Jim Paine was rebuking the speaker. The words were understood by all submariners, and sometimes, they forgot that it would be unintelligible to most others.

"When are you going?" asked Charlie, keeping his voice down.

"Straight after Christmas. Only a short trip as sneakies go, but our leave has been cut short because of it, so there have been a few 'drips' about that."

A new voice was telling them, also in low tones, "What is there to peek at up there? I thought all their defences were hidden inland." Nobody had seen Scouse Peters join them, and his voice came as a surprise.

"He's with us," Bubbles explained to the wary-eyed *Seawolf* crew.

"Some new radar installation on the coast, intelligence reports say. Anyway, that's what it's about. That's what they pay us for," Jim said, looking around now to see if any attention was being directed at their huddle.

"I don't know what you're making such a big secret out of it for." Scouse Peters was about to follow up and put his big foot in it.

"Blokes have been seen in the hills with binoculars. Bloody hell, you can see everything from the Gare loch/Helensburgh road anyway. They know damn well when a boat is going out, which boat, where it's going and for how long."

Peters was drunk and his voice had risen slightly. Bubbles and John started to shut him up and drag him away to the bar before there was any appreciable reaction from the others. They propped Peters up against the bar, wedging him between it and the bolted-down stool. The barman was busy at the other end. For a moment, Peters swayed and almost fell against the fisherman at the bar. Scouse looked up through bleary eyes at the man, who had a distinctive shock of curly blonde hair.

"Sorry, mate," Peters mumbled as his head plopped down onto his folded arms upon the bar.

"He's right, you know. They're not fools," Bubbles whispered to John while they walked back to the table. Apparently, they all recognised the truth of the statements yet nobody was bothered by it. The information didn't change anything; they would still be going North. Nevertheless, nobody ought to talk about it, just in case anyone was listening.

"Did you see Cassandra's prediction in 'The Mirror' the other day?" One of the *Seawolf* crew was starting a new conversation.

"No, what was that then?" Charlie could be counted on to respond and give the right lead-in.

"He predicted a European submarine would be lost with all hands this year. He couldn't say what the name was, but it began with 'S'," The voice stopped, and it had become terribly quiet at the table.

"European, not British," said Charlie, knowing as everyone else there did that the only British submarine beginning with 'S' was *Seawolf*.

"Just forget it. He can be wrong, the same as anyone else," Bubbles said.

"There's a dance on up at the Palladium. You coming, John, Charlie? I'm starving; let's get some fish and chips on the way. See you later." John was already walking towards the door.

"Cheerio." Charlie was going with them. The three of them went out into the cold street and hurried, feeling the bite of this December air. The fish and chip shop wasn't busy yet. A few locals were collecting their supper. A couple of women stood at the counter, discussing the day's events, their hair curlers nodding at each other while slippered feet scuffed back and forth on the tiled floor.

"Her old man will be off the late shift soon. I hope he likes fish and chips." John was nodding at the woman in a purple head-scarf, which only pronounced the angles about her head where the rollers jutted out. Both women heard John's remark and immediately ceased their chattering.

"Lovely evening, ladies." John was smiling at them. They stood, stony-faced, knowing somehow that they had been insulted but not quite knowing how to retaliate.

A blast of warm air assaulted them from the open doors. The pub interior was brightly lit by the coloured fairy lights around the chipped mirror behind the bar.

"You can't bring your own food in here." The burly character behind the bar stood with both fists on his hips in defiant gesture. John glanced briefly at the stale curling pies behind the glass frame on the counter, took one piercing look at the man, and turned on his heel. The other two followed suit.

"It's a pity you don't provide decent food. You won't get much custom with those." Charlie made his parting shot and let the door swing closed behind him.

They turned the corner, eyes down, to avoid stepping into the littered debris. They almost missed seeing Scouse Peters stumbling along, not caring what litter he had to tread through; the blonde-haired, weather-beaten seaman half supported Scouse, halting for the moment seemingly to move to comfortably adjust the sailor's weight. The keen eyes had spotted the other three sailors.

"Where are you off to then, mate?" Charlie couldn't quite remember from where, but had a sort-of-memory that the blonde seaman figure was familiar. Unsure where he had seen him before, he thought it was in the dockyard at Portsmouth. Maybe when loading the newest batch of electric fish. *Not sure, can't worry about it now,* he thought, *might come back to him later, probably not important.* Scouse was staring at the cracks in the pavement, not really sure why they had stopped.

"Good beer, good beer." The blonde man was reassuring Scouse. The three sailors turned into the next street, heading straight for the swinging sign of the next tavern. The next place was more friendly to them. John smiled at the girl behind the bar. She smiled back. She liked to see young men in the bar, spending well. She didn't mind the fact that they were eating. They were buying beer, after all.

A few hours later, the taxi whisked them up the long climbing coast road to the dance. In years gone by, it had been a grand place, and its size was still imposing. From the doorway, they could see down into the Bay and the two still, black silhouettes outlined in miniature against the moonlit waters.

The doorman admitted them, flicking a quick eye over their clothes. The sound of dance music assailed their ears from the inner reaches behind the open door.

"Good evening, gentlemen. Do you have ties?" The doorman beamed in a mock friendly manner. John undid a shoelace and tied it around his neck, smoothing down the reluctant collar tabs of his woollen shirt. Charlie had a crumpled tie in his pocket, and since he had both braces and a belt on his trousers, undid the belt casually, handing it to Bubbles. Bubbles adjusted the belt into some semblance of an uncomfortable knot around his neck. They looked ludicrous, but the letter of the law had been met; it was all that mattered; it would do. The doorman took their money and allowed them to enter. The room was full and warm. Girl's heads turned to see the new arrivals. Bubbles took the belt off and handed it back to Charlie. This was going to be fun and he was going to enjoy himself. The music started up again.

Seven o'clock the next morning saw the crew of *Orestes* at sea once more. There were a lot more happy faces around today. The break had done them good. Life wasn't all work, after all. Some of them would have memories of this place to be indulged at some distant future time. Some of the men had girlfriends here to come back to, and it was sure that they would see them tonight and tomorrow night. The future only went as far as Friday. Just three brief evenings, and beyond that, everything else was uncertain; for the moment that was enough.

The officers' attack training runs continued and the previous day's routine was repeated all over again, except that the pace varied according to the skill and personality of the designated attack leader. Bubbles and his henchman Peters were fortunate, they could catch up on their sleep during the long afternoon. That is, they could rest on their bunks when not on watch. Sleep was something that was usually grabbed in small doses of cat-napping. Sometimes, a man came suddenly out of a deep slumber in a momentary daze, wondering why the boat shuddered and lurched or banked sharply into a steep diving angle. The mind could cope with all the sounds of rushing water along pipes, assimilate the information pouring into the senses and produce a satisfactory answer, finally allowing the mind to slip back into an unfocussed dream.

Now that Jock Brown was no longer with them, Bubbles had split the fore-ends watch-keeping task with Peters. Instead of three alternate shifts, there were two. They could cope since it only involved some four hours each. Dawn to dusk, they were at sea during this week, with the evenings to spend how they chose unless one of them was on duty. They were fortunate in having Charlie as their boss too, since he had made it clear that he would arrange his duties as petty officer of the day around theirs.

Shane had made his contribution by telling Charlie that all the torpedomen were not to go ashore all in one night. He wanted one to remain onboard in case of emergencies. It wasn't his fault there was no replacement for Brown. They would need to cover his duties between them. They knew that on this occasion, the Torpedo Officer was right. The fact that Bubbles had taught a few of the others in the Mess how to operate the torpedo battery alarm system had nothing to do with it. It was quite true; no one else could take responsibility if things went wrong. One of them would have to stay each night, just in case. It seemed that Shane was getting into the swing of things quite quickly. He was definitely becoming more efficient and self-confident. Learning new techniques appeared to come so easily to him and he had taken a lot of trouble to learn the submarine's equipment and machinery. He was often to be seen during the evenings and even late at night with his notebook, on hands and knees, finding out where some pipe or other led to. The notebooks seemed to fill rapidly with newly gleaned data, and the knowledge didn't just go into the notebooks either, they noticed.

The days wore on, each much the same as the one before. Each morning, they sailed at seven, returning on a good day around five or on a bad one, nearer seven, and on one evening at eight o'clock. The designated commander responsible for that delay was not held in high esteem by the crew. Some less enlightened members of the crew saw the four officers leaving on the first liberty boat each evening, chuckling away in a public school manner, recounting the exploits of the day. This was interpreted as the close of play for that particular four. Yes, they were having a grand holiday and could be well away from it all on Friday. What was not always realised by the few was that they were men like themselves, submariners on an intensive and very demanding course. Each of them wanted desperately to reach the top of this particular tree. When it was over, they would go back to their respective submarines and merge into the background, just as this crew did.

Bubbles only ventured ashore in Rothesay once more. He didn't particularly like the place and money was short. Christmas was coming, although that wouldn't mean very much for him. He would be on board during the first leave period. John Bishop, strenuous day though each one was for him, went ashore every night. Bubbles would always stand in for his duties, and John's girlfriend would only see him during the next few evenings. John would repay the duties later, as was the custom. Meanwhile, this was his town.

It seemed, too, that Peters had a girlfriend ashore, or so some of the crew thought, and Peters let them think it, just playing along with any fun poking which came his way. Bubbles thought what a tolerant girl she must be to put up with Scouse being drunk every night. He certainly showed the effects of it each morning.

The last day out from Rothesay on day-running for the Commanding Officers' Qualifying Course added a little more spice to life for *Orestes*. The last of the four officers had completed another successful run, and Jeff Hawks, the Captain, had decided it would be rather pointless to put the less talented through their paces again. His report was already written up. He had made an accurate and fair assessment and it could alter nothing to waste time now. The time would be used to find out something useful about his own officers. The First Lieutenant obviously was already qualified, or he could not have held the position of second in command. Therefore, he did not need the practice at this time. The Navigator, Theo Brooks, as expected, was embarrassed and, as an attack leader, really quite uninspiring.

The hands had been to lunch, and now the weary attack team were closing up again for what they had come to think of as a rather futile waste of an afternoon. When *S12* returned to Rothesay Point to drop their four visitors off into the waiting MFV, it was unusually early, just four o'clock. It was acknowledged that Shane had carried out a brilliant succession of flawless attacking runs.

The least amazed, perhaps, was Jeff Hawks himself. This was what he had wanted to know about Lieutenant Green. There was a promising future in him, after all, but it was early days yet to shower him with praise. That, in fact, would only have had a detrimental effect. Not for nothing had Lieutenant Green been pushed, goaded into finding himself coerced into a required mould. There was, however, still a lot for him to learn. The Captain needed good submarine officers, and he intended that Lieutenant Green would be just that, regardless of whatever other activities had been arranged for him by a higher command. There would, though, be something positive to record in the all-important written report when the time came.

*Orestes* found its way up the Gare Loch that night, in time for the tide, and berthing alongside her depot ship *Maidstone* at nineteen hundred hours on the twenty-first of December. The first half of her crew went on Christmas leave that same night.

# Chapter 8

The joint Chiefs of Staff arrived independently in the drizzle of a December morning, each by a large limousine in service markings. The occupant's Flag Rank pennant hung limply above the radiator, lifeless in the still, damp air. Each uniformed chauffeur held his passenger door open. A white-gloved doorman held the umbrella high and ushered them into the high porticoed entrance. The old Admiralty building bustled with activity behind the scenes, in preparation for the impending conference. The blue-carpeted hall was filled with junior staff officers, general aides and smartly suited administrative civilians. There was a constant flow of briefcase-carrying traffic from one of the four main panelled doors into the hall. All hurrying on to one of the other doors or up the wide curving staircase to the upper lobbies, halls and offices. A military guard in a white helmet stood at ease, but rigidly so, on either side of the towering double doors. In the centre of the carpeted corridor, a chest-high easel carried a permanently fixed board stating 'Staff Meeting in Progress' as if to hinder the unwary.

An American naval lieutenant hurried in, consulted his wristwatch, checked it against the large wall clock above the double doors, proffered his pass to one of the military police and was allowed to enter. The joint Chiefs of Staff were seated at the far end of the room, each in an overstuffed and very old-fashioned armchair. A festoon of small glass-topped tables separated them. These supported numerous folders, each clearly numbered in large black stencils. A handrail-enclosed platform stood close to the only windowless wall, within pointer distance of the already unfurled world map which adorned it. The three senior officers' chairs formed a loose semi-circle around the platform, and behind them, more formally arranged seating ranged across the vault-like room. A group of senior officers were discussing the alarming recent proliferation of Soviet presence into the hitherto western domain and their policy of increasing influence and arena of military activity. Each of the three service chiefs had an open folder across his knees in preparation for the briefing to begin.

"We will need to keep a check on these," the Air Marshal punctuated his statement with a stabbing motion of his fingers at the sheet uppermost on his folder.

"Has anyone looked at this new installation along the Barents Sea?" he asked. Commander Ruskin stepped forward, mounted the platform, picked up the wooden pointer and indicated the position.

"We have arranged several expeditions. From our reports, the key installation will be here at Murmansk, which, of course, is heavily defended. There is another at the island of Zemlya and another over here in the east, at Khabarovsk. The American 2nd Fleet will make arrangements for surveillance of that," the Commander paused, his glance shifting in succession to each of the service chiefs, before continuing. "We believe that Zemlya is only for short range, probably down to sea level and purely defensive. The one which matters most to us is at Murmansk. Particularly so since the build-up of the Soviet fleet." The Chiefs were reading through the report on the latest addition to sea strength.

A rear admiral seated in the next row spoke, "These two nuclear-powered fish factory ships. What is their range?"

The Commander left the platform, his place taken by another, also with a sheaf of papers in hand, who addressed the questioner. "One has already been launched and is due to sail into the North Atlantic at the end of this month. Our report indicates that she is expected to stay out at sea for two years before returning." A low murmur of disbelief was mouthed around the room.

The spokesman waited until the news had been digested. "Naturally, she is not quite what she seems, as indicated by these masts." A slide projector in position to one side of the platform was switched on, and an aerial photograph of the ship was displayed. The speaker went into details of the detection equipment carried.

"This, then, is an extension of their intelligence gathering facility, and of course, she will be capable of transmitting directly to Moscow from any sea in the world. She will be keeping watch in the northern sector, most probably in support of the known spy trawler network, to collate their information." The projector was switched off.

"The second factory ship is expected to be ready around the middle of next year. We expect her to be operational in the southern hemisphere. The American Defence Bureau has already been informed." The speaker finished and waited a short interval for questions before dealing with the list of new military strength.

A general in the third row asked if the significance was known of a vast accumulation of field artillery, tanks and support weapons apparently ordered on the latest Politburo list. The floor was taken by a specialist armed with the relevant agent's report. "This area around Kandalaksha appears to be the destination point for the outlets from factories at Petrozavodsk, Arkhangelsk and Kotlas. As you can see, there are large distances involved here," the speaker hesitated, quickly looked around the room and stated.

"This report is considered absolutely reliable." He paused again for the significance of his statement to be absorbed. "Therefore, we must consider the possibility of an offensive." The officer adjusted his spectacles, shuffled through his papers and extracted a new sheet. "We have not eliminated the likelihood of a landing in Norway from various significant avenues of information."

A number of the officers were discussing the news amongst themselves. The bespectacled officer waited for the talking to subside. "A landing at Trondheim and thence a two-pronged attack at Bergen and Oslo would seem to be the likely course," One of the high-ranking naval officers rose to his feet and interjected.

"An intended seaborne invasion of that magnitude should be a certainty for us to spot long before it could be effected." The naval officer sat down and waited for the reply.

"It's possible the reason for the new radar installation at Murmansk is to give them early warning of our presence in the area, but we don't think so since they already have adequate sources of intelligence gathering. May I now hand over to Colonel Gilchrist of the Royal Marines for an explanation."

The colonel stepped onto the platform, brushed some imaginary dust from his tunic and began. "This radar may not be as conventional as we previously thought." The colonel allowed himself a moment to clear his throat, knowing that his usual hearty gruffness was out of place here.

"Normal radar sends out a beam of a pre-set frequency, and any object appearing in that beam reflects part of it back to the radar scanner. However, these chaps have come up with something out of the ordinary, and we don't yet know what it is exactly. Our experts believe that this Murmansk installation works on the principle of two transmitted beams. One is conventional. What we need to know is what the other one is for. Until we know that, it would be wise for us to keep well away from the approaches in surface craft and, of course, aircraft. They may also have something of special interest installed at Zemlya. We aim to find out soon."

The colonel saw the same naval officer who had asked the question, rising to his feet once more and held up his hand in conciliation and pre-empted the question. "I'm sure, sir, that we can give you ample warning of such an invasion. We have a number of contacts, and we hope to have the answer to this radar problem within a few months." The colonel was satisfied to see the naval officer accept this.

"We are, gentlemen, engaged in a series of tests on a very advanced system of homing-in weapons, which we call Phosphor-Cobalt CV6. This works by using dual beams. Our application at present is in sonar, but it is extremely versatile and the principles could equally as well be applied to radar. It would be ironic indeed if the Russians had discovered one of the applications already. It seems to indicate that they and we are working along parallel lines of the same project." The Colonel raised his bushy eyebrow and smiled broadly. Then, seeing the taciturn faces before him, thought better of making light of the matter in hand. Instead, he collected his papers and vacated the stand.

The Admiral of the Northern Fleet came to his feet and addressed them. "We had best prepare a contingency plan. Some preparatory work has been carried out." The Admiral extended his arm, inviting them to accompany him to the long tables set out along the side of the room, end to end, in a conspicuous array of exercise flags, markers and insignia of ships of the home fleet.

"The code name for this one will be 'Square Peg'." The Captain, apparently already engaged in arranging some pieces on the table, was informing the others, who began to cluster around.

The US naval lieutenant felt himself to be relegated to the fringe of this distinguished assembly. He had no real function amidst the unfolding tactical plan. His orders were to report to Commander Ruskin of British Naval Intelligence. A major of the British Army passed close by, the white shoulder brevet denoting him as a staff officer. "What about this Eichmann trial?" he was saying to his companion.

"Yes, it will all be over soon. The Israelis will execute him for sure," his companion replied. Lieutenant Parker sighted the British Commander, noted the deep furrowed forehead and immediately went to report to him.

# Chapter 9

Lieutenant Theodore Brooks stood by the depot ship gangway, waiting. He had been stood there for some time now. What was it, half an hour? He glanced swiftly at the dial of his wristwatch. The movement had been detected by the uniformed sentry.

"I expect she got held up in traffic, sir." The man was being very proper, respectful to the officer in uniform.

"I expect so." Lieutenant Brooks knew perfectly well that there was no traffic holdup, not on this road. All the vehicles would be travelling the other way, towards Glasgow, not out to this lonely outpost in the middle of rolling hills and very little else. He suspected the sentry was laughing at his discomfort inwardly. The officer didn't say any more, just walked down the gangplank, heading for the compound gate. The rating came very smartly to attention and saluted the disappearing back.

Theodore Brooks was in no hurry, not once he had got out of sight of the conciliatory man on watch. He slowed his pace, just ambling down the lonely road until he reached the wire mesh-enclosed car park. For no particular reason, he stood looking at the cars and wishing that he had not worn his uniform to travel home in. Still, she would come yet, he felt sure.

A car purred softly past in the gloom, headlights flicked up to the sky and lowered again as the wheels passed over the hump in the road, its speed increased and the vehicle departed into the night. The officer stood looking in at the car windows. He noticed the Captain's gaunt features in passing. The Captain was on his way home. He was glad that his commanding officer had not seen him stood there amongst the parked cars. It would have been extremely embarrassing to explain that he did not need a lift and that his wife would be along to collect him soon. The Captain might well have considered him a fool to stand about in the road so aimlessly waiting. He had just time to notice the willowy ash-blond figure driving the car. The Captain's wife was certainly as beautiful as she appeared in the photograph. Many men had remarked on that single, framed photograph above the Captain's bunk whenever they had been summoned to his presence. It was the most startling memory of any such meeting, more so than the business in hand, whatever it was.

Theo's thoughts turned to the fragile beauty of his own wife, Deborah. She had long black, sensuous hair; he liked the way it swished around her shoulders when her head shook in laughter. This wasn't the time to think of these things, he reminded himself. His feet stamped out their cold, numb feeling on the hard ground. He shook his shoulders, trying to generate some more heat, his hands thrust deep into his pockets. Where was she? She should have been here long ago. He wished he had worn a great coat over this lot to keep out the cold, but then, he hadn't expected to be here now. The mist was coming down, beginning to obscure the scattered lights of the tiny houses along the hills. His thoughts roamed back to his own home now, of that inherited Tudor farmhouse with latticed windows How he loved that great ancient house and his Labradors, six of them bred by himself. What a greeting they would give him.

The limousine cruised by, almost inaudible, sliding elegantly to a stop.

"There you are, sweetie. So sorry. Forgot it was tonight. Meant to phone up but forgot. Silly me," her vacuous, giggling voice reached out across the cold stretch of road.

"Nice uniform. Look so handsome. Shut the door. Bloody cold coming in," the pretty, dark-haired girl chattered on at him, and he shut the door behind him. It clicked very gently; he had forgotten how smooth and quiet this car was.

He looked at her, needing to communicate, but she looked straight ahead. "Shall I drive?" He thought she might be tired.

"No." She laughed childishly. "You get to drive a submarine all day. My turn." The car pulled away. He noticed the back seats were window-high with expensive-looking packages. He recognised some of the shop labels from Glasgow. He didn't begrudge her these luxuries, and he could afford them, but he wondered if this had been the cause of her lateness. She wore an evening dress, he noticed. Was that for him?

"Beautiful gown," he murmured softly.

"Silly boy," she began to tell him of her soiree the evening before. She didn't mention why she was still wearing the same dress. Suddenly, Theo felt weary. He leaned back, closed his eyes and pulled his cap down over his forehead, the peak shading his eyes against any possible glare. He listened to his wife, treating him to a long monologue of inconsequential happenings since he was last home.

*Was this what he had waited so long to hear?* He wondered. It was peculiar how the image he held of her during his absences at sea were much more alluring than the real thing. *He must be charitable,* he thought. She was used to having a full social life. She had been brought up in the lap of luxury, taught to expect such things. How incredibly dull life would be for her if she didn't meet new, exciting people every once in a while. Theo supposed that Deborah did care for him in a way; it was just that it wasn't his way. Perhaps he had made it all too easy for her in the four years they had been married. For the moment, he'd really had quite enough. He stopped listening.

The lilting, droning sound of her voice sent him gently to sleep. The superb suspension of the luxury vehicle carried them effortlessly around the tight S-bends and down along the winding road to Helensburgh. Desultory traffic flicked its way past them in the lighted streets but did not disturb him.

Hogarth stood in the railway arch, peering at the platform clock. Another ten minutes and the blue train would be pulling out. He had bought his ticket already. Once more, he felt for it in his pocket and it was still there. The Railway Arms beckoned to his senses from across the road. He had just spent the last two hours in there, but he still had time for another quick one. The sharp acid taste of whisky was in his mouth, giving him a taste for just one more. He made up his mind and made to step out around the bus shelter.

The posh-looking Bentley cruised effortlessly past, hardly bothering to veer away. It narrowly missed him, but there was no attempt to stop. He couldn't be sure since it all happened so quickly, but he thought he knew the passenger. The officer's cap with its scrambled egg-like insignia was pulled down low, but he was still pretty sure it had been the Navvy. *All right, for some,* he thought, *a nice big posh car like that and a chauffeur.* He hadn't actually seen the driver. There hadn't been time.

Big Garth gulped down his quick one for the road, or in his case for the rail, and made a mental farewell to Helensburgh and boarded the train. He found a compartment that was not very full, and he was glad to just sit back and let his tension slip away. He congratulated himself for waiting out the first few hectic hours of his leave. From his seat at the Railway Arms, he had seen each bus come in, absolutely packed with sailors, all rushing, trying to beat each other for a seat on the crowded trains. The rush had diminished only in the last half hour, and the last train to pull out had been about three-quarters full. This one was emptier still, giving him peace and time to think; this was a nice, relaxing way to travel, enjoying sweet thoughts of his waiting family. He had missed the rush; even the civilians had found their way from office and factory, were already at home, perhaps thinking of tomorrow too.

Thirteen stops later, the blue electric train pulled into Glasgow's Queen Street station, and Hogarth descended. Figures rushed past him, almost tripping each other in their frantic haste to catch buses or taxis. Garth glanced at his watch; it read ten-fifteen. He had three-quarters of an hour, time for another quick one. The ticket collector automatically reached to grasp the ticket from him, but he held on with a firm grip.

"Straight through," he said, allowing only a cursory glance from this collector. The streets were busy and well-lit. People in throngs surged along in agonising slowness. Garth dodged around them, walking in the road, clipping past them in long-legged strides. Taxi drivers hurled abuse. Cyclists veered around him, causing more pandemonium amidst the traffic. Garth took no notice of anyone, glanced at his watch and sailed straight into the Buchanan Street Public Bar.

A bleary-eyed Scotsman in a cloth cap tried to engage him in conversation, but the Rangers versus Celtic match held no interest for him. There was just half an hour to catch his train. From the window, he saw a vacant cab draw up outside the empty railway station. He had planned well.

Grabbing his holdall, he left the bar; the doors swung aimlessly behind him. Already, the cab driver had seen him and reversed his flag. "The 11:02, for London Euston, will leave from platform two, calling at Lockerbie, Carlisle, Penrith..." the metallic voice droned on, and Garth no longer listened. This was the slow train; somehow, the timetable had been wrong. He made a dash for the destination board and quickly glanced down it.

He was in luck; there were thirteen minutes to spare for the last fast train tonight. He gave the board a more leisurely look and noted six stops; the second one, Manchester, would do for him. Garth strolled down the wide concrete arena; he towered above the fellow travellers who milled around the station. He had eyes only for the platform numbers: twelve, thirteen, fourteen, this was it. The long queue had started to move through the just-open gates. *Why was it,* he thought, *that they never opened the gates until ten minutes before the train departed?* The railway cleaners ambled up the long platform with buckets and mops, completely disinterested in passengers. His luck still held. The long queue had dispersed throughout all eight compartments. He had this section of compartment to himself and hoped it would remain so in the three minutes that were left. The round white caps bobbed past his window and continued down the platform. He hoped those sailors would go further down the train. He slipped further down into the seat as they stopped and looked around them. He didn't want them to see him; he slid down out of sight, not wanting anyone to join him, but especially not people he knew.

He was on leave now, on his way home, and wanted every minute of these two weeks to be a complete and absolute change. No more sailors, no more submarines, no more crowded spaces, just home and family; that's all he wanted and room to spread himself into. The locomotive pulled away, the comforting shunt of clicking wheels began, and he sighed audibly. The other sailors had got in further down. The girl in the opposite corner seat smiled briefly at him in amusement, in shared understanding of the meaning of his sigh. He smiled back, just a polite smile, and closed his eyes. He didn't want to talk to anyone, not till he got home.

The train rattled along, the speed decreasing, the brakes jabbing, holding and releasing to slow the long line. Its jolting woke the man to see the lights of the long platform slide alongside. His watch showed two-thirty; their arrival was half an hour overdue. There must have been a hold-up for some reason, but he hadn't noticed. The station air was sharp and bracing. He came awake quickly; there was bustling movement about him.

The next connection for Chester was in half an hour, and at least the delay had saved him having to wait around here amongst the hissing steam and littered paper cups. He waited, finding a hardwood seat, knowing the platform would be deserted in ten minutes. The whistle hooted and the wheels began their grinding flow. The carriages filtered past, and the letters along the sides merged in blurring speed. The paper cups rattled about the strewn ground, wafted by a piercing current of air. The tea trolley ambled slowly along on creaking castors and stopped by his outstretched hand. The stale whisky taste had gone, replaced by a sharper, more acidic and less palatable one. He drank the tea; it was hot and temporarily shut out the icy draughts.

Hogarth climbed aboard the almost empty train, glad that the engine's heat was feeding through the ventilation. There was only the most fleeting of stops at Chester. He hardly bothered to look. Soon, the depressing sights of jumbled grey houses would be behind him. He had the coast to look forward to. A long, continuous ribbon of dark blue ocean, clean and unpopulated. Another few hours would see him home. *It was funny,* he thought, *how time became deceptively slow when watching the coast.* He became irritated at so many stops along the route. It seemed as though they had hardly picked up speed before they slowed for yet another station.

He didn't even mind waiting for Gareth's rickety old taxi to pick him up, even if he did take his time to come out. The valleys were just as beautiful as when he had left them, the rolling hills just as high, but to him, they were fresh and new.

"'Tis sad. Needs a new engine, she does," Gareth was lamenting his taxi's condition. "Such a shame to scrap it, though. Good engine she was in her day."

There was little doubt in Hogarth's mind as to what Gareth was hinting at. "Sorry to part with her, I'll be, but nothing else for it, I suppose. Don't like they modern ones, though. No character, not like this old girl." Gareth was being too polite to come straight out with it, but it was certain the speaker hoped the stoker would offer to help. Hogarth was tired after the journey and too close to home to be thinking of engines, but he laughed all the same. The old man was comical in his wheedling way.

"You come by in a few days, and I'll see what I can do." Hogarth was grinning.

"Not tomorrow, not the day after, but in a few days, mind." He wanted to make sure Gareth didn't push too hard, but he really didn't mind doing him a favour.

"Very good of you, Owen boy, I appreciate it, and you don't bother putting your hand in your pocket, not today; see you." Big Garth stood by the gate, waiting for the old car to roll away before starting down the pasture. The old stone house stood as proud as ever against the hills. Smoke drifted from the chimney. *Good girl,* he thought. She was up early to start the chores. She would be feeding the chickens now.

A dog barked, echoed by a higher-pitched yelping from another. The two dogs bounded up the narrow path to greet him, prancing and slobbering over his outstretched hands. The children had heard him now; excited babbling broke out and they helter-skeltered along on unsure legs. The youngest fell, and the nearest girl scooped him up and continued running.

His four children, all excited and incoherent, babbled at him, arms out flung, demanding his immediate attention. That was how she first saw him. A great tower of a man. The twelve-year-old girl draped in the crook of an arm. The two youngest clung to his long forearm, and the other smudge-faced mite fastened tightly to his back. The dogs ran around and around his feet as though to trip him, yelping, creating havoc. Her hair was closely bunched in blond curls, framed around her head, stray wisps escaping at the neck. She stood ridiculously short in the long black gum boots that made her stout figure more homely-looking and fatter than it really was. To him, she looked wonderful.

The First Lieutenant of *Orestes* walked into the foyer of Edinburgh's Waverley Hilton Hotel, strode casually to the reception desk, and addressed the dark-suited figure behind it. "My Mother, Lady Grimes, is expecting me. Which suite is she in?"

The lieutenant, immaculate as usual, brushed imaginary dust from his lounge suit lapel and looked enquiringly at the young man, maintaining the stern countenance he used when dealing with inferiors. The haughty demeanour impressed the young man, who glanced very quickly at the guest register and replied. "The Balfour suite, sir. Shall I ring?"

"That won't be necessary. That will be the top floor, I take it." Lieutenant Grimes was already turning towards the gilt ornamented lift. The receptionist lifted an arm in a silent beckoning gesture to attract the attention of a bellboy.

"Mr Grimes to the Balfour Suite, guest of Lady Grimes," the receptionist was brisk, spoke in quiet tones and discreetly pointed at the disappearing back.

The lift hummed in an efficient and smooth ascent. The floor numbers lit in succession above the door interior, moving on to the suite names. The lift slowed evenly and stopped without a trace of judder. The suite name stayed illuminated above the cage doors. Lieutenant Grimes stood impatiently waiting for the bellboy to slide back the cage contraption. The bellboy performed the duty, knowing from long experience that there would be no tip or word of thanks. The lift descended.

"Is that you, Reginald? Come in, dear." The door opened to reveal the portly woman in an evening dress and gloves. She welcomed her son with the customary peck on the cheek. *How tall he is,* she thought, *so like his dear father had been.* "Will you mix the drinks, dear? I ordered your favourite brandy."

*Such a stern-faced man, her son,* she thought. Obviously, all was not well. "What time is the concert mother? Have you arranged transport?" Reggie asked while bringing the drink to her.

"It is good of you to come with me, dear. I know you don't like opera, but we have a box with Amanda Wilkes, and I do think I may be able to help you." His Mother knew very well that he only attended her out of a sense of duty and would have preferred to be almost anywhere rather than the forthcoming evening concert.

"Mother, you having a quiet word in the ear of a staff officer's wife will not help my career." Reggie was trying to maintain a strict expression, but his mother's wide-eyed, innocent expression was quite disarming.

"Commands cannot be bought these days. I do keep telling you that." His tone was softer, but he knew perfectly well that his words were wasted. His mother would still attempt to coerce her friends, charmingly of course, but nevertheless maintaining the pressure until he had finally become the admiral she wanted him to be.

Reggie desperately wanted to be a lieutenant commander and then a commander, hopefully becoming a captain in the fullness of time, and his mother knew that. "Yes, my dear, but it does no harm to get you noticed." Lady Grimes smiled, sipped her drink and continued, "We have so many influential friends, people who were very fond of your dear father. I'm sure they would wish to help."

Reggie thought about his father, remembering as a child how the gold-ringed uniform had fascinated him so. How very hard his father had pushed him as a boy, exhorting him to greater effort. The four gold rings on his sleeve had been the lure, enticing him ever onward to reach that goal. Reggie smiled to himself, remembering the day the new suit had arrived with its thick gold ring replacing the four smaller ones. His Father had tried to remain quite calm and poker-faced about it, but the household had been mad with excitement, and the servants in white tunics had practically grovelled. *Yes,* Reggie thought, *that power would be his one day.* He hoped.

His mother was holding something out to him. "Here you are, dear. I picked it up this morning, and I was absolutely sure you would want to have it." The package was heavy. He took it from her quickly and unfolded the bright blue packing paper. The book title glared up at him in bold white letters.

"The Campaigns of Alexander the Great," he read the words out aloud, pleased with this new addition to his collection. His mother knew that this was his one great love, collecting information about the world's great leaders.

"And tomorrow, my dear, you may take me to your Military Museum!" She was pleased with his reaction to her little present. *Just like his father,* she thought, *so clever at these military things.* In her mind's eye, she saw her son in lieutenant commander's uniform, a little taller and rather more grey about the temples, just as her husband had looked so many years ago. What wonderful times they had lived through together.

The bellboy knocked discreetly, was summoned to enter, and proffered the message on his silver tray. "Are you ready, dear? The car is waiting." She was in good spirits now, ready to enjoy her evening with her distinguished-looking son beside her. *Yes,* she thought, *she would wait for the right moment and have a word with Amanda Wilkes later tonight.*

The chauffeur-driven car took them smoothly into the Princes Street flow of traffic. Edinburgh was busy this evening, with the streets full of lots of late window shoppers wending their way to some ultimate destination. The flow of cars was interrupted by traffic lights along the whole length of the road, giving passengers plenty of time to view the distant lighted castle upon its hill, take in the details of many statues, and admire the vast shop window displays on the opposite side of the street. Main routes out of the city absorbed the continual flow and were left far behind as the car took them up steep cobbled roads into the old part of the town. The houses nodded at each other across the narrow divide, shutting out much of the sky.

They threaded their way along one-way streets to emerge once more onto wider modern roads, reaching their destination in a remarkably short time. A figure with epaulettes on his shoulders and wearing white gloves opened the door, standing courteously to one side as they alighted.

The hall with its great Corinthian pillars gleamed its whiteness of marble at them, the tier of steps reflecting light from passing vehicles. An usher directed them to their box on the balcony, held the velvet drapes aside for them to enter and quietly left.

"How marvellous to see you. You look divine." The white satin dress rustled as her two hands came out to clasp those of Lady Grimes. "And Reginald. I thought you would have come in uniform; you are naughty!"

She offered a cheek brushing kiss to him.

"My dear," said Lady Grimes, "Where is Sophie? Surely she is in town with you."

"She stayed on at Oxford, darling" Amanda smiled at Reggie. "She is coming up tomorrow. You are on leave, dear, aren't you?" Reggie offered his cigarette case, keeping his head lowered.

"Yes, just two weeks. We have rather a full programme, I'm afraid." Reggie wondered how far the conniving had gone between his mother and her friend. Obviously, they wanted her daughter and himself to get together.

He hadn't yet got over Gillian leaving him like that. Two years, and it still troubled him. He sometimes wondered how instrumental his mother might have been in causing the breakup. They had never liked each other. The lights began to dim in the auditorium. People hurriedly made their way back to seats from the bar. The curtains were opened, and the conductor appeared and made a bow.

Theodore Brooks could hear her voice, light-hearted, trivial as usual, from the next room. He continued to shave, lathered his face again and was startled for a moment at the reflected image of his own eyes in the bathroom mirror. Deborah's voice tinkled on merrily about the party for this evening. She was obviously happy. Theo banished the momentary glimpse of his own haunted eyes from his thoughts and lifted the razor to his chin. *Oh, how he dreaded these gatherings of her friends,* he thought, *but it was her life.* The dress shimmered in the lights and rustled sensuously as she drifted across the room.

"Darling, you're not ready yet. How slow you are. Our guests will be here soon." Her tinkling laugh faded from his ears. She would be anxious for this excitement to begin now, he knew. He heard the gurgle and slosh of another drink being poured. He hurried himself now. He really must snap out of this mood and make the effort for this party, which meant so much to her.

"Nigel darling, I could have guessed you would be first to arrive. Darling Nigel!" Her laughter was echoed by the man. Theo heard the chuckles which followed and wondered for a moment at their private joke in whispered tones. Another car was arriving; the gravel crunched lightly as the vehicle passed slowly over it. Soon, the large, rambling house was full of the sounds of laughter and merry-making. Most of the people were unknown to Theo, and he learnt during the course of the evening that his wife did not by any means know them all herself. He recognised a lot of the faces naturally, mostly because they were previous visitors to his wife's parties. There were very few who were being left to their own devices. Deborah had a natural talent for rounding up all and sundry into the casual atmosphere she seemed so easily capable of creating. Out of politeness, he mingled and talked to these people. They seemed to have a tremendous thirst for knowledge. He had to admit that they were a gathering of very well-informed people, but they asked so many questions.

Everyone was relaxed, a little too relaxed by mid-evening. The drinking habit was taking priority over other pastimes, including dancing. Theo noticed there was much more room now. The floor space was less crowded, and practically all the seats were in use.

He was aware of a latecomer's car arriving. For a brief sweep of the vehicle's progress up the circular driveway, the headlights flickered along the window, throwing its fan-like beam across the room. Deborah was too engaged in a small group of admirers to have noticed the front door chimes. Theo went into the hall, put his glass down amongst so many already littered along the table, and opened the door. He had the vague feeling that he knew the slender young girl with the beautiful grey eyes. His glance took in her evening-suited companions. None of them registered in his memory. Her hand was extended to him in an elegant, feminine gesture; a natural feeling of feline grace emanated from her. He took it lightly and drew her into the hall.

"Please do come in; Deborah has been cornered for the moment." A sudden burst of laughter erupted and floated into the hall.

"Sophie Wilkes," the young girl introduced herself, rested her hand lightly on Theo's arm for a moment, smiled at him to ease his embarrassment, and lightly half-turned to introduce her companions.

"This is Alek, Isaac, and Boris, and my charming young friend here is Binny." Sophie smiled at each of them and, in turn, at Theo. He felt warmer and more relaxed and now remembered who she was. He snapped his fingers in sudden recollection.

"Lady Wilkes' daughter, of course, I should have known!" Her bright, even teeth glinted at him.

"Please don't say, 'My, how you've grown', everyone does, and it makes me feel like an interloper at a grownups' party." *She was laughing at him; her quick mind had seen his at work,* Theo thought. The plump-faced

Binny removed his pork pie hat and thrust a pudgy hand into his.

"Jolly nice place this. Thank you so much for inviting us."

"Please, please do come in." Theo realised he had hesitated too long in the hall. *He really must wake up,* he thought, *and remember his manners.* Deborah had arrived in the doorway, her arms open wide, and hugged the girl warmly.

"Sophie dear, how nice of you to come. Still at Oxford?" Deborah quickly gathered them all in and led them into the throng. Theo stood back in the hall, not unpleased to be left to his own thoughts. The young voice drifted backwards from the room to his ears. "I graduated this summer, dear, and now I am back to stay. I have so much to tell you."

Theo Brooks walked out into the cold night and looked up into the mantle of stars. The coolness refreshed him. The noise of merriment was still there around him, but for the moment, he could shut it out. The real world was out here in a soft, quiet and magnanimous expanse of indifference. One of the dogs whined softly, sensing that his master was near. Theo went out to the kennels and was greeted with a yapping frenzy, a great tail wagging and the ingratiating dip of a Labrador's head, now thrust into his hand. He knew that he could not stay with them for long. At last, reassured and more confident, he returned to the house.

Amongst all the open, bright faces, he saw one which was cool, with inner strength, relaxed and intelligent. She, not unnaturally, held an audience of admirers. "For the moment, I am content to work from a bookshop in Sauchiehall Street, Glasgow." Actually, I am a buyer for a large chain of booksellers. She was gently chiding whoever it had been who made light of her new occupation.

Sophie was very much in control of the situation, Theo noted. Reggie Grimes, his First Lieutenant, was indeed a lucky man; he considered the contrast between the two and pondered on the force which could draw two such unlikely people together. *Strange that he was not here now,* he thought, *but very glad that he was not.* He had found the evening enough of a strain already.

"Stop thinking about work, darling, and come over here." Deborah wafted towards him in a flushed glow of inebriation.

"Tell Alek here about your silly submarine. He's very interested." She floated away and engrossed herself in another group, leaving him in an embarrassing, awkward stance, facing the seated dapper man smiling up at him.

"Deborah tells me you are a navigator. Sounds most interesting. I never could understand those astrolabe gadgets, you know." Despite himself, Theo laughed out loud, a great laugh from deep inside. It came out of him like a great relief, a pent-up frustrated feeling of bubbling mirth much needed and exactly in time to release him from this chain of misery. The very thought of such an ancient mariner's instrument being used in this modern age was indeed ridiculous. The man, Alek, was laughing in a deep throaty chuckle along with him. The thought flickered across Theo's mind that this Alek had intended to relax him. He sat down, immeasurably calmer. To complete his comfort, he saw Sophie treading her cat-like way towards the latest arrivals. She was smiling. Theo suspected nothing.

# Chapter 10

"All hands muster on the for'ard casing." The broadcast was short, giving an explicit order for the men to gather immediately on deck. In fact, they did not gather. Instead, as each one appeared, the Second Coxswain detailed him to take up a position somewhere along the deck. Piles of cartons and boxes stood in irregular bundles about the deck, leaving just enough room for people to get around them without falling over the edge.

"You four space yourselves down the tower ladder; start passing this lot into the Control Room." The Scratcher was being brisk this cold Saturday morning. He knew that this task of stocking the submarine with provisions was always unpopular, and unless everyone moved quickly, it could easily take all day.

"Come on, let's get with it. The crane will be lowering more on as soon we've got space." It was a slow business, but he wanted these unwilling workers to pick up the rhythm fast.

"OK, Noddy." Scratcher was pointing to a yawning figure. "Down the accommodation hatch, start passing the tinned stuff down."

"You four stokers spread along the passage. Make a file somewhere, but keep clear of the Control Room ladder; meat is coming down that way."

Now the petty officer turned to Sudswell. "Right, Bubbles, what do you want to do?"

"How many loads have we got?" Bubbles had only just got up out of bed. As usual, he hadn't bothered with breakfast, and there had not been time for coffee. He wasn't ready to face the day yet. He knew that there must be masses of stores to come for them to have started this early, and the bundle of stores notes in the Scratcher's hands gave proof of that.

"About ten, I should think. On average, I reckon half an hour to each." He was leafing through the papers.

"Are you checking it as it comes down?" Bubbles asked.

"Yes, as it gets stacked, but I think we'll have to do a double-check. Do you want to do the meat? Might make it easier."

Scratcher held out some of the papers. "OK, I'll spell you in a couple of hours."

Bubbles took the notes, climbed down the torpedo hatch ladder and edged his way past the human chain along the passageways. No one needed to be told the faster they could use their arms lifting and pass the loads on, the warmer they would keep. On deck that was an advantage but below, it was quite the opposite. After only an hour the below-deck team was sweating profusely with the unaccustomed sustained exertion.

"Three bleeding days before Christmas, and here we are loading stores. How come it can't wait till after leave? We'll all be here then," the disgruntled voice soon ceased as an extra heavy box was dumped into his waiting arms, driving the breath out of him for the moment.

"We've got to go into the floating dock yet and have our bottom scraped," the reply came from further down the line.

"Ooh, lovely," several voices pretended delight almost simultaneously.

"You do mine, Patrick, and I'll do yours," the remark was funnier since it came from a burly sweating stoker, who had adopted a high falsetto voice especially.

"Well, I hope the first leave party is being left with that chore." The disgruntled one had begun again.

"Quit the cackle; let's get this done and out of the way. We'll worry about that later," someone said. Everyone responded as they didn't want to be here longer than they had to be. The coffee break was non-existent. Nobody wanted to spare the time since it would mean working later. It would only make it harder to start again, too. By midday, sectioned stacks of boxes reached almost to the overheads, all around the Control Room. Another load had arrived in the crane's square metal container, and that was being unloaded on deck.

"We'll make this the last one before lunch. How long do you want?" Scratcher funnelled a hand around his mouth, craning his neck back, attempting to reach the depot ship's crane driver high above. The figure leant out of his cabin.

"Half an hour!" He yelled. The Second Coxswain stuck an arm out, his thumb thrust upward in acknowledgement.

"OK, lads, as soon as this one's clear, go to lunch. No need to change kit; I've fixed it with the galley chief inboard. Willing hands hauled the last of it out and steadied the receptacle on its way upward, back to the depot ship."

"Right, lads," Scratcher consulted his watch. "back here at one o'clock. Go straight to the front of the dinner queue." Scratcher rubbed his hands together and followed the last of the packages into the boat.

"I'll stay here and we'll get this lot shifted." Bubbles swept his arm around the room, indicating the stacks.

"Butcher and Randy in the fridge, are they?" Scratcher asked. Ernie, the cook, was nodding. "One way to get hard, I suppose."

"Come on then." That was the steward 'Randy Sandy' demanding to know why the flow had ceased.

"Got icicles on your nose, have you?" Curly passed a box down, laughing at the frosty red nose which appeared briefly at the level of his boots. The two cooks, steward, butcher and fresh water stoker, who together made up the provisions and stores department, all remained to clear the backlog away into its stowage. Bubbles check-listed each item as it disappeared from view. The store notes were covered in ticks and crosses.

The last of it was going down as the returning men filtered in, standing around, having a quick cigarette before the whole sequence began over again. "You coming up to late dinner?" Bubbles leant over the hatch, shouting down. "No, I'm not eating that muck."

Ernie ducked under a pipe and came into view. He lowered his voice, "I'll do us a fry-up when it's all done, okay?" He was looking up at Bubbles. The Scratcher was up on deck.

"Only another three loads, lads, and that's it," he was telling them. The remaining container loads were brought down in record time, and the Second Coxswain went to report the fact of the task's completion to the duty officer.

"It's Saturday night, and I just got paid. Don't think about the money; don't try to save," Curly, the chef was singing at the top of his voice whilst frying sausages. For once, he had forgotten to put his white chef's cap on, but none of the others complained. They stood around smiling at the galley's fluorescent light beaming down in glistening bright patches on the bobbing bald head.

"Take it away, Elvis!" They were all egging the wiry little man on, and he tipped the sausages with his spatula, beginning to wiggle his hips in mock dance to time with his singing. The white apron danced in still folds, swishing from side to side, in a ludicrous tempo, just clearing the top of his boots. Bubbles and the Butcher sat on the stainless-steel sink and worktop.

Sandy joined in the singing and jiggled his wire basket of chips in the sizzling deep-fat fryer. Cans of beer were going down a treat, and they were ready for their meal.

The Electrical Officer sat alone in the Wardroom, his attention drawn by the sounds of laughter and singing. Obviously, something was going on in the galley. The sounds came from across the Control Room, and he knew that it would not carry from the Engine Room. The plates were being passed back to Ernie from Curly, who filled them.

The Electrical Officer stood and looking in, noted the smudged and smiling faces. He was debating just what action to take since this unscheduled meal was definitely against regulations. Just then, Second Coxswain came up from the bathroom, hair tousled, with just a towel draped around his loins. "Do me an egg sandwich, chef, will you?" He pushed his face in through the door hatch, taking the whole scene in with one glance.

The duty officer was amazed at the man's attitude. Scratcher saw it and spoke, "They worked through the lunch hour, sir. I okayed it." He nodded at the frying pans, now noticeably emptier.

"All right, men, carry on, but let's not make a habit of it, eh?" The smiling officer retreated. The First Lieutenant wasn't on board. The Coxswain was on leave, and if Scratcher said it was okay, well, that was his department. The officer was satisfied. Scratcher winked at Bubbles and went on his way back to his Mess.

The bathroom, for once, was empty. Bubbles and the butcher had all ten bowls to themselves.

"By 'eck! I enjoyed that meal. What times tot coming up?" Butcher asked.

"Don't know. Tell you the truth, I forgot all about it," Bubbles replied. Now that he had been reminded, he would need to go and find out. A few of the blokes thought him a bit strange for not being enthusiastic about the rum issue. As the Leading Hand of the Mess, it was his undeniable privilege to collect and distribute the rum for his Mess. It was a perk that he gladly relinquished to any other killick who wanted to do it. Someone always did, but now that most of them were on leave, he would have to do it himself.

"Is Creeper Swingle onboard?" Bubbles didn't know if Butcher had seen him since he had been busy all day, but it was worth asking.

"He had some urgent paperwork to do on the depot ship, according to him that is." Butcher had heard someone talking about it.

"Funny how it becomes urgent when we're stocking ship." Bubbles shouldn't really have been talking about him; after all, he was supposed to be a responsible rating. He didn't say so, but the man got on his nerves. Creeper seemed work-shy on top of everything else.

They were glad to get their washing done and out of the way. Now, they would have clean gear for another week or two. Creeper was in the Mess, already doling out the tots of rum. Bubbles took no notice. Ernie and Curly were playing cards, trying to decide where they would go tonight.

"Widows' hop, definitely," Curly was saying.

"No. You only get old crones up there on Saturday. The ones nobody wanted on Friday. Have a bit of couth, man." Ernie was trying to put Curly wise to the local goings-on.

"Hey Bubbles, are you going ashore?" Curly thought Bubbles might have a few good ideas. Bubbles was thinking. He had a bit of work to do yet, and he wanted to get it done and out of the way before the first leave party came back. Still, after that meal and the two cans of beer, he was in the mood and didn't want to appear churlish.

"Yeah, why not," he told them. "Think I'll have a few quiet pints up the Rhu Ellen."

"Come on, man, it's Saturday. Get your rags on; we'll go dancing later on." Curly really was in the mood, it looked like.

"Yes, all right. Just let me get this gear out of the way." Bubbles shoved all the oddments of matches, combs, and coins back under his bunk. He had started sorting some of the rubbish out, but he would leave it till tomorrow. At least with the clothes out of the way, there wouldn't be as many bumps to dig into his back.

"You've got a car. I think I'll come as well," Creeper was inviting himself.

"You are out of luck there. You've got urgent paperwork to get on with, haven't you?" Bubbles spoke innocently as though stating an accepted fact. It wasn't easy to keep the nastiness out of his voice, but one thing was sure, and that was that Swingle wasn't going ashore with him.

"Well, I suppose if you two are going ashore, that makes me duty again," Steward was complaining about the two cooks. Sandy was one of those types who loved to complain, even if he didn't mind whatever it was he was moaning about. They knew now that he was indulging his favourite pastime and it meant nothing. If he had really meant it, they would know all right.

"I haven't had my tot yet. Do you want it?" Ernie made the accepted gesture for a favour.

"Too bloody right I do. Give us it here." Sandy would be all right, and since all four of them were going now, there would be more of the 'spillage' left over to share between those who were left.

The gangway sentry sat in his little box, watching the submariners strolling down the gangplank. He knew them by sight, as he knew practically every one of them in the squadron. He wasn't going to leave his nice, warm cubicle on a night like this if he could help it. He pulled the black greatcoat collar a little higher around his ears. His feet were up on the single bar heater, but he ignored the smell of sweltering rubber and went back to reading his cowboy book.

The light was beginning to fade, and the shafts of bright dots of sunlight reflected brilliantly for a split second from the lens of the binoculars being trained downward from the hill. The sentry was oblivious to it all.

The snow was much lower down the hills than the last time they had been in. "Like a flaming Christmas card." The butcher thought his own remark was very droll. He liked to have a little chuckle at his own jokes, just in case nobody else did. Then he wouldn't feel that his effort had been wasted.

"The Parties will all be out in their fur ear muffs and little plastic wellies," Curly was contemplating the picture of the girls he would meet tonight. He was rubbing his hands together at the prospect.

"Kinky sod. Did you bring your whip?" Ernie knew Curly of old. There was no chance of shutting him up once this three-monthly mood was upon him.

The battered old Anglia wouldn't start. In fact, the starter motor didn't want to turn at all. Even Curly jumping up and down in the back seat didn't do much to help except make the springs settle even lower, perhaps. "Somebody give you this for Christmas, did they?" Butcher paused for effect. "Nineteen thirty-five Christmas, I mean."

"Come on, we'll have to push." Ernie slammed the door behind him. The cooks pushed from behind, Butcher on the left and Bubbles pushed on the wheel through the window. They got it rolling down the incline; Bubbles wrestled with the door handle and climbed back in. Somehow, it steered between the lanes of parked cars and out of the compound. Bubbles didn't bother to brake going over the pavement and curb for fear of losing momentum. He looked in the rear-view mirror and could just see the top of Curly's shining head bobbing up and down behind the bottom of the rear window. It struck him as uncontrollably funny. The engine spluttered, coughed twice more and fired, thick smoke belching from the exhaust. Bubbles revved and steadied the throttle, braking to a halt. The others stood by, panting to get their breath back before climbing in again. Ernie noticed the tears streaming down Curly's face; he was still choking on the oily smoke, a large dark streak down his face. Like he was some mother hen, Ernie unwrapped the scarf from around his neck and wiped Curly's face with it. Curly took it and rubbed the grime from his eyes. They were all laughing all the way down the slippery road.

That might have been why Bubbles was driving too fast for the tight bend and why he didn't see the stopped car just out of sight around it. He applied the brakes a little fiercely, and the squealing drums fanned out the liquid rust before holding. They weren't going very fast at all, but the sudden inertia of four bodies going forward prevented the vehicle from slowing enough. The horrendous clash of striking metal bumpers rang out, made louder by the still night. Bubbles was in instant fear of police prosecution, especially since he didn't own a licence to drive. The air was very quiet, and they watched the turban-wearing figure climb purposefully out of the brand-new Zephyr, give a cursory glance at the non-existent damage and stomp over to Bubbles' open window.

"What de hell am you think you is doing?" the Pakistani voice of the man lilted strangely among the Scottish hills. Four voices rang out in loud, open-mouthed mirth, filling the car and pealing far beyond. The Pakistani gentleman was extremely put out, was quite undecided what to do about it, and then silently walked back to his car and drove away.

Bubbles breathed a sigh of relief, noting that his thin, tin-like fender had not even been dented. This was turning out to be some adventure. A day of constant changes and delights. It augured well for the evening. They were all in a splendid mood, laughing at the slightest provocation.

By contrast, the Rhu Ellen Hotel was decidedly unlively, but they still managed to force down two pints. Apparently, their gaiety was not infectious, so they left. The car was no trouble to start this time because the engine was still hot. Another two miles brought them to the edge of town.

It was decided that they would investigate the New L Bar, which was under new management and had just completed its refurbishment. They didn't get in. The new management was trying to attract a new class of clientele. Notably, one that wore decent suits with ties. It was reported that nine millionaires had domiciled themselves in this small coastal town. There were many changes afoot to attract this type of custom. Looking in through the doors of the new bar, the four sailors might well have thought there were forty or so millionaires ensconced within. They took their bedraggled custom elsewhere.

One of the better-known 'dives' of the town gratefully received them and their custom. The house was packed to overflowing, with many familiar haggard faces amongst them. Each small group, mainly of young newly recruited 'old salts' belonging to the depot ship *Maidstone*, vied with other similar small groups. The noise of hurled insults and infantile behaviour deafened the ears of the more sensitive. Curly and Ernie were already half drunk. Butcher was more so since he'd had frequent nips of his secreted whisky bottle.

Bubbles was fed up with the place after an hour, and the beer he noticed was less wholesome than he had remembered. "You going to this dance then, Curly?" Bubbles saw the light of interest stir in Curly's eyes. Curly was back on the one-track thought. Bubbles had no intention of visiting the local hop. He knew that the place would be like a bull ring with this lot charging about. The full bar would remove almost in its entirety to the dance. He wasn't going to be among them.

Bubbles decided, distance notwithstanding, he was going to Glasgow. The nearest post of civilisation where a dance might still be a good place to enjoy himself. He voiced his idea to the others. Curly widened his eyes even further. He could picture the tall, bosomy girls he would be dancing with. Curly had made up his mind. The other two would stay put.

"Lend me a fiver, Ernie." Curly realised he didn't have enough for train fare back in the morning, and he couldn't leave it to chance. Ernie raked some crumpled pound notes from his pocket. There were four, and he passed three into Curly's hand.

"We'll get a couple in." Bubbles crushed his way through the throng, shouted over the din and got two pints and a half dozen bottles for the road.

"See you tomorrow." Curly had bright pin-points of light in his expression. He hadn't been to the big city for a long time. The car was easily found and could be picked out from a distance amongst all the others. It was easily the oldest one among them, hand-painted black all over. It was becoming rare to see an all-black car these days. Bubbles never bothered to lock the doors. The heap was so rusted and battered that no self-respecting thief would have taken more than one glance at it. She fired on the first try, although the red ignition warning light stayed on for almost five minutes before relenting. That was time enough to get them out of town, along the road to Dumbarton.

The bottles of beer rattled around on the floor between Curly's feet. They had, of course, forgotten to get an opener. Three times in thirty miles, they needed to stop and use a handy kerbstone to lever the tops off. Apart from that, the journey was pleasant enough until the outskirts of the concrete metropolis were reached. During the last stop, they examined the map and memorised the one-way systems which had not long been introduced in the city.

The Locarno was busy but not too busy to let two more in. Curly attracted plenty of looks on account of his shining dome and lack of stature, but he couldn't have cared less. He was his usual breezy smiling self, out to enjoy himself, and the sneering looks of taller and glossed-up, bushy-haired louts could not change that. Bubbles had to admire the man's fitness. He watched him cavort with several girls, every one of them taller than himself. He made them all laugh at his antics; he really was amusing, and from where Bubbles was watching, he looked like a big man. They had a few hurried beers during the intervals. The place became more crowded, the smoke haze thicker.

Amazingly, the brass combo sounded better after a while, less strident after each fresh drink. The tall, big-boned girl could hardly control the tears of laughter. Curly, her partner, had just performed an impromptu Cossack dance, forcibly clearing a space for them on the packed dance floor by the sheer power of his exuberant movements. The medley tempo changed, and they moved close together. Neither he nor the girl seemed in the slightest bit embarrassed. Bubbles observed that if the two of them had been that close together outside in the rain, Curly would not have got his head wet. He brought her over to the table after a while to chat. Bubbles was pleased at the girl's bubbling delight in the cook's witticisms. He got up, made an excuse and walked away to leave them alone.

A long aisle stretched before him, formed by the row of wooden chair backs; all of them faced the floor space. He paced slowly down the corridor, eyes fixed on the stage, the band perspiring in contrived musical positions which had no bearing on the music. A lean-backed woman with long dark hair rested gracefully against one of the room columns. He didn't see her face, and merely on impulse at the change of music, he walked alongside and asked her to dance. She looked up, said nothing, but quietly stepped out to the floor. They danced, each with their own thoughts, neither one speaking. After an interval of pained minutes, he made some nonsensical comment on the hall's capacity. She was nervous too, smiled and agreed. This time, the minutes were peacefully held; there was no need to talk. The third dance, the last slow one, came to an end.

"Are you a sailor?" her voice was low and musical. She gazed intently at his surprise.

"Yes, but how did you know?" Bubbles knew that he had none of the brash talk and swagger which usually identified them.

"You were so far away. A certain look. I don't know." The girl's delicate features were soft and warm. Her eyes sparkled. At once, they were at ease with each other and then talked incessantly, all shyness gone. The time flew by, and they were unaware of others in the room. The place seemed emptier for no apparent reason.

"You must be hot." He looked at her flushed face, "and tired."

He added, "Shall we sit down? I'll get you a nice cool drink." The last of the people, mostly men, had drifted from the bar. The shutters were closing.

"Sorry, love, we're closed." The last gate came down and was bolted.

"I'm sorry I didn't realise it was so late. Do you live nearby?" Bubbles wondered if the girl had come with someone else.

"Did you come alone?" she asked him, seemingly reading his thoughts.

"No, I brought that chap there; he is with that girl." Bubbles pointed to the couple.

"Just a minute, I'll get my coat. I'll be back in just a minute." She smiled. Curly came across with his girl.

"Can we take Barbara home, Bubbles?" he asked, "She lives at Ann's Hill." They stood talking, waiting for Bubbles' partner to return. She was only three minutes in coming back, just time enough for him to begin to doubt that she would. He introduced them all, and then they departed, having a good laugh at the awful and aged condition of his car, as well as the empty beer bottles rolling about on the floor. They managed to find a roadside hot dog stall and stayed long enough to keep hunger at bay. Bubbles took the couple home and dropped them both off at Ann's Hill.

Outside her home, they talked, losing track of time once more. Listening to her speak, her softness and warmth attracted Bubbles to her. He was finding out that she had much the same tastes as himself. Her name is Alicia. She wanted to know his name because she was not so comfortable with just the nickname. "Jay," he told her, and he liked that its use would be particular only to her. Really, she was a very quiet person who loved books. She told him about her job as manager of a local bookshop on Sauchiehall Street. Sort of a librarian, really. History was her passion. The real kind, not romantic fiction. She qualified at Strathclyde and worked for the university as a librarian but found the books too limiting for her tastes.

She was actually a part owner of the newly refurbished shop. The real owner, that is, the majority owner, allowed her to name the shop. Alicia wanted to name it 'The Good Book'. Instead, they settled for 'The New Page' the reason being this was a heavily Catholic-populated area that might be offended by the biblical reference. It was quite plain to him that she really enjoyed her work. He was intrigued and knew that she somehow felt the same sense of a new beginning that was creeping over him. They talked for a long time until the church clock reminded them that it was three o'clock. "Yes." He would see her tomorrow. "Here, at one o'clock." Of course, he meant today, not so many hours away then. That brought him a warm feeling. Bubbles felt relaxed and somehow less lonely than he had for some time, in reality, a very long time. He really didn't want to rush into this, whatever 'this' was to become, or not. He drove back carefully to avoid the speed traps.

# Chapter 11

On Sunday morning, the Electrical Officer overslept. He had been up until late going over his reports. First and most important had been the preparation of his department reports in readiness for the coming inspection. He knew that when Captain Submarines carried out his inspection, the electrical staff accompanying him would climb around all over his machinery, go through his records and want to know exactly what condition everything was in. That included an up-to-date assessment of forthcoming maintenance and an informed opinion of what, if any, defects were likely to arise.

Not only that but there were end-of-year character assessments to be made on each of his men. This was always difficult; so much depended on how well he knew them. Naturally, he relied quite heavily on the opinion of his senior ratings. The petty officers had closer contact with the men, and there was less of a barrier between them. They were all from the same side of the tracks, as it were. Always, this was a difficult task for a department officer. The yawning gulf between officers and men made it almost impossible to get to know them. So often, it was easier to look at the man's past record and assessments and simply copy what had gone before. He tried not to do that, however. He had been told once, in a more informal moment whilst having a drink with a man somewhere ashore, that if just one departmental officer disliked a man, then the man could expect his character assessment to read the same for years to come. He had never forgotten that.

The Electrical Officer had been loath to wake up when the trot sentry had shaken him, but the business of the navy had to be seen to. Standing on deck, saluting the flag as it was raised to the top of the ensign staff, the cold gnawing at his face and hands, he felt slightly ridiculous, standing there so stiff and still amidst an empty horizon. That, however, was part of his duty for the day, actually for the whole weekend. It had seemed pointless for two officers to spoil their weekend. One might as well do both days. Since it was Sunday and nothing else stirred through the boat, he had gone back to his bunk in the empty Wardroom.

When he awoke, he thought for one awful minute that this was a weekday, and he had a terrible vision of himself stood up in full dress uniform to face a court martial. He laughed at himself for his fear of authority, which had made him wake so startled. Nevertheless, that fear always lurked somewhere nearby. It was then that he noticed the cup of coffee and saucer. The little blue anchor emblem stood proud on its white background. The coffee was no longer warm. It must have been there for some time. An untidily scrawled note lay beside it. The steward was informing him in his spidery handwriting that he had left the warming plate on, that the coffee pot was on it, and if the duty officer wanted him, he would be inboard. There was a *Maidstone* internal telephone number. The officer thought about it for a minute, thinking what a strange person the steward was. Apart from the grudging way he seemed to have about his duties, he was still good at his job. The Electrical Officer was beginning to understand something of the way these men thought, but they were all a peculiar bunch. He had been in submarines for some years and still he didn't really understand it all. He got up, rubbed his face and thought he would have a wash later. Better to see what was going on first.

Second Coxswain sat alone in the chiefs' Mess, playing solitaire. He might as well have been alone. Two corpse-like figures lay stretched in their bunks, and the stale fumes of beer and spirits encroached on the air in the small compartment.

"I overslept, Coxswain. Is anything happening?" He had another thought. "Are you duty today?"

"The TI should be, but he's not back yet. I am standing in for him until then, sir." Scratcher knew the Electrical Officer was a reasonable sort.

"I let the lads sleep in today on account of all the hard work yesterday, sir. I don't think an hour's work would have made much difference today, but I'll see there's a good scrub out for Rounds tonight." The officer was looking at the cards on the table.

"Red five on black six," he said.

"Oh, yes." Scratcher moved the card.

"I've got some coffee on the go; would you like some?"

"No thanks, I'm going Inboard," the bleary-eyed duty officer looked at his watch "for about an hour, must have a clean-up."

"Right, sir. The lads would like a movie this afternoon. I think they're going to need a treat. Something to make them forget the Christmas dinner the chefs inboard are laying on today." They both laughed. They had a good idea of the reception that lunch would get today. There was a notorious lack of interest in the cookery department during leave periods.

"Yes, they can show a film. We'll have rounds half an hour after completion. Good clean up though, Coxswain."

Sounds of shouting came from the for'ard Mess and the rattling of dice. The officer stuck his head around the door. Four men sat at one table, the big chequered board spread across it. The men were playing Ludo. Only they didn't call it that. The rules were rather different, a bit more aggressive. There was always a lot of enthusiasm for a game of 'Uckers'.

"Who's winning?" The officer asked.

"This black enamel basket," came the reply, and then the men looked up.

"Oh! Sorry, sir, I didn't realise it was you."

"It's all right." The officer was amused. "You are having Christmas dinner today, I believe."

"We will get over it somehow, I expect, sir," one of the men said, smiling.

"I have no doubt," the officer said and retreated quickly before things got out of hand. It didn't do to be too familiar. The men were likely to take advantage of it, making it an excuse to work out their frustrations against officers in general.

The game of Uckers resumed noisily. "Keep the bleeding noise down. There's a matelot trying to get some sleep here," a dull voice came from the depths of a lower bunk. No one took any notice. The game continued. By eleven, the remaining members of the Mess, unable to catch any more sleep, stirred and lazily climbed out to commence the chores of a boring Sunday away from home.

Characters drifted in and out, going to or coming back rather more alert from the showers. In some semblance of dressed order, they waited for each other or a personal mate before climbing the succession of ladders up onto the depot ship to join the queue for lunch. The ragged queue shuffled for'ard down the passageway into the Galley flat. The usual smell of steam and boiling greasy water hung in the air, coupled with that of old floor polish from the passageway decks.

"Wot culinary delights we got today, then?" a voice murmured from along the line. The regulating Leading Hand, 'The Crusher', stood resplendent in a sharply creased white front and immaculate uniform. The gold and red of his crown badge stood out proudly from the serge sleeve. The brightly buffed boots glowed with reflected authority, pacing along to and fro along the ranks. Being on duty to keep order and receive complaints, he naturally had to wear his spotlessly clean white cap that was kept specially as 'best' for Sundays.

"Move up there. Move up there. There's more trying to get in behind ya," he stated loudly in awe-inspiring dignity, directed at no one in particular, encompassing them all. The bright stainless steel 'bosun's call' chain of office dangled magnificently in a double loop from the shoulders, down the chest to disappear, tucked in behind the jersey top bow.

"Excuse me, commissionaire. What's for dinner?" One of the submariners was feeling bored and directed his attention to the regulator.

"Don't be cheeky with me, son," the figure with ginger hair, the cut absent of sideburns, loomed large, not exactly knowing which one of this lot had spoken.

"Christmas dinner, graciously provided by Her Majesty's Royal Navy, as you well know." The crusher was enjoying his role of informant to his captive audience. He carefully enunciated his words, drawing out the last syllables. The long line broke out into muffled laughter. There was much tittering. The figure paced in regimented self-control, the hands clasped firmly, arms straight, behind the back. He had reached the extremity of his patrol at the end of the flat. He eyed the submariners.

"Wot are you a doin' of in number Eights, laddie?" A mischievous grin was his only reply from the addressed figure.

"I am a-speakin' to you," the crusher's voice became earnest. The submariner looked at him, the grin fading, replaced by one of contempt.

"I'm duty, and don't call me 'laddie' either. How old are you anyway?"

The regulator decided not to pursue the matter since he had now noticed the hook badge on the other's arm. He took two more paces. "Wot are YOU a-doin' in Eights?" he said to another, who had just appeared inside the door, as the line moved along.

"Duty," came the reply.

"Where's your chit?" The Regulator had obviously decided to make a stand. His orders were clear. No one was allowed into the dining hall in working clothes. There was always this trouble with submariners. They always lounged about in scruffy gear as though they were a special breed or something. The first figure with the hook on his shirt sleeve stepped out of the line and walked up to the regulator.

"Look," he said, face set in determination, "in your little world, 'chits' might be very valuable. Your world centres around paperwork. We don't have time for that nonsense. Just take names if you must, and then check with our duty officer afterwards, okay?"

The leading regulator stood aghast. He was not used to the inherent authority of his branch being challenged. He had to think carefully. Obviously, he couldn't let this go too far, or the Master at Arms would give him 'what-for' later. The trouble was that this was an old game with the submariners. There were only about six or eight in a duty watch and, therefore, entitled to wear working clothes at meal times. Yet all of them would try it, duty or not. How was he to know which was which?

"Right, I'll do that. What's your name?" The regulator had recovered his poise, aided by his impressive show of producing pad and pencil. He took all the names, but really, it was just so as not to lose face. He'd had this trouble before. Every time he had checked up, the senior rates and officers had stood by their men. It made a regulator's life quite difficult. *Didn't they understand there was a need for discipline?* he wondered.

The meal, when they got it, was all that they could expect. All except two of their cooks had gone on leave. Naturally, most junior cooks were left onboard for the Christmas period, and since they, too, wanted to be ashore, the whole dinner had been prepared during the week.

The submariners returned to their boat. "I thought the pudding was exquisite," one of them remarked.

"Oh, didn't know you liked chewing gum," another joined in.

"Well, it had sixpences in, didn't it?"

"Yes, but they should have scraped the verdigris off first, don't you think?" They were nearly back on board now.

"That was tarnish caused by the brandy." The second one was determined to stick up for the cooks.

"Brandy? That was methylated spirits. The brandy was drunk before they went on leave." This at least brought a laugh as they prepared to get the cine projector out. Christmas onboard was over, except for the lucky ones who had somewhere to go during the remainder of time in harbour.

Bubbles made his escape from the boat during lunch hour, anxious not to face a humour-fraught inquisition about his intended trip to Glasgow. He knew that other submariners of his Mess were quick to note any blossoming romance and could be quite merciless in their constant innuendo and sometimes more ribald remarks. Fortunately, the battered old car gave him little trouble, and in a light-hearted mood, he soon cajoled it along the country road to the distant city.

They were both eager to vacate the dismal streets of Glasgow. They both wanted to suck in the clean air of the hills and lochs of the Trossachs. The afternoon was warm and kind. Their awkwardness in each other's company disappeared as he encouraged her to talk about her beloved books. Bubbles settled into a relaxed crawl along the country roads amidst bleak Scottish hills and warmed to her anecdotes of publisher's parties, as well as the literary world she lived in.

Alicia told him about her friends, prime amongst them being her elder sister and young brother. He was a welder in one of the Clyde shipyards. Her sister acted as their mother now since her own youth had been squandered in memory of the sailor who had long since gone away. There were new friends too, of course, and a young girl had just joined the book department straight from Oxford University. A pretty girl with lovely grey eyes. She was the shop's buyer, actually getting good deals due to her influence with a much larger buying group for the bigger bookstores across the country. Her buyer's name rang a bell with Bubbles. He thought maybe it was the same as the First Lieutenant's new acquaintance. Not that he, Bubbles, would know much about that. Interesting all the same. Their day passed in youthful pleasure of each other's company on this untroubled December day. He hoped there would be more of them. She seemed to wish it, too.

During the weeks that followed; cleaning the boat up thoroughly went ahead in readiness for the dreaded inspection. As time permitted, between carrying out essential maintenance and other work to ensure efficient running of machinery, painted surfaces were scraped, cleaned and painted. Inside, the boat was taking on a resurrected look of smartness and efficiency in its fresh new paint.

First leave party returned and, within a few days, resumed again the life that, for a short time they had forgotten. Second leave party gladly left to take up old associations or maybe find new ones, the first of the new year, in these next precious two weeks which were due to them.

# Chapter 12

Lieutenant Hawks stood in the stern of the motor launch, keeping his eye on the floating dock. The seaman coxswain manoeuvred the fast boat from the pontoon, veered sharply away from *Maidstone's* hull, and throttled the powerful Paxman engine. A cream wake streamed away from the cutting bows, flowing in a swishing drop to spread in churning spumes behind them.

The floating dock stood bleak and grey, towering square against the far shoreline. Halfway across the loch, the boat altered course, aiming for a curving approach against the current to ease gently alongside the landing platform. Jeff Hawks looked upward at the looming cigar-shaped craft bolstered by weighty timbers in the centre of the dock. The submarine was coated in a fresh covering of dull black. Even now, as he watched, a small team of overalled figures dabbed with brushes at the base of the hull. The red coat of anti-fouling paint was going on, swathing a long red line along the lower curve. The bulbous forepeak flared at its base, belying its smooth, slim contours.

Lieutenant Grimes saluted and gave the Captain his verbal report. "We have fuelled and stored, sir. The hull has been checked. Navigator has made his report. The Dockmaster is ready to flood." The First Lieutenant waited. As expected, the Captain asked questions about the crew, recent orders, signals, and if there had been any major amendments. As the two continued their visual inspection, observing from the dock's upper catwalks, they paced the narrow aisles along its top; the First Lieutenant bringing the Captain up to date on all the relevant happenings during the leave period.

"One thing, sir. I'm afraid there is a Patrol Report on Able Seaman Brown from the Glasgow Military Police." The two men stopped.

"We allowed him Leave from Rothesay," the Captain was making a statement, remembering the look on the man's face as he had told him the bad news and given him the Signal to read.

"I'll see him later, once we are at sea. You haven't taken any action?" The Captain wanted to know if Lieutenant Grimes, as acting commanding officer, during his absence, had put any restrictions on the man.

"No, sir. I talked to him and felt that he was quite stable. I think he has accepted the situation now." Reggie thought the whole matter was somewhat distasteful. Fortunately, the Captain would now be able to deal with it.

"All right. We'll begin flooding as soon as the bottom party have finished." The Captain had other things which required his attention. He wanted to get his ship to sea.

The Casing party was on deck, with Leading Seaman Bates directing them. For the moment, there was nothing much to do. They stood watching the water flooding into the bottom of the dry dock in white, raging torrents from the huge circular culverts along the dock walls.

"Water up to the hull, commence checks," the officer gave his information and order from the Bridge. Below, inside the hull, an artificer accompanied the First Lieutenant through the boat to carry out water tightness and air pressure checks. All compartments were sealed, and the flooding continued.

The water swirled in giant eddies, washing against the sides. The black Roman numerals in a vertical line on the dock wall were submerged one by one. Men in overalls manned the winches along the dock top, slowly bringing in the wire cables, hand over hand. The capstan drums turned slowly. One man leant far out from the catwalk, giving hand signals, watching as the great wooden beams floated out from position. The submarine was no longer held fast, no longer held upright by the straining wood wedging steel from steel. They were afloat. "All compartment checks completed. No leaks," the intercom made its announcement for general information and fell silent.

From the Bridge, walkie-talkie communication brought the tugs in closer; the lines were passed. The cantilevered steel struts on the dock front opened, yawning wider, separating the machinery, grinding slowly until they had swung back to their furthest limits. "Let go fore-end! Let go aft!" The order from the Bridge brought the Casing party into action, unwinding the figure of eight turns from around cleats. The berthing hawsers were let slip, to splash loudly and be brought into the dock hand over hand.

The tugs had control lines secured and, by sound signals, began to haul the tonnage of the warship from its encasement. The process was slow and delicate, as minutely controlling corrections were required to manoeuvre the craft safely into mid-stream. Now, the submarine's engines thundered, took over and powered the craft. Lines were slipped, and tugs hooted in short blasts from their sirens and departed. The long black shape slid through the waters, up the loch, heading for the gap known as 'Rhu Narrows'.

The early afternoon sun was bright upon the waters and the men as they worked. A small congregation of amateur fishermen waved to the men on deck from the yacht pier of Helensburgh as they passed.

"Passed Rhu Narrows 1410." The information was carried down the voice pipe to be entered into the log. The time-honoured traditions were observed. All men were at their stations. The Casing party retreated back into the square hole and climbed down the tower, the last one in securing the hatch door.

"Well, how was it in the hospital then, Ginger? Lots of nurses ministering to your needs. Eh, eh!" The members of the for'ard Mess had a new target. The just returned Ginger Bates was in for a ribbing.

"Oh, not bad, you know. Didn't go much on the Matron, mind you." Ginger would play the game with them for a while.

"How did you manage to fall under a bus, anyway?" a new voice entered into the sport.

"He dropped half a crown, and it rolled under the wheels," somebody retorted. They were all going to get as many laughs as possible out of this.

"White Watch, passage routine," the announcement interrupted the hilarity.

"That's me; I'll tell you all about it later." Ginger was back with a vengeance. Straight to sea, and within half an hour, he was on watch. *It gets it out of the way,* he thought, and already his mind was occupied with working out which watch did what in the routine that was to follow during the day. Some new topics would have to be found to provide a little entertainment. The time had to be whiled away somehow.

A few noticed Jock Brown through the torpedo compartment hatch. He was busy polishing away at the copper pipes. He hadn't said much since he had been back. They knew better than to goad Jock. Bubbles took his perch on the curved hatchway and sat pondering the day's work. *It would be a surface passage up around the coast,* he thought. *Couple of days probably, depending on the weather, really.* He would ask one of the radio operators for the weather forecast. He liked to know what was going on.

"Cigarette Jock?" Bubbles offered the packet. The man stopped work and climbed up onto the platform, took a cigarette and placed himself on one of the Derisene motors. They sat like that, smoking for a minute.

"I was in Glasgow a lot last week," Bubbles said. He wasn't going to ask Jock anything about his ordeal, but if he approached it in the right way, he might want to get it off his chest. Brown wasn't about to say anything. He concentrated on the cigarette, rolling it about in his hand, looking hard at the writing along its length.

"I met a girl up there, in the Locarno. Do you know it, the top end of Sauchiehall Street?" Bubbles kept the tone quite light. If Jock didn't want to talk, that was his business.

"I used to go in there a few years ago. They were always closing it down because of razor fights, but I think they've cleared most of them out now."

Jock was still thinking about it, probably remembering those times. "You don't live near there now, do you?" Bubbles thought he would just leave it at that for the time being. It was up to Jock now.

"No, I never did." And that was it. Close of conversation. Whatever it was, the knowledge was going to stay inside his own head. Brown wasn't sharing any secrets. His cigarette was stubbed out, and the polishing resumed, even harder than before. There were a few raised eyebrows when Bubbles clambered back into the Mess. He just shook his head, and no one spoke. Not one of them knew what all this was about. Jock didn't confide his troubles to anyone.

The talk turned to their present destination. Not many of them had been up to the Isle of Skye before, but those who did know what it was like, were not saying much. It was one of those places where if you had managed to make a friend or two, you didn't pass the information on. You had to be invited in to know what highland hospitality was like, and if you valued it, you didn't tell others who might well gate-crash, thereby spoiling it for everyone.

"Blue Watch, ditch gash." The Tannoy still crackled after the voice had stopped. A distant shrieking voice permeated the boat via the open switch.

"Turn the bloody thing off!" There was a short pause and the quite returned. A cold wind blew through the boat while struggling bodies wrestled garbage bags through passageways, trying not to get their noses too close to the horrible oozing mess while climbing through hatches. The 'elephant's trunk', the long grey plastic funnel, had been secured to its circular welded ring and stood like a column around the Control Room ladder. This was how the hellish draught was prevented from sweeping through all compartments. At times like this, though, the floor-to-ceiling long flap had to be tied open, allowing unimpeded access into the vertical pitch-black corridor.

Charlie, the PO on watch, thumbs hooked into braces, was ushering the first four bag-laden men into the tower. One by one, arms were forced upward against the down draught, and the bags were passed upward, frequently banging in liquid mess alongside a head whilst in transit upward. It was always a fervent hope on such occasions that a bag, tied at the top, would not split and cascade its accumulation of soggy debris upon the encapsulated line of men. The man at the top was free from that particular hazard. He merely stood beside the officer of the watch in the small square cubicle, receiving a bag and unceremoniously slinging it overboard. It needed to be hurled way out to clear the ballast tanks and the operation continued until a long line of such white bags strung itself out, bobbing in their stern wake.

"Gash ditched!" would be the cry and they all descended to gather in the Control Room to laugh at whoever had caught the most filth down himself in the seeming jet stream of air rushing past like a hurricane. This pantomime was held once every day at sea, if they were surface cruising.

The coastline took on a dark contoured form as night fell. The coast remained three-mile distant, as *Orestes* ploughed her way north into the darkening sea and sky.

The crew of *Orestes* were completely unaware, as were the other boats of the Scotland-based squadron, that sometimes an Elat trawler would alter course to cross the sub's wake and retrieve floating garbage bags. Sometimes, useful information could be gleaned by the Russians this way.

"Telemotor failure! Telemotor failure! Steering control lost," the helmsman's voice carried clear through the night.

"Stop together," the officer ordered. The helmsman's hands reached upward for the telegraph. The Captain appeared as if from nowhere.

"Belay that. Half ahead together. Inform the Bridge," the Captain spoke, continuing his way into the centre of the room. Already, the microphone was in his hand.

"Engine Room Artificer, Control Room," there was no mistaking the imperative demand in his voice.

"Who's on the wheel?" The officer of the watch knew his voice had been heard, but the helmsman had not replied.

"Able Seaman Simeon, sir. The Captain ordered both engines half ahead, sir," Simeon had not reacted quickly. The suddenness of it all had confused him, and for a second or two, he had frozen completely.

The Captain was leaning over the chart table, examining the last visual fix recorded on the chart. He reached up above his head for the switch to the Bridge intercom. "Officer of the Watch, Captain here. With steering failure, we are likely to roll heavily in a cross-current. That is why it is advisable to maintain speed ahead. You will need to watch for drift."

"Aye, aye, sir. We have three miles sea room, but the current will push us in." The officer had no reference points for triangulation and could only visually estimate the amount of drift.

He spoke again. "Captain, sir. Permission to close up radar."

The Captain reached again for the microphone button. "The Chief is here, sorting out steering. We will know the answer soon. I think we will wait." The Chief straightened, wiped his hands on his overalls and glared at Simeon. He didn't speak but tested the steering and found that it did respond.

He called up the voice pipe, "Engine Room Artificer here, sir. You have steering control now."

The Chief followed the Captain to his cabin to give his explanation. Apparently, the helmsman had been steering with his left hand, the other dangling beside the seat. He had been fiddling and, without realising it, had released the lock on the changeover control lever. Further meddling with idle fingers had shifted the lever out of position, operated a solenoid and shut off the telemotor oil supply. Naturally, enough control had been lost.

Since Simeon was still technically under training, it was decided that formal examination and punishment would not be appropriate. He was, however, reprimanded personally by the Captain, in tones which left no doubt that any subsequent loss of concentration while at his post would be dealt with severely.

Simeon's ears were burning when he eventually came out. His eye twitch was overlooked, as it had come to be accepted as a normal feature of his. Some of the unkinder elements onboard took to calling him 'Simple Simon', and after a while, the name stuck. What had been a minor, really quite insignificant incident was soon forgotten.

The submarine continued its surface patrol, secure in its unvarying routine of changing watches. The craggy, barren cliffs and outcrops of Skye loomed high on the Starboard bow, hardly distinguishable from the mainland. They were in the calm sea of the Hebrides, the sun was shining, and off-watch sight-seers were allowed on deck to absorb the wild view which lay all around them.

Special Sea Duty men were closed up at their stations, including the radar operator. There were so many inlets and passages between the islands, hidden from view, which shielded boats of all descriptions. The likelihood of a trawler or pleasure boat, and especially a car ferry, suddenly appearing from the headland intent on crossing their track was great. All precautions had to be taken to maintain sea room. A few keen amateur photographers took advantage of this unusual and spectacular view from the sea, doubtful though it was that any of the photographs would be instantly recognisable. The more careful, who foresaw this difficulty, made a record of their shots so that locations could be fitted later.

By lunchtime, they were passing into the Little Minch and altering course around the headland. Constant reports came up from radar, as each car ferry was denoted by another dot appearing as disengaging from the land in a flicking procession across the screen. Once Navigator had sighted each from the Bridge, the operator could discontinue reporting, unless he noted an abrupt change of direction.

The Navigator's work was cut out for him, obtaining triangulation fixes for the chart. His eye sight was backed by that of the lookout. Pebble-like islands off the point of Rudh' Uisenish loomed nearer like upthrusts from the sea, resting perches for myriad sea birds.

The First Lieutenant monitored the boat's progress along the chart, ready to pilot the final stage down the Sound of Raasay. They anchored in The Sound, under the lee of high bluffs. The rocky hills loomed perpendicular to the sky. The five-mile distant peak above Loch Portree culminated in a rising patch of tiny white buildings. From this distance, they could barely see the staging pier of the village-sized town outpost.

Leave was granted to half the crew, the remainder ready to attend a dragging anchor if it should occur. Lieutenant Green knocked on the Captain's cabin door and was admitted. Shane took the proffered chair, faced the Captain who rested on the edge of his bunk and waited for him to begin.

"This is the patrol report by the Glasgow Military Police. Have you spoken to Brown about it yet?"

"No, sir, I haven't." Shane took the report, read it and placed it on the cupboard flap, which served as a desk.

"Philip, he is one of your men. I want you to talk to him, find out what's behind it all."

The Captain hesitated; this was a delicate matter. He cleared his throat and continued, "The report gives the hard facts, but since it is essentially a civilian matter and involves his home life, I want to view the whole thing as sympathetically as I can."

Shane was thinking as the Captain spoke. Captain obviously did not want to pursue a hard line of military discipline, not yet anyway. Shane, as the man's divisional officer, would need to defend him and act as his counsel if it did go further. Brown was not exactly an open type, would not confide, and it was even less likely that he would do so to an officer.

"Brown is a very difficult man to know, sir. He keeps very much to himself." Shane looked at the face opposite him.

"You want me to gain his confidence, find out all I can and appraise you of the underlying causes?"

"Yes, Philip." The Captain had been continuing his train of thought as the Torpedo Officer talked.

"I want to know why he acted with such ferocity. That man is going to be in hospital for a long time and probably scarred for life. I want to know what makes a man like Brown do that." The Captain was still thinking.

"He was lucky. It might easily have been murder, judging from this report." Jeff Hawks tapped the paper on his desk.

"The man refuses to bring an assault charge. Otherwise, Brown would be in a police cell right now. It also tells us that there is a lot more under the surface than we know about." Shane was nodding in agreement.

"I think a lot of it has to do with his background. So far as I know, he was brought up in the 'Gorbals'; he was weaned on violence."

"Yes, well, we have got to know about all of it. All the contributing causes must be brought to light. If this isn't handled properly, it could happen again. Brown will be finished, we will have lost a good man, and there could well be other repercussions as well." The Captain stopped for breath, looked at Shane and saw that he did understand the implications.

"That is the task I'm giving you, Philip. If we crucify him now, everyone loses, so let's investigate unofficially first. After that, I will decide what has to be done." Shane closed the door behind him and went away to think the matter over. Coxswain was informed that Brown would be required onboard. Coxswain made sure that he was.

After supper, those who were going ashore went on the liberty boat, especially provided by the Portree mayor's office. The island was prepared to offer hospitality and even welcomed new faces. Visitors were rare enough to be considered as potential friends, provided they didn't come in such numbers that the pace of life would be disturbed.

Shane walked through the for'ard Mess, signalled Brown to follow, and they went into the torpedo compartment, standing by the tube doors so that no one could hear. Bubbles had expected this. Retribution of the law, military or civilian, was usually quick. Putting two and two together, it seemed likely that after this short lapse of time, and with no defaulters process having taken place, it seemed advisable that the personal touch might be used. John and Bubbles had discussed the topic in private. It was a pity, they thought now, that Jock had drawn Shane as his defender. Navvy Brooks would have been a better chance at a sympathetic appraisal, they both thought. Out of their hands, though.

Bubbles leant over from his seat and shut the connecting hatch door, clipping it. A few eager faces, which had peered through the space, now looked dismayed since they would miss the show. Bubbles answered their looks with the one word, "Private."

"This is a very serious business, Brown. You will have to talk about it, whether you want to or not. Now, I am here to advise you, and whatever you tell me will be treated in confidence." Shane realised that his tone was a little heavy; perhaps the fact that they were standing made the whole thing sound more official. He sat down on one of the loading beams.

"It's only confidential until you report to the Captain; he discusses it with Jimmy. You discuss it with Jimmy, and all three of you tell anyone you think needs to know." Jock could feel the anger and frustration rising in him as he spoke. Shane merely looked at him, cool and unspeaking.

"This is a personal thing. I don't want to discuss it, sir." So far as Jock was concerned, that was all he had to say.

Shane thought for a minute he would have to change his tactics. "We know that this involves your wife, but you can't just half-kill a man for that reason." Shane meant to continue but was cut short.

"Look, sir. Are you married? No," Jock answered himself, "and your experiences don't equip you to know about my problems. Just leave it be. I can handle it in my own way."

Shane decided to overlook the insult. "Your way of handling the situation is going to get you in a lot of trouble," he said. *It was time for a cigarette to ease the tension,* he thought.

He offered the packet and lit them both. "You have been in the Navy long enough to know that the system only works because everyone takes orders. We would have anarchy if people took the law into their own hands. Can't you see that?" Shane considered if he would get through.

"I'm not stupid, sir, so don't talk to me as though I am. I know what the law can do and what it can't do. It doesn't protect people in this situation. A man has to take his own satisfaction. Where I come from, that is the law." *Well,* Shane thought, *at least we have got around to the subject of his background.* He would just have to stand here and suffer the insults for the sake of the Captain's directive, to get some information. They talked for well over an hour. The officer elicited everything he could and had to deduce a lot from it. Brown would not tell him any direct facts of the case, but at least now Shane began to understand something of the slum land he had come from and the basic creed of that jungle. Jock only told the officer what he thought would be enough to get him off the hook. *Why didn't they just leave him alone,* he thought.

Lieutenant Phil Green made his report to the Captain, who advised the First officer. Captain relented and removed the ban on shore leave for Brown. Captain was not entirely satisfied, but they understood the situation better. In this case, they would just need to wean the man out of it. He was, after all, a victim of his upbringing.

The submarine remained at anchor for three days. The periscopes saw a lot of use, during this time. Some of those who couldn't or didn't choose to step onto dry land whiled away their time observing, undetected, several of the young couples who climbed the high hill of Ben Tianavaig. It was an entertaining sport. It appeared that the newest generation to be born on Skye would have some fewer red-haired progeny amongst them.

On the third day, half the crew went ashore, and with them was Able Seaman Brown. This small corner of the Island was just beginning to lose its patience with the ways of the mainlanders. The sailors went looking for adventure. If there wasn't any, they made it. It had at first been a treat to see so many boisterous and entertaining men bent on enjoying themselves, and the drinking, it was understood, was part of that, but the islanders were not pleased with having their haven treated as a holiday hostel. The welcome was wearing thin.

An enterprising fisherman had some time ago fitted out an old motor caravan as a mobile fish and chip shop. He was a local of Portree, and when the climate was right, if the fish weren't running too well, he could always make a few bob, making instant suppers around the island. Mainland commercialism had come to Skye. The fish and chip van had a roaring instant trade by the small jetty from the hungry returning sailors. Jock Brown had a tendency to compensate himself with an excess of booze. He was drunk and in a temper, not much caring for the high price or even the quality of the supper. The fisherman, not one to mince his words, was abusive, and Jock promptly leaned into the cab, released the handbrake and sent the vehicle straight over the edge of the dock.

On news of the incident reaching the Captain, he dispatched Lieutenant Green to ascertain the facts from ashore. Sailing had to be delayed by one hour. The submarine commander was not amused by his officer's report. Retribution was swift. Jock appeared at the First Lieutenant's defaulters table, was summarily heard, and the facts recorded and passed onto the Captain's punishment table.

"What did you get, Jock?" he was asked when he showed up again in the Mess.

"Seven days number nines." Jock was not bothered by this particular punishment. He liked work anyway. It made no difference to him that he now had to work late and get up early for the next week. Most of the time, he occupied himself thus, anyway. It was a flea bite in this game of life.

The trip south was uneventful, except for the intended excursion for which they had come this far. One of the deep lochs, in fact, the deepest, served the submarine's purpose. A resident station had been set up long before to monitor a submarine's noise levels when dived. At the same time, the onboard sonar operated during many submerged transits of the loch. The purpose of the visit was to carry out sonar trials. A team of scientists came aboard to monitor all sets, making recordings to ensure that they functioned according to their specifications. The mysterious Mr Gray was with them, and yet to the sonar crew, it was obvious that his task was even more specialised. This time, he had much more equipment with him, including a padded box, securely locked. The box held some vital new transmitting coder for one of the Asdic sets. So, the rumour went around the boat. The trials began.

The professional 'Pingers' were involved in the long process up to its final conclusion. John Bishop, more resilient and easily the best of the operator's team, did not feel the strain quite so heavily.

The Captain, in conference with his First officer Shane, and the scientist Mr Gray, decided that only Bishop, the best pinger they had, would receive special instructions from the scientist on how the new Asdic link would be operated, but that was all, simply the operating instructions. It was deemed unnecessary for anyone else to know even this much. After each day's run through the sonar range, the scientist and John Bishop locked themselves into the sonar shack. Nothing was said amongst the crew; it was not openly discussed. Only a few realised that this procedure was abnormal.

The days of trial that constituted at least one run, and usually two each day, required only Bishop and the scientist to be in attendance. The other operators could take a rest. Nevertheless, after such long periods of intense concentration, some of them were mentally drained, the signs of weariness apparent to all. John was concerned that Simple Simon did not appear to be improving with time. His techniques, or lack of them, remained consistently low. John still had serious reservations about setting the ball in motion, which could so easily terminate the man's chances. He continued to keep a careful but unnoticed eye on him. For the moment, he was glad that the submarine was on its way to Campbeltown, which had always been one of his favourite haunts. *With luck,* he thought, *they would be there tomorrow, early.* He made a quick calculation and decided that maybe twelve to fourteen hours of surface cruising would do it.

In the late afternoon, the for'ard Mess was indulging in a game of Uckers. Actually, there were four players and around six onlookers who shouted encouragement or tut-tutted an unwise tactical move. A dishevelled character appeared in the doorway, bag of tools in hand.

"What do you want, Spider?" One of the players, noting the tools, had a strong suspicion of the electrician's intention.

"Can't help it, lads. Got to do me battery dips." He smiled a tongue-in-cheek sort of expression. Long ago, he had learnt to sway before the onslaught which came his way. *Part of the 'battery king's' life, really,* he thought.

"Look, I'll do this side first, right? Then you can all move across 'ere, and I'll do t'other, right?" He had a merry twinkle in his eye.

He knew they weren't going to give up just like that. "Come on, man, you're going to ruin the game." This appeal to his sense of decency had no effect either. The man just stood there, hair all tousled as though he had just woken from sleep, cheeks ruddy. He always looked like that. His tattered shirt, full of grouped frayed circular holes, like miniature bullet holes, revealed pink flesh beneath.

"Aw! Come back at midnight when everybody is turned in," the voice argued in a somewhat hostile tone. Spider stopped, shook his head in slow, deliberate turns from a complete left to a complete right, and repeated.

"Can't be done, Matey. Got to do t'dips. Charging batteries overnight. Got to know condition and SG, right?" With no more ado and definitely closing further discussion, the electrician began to unbolt the two right-hand tables from the deck. Then, the seats, and by this time, three others were helping him to store the heavy gear in a corner.

"Fags out, gents!" the final phrase was mouthed over his shoulder while on hands and knees, lifting the battery hatch flaps. A whole line of gleaming copper bands linked the row of secondary batteries beneath the decks. The man disappeared below, taking only his hydrometer and an insulated tool. Spider Webb was as popular as usual, even in his absence. Nobody minded, really, just a hint of minor irritation blown up into a hostility game that everyone knew was harmless. Spider was a mischievous, cheeky character, and they liked him. He was one of them. By the time he came out, there were a few more acid burns on his shirt, which would rot away the material into another little hole or two.

*Orestes* churned its way through the night, encountering only one freighter at close quarters in passage through the Atlantic Ocean. They sighted and exchanged signals, giving identification and destination. This interchange occurred off the coast of Coll and Tiree. The facts were registered in the ship's log accordingly.

After midnight, the Electrical Officer informed the Captain of the batteries' charging levels and the fact they would be gassing at high rates until morning. The message was passed along the boat amongst those who were still awake, and 'No Smoking' boards were hung in prominent positions along hatch accesses. Some slumbering creatures, whose habit it was to light up first thing in the morning, even before opening their eyes, were greeted with the intercom announcement.

"No smoking throughout the ship, batteries gassing." John's estimate of arrival time was sadly mistaken. Unknown to any of them, the submarine had received a signal in classified code. The officer of the watch received his instructions in the Captain's cabin prior to climbing the tall tower for his tour of duty.

# Chapter 13

The detour up the Firth of Lorn to lie off in wait at Kerrera was accepted when the news broke as routine business, transferring the Whitehall big wig from one place to another. John Bishop, as the present helmsman, noted the agile black-coated figure emerge from the elephant's trunk and step into the Control Room, to be immediately ushered into the Captain's presence. John said nothing and passed no comment to the log-keeper. So far as he was concerned, the answer was simple. Duly, the log keeper entered the pick-up point, and the guest was recorded as a Government Official, as per instructions.

The Cabin door firmly shut behind him, and the new arrival stiffly saluted the lieutenant who was the commander of this submarine. He felt uncomfortably close. The cabin was barely bigger than a broom cupboard back home. *These British sure lived in cramped conditions,* he thought.

"Lieutenant Palmer, US Navy, sir. I have orders from your naval intelligence." The young American was reluctant to say more, and Jeff Hawks sensed this.

"Please sit down, Lieutenant." Jeff Hawks proffered the only chair by his desk bureau. He cast a measured glance over the man and let his gaze rest on the officer's cap, which now adorned his desktop.

"Orders, sir." The American had noticed the look and was smiling broadly. The New England accent was barely distinguishable from the English spoken in Surrey or Kent.

"While in transit on British government transport, I am to wear British uniform. I have to remain as inconspicuous as is possible, you understand, sir." The young lieutenant noticed the ornately framed photograph of a striking ash-blonde woman, presumably the Captain's wife. The Captain read the letter addressed to him from a Commander at Box Ten. The signature was meaningless to him. However, he had been informed of all that it was necessary for him to know through official channels, but thought no harm would come of making a casual enquiry of the American.

"All I am able to say, sir, is that my team of commandos has a mission to recover certain useful Russian equipment. I believe you will receive orders soon for your submarine to get us in, and hopefully out, with the prize. More than that, I am instructed I must not reveal. Really sorry, but Top Secret, I'm afraid. The Captain had to be satisfied with that and he invited his temporary guest to the Wardroom.

The journey continued, most of the crew remaining in ignorance of their passenger. John had his doubts that they would, in fact, continue to Campbeltown under the circumstances. Once more, he was wrong. Later than originally planned, they skirted to the starboard of Davaar Island and proceeded up the channel, past the fishing boats, and alongside the wooden stage platform on stilts.

A large black car drew up alongside the storage tanks. That was as close on the road as it could get to the arriving sub. The gangway was thrust out, sliding to rest on the wooden jetty. Almost before it stopped, the Captain and the tall, lithe officer tramped down it together, their synchronised steps causing it to bounce in time. At a brisk walk, they headed straight for the car, got in and were gone.

"Who was that bloke? Never seen him before." Petters had temporarily been seconded to the Casing party and stood by the gangplank, gaping. The First Lieutenant belatedly climbed down from the tower. He should have been there to salute the Captain leaving the ship. For once, he had not been informed and, as a result, had missed the departure.

"Never mind that Petters. Get on with your work. That gangway isn't secure." Jimmy, dwarfed by the slow-thinking hulk, turned his back and returned from whence he had come. Ginger Bates had tried to warn Pet Hulk not to say anything, but it was too late for that now. He wondered himself where the new lieutenant had come from, and besides that, since when did a junior officer accompany the skipper off the boat on what was obviously an official trip, what with the car and all? Well, he wouldn't get any answers, so it's best to forget it.

The liberty men were already tumbling out on deck. "Come on, tie the rotten gangway up. I want to get ashore before the fishing fleet gets in." That was Peters, the so-called physical training instructor. *As fit as a flea, he is,* thought Ginger. A lot of the men went out on the town that night. Submariners were well known here, especially by the fishermen's wives. They might even throw an impromptu hop up the village hall.

There was already a rousing chorus going in the bar when John and

Bubbles stepped through the door. The first sight which greeted them was the steward, propped against the bar, shovelling whisky down his throat as though afraid that the bar would run out. The hooked nose already had a faint pink glow to it, and each time the head went back, his banana leaves style hair cut clipped upward and back into place as he finished the gulp.

"Take it steady, Sandy; we're only in till tomorrow." Somebody was trying to dampen the steward's style.

"I know that. It's why I'm having tomorrow's now!" Randy Sandy was ordering another drink. He was quite happy to stay up at the bar until it closed. A lot of the others were not. The news got around that a group had been got together, the rickety old wooden village hall had been opened up, and that people were coming in from all over the place. Many of the men knew that if this followed the usual procedure, there would be no bar at the dance. For some strange reason, drinking wasn't encouraged. Most of them bought a half bottle, just big enough to still fit into a hip pocket but not big enough to be obtrusive. John, Bubbles, Charlie and the rest of them gathered together and sauntered up the narrow streets to the outskirts of town.

It wasn't easy to miss because the group's sound vibrations carried clear across the hills and the makeshift harbour. There were two or three small tables, obviously brought in from people's homes, especially for the occasion, and maybe half a dozen kitchen chairs. Necessarily, the two hundred or so incumbents occupied the floor in small groups at talk or shuffled in indistinguishable huddled pairs. The stage, wooden like the rest of the edifice, rattled to the strains which emanated on its top. Apparently, the stage was a permanent fixture. A couple of keen-eyed organisers watched to try and catch the surreptitious flash of a quickly tilted whisky bottle. They had little success and yet still wondered why the toilets were in such heavy demand. Liquor was not allowed in the island halls, even for an impromptu music gathering or dance, usually put on for visiting sailors such as this.

Several couples slipped away early, unnoticed; the spaces they left were soon occupied by new arrivals. Within a couple of hours, the dance deteriorated into a stagnant chat show. Virtually no dancing went on, and the band might just as well not have been there. Little attention was paid to them, and the declining number of females were much in demand.

When the band packed up their instruments and went home, it appeared that most of the remaining milling figures in the place were forlorn husbands and boyfriends. Very few of the submarine crew were to be found, but Randy Sandy staggered in magnificent time to the non-existent music, his nose in vibrant, full-blooded glow. At this moment in time, apparently, he belonged to Glasgow.

A cluster of irate civilians gathered on the roadway, semi-surrounding the three or four sailors. John Bishop stood on the fringe with the girl, who nestled comfortably into his shoulder. Bubbles, at the centre of the group, felt decidedly drunk from the effects of the unaccustomed raw spirit and wondered briefly if it was homemade moonshine, good quality though it undoubtedly was. He also felt reckless, not for the first time in his life.

The civilians argued, the gestures becoming angrier. It seemed that a stag fight was about to commence. *Campbeltown rutting season,* Bubbles thought, *and the leaders of the pack objected to the rogue male stealing their female.* In his mind, Bubbles waxed lyrical, and watching the frightened and shy girl, he felt suddenly romantic. John, quite, quite sober, was anxious to be gone, preferably with his prize. Bubbles looked at the men, the hubbub of voices rising around him, lost in unintelligible island Gaelic gabble. The meaning was obvious, but the words were lost. He looked at the couple, at the hunted look they shared. For this occasion, in a once-only performance stand, Bubbles would become Sir Galahad.

The voices had momentarily subsided, allowing the injured party to vent his intense displeasure. At the same moment that Bubbles launched himself, fists flailing, he realised that this was not the husband but an additional boyfriend. He felt no sympathy at the slamming impact of his fists on the man. The numbers ensured that he held no permanent supremacy. As he went down, he had time to see John take advantage of the distraction and scarper with his prize. Bubbles had acted on impulse and had not stopped to calculate the likely outcome. However, Charlie and the cavalry had departed unnoticed by him.

The cold wind stirred, rustling about the curled figure on the ground. Biting wind stung his face, and he shook his head. That was a mistake; the pain shooting arrows through it brought his hand up to explore the damage. Cuts stung intolerably, leg muscles creaked while he dragged himself upright. The area was deserted, village hall dark, locked, empty looking. His left hand came away covered in blood, and there was a deep throbbing furrow down one cheek from just below the left eye. Everything else was all right, apart from the sense of departed strength. Bubbles' head cleared in the coldness of night. The alcohol fumes had gone; only the numbing effect remained, acting as an anaesthetic. In a weaving, uncoordinated shamble along the streets, he made his way unseeing through an alleyway. A dark, outlined figure wafted towards him from the light.

"Christ almighty, you're in a mess! Come on, son. You come with me; I'll fix you up," the voice, gruff but kind, talked at him. Like a wounded animal, he responded to the offer of assistance, being led into the unknown.

The shadowy figure reached into a box and poured a small amount from a bottle onto a wad in his hand. The cotton wool came away with clustered speckles of clotted blood. The warm feeling pulsed through his cheek, so he looked around the tiny cabin to distract his thoughts from the pain. Papers and clothing lay in scattered heaps around the bunks. An overpowering smell of oily dirt and fish assailed his nostrils. The smell of fish pervaded over all others, persistent and nauseous.

Dimly, he was aware of a second fisherman, or so his clothes denoted him to be, somewhere in the darker reaches of the cabin. Bubbles had the vaguest feeling that he had seen the blonde-haired man before, possibly at Portsmouth dockyard. It was too painful to think just now.

"I expect you'd like something to eat. You were lucky there, you know, another inch, and it would have been your eye," the gruff voice stopped, and the man went away to get food. Bubbles heard him moving around in some cubicle behind where he now sat. He listened to the gentle lapping of water against the trawler's hull. The weather-beaten figure just sat, saying nothing, sewing a shirt or something. Bubbles could not see what was in the man's lap.

"There you are, mate, get that down you; you'll be all right." The figure came into view and, crouching, took the seat opposite across the table. The soup was thick and oily, its steam rising from the chipped mug stung at his face. Bubbles ate the sandwich also, feeling better by the minute. Now, he felt sheepish to have done such a stupid, senseless thing. He wasn't a fighting man; he didn't like violence, and yet there had been an instinctive, primitive satisfaction in that brief bestial barrage.

"You're from the submarine, aren't you, mate?" The gruff voice laughed. "'Course you are. No other ships here. Strewth John, your uniform's in a mess." The man looked concerned. Bubbles felt the lurching of the small fishing smack as the waves rolled it backwards and forward against the jetty. He felt queasy, the pain in his head had returned and a mist seemed to be closing around his eyes. Dimly, he could hear the man talking.

"Oh yes, I recognise that badge." The kindly fisherman was helping him off with the jersey, a sponge in hand. He dabbed at the mud stains and looked closely at the badge on its right arm. Bubbles opened his eyes to see the gold crossed torpedoes and the harpoon through its middle. Why, he wondered, were they so interested in the badge? He could sense that the other man had come closer to look. His head was hurting dreadfully. *The rocking of the boat must have something to do with it,* he thought.

"Torpedo and anti-submarine branch, eh, John?" The fisherman was grinning. Bubbles tried to think, but the effort was unrewarding.

"Why are you calling me John?" he muttered. The other man spoke for the first time.

"What this letter?" the clipped tones seemed unnatural, foreign even to Bubbles, but somehow, everything seemed vague, unreal. *It was not the sound of these islands' usual lilt, somewhere further north or east,* he thought. Couldn't place the accent, though. He couldn't feel his legs. They seemed like rubber.

"What this letter, eh sailor?" The man was shaking him roughly by the shoulder. Bubbles opened his eyes, the jersey uniform jumper and its badge floated there in front of his vision. The golden stitched 'W' stood out clear beneath the harpoon.

"Weapons." It seemed such an effort to get his tongue around that single word. Then he faded into a black world, where even the rocking of the boat ceased.

A cold wind blew across his face, stung grievously at the wounded cheek, and battered at his now open eyes. Bubbles lifted himself onto one elbow and stared at the empty street around him. The first light of morning was coming up. He felt his head and rubbed his hands through his hair. His cheek was raised and jagged. He could see the lump; the great swelling stood out beneath his eye. Cautiously, Bubbles pulled himself upright onto his knees, tested his balance, and waited to see if his head would rock with the pain he expected to come. After perhaps a minute, he realised that it would not taunt him further; the pain ebbed, thankfully. He stood and, to give time to gain confidence in his ability to balance, idly brushed the dust from his suit. The caked mud would have to wait for now. His hand swept over the badge on his right arm, and a memory of the events of the night before rushed in.

It was relatively easy to find his way back to the submarine. He merely needed to follow the line of the hill and take any street that led downward. Inevitably, it would lead him to a place where he could look out on the sea, and then the extended wooden jetty would be easy to find. He tentatively took the first few steps and then picked up his pace as his muscles responded without too much complaint.

Bubbles began to put the events of his experience together. For some reason, they had thought he was John. That in itself would have meant nothing except that they showed an interest, in fact, a great deal of interest, in his badge. Fishermen were never concerned with things like that. It suddenly came to Bubbles why they had been so interested. Only he and one other of the submarine crew wore that particular device of a gold thread star above and one below the harpoon. John Bishop, he was the key to all this! The one difference was that John had the initial 'C' in gold thread beneath his badge. That was it! Those fishermen, or whatever they were, had thought he was John Bishop. What was their interest in him?

Bubbles was nearing the submarine before he realised that the whole incident with the irate boyfriend the evening before had been set up to trap John. It just remained to deduce why such an elaborate plot had been hatched to appear sympathetic to a sailor whom they must have arranged a beating for. Coxswain dressed the cheek wound and listened to the story. Bubbles could tell that he was dismissing it as a pure flight of fancy. However, the more Bubbles thought about it, the more it made sense. He must keep it in mind to mention the episode to Shane when the opportunity arises. For now, it was best forgotten. He had learnt something, and he had been lucky too. Now, it was put down to experience and belonged to the past.

Pet Hulk had the early watch on deck. Most of the late returning revellers were asleep below. The sun was rising, sending bright waves across the sky. It was time to be up and about; a new day had begun. All was in readiness for sailing, and yet they had to wait. The Captain had not arrived from shore. The First Lieutenant treated this as a normal working day until his commander returned. The men were busy with their tasks.

Petters walked to and fro on the casing with nothing much to occupy his mind. He wondered idly how West Ham were doing in the Cup. Then, he saw a dishevelled figure ambling up the long wooden corridor towards the boat. By the way he was dressed he was obviously a fisherman, and he looked a little the worse for wear. *Nothing better to do, I suppose,* Petters thought. The Hulk continued to watch as the man approached furtively. Petters strolled to the gangplank and started to walk down it. For a moment, it looked as though the bloke was going to come on board.

"Have you got a man, name of Peters on here?" the fisherman spoke with a very thick island accent, made worse by his condition of drink. Pet Hulk stood there, quite at ease.

"Yus, that's me." He wondered what this was about. The haggard face screwed up into a sudden rage. The fisherman charged in like a bulldozer, arms swinging in giant haymakers. Petters took the first two blows on his massive chest before he realised what was happening. The blows had no effect, not even rocking him, but were enough for Petters, who lashed out in effortlessly gathered strength, connected with the tired face and proceeded to immunise him from all possible further thoughts of violence.

The man lay in a bedraggled heap where his senses had left him. The Hulk scratched his head in bewilderment, not understanding what it had all been about. Nevertheless, he dragged the prostrate body up the jetty and lay him in a quiet shadow out of sight. It wouldn't do for one of the officers to see this. A head popped up from below in time to witness the incident, said nothing and made a hasty retreat. Disappearing again before the sentry saw him and then returning to the for'ard Mess. The Mess was full, all of them vying for the few cups so they could get their share of tea.

The Liverpudlian was in full conversational flow. "Well, we left early, see, and was looking for somewhere quiet, like." Nobody was all that interested. Scouse was embroidering a story on his previous night's experience.

"So, we goes into the graveyard, you know, 'cos there's nobody about, but she doesn't go much on the cold headstone on her backside, see what I mean?" There were a few laughs at this part of Scouse's story. He could certainly invent them, they thought, but he was holding their attention now.

"Well, we goes back to her place, and she reckons her old man won't be back till midnight." Scouse interrupted his story to observe the effect.

"Go on." Somebody was getting impatient at the delay.

"There I am with all me gear off, and we hears the front door open. 'Oh God,' she says, 'that's my husband!'" There was another pause. "So, I grabs me clothes, tucks 'em under me arm, and climbs out the window, just as he comes in. I got away all right, and he didn't see me, but I bet she didn't half cop it." Scouse Peters looked around at the faces. A few of them wanted to believe it, but a lot of them looked quite bored.

"Hey, do you know what I just saw up top?" a new voice held their attention, and when the story was told, the whole place was in paroxysms of laughter.

"Captain, coming aboard," the announcement, localised to the Control Room and Wardroom circuits, was hurried. For the second time, Reggie was too late to observe the customary formalities. Petters received another ear full of veiled threats from their irate First Lieutenant.

They got under sail in minimum time. The Engine Room crew had been standing by for two hours. The submarine made all speed to round the Mull of Kintyre, passing through the Irish North Channel and proceeding out to the Atlantic. The task force with which they must rendezvous was already in the designated area, on station, waiting for *Orestes*.

Exercise 'Square Peg', due to start on the fifteenth of January, was delayed by one day due to unforeseen circumstances. All the commanders in the task force opened and read their exercise orders. It was clear from these that the prime object was to give a cruiser, two destroyers and three frigates practice at submarine attacking.

The second phase would be centred around an aircraft carrier, using its Buccaneer jets to simulate attacks on a squadron of ships to be known throughout as 'Orange Force'. The carrier and all submarines to be known as 'Blue Force'. Due to a shortage of ship availability, a number of royal fleet auxiliaries, patrol craft and minesweepers occupied places in the exercise. On paper, they would become cruisers, assault ships and landing craft.

The second phase completely reversed roles, whereby the ships would deploy on a screen to protect the one capital ship. In this case, the Orange Force capital ship would be a helicopter-carrying frigate, but for the purposes of the exercise, it was designated as a commando and helicopter-carrying carrier.

The submarine's task was to penetrate that screen in whatever manner became necessary in order to sink the guarded ship. Naturally, this was a simulated battle, but that did not alter the objective nor the amount of skill and daring which must be used in order to achieve it. This was vital practice in the event that one day, those talents might be required for real in the defence of their country. To the officers, total commitment to participation in the war games was essential. For the crews who carried out all the constituent functions of each craft which made the games possible, it was merely another two weeks at sea. They did not see the overall plan nor the strategy, nor did they appreciate the tactics involved; their tasks were technical, repetitive and often menial. This is how war games are fought, as though for real.

*Orestes* sent her 'arrival on station' signal, and prepared to dive. Her function during that first week was simply to avoid detection, transiting from one area to another in compliance with her orders. At a predetermined time on a particular day, she must be in a certain sector. Apart from that, her commander had complete freedom of choice about how and when to comply. The onus for obtaining early warning of enemies in their area lay with the sonar operators. John Bishop became the lynchpin around which information was gathered. Two hours was considered the maximum time allowable for full concentration in any one period of 'listening'. The Watches were operated accordingly. The submarine was in transit at depth, maintaining slow speed and listening.

"Silent Running. Long-range listening." The intercom fell silent. The crewmen who were not involved had been informed. They knew that they must only undertake such activities which would not infringe the rules of silence. This was a golden opportunity for some to climb into their bunks and read. All unnecessary machinery was either shut down or used only as required, with minimum use of operation being the criteria. The chefs prepared their meals in silence, with no heating, no cooking; everything had to be cold. Exotic names were concocted for the salads, which varied from meal to meal with only minor changes. The names were intended to make the sameness acceptable but usually fooled nobody.

After a number of days, the crew lost track of time; day became night. Each, in his own way, found a means of filling in that time. Many of the men gathered together pieces of wood, plastic and cloth, any scrap material which could be utilised, and were made into toys for their children. Movement through the boat was done quietly and restricted to the minimum.

The First Lieutenant decided this was an ideal time to test the knowledge of the trainees. Simeon and Harman, along with the others, were summoned to the torpedo compartment and thoroughly questioned on its apparatus. In turn, they went through each of the six compartments, all their knowledge being elicited by the questioning officer. He was not satisfied with their progress, deciding that extra instruction was necessary over a period of a month, at which time he would test them again.

Simeon missed his Watch in the sonar shack through no fault of his own, but it meant that another had to take his place. John was annoyed at the disruption. In fairness to the man who had taken Simeon's place, Simeon would now have to act as number two in the next Watch. Unwittingly, the First Lieutenant had removed Simple Simon from John's watchful eye and his custody. The number one operator maintained long range and also medium. At present, under these circumstances, all concentration was centred on long range. Meanwhile, Simeon, the number two, operated on short range. One of the enemies was near, lying in wait, engines silent, using her sets to listen. The submarine had lost contact; they didn't know where the ship was, except that she was within a five-mile radius of them.

"Ultra-quiet routine," the Captain ordered. All departments closed down everything that was not essential to the boat's motive power, except for the minimum of lighting. The bathygraph gave constant readouts of sea temperature, and the submarine continued to crawl forward through The Deep. Orders for changing depth, coupled with gently eased alterations of course, were given. The Captain observed the bathygraphic read-outs until he found what he was looking for.

"Layer of warm water," there was a slight note of triumph in his voice.

"One hundred and twenty feet, stop engines," he ordered and moved to stand between the two planesmen, watching their manipulations of the fore and after hydroplanes. Satisfied now that they were settled on depth, virtually still and requiring only minimum adjustments to maintain their level, the Captain went to the sonar room. With headphones settled on his head, Jeff Hawks listened for the echoes transmitting from somewhere on the surface. He smiled gently to himself. The transmissions had stopped. There was nothing left but to wait it out.

An hour passed, and nothing happened. The heat generated by machinery and personnel built up in the enclosed space. Men's faces shone with sweat. Simeon felt distracted by the Captain's presence and his own ever-present fear of being encased within this steel tube. He didn't so much mind being shut in, but his imagination played tricks, conjuring up situations of panic. They filled his head with visions of water rushing in, hearing it, and not being able to see where it came from. So far, he had been able to stifle the images in time before they took over his mind completely. Somehow, he always managed to force his attention away from the pictures to focus on the practical task at hand, yet still the fear remained. His concentration had slipped. There was nothing to listen to, so it didn't matter, but if it had started again, his reactions would have been slow. The Captain's presence irked him; he felt watched, spied upon. He felt closed in, and the visions were coming back; his nerves were beginning to shriek at him inside his skull.

The time had come for action. Captain took up position in the centre of the Control Room. "Easy does it," he was instructing the blowing panel chief.

"Blow, three and four main ballast. We are coming up to sixty feet." The chief cracked open the valves until a blowing hiss of air emanated, then opened wider. The deafening roar closed in on their ears after the silence. The Captain's hands indicated a downward movement. They shut down the air blow valves and watched the depth gauge, its needle flicking to the left, gently following the numerals down its scale.

"Up periscope." The Captain was gesturing. The Second Coxswain felt relaxed now that they had broken silence. He gently manipulated the hydroplane and glanced around at the other petty officer. His planes control was steady. A strange pulsing noise came from somewhere not too far off but not yet identifiable to the planesman. The Captain's hands flicked upward on the periscope handles, closing them into the vertical with a sharp click.

"Dive! Dive! Six degrees bow down bubble. Two hundred feet. Flood main ballast. Flood Q. Down periscope," the Captain's order was calm, even-voiced.

The pulsing became a dull thud.

The reaction time of the Scratcher, who was the for'ard planesman, was appallingly slow. He had been watching the depth gauge for some reason, fascinated by the flicking, vibrating needle.

"Dive!" The one word was accompanied by two swift steps by the Captain; his right hand reached out swinging. The open hand caught a terrific stinging blow to the side of the planesman's head. The Captain's hand then darted forward to plunge the control bar downward to its full extent. The Second Coxswain's hands belatedly took over.

The rush of flooding water into the main tanks stopped. A vibrant thrumming sound filled through the chamber, reverberating through the steel hull, coming closer, louder. Simeon sat spellbound; the echo could not be real. His mouth dropped open, and he froze. The deafening roar of hissing air blanketed everything.

For just a split second he thought he had heard something. His tongue was dry, clinging to the roof of his mouth. There was no need for headphones now. Everyone in the steel chamber heard the slow whirring thrum of bronze propeller blades thrash their way through the sea. They stood, every one of them waiting for the tearing crash that must come. The boat was in a steep, inclined attitude. She moved, diving but so slowly, there would not be time. The boat inched her way deeper; the sound was on top of them, filling their lives.

After what seemed an eternity, the moment passed, the seconds ticked by and no rending tear of twisting metal came. The flutter of churning water faded further and further away. The sound of each man's heartbeat took over the drumming sound, subsiding but slowly as the danger faded away. Nothing was said, everyone returned to their duty.

The submarine slipped quietly away, heading into the next sector. No one else found them in the remaining days of that first week. *Orestes* surfaced on schedule, shut off from diving, having successfully evaded the opposing force.

Signals were exchanged, and ships dispersed to carry out their individual assignments until the second phase began in two days' time. *Orestes* nosed her way around Inishowen Head, through the wide bay of Lough Foyle and up to the landing stage within the environs of Londonderry.

# Chapter 14

Shane had considered the matter thoroughly and was now convinced that the incident involving Leading Seaman Sudswell at Campbeltown, was indicative of foreign interest in the new secret sonar apparatus. He did not have enough overall knowledge to decide which foreign power was involved. Yet it had to be the Soviets, surely! All he could do was report the matter to those in a position to make such an assessment. Lieutenant Hawks granted his Torpedo Officer permission to send the Signal in code. It had been made clear to him recently that this was a facility which he must extend to this officer, like it or not. He certainly did not accept the idea readily. This was a most unusual order to receive through Captain SM. Though it was clear to the Captain it had to be intelligence work, and yet he was not himself in the loop.

The crew rested for the weekend living within their steel shell. Then venturing out along the broad main road to town after a few jars in Cassidy's, their favourite haunt. Most of them didn't bother going anywhere but the pub across the road, so close to them and next door to the betting shop. That was relaxation enough and besides, the English were never popular here, not since the early troubles. A few, but only a very few, were granted special leave to take the rail journey to Belfast and thence fly home to Glasgow. They were the few who could afford the fare, needing to justify the visit to their officers, and to themselves. They needed to weigh up the cost of travelling home for just two days and return for Monday morning.

The telephone call, only hours after their arrival alongside, surprised Shane. At first, he did not recognise the voice suggesting a meeting at a Londonderry hotel. The name meant nothing to him. "I want you to meet me at eight o'clock tonight, in the Victoria Hotel, Shannon Street." The request was terse and stilted. The Welsh voice was unfamiliar, distorted through the telephone speaker.

"My name is Clover. Do you remember me from the Astoria Hotel?" The memory of an unshaven chin and a shabby ginger-haired man crossed Shane's mind. He now realised that this was the response to his coded message. The voice seemed to have sensed his recollection of the prior meeting.

"Ask for room thirteen. You will not be in uniform." The click of the receiver sounded loud in Shane's ear. The caller had gone, and there had been no chance to say anything other than his name when first answering the call. It would not, in any case, have been sensible to have worn a uniform in this place. It was too close to the border of Southern Ireland, and an Englishman could so easily draw antagonism. The Troubles were well remembered if superficially hidden for the present.

The taxi brought him to the town square, surrounded by its shop displays and tavern lights. The officer, uncomfortable in this strange place, in such casual clothing, paid the driver and waited for it to turn around the square and disappear from sight. There were very few people about on the streets. In any case, Shane did not feel like asking for directions. He felt cold, and the cause of it was more than the weather. The atmosphere around him felt hostile, but he tried to shrug it off. Before long, he came to the post office, and as luck would have it, a town map was displayed in the window. He did not have far to go.

A few bottles of brown ale stood amidst the dust of the table. The man seated behind it still looked dishevelled, bleary-eyed and unshaven. The puffed eyes might only have been the shadows thrown in from the lights of a sign across the narrow road. Shane knew that the man called Clover was shrewder than he looked. Still, he refused the hospitality.

"What happened, exactly?" Clover poured one of the bottles into his stained glass and gulped the brown liquid, belying the fact that he was listening to Shane recount Sudswell's story.

"What is all this about?" Shane did not like his companion, who appeared not to hear what he had told him, preoccupied instead with his drinking. His hands stopped playing with the glass, and both elbows came to rest amidst the dust and spilt liquid, hands clasped together, fingers entwined. For the first time, those eyes gazed intently at him, shoulders hunched forward.

"The Soviets are creating an empire," Clover's voice had softened, but the face was like steel, in earnest, for once alive. The eyes were bright as he continued.

"To accomplish this, they need military superiority over the West. You know their history." Shane nodded. He was not easily overawed by anyone, but now he admitted that perhaps he was impressed by this man's zeal. Clover seemed to be examining the officer's expression. "Soon, they will overtake the free world in sheer weight of arms, and they know that it is necessary to produce more advanced weaponry, technology, and science." Clover hesitated, searching for the right phrase.

"The quantity is equal, the quality is not, but soon, my friend, it will be." The head nodded, confirming the statement. Shane noticed how white his knuckles had become.

"They advance on many fronts. Their science is growing. Now to answer your question." The fingers relaxed, and the voice was calmer.

"The Soviets are experimenting with a very sophisticated guidance system. They feel so sure of it that they are already discarding some production of conventional weapons, guns, tanks, and artillery, mostly so that the factories can make missiles. America has missiles, Russia must have missiles, but there is a difference. There will be a new generation of missiles soon. The experiments will show that it works on a new principle. Now this, my friend, is the irony." Shane wondered if the Welshman's anger was at himself, the world or with him. No, he decided it was not anger nor frustration, but incredibly, it was pleasure. Shane was repulsed by the man's exuberance, reverence almost, as he talked of the prelude to Armageddon.

"It is a race, my friend, to see who will find the answer first. We have some of the jigsaw, and they have some. We want their pieces, and they want ours."

Clover stopped speaking to refill his glass. Shane thought deeply about what this information meant to him and everyone else in the free world. "You will not see your Mr Gray again. He is too valuable now and not even safe in his laboratory at Portsmouth." Clover finished the glassful and wiped his mouth with a sleeve.

"They will try again as they are desperate now in case we find the answer first. Even the smallest detail is important. Be on your guard." Shane was not unduly concerned. This grubby little man seemed hardly able to take care of himself. He wondered perhaps if the man delighted in exaggerating the situation and, hence, his own importance. How much truth was there, he wondered in this answer to his question. Shane left the unfriendly room, knowing that he could not discuss this evening's events with anyone unless authorised through his chain of command channels.

The Second Coxswain was angry, and volubly so, in the Mess. "An officer can't get away with striking a PO or anyone else!" Scratcher sounded peevish. No one else in the Mess had any sympathy for his attitude. If it happened under different circumstances, then they would very probably have supported him. Coxswain, responsible for discipline, didn't even like being present while Scratcher was on his dignity. Somehow, he wanted to calm the man down and prevent what he thought was likely to happen.

"PO." He had attracted the man's attention and now meant to tell him just where he stood.

"The fact remains that you did not obey the order fast enough," Second Coxswain began to bluster, trying to interrupt. Coxswain's position of authority could not be challenged in this way.

"Be quiet. I am talking for your own good. The situation is this. The Captain was the only one in a position to know what was happening; he gave orders, and they were not obeyed promptly," he paused, and the chiefs' Mess remained silent.

"The Captain has absolute responsibility for the safety of the ship, and he took the action that was necessary. Now, nothing has been said since then, so if I were you, I would leave it well alone. Just forget the whole thing. That's my advice, and another thing, I don't want it talked about outside of this Mess." The Mess members privately agreed that the Coxswain's assessment was right. If there had been official repercussions to come, then they would all have known by now.

Scratcher felt that he had lost face in front of the men. The situation was intolerable to him, and the only fact that he seemed able to recognise was that an officer had struck a senior rating, and obviously, that was a court martial offence. The Second Coxswain was not satisfied and went to see the executive officer to state his complaint officially. Reggie knew that it would be useless to attempt to deflect the man from his purpose. Regulations had to be followed. The complaint had been stated officially and must be passed to the Captain.

Scratcher had hardly sat down again when he was summoned to the Captain's cabin. "PO Quill, I realise that you feel you have been unjustly treated; sit down there, and I will tell you the real issues involved," the Captain spoke softly; he was completely calm and relaxed. The cabin door was closed behind them.

He began speaking, "Five officers and sixty-three men came very close indeed to losing their lives, and a valuable vessel would have been lost."

The voice silenced, and the eyes pierced intently into those of the petty officer. The man did not dare to speak.

"Quite probably, that did not happen because you were slapped on the face once. If I had not done so, and you had remained inattentive for just a few seconds more, the chances are that we would not be discussing it now. You and I, and sixty-six other men, would be at the bottom of the sea." The Captain paused, but the other man didn't speak, was still thinking. Captain was also thinking. This man had been given his chance to retract the complaint, to admit that he had been wrong and that he had provoked the incident himself.

There was nothing else for it. The Captain spoke, "What matters now is whether you can still take orders on my ship." There was still no answer. "And if I still want you on this ship." The Captain waited. The Second Coxswain would not admit responsibility. All he could see was that he had lost face in front of everyone. He explained his stance, and they discussed it behind the closed door.

The Executive Officer and the Coxswain were informed later that day. Coxswain told no one what arrangements were to follow. Untypically, there was very little interest shown by any of the crew in this new development. The general opinion was that Scratcher had made a mistake, had pushed his luck, and compounded the error by voicing his opinions. Nobody wanted to listen.

The weekend drifted leisurely along, and Monday arrived too soon. The submarine sailed for phase two. This time, she was the stealthy attacker. After the initial transit period and preparations for the search had been carried out, the black, cigar-shaped vessel glided through the quiet, deep waters in a preconceived search pattern. The emphasis lay almost entirely on the need for absolute quiet. Night was turned into day in a continual cycle of two hours on watch and four hours off.

The first two days drew no sign of the enemy convoy. On the third it was found. From here on it would remain a cat and mouse game, alternating in aggression between them and the destroyer escort.

Submarine *Orestes* lay shallow, quiet and listening, waiting for the cover of night. The outriders of the convoy were slowly disappearing. The cavitation noise of their propellers grew fainter. The sonar crew grew tired just waiting. Their commander waited, knowing that the surface ships' lookouts would not be able to spot the wake from his periscope, running at this speed from periscope depth. This would be his best speed dived and that was what he wanted. Slowly to intercept at close quarters. The commander pored over the charts, waiting for the news his sonar crew could report. Soon, he felt sure, the destroyer would turn and retrace her transit across his path.

John Bishop lay back in the chair, one foot resting against the sonar shack door. His eyes were closed and he was intent on the fading flutter of noise in his headphones. He had guessed what they were waiting for. If the Captain did not stalk, then he must be expecting them to come to him. John knew what to expect. He would know the moment they started their turn so long as it happened in the next five minutes. Already, his second operator had removed headphones and was rubbing his ear lobes where the constant pressure of the foam lining chaffed. He had lost the ship sounds. John signalled him to replace the headset. Simeon's eye twitched spasmodically in anticipation.

For a moment, his senses played tricks. The dying sonar flutter was overlaid with several others, too far away to count, but the pitch was different, certainly a deeper note. John sat bolt upright and looked across to his Second. He hadn't heard it yet. The man's face grew anxious watching John. Something was up, but he didn't know what. The hydroplane effects were approaching, growing more distinct. John tried to count them, but he couldn't tell. There must be a great many for that sea-whipping noise to rattle and distort what should have been a distinct crisp note. Already, his thumb was on the intercom button, but he paused, needing confirmation that his second heard it, too. No response. He couldn't wait any longer.

"Sonar reports HE approaching submarines, repeat submarines, closing." Before John had released the button, the sonar room door was flung back; the door hinged at its centre and caught John a glancing blow on his lolling knee. Their Captain stood glaring.

"Submarines!" he spluttered only one word. The second operator was nodding now and touched John on the knee, confirming.

"At least twenty, approaching fast, ten miles to eight miles. Could be layers." John removed the headphones and handed them to the incredulous Captain, who donned them. He was thinking furiously. If they were indeed submarines, were they below him? How long did he have? Fifteen minutes, twenty, half an hour? He couldn't tell.

The Captain dropped the headphones into Bishop's lap and stepped out of the shack.

"Flood Q. Maintain bubble at three degrees," immediately after the Captain's order, John's voice broke through the intercom.

"Nuclear. Closing fast."

"Stop flooding Q, open main vents one, three, four, six, seven." The blast and gurgle of escaping air was screaming upwards to the surface. The sonar crew were now deaf to the outside world. They could hear nothing but the jagged, piercing noise of escaping air from the tanks along the length of the hull. They both sat ashen-faced, having torn off the headphones.

The boat was going down like a stone. "Flood two hundred gallons for'ard to aft," the Captain ordered the Engine Room, trying now to even the keel.

"Shut main vents." The stream of hissing air slowed and finally halted. Not enough room, he was thinking. He couldn't bottom the submarine. The Captain just prayed the nuclears were not deep enough to pass underneath. The mighty whirr of propellers thrashing through the water came to them all now, passing on both sides. It was incredible that there could be so many without adequate warning. Jeff Hawks was calculating their speed from the time of interception until now. Nuclear, without a doubt, he was thinking, to have that turn of speed. He wondered idly if they had known he was there prior to his flooding and blowing air. They would certainly have identified that. How close had they been to a collision? It had never happened yet, though the threat of it was ever-present at sea.

Everyone else was counting the individual cavitation noises as they went past. *Orestes* was still going down, but level, and she was slowing. Jeff Hawks wondered what the destroyer and other outriders had made of that. The Captain made a quick note of the time, position, number of craft and type, heading and speed. This Signal would go at the first opportunity, he decided.

The crew discussed this incident at great length. No one had ever heard of so many submarines being grouped in one place at sea. Perhaps not even during the war had there been a pack of thirty. They all knew that they could only belong to one nation, Russia. The West kept each other informed of submarine locations. The Captain made an announcement. This information was privileged. It must go no further and must be considered secret.

During the ensuing days, the Captain gave his officers a chance to practice their skills, retaining the more difficult and daring penetration runs for himself. The one destroyer kept eluding them. Jeff Hawks felt certain it was the same one which had nearly and inadvertently run them down in the episode during phase one. He decided to change his tactics. This destroyer was the biggest challenge, and he decided to tail this one, leaving the cruiser strictly alone. So far, they had made three successful simulated hits, but the cruiser remained immune under the cover of her escort. It seemed reasonable to leave his attack upon her until the last moment, and by that time, her Captain might well be congratulating himself on being undetected and unscathed. *Orestes* duly kept track of the destroyer's movements, particularly at night from the periscope. There was no chance of matching her speed; it was all a question of anticipating her next move and trying to get into position to take advantage of it.

The game continued for two nights and a day, during which time the submarine was detected a number of times and twice nearly caught. On each occasion, quick thinking and an instinctive skill put the submerged craft beyond reach. It happened just often enough for the submarine commander to pinpoint the destroyer's weakness. At times, her sonar crew were good, very good, and yet at others, the technique of search was quite sloppy. It seemed that the destroyer Captain did not close up his attacking crew for every pass. Therefore, Jeff Hawks reasoned, if he could get close enough without being picked up, he might well be able to get in a strike if her Captain reserved his best team. On that assumption, he pressed on with hounding tactics to draw the destroyer, keeping her fully engaged for several stressful hours.

Eventually, the pattern seemed to change; her Captain had been fooled into believing the submarine was at bay and accordingly stood down his attack team. Lieutenant Hawks demanded a final effort from his own team, knowing that he had driven them hard, but now would come the prize.

He emerged from the perfect position of surprise, from under a dense layer of warm water. The run was fast and straight, without the slightest possibility of a miss. Computer trace would confirm his victory at a later time, on return to harbour. For the moment, he was satisfied and ordered a green flare to be fired. He wanted his rival to know he had been tactically 'killed'.

Of the few days left to complete the exercise, much time was wasted in avoiding the escorts which had already been defeated. Nevertheless, they remained in play to confuse the issue. Avoiding tactics had to be taken on an assumption that the attacking vessel might be one other than those accounted for; there was no way of knowing.

At the close of the week, the Capital ship had not been successfully attacked due to the hindrance of its screen. The merits on each side would be determined at the 'Wash up', a conference to be held ashore with all competing trace records from the computers to corroborate each claim.

The task force dispersed, and *Orestes* returned to her base port at Faslane alongside *Maidstone* in a trot of three submarines. The crew of *Orestes* had time for a weekend at home. Two of the three Watches made private arrangements between them, individuals made duty swaps in order that more of the men would be free for the two days. Always, there had been a rivalry, not always good-natured, between men who lived locally and those who lived beyond reasonable travelling distance.

The long-distance travellers reasoned that since they rarely got home, apart from periods of leave, they should get priority for the very few weekends in which they might get home. The locals countered that they needed time off just as much, and since the submarine alternated its business from one end of the union of countries to the other, it worked out fairly even enough anyway. The impartial observed that any crewman, according to his circumstances, had the choice of moving his family nearer to the base port, and if he didn't choose to, then he accepted the consequences. As always, the strength of a disagreement was loaded according to personal bias, and there was always a tussle to decide who would go on weekend.

The submarine had been allocated a whole week in harbour for the forthcoming inspection. There was too much work to be done and not enough time to give more leave. Each department sorted out its priorities and worked its men accordingly, but in every case, it was necessary to employ them far into the night, every night. Wives who lived in married quarters only five miles away found it hard to believe that their husbands should return home at midnight, worn out and not inclined to listen to their point of view. In the morning, the whole thing started once more, and it was useless to explain that they were the lucky ones. Others who had no homes nearby might well still be working until the early hours.

The day of their new ordeal dawned. The boat was spotless, all surfaces gleaming, and the floors glistened with new wax polish to complete the facade. Uniformed figures held themselves upright in tiredness, ready for the Captain of 3rd Submarine Squadron to arrive with his retinue. A superficial inspection by the Captain and a thorough one by his staff progressed from for'ard along all six compartments.

By mid-day the first phase inspection was completed. After lunch the technical inspection team arrived, overall-clad, to begin their searching, detailed enquiries. Even the bilges showed resplendent in new coats of paint. Not a sign of waste oil or water showed itself anywhere. A handful of key personnel stayed behind to minister to the team.

By late afternoon, the crew had assembled on the quarter deck of the depot ship in full dress uniform, immaculately pressed and decorated with medals. Captain SM inspected the drawn-up ranks, halting at intervals to converse briefly with a bemedaled figure or the holder of an unusual insignia or badge. Where a slovenly sailor could not be found, and on such an occasion there never was, a figure would be picked out at random.

The fate of that individual was to provide a complete kit for inspection. No man onboard *Orestes* had a full kit. Most of what were considered unnecessary items had been given or thrown away long ago. There was no stowage space aboard a compact craft, crammed as it was with machinery and little enough room for its men. The one consolation to the man chosen was that he knew that if he just sat down and waited for the parade to finish, the other members of the crew, on returning, would ransack their own gear to provide an apparently full kit between them.

The ordeal was over, and *Orestes* received a "Well done." The engineering and electrical departments were more fortunate. They received an, "Extremely well done." It was late when they finished, and each man went about his own business that night.

"First Lieutenant speaking. We have received a signal from Captain SM. It reads, 'I was very impressed with your turnout. Well done.' I would just like to say that now we have achieved this high standard of cleanliness throughout the boat, we must all strive to maintain it."

The men were back onboard, changing into working clothes from their going ashore outfits. Many had stayed in uniform overnight so as not to waste time in getting ashore. Now, they stood listening to their 'favourite officer', and some of them grimaced. The loudspeakers crackled again.

"First Lieutenant speaking. In view of all the hard work that has been put in during this week, particularly by the engineers and electricians, there will be a general 'make and mend' this afternoon. You are reminded that we sail tomorrow morning at 0800. That is all." At the first hint of what was coming, some of the men became exuberant, 'ecstatic' would not be too strong a word to describe the way they greeted the news of an afternoon off. Exultation was dampened by the singling out of two departments, however, when everyone had worked late. There was still some grumbling going on in the for'ard Mess. Bubbles saw the effect on the men and knew that something had to be done.

"Right, last chance for a run ashore in Scotland. I'm taking it; who's coming with me?" He looked around at the faces. The looks were changing. The thought of beer and a few extra hours of freedom was heady stuff.

During the afternoon, when it was quiet and only six or so men of the duty watch remained, the Second Coxswain left the boat with all his gear. He was not seen again on this submarine. There was no replacement designated for him, as no one could be spared. Leading Seaman Ginger Bates was informed later that he would take over those vacated duties permanently. No replacement for Ginger either, but in a few days, an able seaman substitute would be found.

Next up – Sea Trials.

# Chapter 15

The granite fortress of Box Ten coolly collated information from the extremities of its network around the globe, assessing, compiling, stacking volumes of priceless espionage information onto ever-expanding shelves of accumulated intelligence. Deep within its maze of passages, a small group calmly received its latest news.

"Signal from Commander-in-Chief, Home Fleet via task group North Atlantic. 2100hrs, 23 January, group of thirty Soviet nuclear submarines detected, group course one nine zero..." Commander Ruskin took the signal from the lieutenant and continued to read it himself, noting the speed and identification of the group classes. He realised that the naval sonar school in Dorset would have checked its bank of tapes against those recorded of the Russian group. No doubt the identification was correct, but nevertheless, he wanted it confirmed.

"Send this for transmission by scrambler phone. I want this confirmed as soon as possible." The Commander had written his request and handed it to the messenger, who now hurried from the room.

The Commander's brow deepened in thought as he stared at the wall map. He considered recent world political events. The impending resignation of the Premier of Tanganyika did not seem a likely reason. For the moment, he could do nothing to anticipate this sudden turn of events. *They had slipped-up badly here*, he was thinking. No warning at all of this one. It was the first time, to their knowledge, that any sizeable Russian force had broken into the North Sea. Absentmindedly, he received the new message.

"Confirmed report. *Stickleback* killed. Sector 3 to cover assignment soonest. Full report follows." The Commander again looked at the map, passed the message to the lieutenant, who now crossed to the blue telephone.

"Scratch *Stickleback*, Sector 3." The lieutenant replaced the receiver, thinking of the blue-topped pin, which would very soon be removed from the relevant sector map in an operations room below.

Something was prodding at the Commander's memory. One political incident which had occurred in the last few days must have been significant to this submarine group. So much was happening here. They needed more staff. He would have to see the Director about this soon.

"Do you have a copy of the weekly event chart?" Commander Ruskin paced the room in thought. On reading the chart, the implication suddenly hit him.

He read aloud, "29th January, the three-power conference on nuclear weapon tests had failed to reach a satisfactory resolution in Geneva." *That was yesterday,* he thought.

He turned to the lieutenant. "See if you can expedite the Geneva nuclear talks report. We want that today." The Commander continued to pace; he was reading an agent's assessment of the USSR and Cuban trade pact agreement. Obviously, this was the normal thin diplomatic cover for an aid programme.

He would need to contact Washington over this one and find out how many men they had in Havana. Was this the significance? He wondered. The submarines certainly had the range. He had the feeling that this was of paramount importance. He must contact Whitehall and Washington to arrange surveillance. Was it conceivable that the Russians were about to deliver and station missiles in Cuba? The Commander made his way down to the fleet display room. There was nothing in the area capable of tracking the Soviet subs.

"Contact Nimrod Command, see if they can divert over this area." The Commander paused. "With infrared cameras."

It occurred to him that the subs would come shallow at night. The cameras would give a vital indication of their course. "Request US nuclear submarines cover to intercept by arrangement with RAF Nimrod Command, Edinburgh."

Commander Ruskin was satisfied for the moment. What a splendid stroke of luck that operation Square Peg had been exercising in precisely that spot. The Commander allowed himself a thin smile. "Contact home fleet C in C. Transmit to submarine *Seawolf* first opportunity as follows: 'Warning Red nuclear submarine activity your area. Extreme caution.'"

The lieutenant had yet another sheaf of papers. The Commander sighed as he took them and wondered for a moment why the lieutenant was grinning. He soon saw why when he quickly glanced through the sheet and picked out the keywords. Yes, he could afford to grin. Apparently, Soviet activity had declined. Every sign was that amassed vehicles of invasion were being dispersed from the border area. The Russians, it seemed, had been daunted by the preparations of the western forces. It looked as though the Norway invasion was 'off'. The Commander thought about this. Had it all been a game to test the West's resources and commitment? At times like this, the Soviet network positively aided the West. It was certain they would know of the forthcoming NATO exercise. Temporarily, at least, they had been frightened off. Both men were grinning now.

# Chapter 16

First Lieutenant Grimes released the microphone button having announced the afternoon's make and mend. He was pleased with himself. He too was looking forward to taking this afternoon off. For the first time in a long, long while, he had a pleasant anticipation of spending the rest of the day with lithesome, intelligent and understanding Sophie.

The inspection had gone well. The Captain was pleased, and it would certainly redound to his own credit. He was the one responsible officer to whom the glory would accrue for an exceptional inspection report. Reggie could feel his foot firmly placed on the next rung of the promotion ladder. He had every hope that he would not be passed over this time. His promotion review was due shortly. It could only help that his girlfriend was the daughter of a staff officer.

The book buyer from Oxford stood alone, leaning so elegantly, so casually, against the sports car, her hair being whisked away from her pert, oval face. *She was stunning, beautiful,* Reggie thought, now pleased rather than irritated at their mothers' matchmaking. They shared at least an admiration for the same dominant personalities who belonged to military history. They held something in common, and in some way which Reggie dared not analyse, she helped to ease the single pain which had become part of his memory: that of his lost wife.

She waved to him as he crossed the depot ship. Many eyes were upon her slender body. Imagining the softness of her arms, Reggie brushed a hand back over his greying temples, pulled his cap a little lower over his eyes and was careful to tauten the expression on his face. He must remain as impassive as ever, essentially present a figure of authority. He bathed in the new respect he could feel coming out at him from the depot ship sentry. The man saluted smartly. Reggie marched down the gangway, measured but unhurried and in regulation strides towards her.

"My handsome sailor, my handsome commander." The grey eyes fluttered in mock servility. "Shall I drive, weary hero?" She kissed him lightly on the cheek so that he would not suspect the offence she intended.

Reggie was thinking of the four gold rings on his father's suit. For an instant, he was that child again staring upward at the barrel-chested figure of his father in his dazzling uniform. She drove expertly, the car speeding along the winding road to Glasgow. Her dark hair whipped around in the rush of breeze, the grey headband emphasised the colour of her eyes, and she was smiling.

"I hope you don't mind, darling, but I simply must dash into the bookshop. I won't be long, dear, really." The car slowed; she pulled into the curb and ignored the single yellow line. She knew well that within ten minutes, Lieutenant Grimes would feel compelled to drive the car away from that offending yellow line. He would circle the block continuously or telephone her from some suitable place of safety later.

Three men were waiting for her in the small private office at the back of the building. She needed to be careful in her dealings with the bookstore manager. She was a nice girl, and Sophie liked her. Not particularly bright but sensitive, and sensitive people could be dangerous to her. Isaac stopped speaking, shook her hand and inclined his head in a formal little bow. Isaac always administered these little niceties, a part of his orthodox homeland upbringing.

"The internal committee has ordered we increase our initiative. It is vital." The clipped Jewish speech was rising to a crescendo. She interrupted the flow.

"There is only one way. Binny must be got onto that submarine." She glanced briefly at the other two men before continuing, "Fortunately, they are a man short, and they will be searching their draft list for someone suitable. I have been in contact with our man in Gosport. He has access to the right person and can arrange a transfer without anyone suspecting."

The two men who sat on the desk edge had listened to her words, content that she was a clever and competent operator. She had only made one mistake so far. One of the men stood. "I had best jolly well wend my way south then. Arrangements will be simple enough." The overweight man clasped his pudgy hands around hers, his eyebrows raised in question.

"You did well, Boris." Sophie looked past him at the seated figure.

"To have acted promptly on advance information and got our friend here into the submarine service when you did." Sophie was smiling at the man.

"I was the Cell Head before you came, my dear comrade," Boris tinged his remark with an acid grin, almost a smirk. He resented her, but Party discipline required him to accept her leadership. Now she was angry. She had warned them countless times not to address each other in such terms; however, she could not reprimand him now. She must, at all costs, keep calm and in control of the situation.

"It is settled then. What news from the East?" The agents gave their latest intelligence on the arms agreements so far reached in Cuba. The Politburo had not yet told this spy cell if missiles would go to Cuba. They went on to discuss other ventures into Russia's political intrigue.

She heard the car start up; its loud crackling spurt of power drew away into a throaty purring acceleration, halting momentarily in a rapid succession of gear changes. She relaxed. She thought that the other girl working here, whose new boyfriend also served as a rating on Reggie's submarine, had an inkling that she was involved in something not quite right. She must not be able to make too many connections. Already, she, Sophie, had drawn the net a little too close. It was a very tight game, but these were desperate times, and risks must be taken to get her information out to her friends abroad. The car horn sounded twice; the sound was strident, impatient. Sophie glanced at the clock. The lieutenant was perhaps not so predictable as she thought him. Reggie had left as she knew he would, but as rapidly had returned and worse, was now impatiently drawing attention to the fact. She could not risk him coming into the shop. *He could pay for the fright his unexpected return had given her later,* she thought.

The Casing party stood to attention, waiting, as the Captain clambered down the steep steps of *Maidstone's* accommodation ladder, crossed the first submarine gangplank, and on towards them. A sound of bosun's call pipes filled the air at the departure from the ship, subsiding into stillness as he crossed each boat's gangway.

"Pipe!" The First Lieutenant stood rigidly to attention, saluting as the ordered official welcome siren of three distinctive notes from the bosun's pipe sounded.

"Good morning, number one; let's get under weigh." Captain briskly stepped onto the casing and up the ladder into the conning tower. Ginger Bates had already singled up the berthing lines, and now only one neatly cleated row of lines held them.

"Off breast ropes." The First Lieutenant was in a bad mood for some reason and snapped the order to the casing officer, who nodded to Ginger.

By this time, the executive officer had also disappeared, and Ginger nodded to the two men to get on with it, as usual.

"Main engines ready." The telegraph call from the Engine Room to the Control Room was echoed up the voice pipe by the Coxswain. *S12* foamed its way down the loch, aiming for the Rhu Narrows gap. Below decks, Swingle, the LRO, was sorting out the morning mail. It had been a close-run thing this morning. For some reason, there was a reorganisation going on inboard, and that had delayed mail collection. All this should have been done an hour ago. The letters and packets were arrayed around the table in tidy bundles; the two blue nylon mailbags were neatly folded beside him. *Only six letters for the for'ard Mess today; obviously, this lot didn't write much,* he thought. Two for Sudswell he noticed, both by the same female hand, it looked like. At this busy time of sailing, there were only a couple of men in the Mess. Nothing for them, he told them, but pass these two on to Bubbles. Bubbles leant through the hatch, took them and put them both in his pocket.

In unusually quick time, the Casing party was below. Ginger had organised things so that everything wasn't left to the last minute. Somebody was making a pot of tea now that the Mess was filling. The making of a big pot was justified.

"See you've got a casing officer again," somebody decided to rib Ginger. It was a sore point with him as they all knew what they were doing and didn't need one; it was just an extra duty for entering or leaving harbour, which alternated between Navvy and Shane.

"It won't last long. I'll soon see to that." Ginger was smiling grimly.

"I thought Shane managed to talk his way out of it. Told Jimmy it wasn't necessary, what with an officer being on the Bridge anyway and able to see everything," Harman was talking. He had settled into routine now, taking an interest in all aspects of submarine life. He noticed that he was no longer treated like a new boy since he had adopted this attitude.

"It's only 'cos Scratcher went after being slapped, and 'Pussers' like that when a job passes to somebody inexperienced." Scouse could be relied on to get his tuppence worth in. Ginger knew Scouse was trying to goad him, but he knew how to put him down.

"I'm experienced enough that they know I'll do the job properly, and if I say it's done, then it is. If they don't know it yet, they soon will." Ginger was making an oblique thrust at Scouse, who wasn't entirely reliable.

Bubbles turned around on his hatch, faced into the Mess and looked at Bates. "Do you reckon they'll rate you up then, Ginger, to go with the job?"

"No, Coxswain says we're overborne with senior rates, even with Scratcher gone. Besides, I'll still have to do seaman watches at sea," Ginger finished talking, and they all thought about it. It was true enough that without a replacement, there was no one else to make up radar watches. He obviously couldn't do that and the PO of the watch as well.

"Hard luck, mate." Scouse thought there was an opportunity to get another dig in. It drew no comment.

"Now that we are fully operational, we can expect an easier time of it, anyway. No more trials or inspections." Harman thought about this statement by one of the old hands of the crew.

"Does that mean we get more time alongside?" he asked.

This was greeted with a few desultory laughs, and one of them replied, "In theory, mate, but I wouldn't make any plans on it if I were you."

Bubbles was thinking about the letters still unopened in his pocket and about the girl who had written them. She is a lovely person, so caring and kind. He couldn't let her waste that on himself. Didn't want to see the disillusion come into her life over the years if they stayed together. Bubbles thought about his own past, what there had been of it that was worth remembering. He could not contemplate a repeat of that failure and so he had decided not to risk it with yet another new romance. Permanence did not seem to suit his lifestyle. He only needed to look around at others, of this and other submarine crews, to see the futility of those relationships. How could he put that upon her? Really not fair. Best to leave her life as untouched as it was before he came into it. He would have difficulty writing that letter to her tonight.

The intercom spluttered into life, interrupting their individual thoughts. "Captain speaking. I want to thank you all for the long hours of hard work that went into the preparations for our squadron inspection. That hurdle over, we are now fully operational, which means that we will be involved in rather more exercises. You will have seen from the programme that we are scheduled for exercise 'Red Triangle', followed almost immediately by the NATO force manoeuvres," the voice stopped, enjoying the moment of suspense. The key was still held down, and crackling static filled the boat. Everyone paid attention.

"I have received permission for us to have a 'jolly' between these two exercises at Barry Island. I am sure this will come as a welcome surprise. Well done, everyone." The sharp click denoted the end of the message; the intercom went dead.

The boat ploughed its way south through deteriorating conditions. The sea swell was rising. Bad weather was forecast for the Irish Sea area, extending south. It was expected that there could be squalls, and if the ionosphere dropped, a major storm might break. Engine speed was increased. As much time as possible had to be saved during surface passage. The crew were understandably pleased at the news of a week-long break in a foreign port. Any place outside of normal UK ports was considered as being 'foreign'. This was the new fascinating topic of conversation on the Messdecks. It drew their minds away from the immediate prospect of three weeks of monotony under the sea. Necessary routines filled their time while they made tentative plans, invoking pleasant thoughts for the holiday to come.

"Expecting rough weather Bubbles, the sea's rising. Forecast says possible Force 8." Charlie walked down the plated aisle, looking at the long blue and silver monsters on their racks.

"We've lashed most of it down and I've checked all the securing loads. Those fish won't move," Bubbles told him, wiping his oily hands on the rag. The boat was already beginning to roll, not enough yet to make it uncomfortable, but trickles of oily water were running out of vent pipes down the clean paintwork to form shuffling patches on bilge decks.

"Are those loading trays locked in?" Charlie knew, even as he said it that the leading seaman would not have overlooked such a thing, but it did no harm to check. He would be the one to carry the can if this lot started jumping about. The TI wasn't about to take chances like that.

"I think we had better get the engineers to pump out these bilges, or we'll be forever mopping up." So-saying Bubbles gave a shout to Jock Brown, who was nearest the intercom.

"Control Room, Fore-ends. Permission to pump out fore-ends bilges." Jock waited for the answer to come.

"Fore-ends, Control Room, open AIV bilge main suction valve."

"Fore-ends, Roger." Jock went and opened the valve. The PO of the watch set the pump order on his indicator panel, waiting for the display light, which was operated from the Engine Room, to come up.

"Scouse, stick your hand down that grid; see the filter is clear, will you?" Bubbles stopped Jock in his tracks, who was on his way to do just that. Jock looked at Bubbles, saw that he intended that, for once, the other man should get his hands dirty, shrugged his shoulders and went back to what he was doing before.

The fore-end of the boat started to lift in gradual sweeping arcs, and as the water dropped away from under, it suddenly fell back into the empty trough in a downward shaking plunge. *Well, this is only the start of it,* Bubbles thought; he had better go around the compartment again and make sure nothing was loose.

"Charlie," he said, drawing the P.O.'s attention. "do you reckon we ought to tighten up on these torsion bars?" Charlie came over to have a look. They were certainly a bit slack. The long bars stretched between the torpedo beams. He thought about it. If the boat hit a really bad patch of weather, she might try to corkscrew and that kind of pressure could impose tons of strain on the individual beams. They would act against each other and try to buckle.

"No, I think we better let them have some play, or we might rip the threads off. Leave them as they are; it'll be okay." Charlie went away, thinking that sometimes Bubbles must go around looking for extra work to do. What with him and Jock, he had a good team, even if they did have to carry Scouse. He would have to see what he could do about sorting him out. The sooner they got rid of him; sent him to that physical training school, the better.

"Permission to relieve 'Lookout'," The helmsman had to lift his voice and repeat the shouted request up the voice pipe before he got the required answer. A noisy, bustling blast of air emanated from the flared end of the pipe, giving a perpetual draught down the back of his neck. The helmsman was having a job to fight the sea, finding that the boat rolled less if he allowed it to waver off course, waited for the rolling wave to subside, and then put opposite wheel on to bring it back. The ticker-tape trace rattled past behind its red Perspex cover. He wondered how long it would be before the officer of the watch noticed it on his compass repeater and told him to stay on course. Almost as if by telepathy, the First officer, as officer of the watch, bellowed down the voice pipe for the helmsman to do precisely that: stay on course.

The new lookout emerged from the tower, the icy blast dragging at his clothing. Immediately, cold air streaming over the Bridge top struck him in the face. His head ducked to find the narrow-hatched passageway back to the lookout position. There was just room to crouch through, emerge to straighten upright and turn around. The other figure, hood up, wasted no time in turning over his report. "Lighthouse Red eight zero. Another lighthouse on the starboard bow, about Green five."

The new watcher was still trying to adjust to the elements. The daylight still dazzled him, and he couldn't pick out distant objects yet; his eyes weren't focussing in the unaccustomed open light. The other man was anxious to be gone. "On that promontory, a white tower just on the edge, can you see it?"

"No, but I'll get it in a minute; I can see the land. What else?"

"Three ships astern. Two tankers and a freighter, nothing coming up this way." The man pointed astern, his arm wavering in the wind.

"OK, I've got them." The new man felt queasy from this rocking platform, but it would pass.

"Permission to go below." The hooded figure appeared beside the officer.

"Yes, please do." No sooner were the words spoken than he was gone into the dark void, boots ringing on steel rungs. White caps on wave tops grew larger angrier, the roiling tops forcing upward to shed white spume in far-flung spray.

Despite their terylene penguin suits enfolding the two figures, the hoods drawn tight to cover head and neck, surges of water battered upward along the outside of the boat's tower, drenching them. As the waves reached higher, the yawning distance between them spread larger. The boat straddling them dipped even lower into the trough, thence to ride the crest of a looming wave. Each shuddering quiver of the steel hull extending over an abyss rattled the smaller internal parts to give warning of the ensuing plunge. A forming wave smashed into the curved ballast tank, absorbed the pressured energy and reached further upward in a thickening column of water.

"Hold on!" the words whipped away by the whistling wind, flashing past the lookout, were lost amidst the crashing movements of the sea. The thundering drive of water funnelling down drew all eyes in the Control Room. Men stopped in their tracks, turned towards the noise, and saw a deluge of spewing sea gush out of the trunk to rush across the deck.

"Bridge," the Captain's voice funnelled upward. The noise of flailing water, dashing from one side to another as the boat rolled and tried to drown the sound of voices.

"Turn into the sea; try to hold us into each forming wave. Captain coming up." The water diverted in parallel lanes around the men's legs, following the gravitational slide of heaving floor.

"Emergency Stations. Open up for diving. Coxswain to the wheel on the double." All through the boat, the clanging sound of between compartment hatches being slammed shut, told all that something dramatic had happened. Those who had not seen or heard the invading sea waited for the expected crash of a ship's collision. In rapid time, all hands leapt to the task of turning valves and uncottering main vents. Various watchkeepers reported to the Control Room when ready.

"All hands not actively engaged in diving checks muster for'ard with bailing equipment," Navigator sounded tense over the speakers. The Captain had gone to the Bridge to assess the situation.

"Shut lower hatch," he bellowed down the tube, and someone leapt to reach into the tower, bringing the heavy circular disc down in ferocious slamming motion. A drumming fall of water bounced upon the locked access and tumbled away inside the fin. A dozen men with assorted mugs, dustpans and buckets bailed the salt water into whatever large containers they could find, pouring it into sinks and bilges as fast as they possibly could. Two electricians rushed through the accommodation space to check that battery hatches had been securely battened down. Fortunately for all, they were securely bolted. No salt water had passed below. A potential crisis of producing lethal chlorine gas from the below-deck batteries was over.

Despite the tendency for the craft to roll on a rising swell, the men worked rapidly and in concert to remove the swilling mess. "So much for Jimmy's polished deck!" one of them remarked.

"Don't worry, he'll soon see we put a fresh polish down, must have it gleaming, you know. Got to keep it up to inspection standard," the mimicry of their First Lieutenant was accurate enough to make them laugh. The between-compartment hatches were quickly shut after any man who needed to pass through. For once, and quite alien from all tradition, the officer and accompanying artificer carried out a checklist, accepting verbal confirmation of each task from the senior man in each machinery space. This unfamiliar routine saved valuable time that was required to check for themselves. The whole procedure was quite unprecedented. The Captain, however, had confidence in his crew and wanted to dive under the prevailing sea conditions just as soon as he possibly could.

He regretted now that he had not taken sufficient notice of the storm warnings. The time he had expected to have for deliberation had not been given him. Now, he would need to accept the delay imposed by carrying out his passage dived. It could no longer be helped; the risks involved in surface passage were no longer tolerable. In record time, just under twenty minutes, the Torpedo Officer reported that the boat was ready.

"Right, get the LRO up here to take a radio message." The Captain walked away to the chart table intercom.

"Bridge, Captain. I expect to dive in about ten minutes. Send the lookout down as soon as you are ready," a distant voice replied, the wind carrying the words away from the microphone. Some separated words came through, but the response was intelligible. Wind... shifting, suggest... two points... port... lookout... shortly."

"Ask him to confirm by voice pipe," Captain told the helmsman, "and then give his instructions to the Panel Chief. There is likely to be a heavy roll on the way down, chief, so I want to go down level if we can. Tank one, seven, two, six, three, five, four, that's the order, and you had better use your number two man also this time. Get the boat down as fast as you can." LRO Swingle arrived with a pad and pen, ready to take the message.

"Signal classified six. To: Commander-in-Chief Home Fleet; Captain SM1; Captain SM3; Operations Room Dolphin; relay to ships on Red Triangle, from Captain *Orestes*. Message reads. 'Due to heavy storm conditions Irish Sea, estimated time arrival delay approximately six hours. Am completing transit dived until conditions improve.' Time 1600, date, code and position."

"Do you want that scrambled, sir?" The pen hovered over the paper, ready to note the cypher index."

"No, that won't be necessary. Get it sent as soon as you can. I want to know as soon as you've completed." Jeff Hawks turned next to the Navigator at the chart table, who was already laying off the courses for deep water along his charts.

"Control Room. Radio. Message sent and received, sir, by patch link." The Captain was busy thinking; his hand reached for the microphone and tapped the button down twice to denote he had heard. In almost the same instant, he reached for the klaxon.

The deep, agitating tremor of sound lifted above all others faded and sounded for a second time in rapid succession. A clatter of hurrying feet was heard descending the tower, in company with the disturbed air flapping the plastic trunking. A sodden shape arrived, binoculars draped from his neck, the water still tumbling from folds in the close-fitting foul weather suit. The moment he arrived, a man leapt up the first few rungs, grabbed the short rope, pulled the hatch shut and locked the outer keyed ring, all in a well-rehearsed motion. They were submerging; the hiss of escaping air could be heard from within. At exactly the wrong moment, heavy seas gathered in, rolling at the Fin, attempting to push the black cigar shape over. Two pairs of hands rotated the valves as fast as they could.

Off centre, the boat slid between the crushing forces as they rolled upon each other to fill the vacated space. In each Mess deck, cups, plates and other loose items on table tops hurled themselves into bunks. The deck tipped to an ominous twenty degrees and hovered like that, as though debating whether to reach even further. They slowly descended, attempting to compress sea beneath them. Gradually, the tower acted as a stabiliser, correcting its stance and easing the boat back into a level and upright position. A few sighs of relief escaped from barely open mouths, and then the men steadied themselves to the business of retrieving the lost crockery and utensils.

Once beneath the waves, the fomenting forces at the surface could no longer affect them. The course was set again for Portsmouth, the starting point for their next trip. The unexpected delay spread the journey over an extra day, and in the evening, to pass the long hours, permission was sought and obtained to show a film. By coincidence, the film was an American made, wartime submarine adventure. Naturally, the melodrama was reacted to with criticism and good-humoured ridicule. Nevertheless, they were in need of light entertainment, and the plot was very entertaining. Perhaps in part due to a similarity with their present situation. In some aspects, it was like looking into a mirror, a mirror image of their own experience.

Afterwards screen and projector were stored away. The guest stokers returned to their own quarters aft, and the aftermath of debris was cleared away. Charlie and a couple of others from the chiefs' Mess had sat in by invite. The busman's holiday of a film was reviewed in depth by discussion amongst the torpedomen. They lounged comfortably around the torpedo compartment platform, using the machinery for seating as usual. So far as they were concerned, the most interesting aspects of the movie had been where the action was centred around the torpedoes. In some strange way, the fact that *Orestes* was not engaged in war made the actions of the torpedomen in the film more intriguing since they were. Casually, they sat in loose groups of five, smoking, discussing the details of a particular scene where a torpedo had been shaken from its rack and had fallen and crushed a man. The conjectural situation held some morbid fascination for them.

It was late into the night, and Lieutenant Hawks ordered a change of depth. "Sixty feet. Up periscope." It was time to observe the surface weather conditions. As soon as they improved, he wanted to surface and make up some of the lost time.

"Sonar. No contacts." The sound of that report was reassuring; he wanted no other shipping anywhere near him when he came up. The depth gauge needle flickered upward. The boat began to rock gently from side to side, the wave pressure ridges buffeting them the nearer to the surface they came. Alternating pressure and suction forces made the job of handling the hydroplanes extremely difficult. Constantly moving controls filled the Control Room with the hiss of hydraulic fluid under pressure. Visual inspection by periscope lasted only a minute.

"Down periscope. Two hundred feet." Captain was disappointed, but he would take another sighting in a few hours.

There must have been an unusually large wave forming, gathering strength from beneath the for'ard part of the hull. Regardless of the planesmens' attentions, the boat came lurching upward to break surface, bows up. Immediately the full violence came to bear on exposed metal, forcing a complete reversal. The bows were mightily thrust down and the boat kicked downward in a diving angle. Momentarily, the stern came too close to the surface and the same pressures exerted themselves on it. Confusion broke out; men awoke sweating from these unexpected happenings. In the fore-ends, the torpedomen held on to anything that was firm. The boat plunged, bucked and reared, even as they were sinking into calmer waters of safety. A strange, ominous creaking acted upon stretched nerves.

Charlie reacted swiftly to save himself. Some inner warning sense told him what must be happening. A thundering mass of blue metal juddered and catapulted backwards in a perfectly straight line to crash through pipes, embedding itself into the fractured remains. Even before it had come to rest, the monstrous torpedo tail occupied the place where Charlie had sat. Three of the men nearest to the hatch scrambled through it simultaneously. There was no chance at all of the three getting through together, and they sprawled stomach down across it, wedging each other in. Charlie, the fourth man, dived into the gap above them and, by some miracle of effort, cleared the men to land in a sprawled heap upon the Mess floor. The fifth man, Bubbles, who had been furthest away, had made no attempt to escape. He sat on the other side of the platform from the crashing 'fish'. He had instinctively recognised that, for him, there had been no danger. All of them became aware of their ridiculous position, and the tension of the moment was relieved by peals of laughter directed at each other and at themselves.

The torpedo was wedged firm, but they still shackled the winch to a strap around its middle. The submarine regained stability as it went deeper; there was no further risk. Supported by guide ropes, they eased the torpedo, quite undamaged, back into position. On examination, they found that all the boat's shuddering under the forces of the day had shaken loose this particular set of securing bands. For no apparent reason, its position had become the focal point for the vessel's vibrations.

A technical enquiry was held within the hour, late though it was into the night. Lieutenant Phil Green stood behind the others in the fore-ends, listening and taking careful note of the voice tones and attitudes of the talking men. There seemed to be no obvious reason why those steel bands should have come loose. Lieutenant Grimes also listened to the artificers discussing the possibilities, but he was less inclined to reserve judgment.

"I would say that it seems very unlikely that this could have been brought about by vibration." That was his first announcement to the assembled team. It was clear to all of them what must come next.

"It is much more likely to be a simple question of negligence. I don't think the torpedo was secured properly," he finished and everyone fell silent. The implication of Jimmy's assessment was quite obvious to everyone.

Shane was disturbed by Reggie's manner; it was far too strained. The man had been irrational in his behaviour lately. Probably whatever caused it was also responsible for the considerable irritation he often showed for quite minor incidents. Shane had recently begun to doubt his superior's rationality. Neither of the officers knew enough about this torpedo incident to make such a pronouncement.

Shane cleared his throat. "I was in the fore-ends just before sailing and saw the preparations for sea being carried out, sir. I didn't see the torpedo checks being made myself, but the Torpedo Instructor here made a full report on compartment readiness. The message was passed to me by LRO Swingle, who happened to be in the fore-ends at the time. As you will know, being a large space, it is quite often used for relaxation by some of the for'ard Mess crew, their quarters being so confined."

The executive officer looked slightly aggrieved at the Torpedo Officer's intervention. Personally, he thought discipline was very lax. He was quite against this easy-going attitude amongst the men. It seemed to him there ought to be a more clearly defined military authority on this submarine. An example ought to be made here to show these shortcomings.

"Did you personally check this Petty Officer?" He looked sternly at Charlie. All of them noted the official tone of voice from the First Lieutenant, which wasn't at all the normal sort of approach unless the man addressed was in severe trouble. Charlie realised there was a need for caution here, but at the same time, there was also a definite need to back Bubbles.

"I was here when it was done, sir, as I always am when any important work is carried out in the department. Leading Seaman Sudswell and I discussed the arrangements for sea stowing in some detail."

"Petty Officer." The First Lieutenant had a peculiar, frenzied appearance as he spoke. "You do not 'discuss' with junior rates; you give orders. What orders did you give?"

Now, Charlie realised that he was in trouble. If Jimmy decided to take the official attitude on internal relationships between ranks, then there was nothing he could do but follow that line himself.

"We discussed details. I ordered the compartment to be secured for rough weather. Some of it I checked myself, some I did not. This is a large compartment. Leading Seaman Sudswell reported to me that the compartment was secure." Charlie kept a completely level voice, staring straight back at Jimmy.

"Also, I have every confidence that it was carried out properly," Charlie added the statement as an afterthought, in a last-ditch stand to deter the officer from taking the next step towards instigating a court martial. It might not be sanctioned by their captain, and there was no evidence for such a procedure, but that would all be in the draw of providence or luck.

Shane had been doing some rapid thinking. He knew that there was no evidence, no support for the First Lieutenant's implied allegations, and also that there was none to be brought in defence. Those things had to be taken on trust. If all this went to court martial, it could go either way and more probably, the charges would be dropped. That, though, was not the essential point. Irreparable damage would have been done to the efficiency of the department and the morale of the entire crew.

"In my opinion, and I shall recommend so to the Captain, this is a clear case for…" the First Lieutenant spoke in loud tones, out of all proportion to the circumstances as they were a small gathered group, standing close together and could hear each other without any need for raised voices. They all felt the tension and sense of impending doom. The statement was cut short by a quiet but ringing voice behind them.

"I checked it personally during evening rounds." The room went perfectly silent, and all heads turned to Shane, hardly able to believe the words from his mouth. The moments of inactivity seemed endless, during which time Reggie's face tried to control several contortions.

"I think we had better talk about this in the Wardroom. You are all dismissed." The two officers walked away, and the rest relaxed, leant back on beams, and began smoking. The past fifteen minutes' events called for some thought.

Every one of them there knew that Shane had perjured himself. No non-technical officer took a tool into his hands and did something himself, and that was the only possible way to check the thing. Shane increased his stock with the men immeasurably with that brief uttered sentence. They respected him for having stood by his men, demonstrating complete confidence. It was so unlike him, and it was hard to realise that he had done so. Lieutenant Green stuck to his guns and maintained the lie. He felt that the unusual circumstances, the implications of not doing so, and the executive officer's unreasonable behaviour warranted it. He had perhaps made an enemy of his senior officer, but that had been a cross that he had become used to. The First Lieutenant surely would not dare to question the veracity of his assertion.

Lieutenant Hawks listened to his First officer's report and said nothing. After he had gone the Captain reflected on the matter, considering the seriousness of the accusations. He knew very well what was going on, had seen the gradual change in personality and had seen the books his first officer read. At this stage, he did not want to endanger the potential career of either of the officers. He decided that the whole thing would be kept under wraps, but as soon as he could, on arrival at Portsmouth, he would arrange for a full and secret technical investigation on the torpedo incident. Whatever came of that would decide what subsequent action he would take.

Lieutenant Grimes was marked. He did not know it, but all hope of the long-awaited promotion had gone. Unknown to him, the Captain was writing notes, which would be incorporated in a formal report on arrival in harbour.

# Chapter 17

The submarine surfaced at dawn in the English Channel. The storm fury had passed on and was travelling south. The weather report said it was diminishing in force and would be likely to dissipate itself during the following day. The relatively calm waters of the channel made the submariners more relaxed. The tensions of the night slipped away. Their first sight of Portsmouth harbour was the long, high-walled breakwater, which culminated in the tall fortress walls of *HMS Dolphin*. A slow left alteration edged them nearer to the bottleneck harbour entrance. High defence walls loomed to left and right, the circular watch towers of the old town passed to starboard, with waving civilian visitors crowding the wall walks at its top.

"Attention on the casing. Face to Port," the voice from the Bridge carried to the Casing party men scurrying to line up on the for'ard casing. Forming the line were five figures in white sea jerseys and just off-centre, one in a pale pink jersey. A small lone sound bridged the gap from the castellated sea wall to their left.

"Carry on." The Casing party, as one man, turned right through ninety degrees, stayed to attention for a brief pause, and dispersed to tend the ropes. The long, slim hull purred its way past the fort to slip alongside a trot of two identical boats, sisters of the sea.

The duty radio operator carried a message to *Orestes*' duty officer later in the day. 'Why was one of your Casing party in pink?'

"The casing petty officer told me he didn't have time to send him below to change it. Apparently, Harman's new wife put his sweater in the twin tub with a non-colour fast red skirt, sir."

"New twin tub, was it?"

"I believe it was, sir."

"All right," the Captain said, "a young wife and a new twin tub. Not a good combination. I will see what the Port Admirals Office have to say. No further action, I think, Number One."

A small, smart figure holding a much-used leather briefcase, a black rolled umbrella resting in the crook of his arm, stood on the jetty peering down at the submarine. The Casing party, idly standing, their work done, were attentive to the unusually dressed observer. He looked, they thought like a diplomat or possibly a high-ranking civil servant.

"I say you chaps, is that *Orestes*?" the deep, plummy voice, trained by some public school, resounded across the intervening space.

"Yes, sir," Ginger Bates shouted. He wasn't sure about the 'sir' bit but added it as a precaution. The man could be an officer. The portly pin-striped figure lifted a casual arm and raised the homburg a fraction above his head in salute to them.

"Well mannered, ain't he?" One of the Casing party observed. The black mohair overcoat of very conservative style swished as the man climbed to the awkward angle of descending gangplank and gingerly side-stepped down the incline. His progress was slow and deliberate, and halfway down the trot, the sentry of the first boat climbed up and offered to take the impeding briefcase.

"Oh, would you? That's extremely kind," the rich, plummy voice floated across the decks. Heads turned to look at each other.

"We got a right one 'ere," someone remarked. The sentry tripped lightly down the three gang planks, deposited the briefcase and stood to one side, allowing the large waist to pass. Ginger picked up the heavy briefcase and held it.

"Do you want someone from the Wardroom, sir? Do you have identification?" Ginger was eyeing the twinkling blue eyes, set in a pudgy face and moved down to the pear-shaped cleft chin as it gave way to a smile.

"Don't think the Wardroom is quite me, old man." The hand reached into the breast pocket and withdrew a blue plastic-covered card.

"Name's Blinveld. No need for the 'sir', old boy, I'm an able seaman, call me 'Binny'." The smile widened to a huge grin. Ginger couldn't help himself; despite the thought that he had been taken for a ride, he couldn't suppress the laugh. They were all laughing, all the men standing around on the three boats' upper decks. Binny's appearance and manner had the same stunning effect on all of them, and the Second Coxswain in particular, who thought this was a joke being played on him. He scrutinised his identity card closely.

"Why are you joining the boat in civvies?" he asked. He was going to turn this into a bad joke for this man if he was having him on.

"Actually, the regulating staff made a 'B' error, Coxswain. They sent me up to Helensburgh to join the boat, but when I arrived, you had already left. I had a spot of leave to come, you see, so I came direct from home." Blinveld was smiling, a dangerous lack of respect, when aimed at the Coxswain.

"Are you taking the mickey?" Coxswain was astounded at the man's effrontery. Blinveld had experienced this reaction to his mode of speech and style of dress on many occasions and knew exactly what effect he was having on the other man.

Blinveld had studied the part to perfection. It was the perfect cover. By being so completely different, he would remain so conspicuous that he would be beyond suspicion. Soon, they would accept him as merely an amiable idiot. It would give him adequate protection. Blinveld knew himself to be a good actor, and he knew that in this close community, he was going to have to be.

"No 'swain, absolutely not." The Grocer had no choice for the moment but to accept the man at face value, but he would soon get to the bottom of it.

"Got your travel papers, discharge note, leave card and leave pass?" The Coxswain was business-like; he would soon know if the man was lying. Surprisingly, all the required items were placed in his hand. The Coxswain relaxed.

"Right, go and have a cup of tea. Leading Seaman Sudswell will fix you up with a bunk, etcetera; he's the killick of the for'ard Mess."

The large stout apparition filled the doorway. "I say, chaps, any chance of a spot of tea? Just joined, you know, to replace a chap called Bates." No one knew whether to laugh or not; it was so unbelievable having a public-school twit in the seamen's Mess. They soon learnt, however, that the new man was not a twit and that his voice and manner were quite genuine, made all the more confusing since he played up to his audience and even contrived mild eccentricity at times.

"Well, Binny, no bunks in the Mess, I'm afraid," Bubbles explained the situation briefly that Ginger Bates was not moving up in the world and would still require his bunk.

"Have your cup of tea, and I'll take you to see Randy Sandy; he's the steward. You'll need to take one of the Wardroom passage-way bunks for the time being." Bubbles wanted to get the man settled in as quickly as possible since he might want to go ashore, as he himself did.

"Sling your gear on that one, you can have any of them, but that one's mine." Sandy was being his usual, well-loved, terse self. Blinveld opened the briefcase, holding it sideways on the steward's draining board. The steward looked bored, washing out some wine glasses. They noted his eyes were bleary again. His glance flicked over the briefcase.

"Not another bleeding intellectual." He sniffed and put the upturned glasses down to drain. Books came out of the briefcase in handfuls. Sandy was reading the titles.

"'Sudden Rides Again', 'Sudden at Black Creek', 'Sudden Strikes at Dry Gulch'."

"Here, I haven't read that one." Steward had accepted the posh-speaking newcomer. More books came out of the leather space, and finally, right at the bottom, a crumpled pair of underpants were withdrawn.

"You'll be all right for a kit inspection," Bubbles commented, noting the lack of other clothes. "I left a bag at the station, a toothbrush and whatnot. Mater will send the rest on from the old ancestral home, what?"

Bubbles wasn't taken in; he had already sized up Binny. He was what he appeared to be: well-educated and from a good home, probably well off also, but he played up on it, too. "Well, put your clean pair of knickers on, and we'll go ashore to meet your boss." Bubbles thought about John, who was already propping the lounge bar up at the White Swan. He wanted to get off with the barmaid apparently and was devoting a lot of time to the task.

# Chapter 18

The Captain and key officers came away from the briefing room. It was going to be a complex exercise, with so many ships involved, and the meeting had lasted much longer than usual to deal with the intricate details. The whole show had been upset, but not devastatingly so, by the late arrivals due to storm weather. It was to be an early start in the morning, leaving the harbour empty again. The numerous publicans of Portsmouth would probably not show much of a profit this week.

Lieutenant Hawks went to his rendezvous with an old colleague, who was now the 'big wheel' at a metal stress analysis laboratory. "Well, from what you tell me, Jeff, it sounds possible, but without doing a whole series of related tests, I can't really be specific." Lieutenant Commander Edward Gibson knew perfectly well that his old friend wanted him to use the laboratory facilities to clear up the matter.

"You see, Teddy, it isn't so much the incident that matters, but the issues that have resulted from it. That is particularly why I need to know." Jeff Hawks paused for thought.

"From the navy's point of view, it would be useful to know if this phenomenon would be brought about under similar conditions again. It would be necessary to carry out modifications to prevent it happening in future."

"Yes, of course. Well, as you want it done on the quiet, for the time being, I can incorporate it into my present studies. It's sort of semi-official if you see what I mean. Unfortunately, we don't know too much about stress factors causing vibration patterns. There hasn't been a terrific amount of work along those lines. Still, it's interesting. I'll see what I can do." Edward looked at his watch; the night was flying past and he had other appointments to see to yet. Jeff Hawks stepped out into the cold night air. He had a place to go, and he didn't intend to spend what was left of the evening out here.

To the petty officer and his staff of three at the pier head, the whole morning seemed to be filled with the customary ceremonial piping of a procession of ships leaving harbour. A group of two or three would go out, the men would all stand there stiffly to attention, and no sooner did they get back into their glass-covered shelter to get their hands warm, then the lookout would warn them of more ships coming up to leave harbour. Submarine *Orestes* left harbour in company with two others of the Oberon class. For a few days at least, they would form a close operating liaison.

The force dispersed out into the Western Approaches according to their separate orders, fanning ever wider out to sea. At the close of the second day, the complicated attack sequences began, trying out, in turn, all the modern techniques acquired in recent times. Numerous different combinations were attempted to increase the dividend of knowledge. *Orestes* crew were kept amused by the eccentric new pinger. Delegations of stokers arrived from time to time from out of the nether regions to sit, sup a cup of tea and be entertained by the posh bloke up for'ard.

"Mater was enthralled when I informed her I'd joined the Navy. She said, 'Oh, how marvellous!' Well, you see." Binny turned conspiratorially to his next-door seated companion, one hand raised to his mouth in mock simulation of privacy.

"One of the paternal lines of our ancestors was an Admiral and Mummy so likes the uniform." Most of the Mess sat there attentively as though listening to someone read a storybook at bedtime. John Bishop lay on his back, withdrawn into the confines of his bunk, trying to read and ignore the rambling tale below.

"Then I told her I'd joined as a common seaman. Poor old deah! Needed smelling salts for the rest of the afternoon. Absolutely ruined the croquet tournament, great pity." Blinveld was enjoying his fame tremendously, thriving on the attention which came his way. Most of them had no experience at all of someone like him, with his background. He came from a different world, and they were fascinated.

*So far, so good,* Blinveld thought. They were learning to accept him as an eccentric, which would be a useful cover for a multitude of mistakes should he happen to make them. His background was indeed authentic, and it would be an acceptable explanation of why he didn't understand as much of their navy jargon as perhaps the role required.

"Action Stations! Attack teams close up." The dreaded pipe came over the air. John heaved himself upright, tucked the book away under his pillow, and climbed down, feeling for his boots amidst the huddled feet. He wished this clown would find somewhere else to entertain his audience. Still, it wouldn't matter to him for the next hour or two anyway. Pity, though, that this Blinveld character was part of his sonar team. He could have done without that.

During the first week at sea, the food was as varied and palatable as the two cooks knew how to make it, and there were no serious complaints apart from the ones they received at all times, from the one or two who knew no better. After the first week, at the point where every day and night were so like the ones before that only fixed reference points in time became the meal times, it became apparent that there were serious shortcomings in the staple foods.

This was first noticed when Big Garth came for'ard to borrow a packet of tea. Everyone had grown so used to this once-weekly occurrence that it was no longer regarded as anything out of the ordinary. He was just about the only stoker who could be relied upon to repay the debt, and being such a natural, easy-going kind of man, they always gave it to him. "Coxswain is being stingy again, lads. Do you think I could borrow another packet? See you right in Barry Island, I will." The unfamiliar Welsh accent, always conciliatory, sounded cheerful.

"Won't be long now, eh boyos?" Hogarth was so obviously enthusiastic at the prospect.

"Bet you've got your train connections worked out already, Taff." There was no bitterness in the remark.

"Oh, looking forward to it, I am." Garth looked really pleased.

"Engineer's let me have a week's leave. Got a lot of work to do on the land at home. Time for planting, isn't it." Somebody was looking through the cupboards for the tea while the others looked up at the smiling, gentle giant. A few envied him his simple outlook, the honest pride in his family and the love of his piece of land.

"Only one packet left. What's happened to all the tea then?" the searcher enquired of the Mess in general.

"You run out altogether, Taff?" Bubbles asked. He had forgotten to draw the consumable issues this week.

"Yes. That is, we are on the last one. It might last us out the day, but I doubt it. We've had this week's already. Thirsty lot down aft, they are."

"Never mind, Taff, have this one." Bubbles threw him the packet, looked at his watch and decided the issue would have to wait till tomorrow now. He would go and see the steward in a minute. Randy always had a packet or two hidden away and he would give him one, provided he didn't say where it came from.

The next day, Coxswain handed out the tea that was left and made up the issue with coffee, and a few days after that, the bread ran out. The next thing they noticed was that the evening meal, the hot one of the days, was made up with tinned potatoes. There was no fresh left in the vegetable locker.

"We were only in Portsmouth for one day, and the stores didn't arrive; that's what Coxswain says." Someone had braved the Grocer's wrath and was now reporting back on what he had been told.

"This isn't on; we'll starve at this rate," one person at least objected.

"No, you won't; Ernie and me are going to start baking bread at night," Curly told them, not too happy at the prospect of losing more sleep.

By the end of the second week, all the tinned milk had been used up, as well as the sugar. It became common practice for a cup of strong black coffee to be taken with a spoonful of syrup in it for sweetening. Nobody liked it much, but it was that or nothing. Only the next day, all the yeast and flour went, so at least Curly was able to regain his normal sleeping habits. All the greenery which had survived was limp and unappetising. There were distinct rumblings of discontent in more than one sense. Butter was a thing of the past, but was replaced with one abundant item, that of tinned margarine.

Haunted shadows were seen at night, reaching down behind torpedoes, filching packets of shredded wheat from the Coxswain's stowages. Shredded wheat smothered in margarine became very popular for a midnight snack on that trip.

With just four days of the exercise left to run, a signal came in which shook them all out of their subjective concerns. A West German submarine was missing, believed lost. Her name was '*Seeadler*'. She had missed her surfacing signal by three hours. This was grave news indeed. Translated, the submarine's name was '*Seahawk*'. The exercise was terminated, and all ships and submarines in the vicinity were ordered to look for her. A daunting task since it was thought Soviet submarines, nuclear at that, might well still be in the area. No firm assurances to that effect as such. An unlikely coincidence, perhaps; who could say?

Three days passed before she was located, silent, no sounds of machinery or life, at a depth of one thousand feet. There could be no one left alive inside the *Seeadler*. Nothing could be done; there were no facilities for divers to go that deep. Sound equipment was lowered by a ship, especially brought in, but everyone knew that it was hopeless. There was nothing more anyone could do, and the matter was reported to the Federal Republic Authorities.

Some of the men aboard *Orestes* remembered the prediction they had heard whilst in Rothesay and how they had wondered if it had referred to the *Seawolf*, which was still out on patrol. Those who had friends aboard *Seawolf* felt easier, assuming now that they would be safe. Despite that, there was a deep sense of loss for this unknown craft with a crew they had never met. It was a question of sharing a certain way of life with those men which brought the catastrophe so much closer. It was indeed a great tragedy, foreigners or not.

Due to the established misfortune and nothing more to be done, *Orestes* left the area one day early and made her way up the approaches to the River Severn. Their arrival in Barry Island was unexpected, and the welcoming committee took a long time to wind up its machinery to provide the customary services. A few of the lucky ones avoided the long wait, being allowed to go on their special leave, even before the car arrived to take the Captain on his courtesy visit to the town hall. It was by long-standing precedent, that the Captain left the ship first on entering harbour.

Within a few hours, a team came out to connect up the shore telephones, and an old crane trundled along its rusty tracks, carrying a robust gangway to replace the boat's aluminium plank.

Steward was the first one back from ashore. His visit had been on a duty trip to obtain some items that the Captain had asked him to get. It was obvious from Sandy's appearance that he had already made a preliminary investigation of the pub life. His arrival in a somewhat dishevelled suit coincided with that of the railway truck, shunted from a disused siding along the ancient rails to be left opposite the gangway. A whole network of intersecting rails stretched from the jetty far across the wasteland of an isolated dock area. The provision of one sliding-door type empty cargo truck was all part of the laid-on service. It was intended for the disposal of rubbish. No one quite knew why it had been deposited so close to the submarine; it was assumed that the intention was for convenience. Fortunately, it was still cold and the sun was not too strong, and so the smell of the piled pyramid of refuse in the centre of its compartment did not pervade so overpoweringly as it might have done.

The allotted span of time for sentry duty on the casing was not reduced, even though by popular request of the duty watches. To have shortened the ordeal would have necessitated two tours of that abominable duty being kept by each man. The weekend came and went, and with it, a large number of the crew, some taking the unfamiliar trek across country to be at home, and others to enjoy the fleshpots of Glamorgan, or the ones they could find in this corner of it. It was lamented that it was necessary to walk some two miles to reach the borders of dockland. It became a regular excuse for preferential use of the ship's single, temporarily installed telephone; ordered taxis making a roaring trade during the brief interlude.

The taxi screeched to a halt at the gangway; its skidding stop throwing clouds of gravelly dust into the air. The driver slammed his door, hitched up his trousers and shuffled up to the plank. "Got a cab for a squire name of Blunderfelt, Blunderbolt, something like that," the man sniffed loudly as he spoke.

"Binny's taxi's here," Bubbles shouted down the accommodation hatch. Within a minute, Blinveld appeared on deck, resplendent in pinstripe and homburg, his walking-out kit.

"Oh, splendid. Just hang on a mo." The companion he waited for was the LRO, Swingle.

"Where are you off to?" Bubbles asked while they were waiting.

"London, a bit of night clubbing, I think, just for two days, you know." Blinveld opened his cigarette case and offered one to Bubbles, who took a quick glance around, took one, and lit it. He shouldn't really, since he was on watch doing first trot sentry, but there was nobody about.

Swingle climbed the ladder. "If the mail arrives during the next two days, sling it on my bunk, will you? Radio Supervisor will take care of it if you let him know."

"Yes, okay," Bubbles replied. *It hadn't taken Creeper long to take this opportunity of increasing his social status,* he thought.

"Right, my man, we are ready. Cardiff, if you please." Blinveld stepped jauntily over the gangplank carrying his umbrella. The briefcase was not going along on this trip. Swingle followed on, looking quite vulgar in a purple shirt and white tie beside the elegance of Blinveld. The car roared away, tyres screeching. Bubbles cupped his hands around the cigarette to hide it from view. He wondered who this gaggle of pedestrians were, strolling between the railway trucks towards the boat. As they came nearer, he recognised both the Navvy and Shane, escorting three female guests. *I hope they're not coming back for lunch*, Bubbles thought. Not long before, he had seen a red-nosed steward ditch what was left over from the officers' meal into the railway waggon.

Bubbles saluted the party onboard, hoping the cigarette wouldn't burn into his other closed hand. He remained quite poker-faced, hoping they would take the hint and not stop to talk to him. The party climbed down the ladder, with lots of chuckling and tittering at the girls' difficulty in negotiating vertically aligned rungs. Apparently, they were all tipsy. About ten minutes passed and Bubbles heard the steward coming; his bedraggled spaghetti-style hairstyle appeared.

"Bleeding pigs, perishing guests this time of day." Sandy appeared with a silver tray and a white napkin.

"Lunch for five, steward." The steward imitated and stumbled off, muttering obscenities. Sanderson was still a little drunk himself and wanted to get ashore to become drunker still by the look of it. In the next moment, the gash truck door was being slid back. The little man was on his hands and knees in the middle of the stinking rubbish, selecting the rather less battered pieces of whole fish and wiping them, one at a time, on his nice clean napkin before arranging them tastefully upon his silver dish. Having selected five pieces of this delicacy, he filtered through handfuls of the top layer of chips, eliminating tea leaves and other unwanted muck, placing them in soggy piles upon the silver tray. Satisfied with his artistic arrangement, Sandy hopped down, shut the door and gingerly flicked the assortment over with the napkin.

"Hope it bloody well chokes them," steward muttered on his way past. All he needed to do now was to warm the tray up for about ten minutes. Grinning all over his face, Randy Sandy appeared a half hour later, still in the same scruffy suit on his way ashore. He was still muttering as he walked away down the jetty, only this time it was a comic take-off.

"Lovely meal steward, at such short notice. Best I've tasted for a long time. Particularly enjoyed the mint. Mint, ha! Bloody tea leaves. Bleeding fools." Steward was quite happy in his peculiar way, wandering off towards town to compensate himself in the way that suited him best, quite alone and uncaring for anyone or anything. Bubbles kept the information to himself. Creeper, the biggest danger, had already gone ashore, but a story like this would go from mouth to mouth in no time and might get back to the wrong people.

Later that night, Bubbles got Pet Hulk to take over the watch and went ashore with John. After so long at sea, and especially being on duty the first day in, made him want to get ashore, try and unwind. It was even worse if you had to stand and watch others going to enjoy themselves. Some mainspring somewhere in the delicate balance of the mind started to unwind. All of them, the whole crew, seemed to experience the same thing. Nobody stopped to consider why it was, but they all got drunk, and most of them stayed that way for the whole week.

John was chatting up the girl who served them in the lounge of what had become their local. The pub was seedy and run down, in keeping with its setting on the dockyard fringes. After a two-mile hike, it was the first drinking house ashore and subsequently became a meeting place for the submariners. It was the last day in, and some of the returning men from leave were experiencing the local beer for the first time.

"Good leave then, Spider?" Bubbles watched the cheeky face approach.

"Not too vile at all." Spider was always chirpy, no matter what came his way.

"I suppose you went back to Faslane." Bubbles sipped his beer; for some reason, it didn't taste right, but he had drunk so many he couldn't be sure, and nobody else seemed to have any qualms about it.

"Yeah, went home to be with 'trouble and strife', didn't I."

Spider ordered a pint. "You all right there then, are you?" Spider was nudging John's elbow, nodding towards the shapely girl, who even now was getting his drink.

"I was till you came in," John had a habit of making cutting statements which could be taken more than one way, especially if someone looked likely to cross him.

"Touchy, touchy, say no more." Spider was too likeable to be offended. He wasn't about to try and beat anybody's time. He drifted away from the bar and took a seat.

"ere Bubbles, know what 'appened up there'?" Bubbles didn't.

"*Seawolf* came in, tower all smashed in, 'alf of it missing. Nasty do." All those within hearing range were immediately paying attention to Spider Webb.

"Your mate, Jimmy Paine, told me on the quiet like," Spider lowered his voice, and they all moved in closer to hear better.

"Their skipper told 'em all to say they came up under the ice, you know, if anybody asked, and you know, well, with damage like that, people going to ask questions, ain't they?"

"What really happened?" One of the crew asked, and they all hunched forward to hear the answer.

"Trying to bring her to the surface, weren't they? Don't know exactly what it was they was dropping over the side, but they weren't firecrackers, were they? Know what I mean?" A few heads turned to look at each other. This was highly unusual; boats went out to relieve each other on station all the time, but nothing like this had happened before. Could it have been depth charges? Nobody used depth charges any more. Bubbles had been thinking something here didn't ring true.

"Did you see *Seawolf* yourself, Spider?" he asked, looking carefully at the man's reaction.

"No, mate. When I goes home on leave, I don't go for trips up the loch to look at submarines, do I? I'm just telling yer what was said."

"So, you don't know how bad the damage was then." Bubbles was driving at some particular point, but they didn't know what he meant. John Bishop had heard most of it, and when the talking went into whispers, he had sidled over unnoticed. He knew what was going on.

"If half the tower was missing, they wouldn't have got back." John looked at them as he spoke.

"Damage like that would have to crack the periscope watertight glands. The boat would flood in no time with five openings like that in her." Spider was blushing, a cheeky grin on his face.

"So, somebody exaggerated, but I'm telling yer, something 'appened. That's wot they reckoned themselves."

Figures started to drift away. Apparently, the event had not been so dramatic after all. They carried on drinking their beer, starting new conversations. "You had everybody going there for a minute." Bubbles smiled; he didn't want to upset the man.

"Soon, find out when we get back, matey," Spider was going to have the final word; if they didn't believe him, that was up to them.

The drinking went on until late; the place got noisier until it was hard for a man to hear himself think. It appeared that, for once, John was wasting his time. He took some persuading, but eventually, he, too got tired of the place. The taxi took John and Bubbles, plus a few others who crowded in at the last moment, on to the casino in town. As soon as they walked in, they realised they had made a mistake. There was practically no one there but the croupiers and the girls in scanty uniforms trying to distract a gambler's attention.

Bubbles and John realised immediately that this was a specially set up operation geared to high mobility. Judging from the entrance to the shabby house, it looked like a temporary arrangement in an unused semi-detached that had seen better days. True, there were drapes hanging on the walls to lend a veneer of sophistication. The croupiers' dinner jackets and bow ties were smart, but where was the custom?

The first ordered drink came, ice clinking in the tumblers. It was even more suspicious that the first one was free. Some of the drunker matelots huddled around the green baize. A long ivory-coloured spatula flipped cards across the table, turning them face up in the flick of a wrist.

"Sod this, I'm off," John had pronounced his intention.

"You are leaving, sir?" The tall figure smiled laconically, eyebrows raised in mock servility. They noticed how the jacket bulged.

"The free drink, sir, is for patrons who play the tables," the voice was filled with sinister and sneering malice.

"So, we'll pay for the drink." John was not easily intimidated.

"That will be fifteen shillings, sir." The smile was a thin mockery.

"What?" said John, his voice raised.

"Each." The smile continued, but the clasped hand knuckles were clenching. John looked at the table.

"What is the minimum stake?" he asked, and his voice was not gentle.

"Five shillings to play, half a crown for a card." The suave bow tie bobbed slightly with the smoothly uttered phrase. Five shillings went onto the table.

"Just a minute." Bubbles placed a half-crown coin on the baize. Neither of the men bothered to sit down.

"One card." John didn't bother to look at it.

"You win," he said and turned on his heel. The guard opened the door and let them both out.

"Pleasure to have your patronage, sir." The sneer continued, but the door was closing slowly. The man was smiling; he thought he had won.

With the timing born of perfect reflexes, John powered a scrawny fist through the diminishing gap to land with all the power of his lean shoulder behind it. The nose flattened and gushed red as the door slammed the last few inches, but too late. John had withdrawn his arm just as fast, and the two of them were running.

They still found some small clubs to drink in. By the end of the day, the place looked like the for'ard Mess. Nearly all of them had found their way in, in twos and threes. The place didn't shut until six in the morning; it had stayed open, especially for them. The normal closing time was two o'clock, but as the proprietor had remarked, "Too good an opportunity to miss. Don't get boats down here often."

A weary and well-sozzled bunch straddled the old railway tracks in a continuous line back to the submarine. Two hours later, they were at sea. A heavy swell was running, which tended to make the boat roll. That, in turn, made many a stomach queasy, but at least they'd had their fun ashore while they could.

The Captain was not going to be caught unprepared again. He ordered the boat to be opened up for diving immediately upon clearing harbour. The fore-ends crew stayed closed up at their diving station, as sick as they felt. They were all of one company, green in the face, including their officer.

Shane, too, had been on a spree and now suffered the consequences. He hadn't thought that he had consumed all that much. A few brandies a bottle of wine with lunch, shared with the guests, of course. What had they drunk during the evening? Shane found it difficult to think back, and yet it had only been a few hours ago. Yes, he had it now, knew what it was. The beer had been off in that dirty little bar outside the yard. He could taste it now, vile stuff that it was. He had been a bit too well on the way to being tipsy to have noticed it before.

Shane leant out over the bilge, the vile taste in his mouth. Echoes came from all around the compartment. One from the port side of the tubes, that was Jock Brown examining the TOT tank vent. A regurgitating sound came from the Starboard side also. Scouse was trying the mechanism of that vent also. Charlie, the TI, had held out as long as possible and suddenly rushed off somewhere, fingers spread across his mouth. Shane wondered for a moment where Sudswell had got to until he heard the groans from the plated trench down the compartment's centre. He was checking the Q Kingston bilge. All here doing our jobs. Shane grimaced to himself, trying to hold back the green feeling which threatened to grip him.

Blinveld's breezy cheerfulness was more than anyone could take this morning. They hated him, albeit temporarily, for being so hearty while they were so close to the grave. John managed to talk him into doing his job for leaving harbour. John had given up the ghost entirely, reclining in a comfortable, reassuring foetal position in somebody else's bunk. He had to take one of the coffin bunks to escape detection while Jimmy perambulated himself with his Tiffy checking the boat. Somehow, sickness passed away into sleep. He was still there when the table flaps went up, and the Mess became busy with the sorting out of meals for the next watch on. Some vague sniffing disturbance brought John awake. The nauseating smell of oily gravy had an immediate reaction upon him, but he was trapped. The table and seat flaps held him in; there was no release. Somebody came into the Mess straight off the casing. Pet Hulk's hand pressed his round hat into his bunk between the curtains. Saved in the nick of time, John satisfyingly made full use of the proffered gift as quietly as possible.

Later during the day, Petters, looking agitated, came off watch, strode into the Mess and addressed them, "Anybody seen my hat? I've lost it." Petters looked confused and agitated at the same time.

"What does it look like?" John was feeling okay now and sat upright at the table adjacent to his recently abandoned bunk, enjoying his coffee. The big sailor nearly fell into the trap, about to explain that it was white and round, then he grinned sheepishly.

"I thought I left it on my bunk." Nobody seemed to know anything about it. John sat still, ignoring the proceedings while Pet looked through all the bunks and behind all the water pipes, where hats usually ended up. John felt safe, knowing that the evidence would be floating about two miles astern by now in one of the neatly tied white gash bags.

"Chef said something about not having a dish big enough to make a cake in." John was adding insult to injury, but Pet was slow to get his meaning.

"It was only a joke, only a joke!" John stood up, realising that he had overstepped the mark. Petters's face was settling into a mask of rage, and he was a strong man, too strong perhaps to play these games with. There was an uneasy truce. Bubbles smoothed it over, but he didn't yet feel well enough to cope with this sort of commotion.

The NATO exercise began, and having work to do, everyone settled into a routine quickly. Bubbles went to see the Coxswain to find out about their stores situation. Coxswain had a bad head and didn't take kindly to the implied criticism. He was not forthcoming with information. The butcher was more helpful. "Yes, well, he's in the Red for the audit period, you see," the able seaman explained, "so he's cutting back on stores where he can. Don't worry; we've got enough fresh stuff on for this trip."

"What about tinned milk?" Bubbles wanted to know exactly what was likely to run out. Butcher looked around to see no one was eavesdropping.

"Well, I can help you out there with a few cans, but that's one of the things we're low on. He's got to make it up on the consumable stuff. There is going to be bread rationing 'cos he didn't order enough, and tea is short as well." Bubbles got an armful of tinned fruit and sponge pudding tins, took them back to the Mess, and confidentially told them what the shortages would be. The contraband was hidden in various spaces behind air conditioning trunking. During the trip, everyone got into the habit of hoarding food. The last trip, when practically everything of value had run out, taught all of them to cache away any extras that they could lay their hands on.

The bread issue, all two loaves of it was brought up in the morning. Very few bothered with the formality of breakfast, but henceforth, if it wasn't had at breakfast, a slice or two of bread went under each man's bunk for later consumption. The table lockers stayed empty. There was no longer a food surplus to be kept, not one that anyone would want anyway. Lockers didn't lock, which in itself was a laugh. Nobody ever stole, but when food was short, who would take the risk? A man's bunk was a different matter that absolutely was untouchable.

The First Lieutenant was in a sullen mood, and he had been brooding since the Captain had informed him whilst in Barry Island that the promotion review board could not be convened. Lieutenant Grimes had been passed over for the third and final time. Effectively, his career was finished. He was entitled, of course, to officially request an interview with Captain SM and be able to put his case. At this point, he would be acquainted with their lords of the admiralty's reasons. Reggie felt sick at heart. His career was floundering, and his personal life was not very satisfactory either. His relationship with the beautiful Sophie Wilkes seemed to be growing cold. Her affection towards him had waned and she had refused to see him several times. The excuse was pressure of work, but he didn't believe it. Work must be his panacea, too, for the moment.

The First officer decided the time was right to hold part three submariners' examinations. These were the as-yet unqualified submariners who had yet to prove themselves.

Coxswain informed the part threes of their time to muster in the torpedo compartment for an examination.

Lieutenant Reginald Grimes walked for'ard and buttonholed Bubbles. "I want you to rig the fore-ends for escape, Leading Seaman Sudswell, to make it more realistic for the exam." Bubbles had already got doubts about Reggie's sanity. He stared at him with a dull expression, thought about it, and then expressed himself.

"As you can see, sir. The Coxswain's food stores are scattered all over the place. Where am I going to stow it all if I need to move the deck plates up to the centre level? It also means rearranging these torpedoes. It's going to take all day."

"Use your initiative; you are a leading seaman. You could pass all the food into the Mess. I want it done by five o'clock tonight. Is that clear?" When Jimmy used that imperious tone of voice, it would be like banging one's head on a wall to argue with him, and just as dangerous. Bubbles went to see Charlie. Jimmy had neglected the formality of discussing his intention with the Torpedo Officer or Torpedo Instructor.

Charlie knew nothing about this new directive and agreed with Bubbles that if all the stores went into the Mess, the men presumably would have to be stowed in racks alongside the batteries underneath. The Torpedo Officer thought about this news and wondered if this was a plot to bring himself out into open opposition with the executive officer. There was no doubt that Reggie had been peculiar in his thinking for some while. Nevertheless, he would not fall into this apparent trap.

Shane talked with Jimmy, who remained quite adamant. There was nothing else for it; it would need to be done. Bubbles put it to the Mess, and everyone off watch gave a hand, even Creeper Swingle, who could not pretend that he had signals to send whilst they were in radio silence.

Two torpedoes were moved by winch, and steadying hands, from their inboard central stowage rack to an upper level. Most of the food stores were re-shuffled around the compartment and stowed behind or on top of the tin fish. The rest of it was handed along the human chain until the bunks were full of it. Aluminium deck plates had to be unscrewed and removed.

The torpedo hatch ladder, big and weighty, came down, presenting something of a problem to be rid of. In the end, that, too, was passed into the Mess to fill the floor space. It became quite certain that the Mess would be completely disrupted for the rest of the day and some of the following one as well. Bubbles and Charlie discussed the problem and decided that, as in a real escape emergency, all the loose bags of rags and other conglomeration of essential items in the deck trench would need to be lashed down.

It was quite obvious to them both that 'Raging Reggie' would only insist that it be done, so they might as well do it now. Three hands undid the securing bolts to pull down the escape trunking, it too being lashed into position. "He wouldn't like us to open the escape hatch and let a bit of daylight in, I suppose, just for a bit of realism, like." Sarcastic the Scouse was, his remark received a fair amount of approval and mirth at its absurdity.

The whole operation took three hours, which was fine, considering that fifteen men helped, and on the very rare occasions it was carried out as a drill, it was normally done by three or four men.

The First Lieutenant stood on the platform during the last ten minutes of the preparations, seething, with dark, angry, fluttered eye-brow movements. "I said five o'clock. It is now ten minutes past five." An angry tick appeared on the officer's cheek, the muscle twitching out of control. The men stood, sweating with exertion in the already thick atmosphere. They looked at each other and back at him, but nobody spoke.

"Where are the breathing masks? You haven't taken the masks out of the lockers. I want them plugged into the BIBS system." A few of the faces cracked into a nervous smile at the almost tantrum-like statement of the officer. Charlie climbed up onto the platform and faced Jimmy.

"Do you mean you want all of them broken out, sir?" He stared straight into the officer's eyes at about six inches range.

"I said I wanted realism. Yes, I want them rigged." Jimmy had not flinched at the PO's nearness.

"Well, I think I had better go and get the Torpedo Officer and also the air Tiffy, sir, before we go any further," Charlie finished speaking and ducked through the hatch before he could be stopped.

"Hand me that wheel spanner," the voice of Jock Brown echoed out in the silent room. Someone handed it to him without thinking. Bubbles realised what was about to happen and tried to intercept the tool.

"What do you want that for?" he asked and then wished he hadn't because it gave Jock the lead in he wanted.

"I thought I would open the compartment flood valve and see if we can't get a bit more realism into it. We're only at two hundred feet; nothing to worry about, really." It was too late; the full effect of Jock's flippancy broke the tension in the fore-ends. Everyone, except the officer, burst out laughing. He alone remained quite ashen-faced.

"Brown, report yourself to the Coxswain immediately." The First Lieutenant had relinquished control over his muscles. His face had gone scarlet, and the nerve twitched more rapidly. He turned on his heel and disappeared to confer with the Coxswain on a charge report for Brown.

Charlie came back with the Torpedo Officer and air chief, but not soon enough to forestall the incident. Even Shane, though he tried to hide it, was amused when the tale was recounted by the still-smiling men who had witnessed it. Shane went to discuss the First Lieutenant's plans with him and was instructed to carry out the examination himself, thereby saving face by not rescinding the order.

The four trainees spent a busy session under the Torpedo Officer's tutelage, whilst those in the Mess who could find room perched themselves to wait until the Mess could return to normal. Shane compromised, a tactic that he was becoming adept at. He conducted what could reasonably be assessed as a thorough test but, at the same time, minimised the inconvenience to the men. Before finishing up, he authorised the stowing of equipment. So far as he was concerned, two had passed, and two had failed. The two unsuccessful ratings being Simeon and Harman.

# Chapter 19

The first week of the exercise had gone smoothly enough, despite some minor communication problems between ships of different nations. Phase two was about to begin, but *Orestes* had found herself at the furthest reach of one sector, at a time when she needed to be further west to complete transit in time.

Lieutenant Hawks ordered high speed for the transit. He was just working out the amount of time which would be lost. He stood at the chart table, dividers in hand. The Engineer Officer hesitated and stood inside the Control Room, his white overalls smudged with oil at the sleeves. *There was no way to avoid it,* he thought. He couldn't take the risk; the Captain would have to be informed.

"Excuse me, sir." The engineer was at the Captain's elbow, looking down at the calculation. The smoothly brushed hair gleamed in the dim reflection of the chart table light.

"I'm afraid we have trouble with one of the port shaft bearings. I would like to shut down that side for examination."

"Damn!" The Captain's hope of regaining the lost time was gone.

"Sorry, Engineer. How bad is it?" The Captain's mind was already churning over all the possibilities.

"The vibration is only just visible, but we have the beginnings of a high-pitched whine. With luck, it is only a badly packed bearing. Until we can take it apart, I'm afraid I can't report on the extent of damage." The engineer showed genuine concern; he knew quite well that this was the bane of command. The Captain also realised that in this turbulent sea state, he would need to alter his heading away from the designated position.

"Let me have your report as soon as you are sure, Engineer."

"Stop port. Slow ahead, starboard. Thirty degrees of starboard wheel. Steer one three zero degrees," the helmsman repeated the orders as his hands got busy turning the handles.

"Bridge, Captain. I've ordered one three zero heading. Amend that as necessary to keep a sea heading. The engineers are closing down the port shaft for inspection." Two hours later, amidst a clutter of tools between overalled figures, the Captain knelt beside the engineer.

"It isn't badly scored yet, but I'm very much afraid there will be some ovalling." The engineer smeared the contaminated grease between his fingers, feeling the grit in it.

"The shaft is out of alignment by some three thou'. It is bound to deteriorate, sir, even with re-packing."

The word soon went forward that the rest of the exercise was off and that the boat would need a dockyard for repairs. The Captain sent his signal, set a new course for the coast, and waited for the reply.

"Do you hear there? Captain speaking." All the men gathered around the loudspeakers. This was an announcement not to be missed.

"We have damage to our port shaft, which requires dockyard assistance. The only yard which can fit us in at such short notice is Chatham." A lot of the men were disappointed. Nobody aboard lived in Kent, and a lot had hoped that they would be going back to Scotland.

"We should arrive in two days, weather permitting. Main leave arrangements will be as previously scheduled." Some of the crew were starting to grumble, wondering how they would manage to find the fare to get home for leave.

"We shall bring all the pressure to bear that we possibly can on the dockyard to complete the work as quickly as time will allow. We must still keep our patrol commitment. That is all." The switch went off, and the static faded.

"Well, if I know dockyard maties, we won't be out in time for that patrol, anyway." Ginger Bates was voicing his opinion, and the laughter indicated that some agreed with him.

"You must be joking." John's head peered out from behind the bunk curtains.

"All that overtime, they'll lap it up. Fat pay packets for working at night, of course, they will."

"Yes, but the work they do at night will be the work they should have done during the day." There was a lot more laughter at this.

*S12* limped up the English Channel on one engine. The journey would take as long or longer than if they had returned to their base in Faslane. Those who lived in the midlands and south of England were pleased. The crew who lived in the north were not.

With only two days left to reach harbour, no one was particularly interested in the lack of food variety and hardly noticed those deficiencies.

The First Lieutenant ordered a muster of all junior ratings not on watch, to take place in the fore-ends. This was the only compartment large enough to hold them all. The appointed time arrived, and the men jostled each other for the limited space. Lieutenant Grimes arrived and took his place on the raised ladder platform. A sea of inquisitive, questioning faces looked up at him.

"As you all know," he began, a vague glint of restrained fury in his eyes and with a deep and pronounced harshness to his voice. "The domestic refrigerator in the accommodation space is for the use of the whole crew." Lieutenant Grimes paused. The assembled men turned to look at each other. He was right; they did all know, but they had no idea what all this was about. "However, it is well understood that the top shelf is for the exclusive use of Wardroom officers."

Reggie halted his speech to take a deep breath. The fury was trying to unleash itself. The men silently agreed. They all knew the top shelf belonged to the officers. It would, naturally, being the coldest. "Which means," the speaker's voice had risen an octave, "that everything on the top shelf belongs to the officers. There was a Stilton cheese on that shelf." The eyebrows lowered in a grim, brooding arch. His voice sounded like a parody of itself.

"We, the officers, supply ourselves with delicacies paid for from our own pockets." Another pause. "Some individuals have taken it upon themselves to appropriate that Stilton cheese and I want to know who was responsible," the speech had ended on a note of determination.

The sea of faces moved in a strict bending phalanx, from side to side, swaying with the gentle rocking of the boat as it altered course. The expressions were empty. *Someone amongst all these faces knew something about it,* Reggie thought, *but they were so densely packed, so many of them, that no guilty individual could be selected.* "I know where the cheese has gone," the officer's words were loud in their sudden burst upon the silence, "its remains were found in the Wardroom gash bucket, out in the steward's passageway. I want to know who was responsible." The flow of words was greeted with total silence and some creeping apathy. He could see from the vacant expressions that no one was in the least concerned.

"Some of you know who did this. It is stealing, no matter what you might call it; this offence is a serious one, and any one of you who knows who did it must speak up, or you are condoning his theft." The words evoked a mutter of ill-tempered oaths from the gathering. The accusation apparently was being levelled at them all, and it was resented.

Reggie looked down from his lofty, superior position. It became obvious to him that he was alienating them. This rabble did not intend to support him and were not eager to have the culprit known. *An ill-disciplined and loutish bunch,* he thought. Reggie decided to change tactics and shake them into a response.

"I know who did this dreadful deed," the voice resounded, and now he had their full attention. The words followed quickly to capitalise on the shock.

"We have the teeth marks embedded in the remains of the cheese." There was a vague titter of laughter from somewhere amongst the crowd.

"Teeth marks can be matched against dental records," the voice was rising to a crescendo. Reggie sensed that the expected impact would not materialise. He was losing them, and now his own words had taken on a quality of desperation. "A FULL SET of teeth marks, both rows of teeth, where they had bitten into the cheese. The culprit will come to light when they are matched with his dental record. There can be no doubt."

A bubble of constrained ridicule broke completely free from the numerous spluttering mouths, almost drowning the last spoken sentence. The laughter broke spontaneously at the ludicrous display, quickly becoming infectious. The whole room rocked and swayed in deep belly laughter. The figures bent, doubled in paroxysms of mirth, crowding in upon each other with hardly room for anyone to move.

The executive officer stood speechless, reddening in the face, the suffusion quickly bracing into scarlet. He looked down at the assembled crewmen, but to him, they represented a mob, and he felt powerless to influence them. He could no longer make his presence felt. There were too many, just too many individuals en-bloc for him to cope with.

A pulsing itch irritated his hands and face. A brief dart of adrenalin seemed to pump into his legs. There was an overpowering urge to flee, but some twitching nerve in his head would not allow him to. By what method, he did not know, but he managed to stand his ground. The man had failed, but the uniform stood firm, shouting its unmoving symbol of authority. Because he stood his ground, the laughter began to wane. Each, in turn, regained his senses. Euphoria subsided and individual freedom vanished. They were again respectful of the uniform's authority. He had their attention once more.

"You will all pay." Lieutenant Grimes looked over their heads, still not able to look into any eye.

"The value of the cheese will be stopped from your Mess funds," a few splutters started again. The officer turned and left the compartment, quitting while he was ahead. Content to have the last word. He just had time to hear the one comment behind him; but did not stop.

"He's lost his marbles," one voice was raised among many, and no chance of identifying it.

"He can't stop money from the Mess funds," another voice spoke. This time close to Bubbles.

"No, of course, he can't, especially since we haven't got one." Bubbles smiled at his own remark. Mess funds were illegal unless authorised by an executive officer. Nobody ever bothered with that detail, but Bubbles knew the sort of trouble which could arise from running one for the Mess. So, he himself had stopped the last one, and a Mess fund could not be operated without his knowledge. Apparently, Jimmy just supposed that he ran one. *Well, if he tries to follow up, he'll get a shock,* thought Bubbles.

Nothing more was said about it. Not until much later, when the tale became part of folklore, recounted in numerous bars ashore with friends from other boats. In this slow, repetitive routine, the incident was forgotten. There were other more immediate considerations to block out its memory.

The Coxswain was in a foul mood. He now needed to reroute all travel warrants for the first leave party, besides coping with new requests for the precious travel warrants and those nuisances who decided that they didn't need one after all. With all the extra paperwork required, he decided to rope in Leading Seaman Bates to give him a hand.

"Hold on 'swain. I'm working seaman watches, remember, not PO of the watch." Ginger knew the protest would not register. *Like talking to a brick wall,* he thought. Coxswain was scowling.

"Bates, you are acting Second Coxswain, and doing paperwork goes with the job; sit down there and cop hold of this lot." One of the POs was busy in the opposite corner of the Mess.

"Is it all right, Bill?" Charlie, the TI, was pointing whilst looking at the Coxswain. Coxswain nodded assent.

"There you are, cocker. Get that down you. If you're doing Scratcher's job, you might as well have the Scratcher's beer." Charlie placed the pint pot down by Ginger's hand and winked. The gesture said you're not getting paid for the job, so get paid in perks instead.

"Now, where did I put those paybooks?" The Coxswain had gathered all the crew's pay books in. In these was kept the used allowance of free railway warrants, along with a record of the man's leave. They had all been collected so that the official red line could be inserted to denote that all three basic and two separation warrants had been used by the end of March. If they were not, then they were forfeited anyway.

"You put them all in gash bags, round by the battery board 'swain." One of the chiefs had a memory, anyway. Due to the unexpected change in plans, the Coxswain would now need to make amendments to the pay books of those who now required a warrant.

"No gash bags near the battery boards 'swain, nor anywhere else either," Ginger reported his search result, beginning to realise what had happened. The leading hand of the gash-ditching watch for that evening was sent for. Petters didn't know what all the fuss was about. Well, yes, there had been a half dozen bags more than usual, but he hadn't taken any particular notice of that fact. Not only had Pet Hulk unwittingly sent all their paybooks overboard, but although he had not known it, he had also passed his own hat up to be sent over with all the rubbish.

Blinveld kept very quiet but mentally breathed a sigh of relief. He had seen the opportunity and taken it. It was he who had passed those particular gash bags out along the line. Fortunately, no one had noticed. The paybooks he had secreted away from the bags could be very useful to his network. Several identities could be duplicated from the information contained in each, especially since a paybook carried the men's photographs. So far, there had been no luck with the sonar device. John Bishop never let those keys out of his sight. He had also cultivated Swingle, who could probably be useful when the time was right. Swingle had many weaknesses, but one in particular which could be exploited. Blinveld was content for now; he could wait.

The Mess members were not amused when informed that the Coxswain since he had no separate record, would assume that all that year's entitlement of travel warrants had been used up. As a special concession, he told them, he would allow them to use one from the new entitlement, which began on the first of April. John and Bubbles both immediately saw that the Coxswain had taken advantage of this unfortunate incident to reduce his own workload. John went to see the Navigator, nominally his divisional officer, to discuss this new development and point out the injustice in the Coxswain's decision. John knew better than to make an official complaint.

Theo Brooks was loath to approach the executive officer with this problem since the Coxswain was, in effect, an extension of the First Lieutenant's authority and, in matters of discipline, acted in his name at his own discretion. As expected, Reggie took the view that it was a departmental affair which was quite within the Coxswain's jurisdiction.

Independently, Bubbles had discussed the dubious deal with Charlie, who in turn represented the matter to Shane. Lieutenant Phil Green was not afraid of the First Lieutenant and, in this instance, took up cudgels on the long-distance travellers' behalf. He pointed out to Reggie quite forcefully what the effects of the edict would have on morale generally, and on cash resources for the individuals concerned.

Lieutenant Grimes was not inclined to discuss functions of administration with Lieutenant Green and forbade further discussion. The Captain, who always kept his ear close to the ground, heard the rumblings of discontent and acted accordingly. His considered opinion was that the crew, through no fault of their own, and without sufficient time to plan for it, found themselves at the opposite end of the country. He upheld the view of his Torpedo Officer and reversed the First Lieutenant's and Coxswain's decision. In order to soften the blow, he produced a compromise whereby the men travelling north of the midlands would receive a free warrant, extra to the new entitlement.

The Captain considered his First Lieutenant's behaviour in recent episodes of the trip. There could be no doubt now that the man was unstable. He would have to recommend psychiatric analysis. That signal was transmitted even as they approached the harbour, asking for a replacement.

On arrival at Chatham dockyard, *Orestes* went immediately into dry dock. Negotiations began with the dockyard administration at the same time that teams were being formed to commence work. First leave party rushed, late though it was, to catch one of the last trains for London.

# Chapter 20

The train shuddered to a screeching stop at Waterloo Street, the remainder of its doors opening wide to disgorge packed compartments. Clouds of steam and hissing air floated upward around the feet of alighting passengers. Three men ambled up the long platform to the high gates and weary-looking ticket collector. His gnarled hands attempted to snatch the three tickets, but they all held on with a firm grip. All three were travelling on northward.

Thronged ranks crushed through the barrier, dispersing into thin beads of rushing humans. Six separate speeding lines of clipping feet spread across the open space to different destinations.

The lights in red and yellow beckoned from the buffet bar. Without spoken thought, John, Bubbles and Blinveld headed for this oasis. "First one today!" John gulped his beer, catching a glimpse of his own haggard, lean appearance in the scratched bar mirror.

"Piccadilly or Wardour Street?" Bubbles diverted his friend's attention from his reflected nightmare.

"Why not both? Bright lights and seedy backstreets, just like home." Binny leaned on the bar, watching his own cynical reflection. Scruffy, sad-eyed individuals drifted past with all the painful marks of human experience etched into their faces.

"Watch your holdalls." John eyed the furtive figures, crouching for cigarette ends, sidling their way between the seats.

Four foreign-looking types, dressed in the ragged style of the world's merchant seamen, sat discussing a camera that one of them held. They were trying to decide how much it would fetch on the street market. From the interest shown in it and the way it was closely examined, passing from hand to hand, it appeared that one of them had just found it.

The two sailors gripped their holdalls between their feet, the third quite nonchalant about these proceedings. Binny carried nothing but his umbrella. "Another?" His eyebrows raised in enquiry, an empty glass in his hand, the hatted figure made as if to stand.

"Too pricey here, full of dead-beats and layabouts." John drained his glass and stood, taking a firm grip on his few belongings, thrown casually at the last minute into a bag.

The station had virtually emptied, save for loitering figures and a few late travellers seated in silent anguish along some benches. "Let's get going before the next train arrives." Bubbles shouldered his way out of the door, heading for a taxi rank.

"Think we ought to book our rooms first, old chap." Blinveld, homburg at a jaunty angle, strode out down the incline, umbrella swinging to time with his march.

The sailors' hostel welcomed them in dusty silence. Without a word, the desk clerk listened to their request, eyed identity cards and thrust the register towards them. Three keys came down from a pegged board behind him. In bored silence, the club went about its lonely business. Aged, wooden-like men sat in regimented rows, waiting for something to happen. A few looked up as the three passed by, but nobody spoke.

Blinveld's umbrella was used successfully to bring a cruising taxi to a sliding halt beside them. The much-used, musty smell of dust and leather wafted up as the doors opened. They climbed inside and watched the panorama of London streets unfold.

In the uncaring emptiness of a crowded bar, the liquid worked its magic in record time. Soon, they were laughing, forced enjoyment bubbling from the three as more and more of the brown fluid passed their lips.

The second taxi they took threaded down closeted streets in numerous turns to take them into Wardour Street. John challenged the driver about the fare, but it made no difference. They all thought the route had been too circuitous, just to pace out the meter to a larger profit. They had only their suspicions and no hope of proof, so they paid. The Cabbie mouthed abuse as he pulled away, not happy at receiving no tip.

Blaring, lively sounds of music hailed from some hidden basement. They went in, paid the club membership, and found their way downward along narrow stone steps to emerge among bright flickering lights and a convulsing throng of people. The night lingered onward in raucous blasts of jungle harmony, lights low, people milling, an agitated smell of heat generating throughout the room. There was no friendliness to be found here for three out-of-town strangers. This lonely city engulfed them, but they were not part of it. At three o'clock, they could hold no more of the expensive drink nor throbbing rhythmic pulse in the head. They returned to the empty corridors of the seamen's hostel, each door equally spaced along its passageway, uniform in colour and size, and a forlorn sameness about everything.

In the morning, cheerful rumblings of the canteen staff brought light into the room. A good, filling breakfast put all three in a better mood for the start of a new day. They made tentative plans for meeting later in the week, and each went his separate way. Bubbles joined a long queue, waiting for those gates to open.

He looked idly around in the busy station at so many preoccupied faces rushing this way and that, all ruled by the clock, darting worried glances at a wristwatch, a frenzied search for a wandering child, a few with the lofty pride of a bowler-hatted head.

A railway official arrived, pulled out a watch on its chain, examined and tapped its face, and slowly opened the gates. The queueing throng dashed along the platform to take possession of an empty railway compartment. Ten minutes later, they were all full, every seat taken. Bubbles ignored the sullen faces, leaned back and closed his eyes, waiting for his journey to begin.

The train moved, gathering momentum, past platform signs and briefly glimpsed bill hoardings. Morning sunlight cascaded into carriages, momentarily blinding its occupants. Faces were hidden in opened newspapers, rows of black print on sheets of white jiggling up and down in unison with the train's hurried motion. Countryside unfolded in a patchwork of green and brown, rows of trees flanking between. The sun darted from behind one to another, causing bright stabs of pain in Bubbles' eyes. He became intrigued at the distant crawling struggle of miniature vehicles, twisting upon bands of curling road. The houses became fewer and fewer, the long rows of terraced blocks giving way to broad expanses of open ground.

A ticket collector bumped his way from row to row, summoning all to present their squares of green pasteboard. Bubbles listened to the dull-voiced approach, timing the intervals between each metallic click before the man gathered attention to himself once more. Bright sunlight settled on the faces, warming them and making many drowsy. Wandering thoughts pursued each other from hour to hour, jerked temporarily back to the present with each grinding halt at a swarming platform. The banging and rattling of doors and windows, the scuffing of feet and exhortations to hurry filled the carriages, shattering tranquil thoughts, banishing dreams, parading the cold reality. Shuffling ceased, faces relaxed, the tension ebbing away as a whistle blew and the shunting clatter of rotating wheels sent pulses of vibration through the floor and seats.

Uneasy rest resumed, thoughts turned again to personal things, deeds done and opportunities that had not been taken. The image of a face crystallised into sharp detail behind his closed eyes. The smiling face and welcoming eyes shone out at him, asking him where he was going. "Come back," the face seemed to say. "I am waiting."

"York Station," the strangely clipped words echoed at the back of his mind.

"York Station," the sound seemed nearer, stirring some forgotten thought in the sleeping mind.

"York Station," the monotonous voice penetrated his mind and brought it to the surface. Two clipping paces of measured feet and the two words were flung out into the air again. Bubbles realised what the words meant to him, and he galvanised into wakefulness, grabbed his brown bag and forced it against the incoming tide of strange faces.

"Nearly missed it, son!" the porter uttered the words in a barren monotone and continued his pacing steps along the platform. Bubbles rubbed his eyes, shaking the last vestiges of sleep from his head. The bitter tea from the buffet bar refreshed him and brought him to his senses. Foreign lilting tongues all around him were a reminder of his presence in this strange place and the reason that brought him. The long, curving road was filled with lunchtime traffic. He walked along the wide pavement, going against the stream of pedestrians hurrying past. He began to despair of finding a cafe that wasn't filled, but eventually, he did, probably because the inmates were now in a hurry to get back to work.

After the meal, not sure of his way, Bubbles needed to ask a passer-by, who thought him strange for not knowing where he was. As instructed, he followed the long continuous stone wall, not being able to see over its high top, and only realising when he came to the tower gate that the wall was an ancient fortress defence around the city. Threading his solitary way down narrow streets, unlike others, he was not interested in the Cathedral or quaint shop fronts and was not inclined to steep himself in historic atmosphere. He only wanted to find the right number, having never visited the house he was looking for. In a narrow passageway which led from a cobbled street, through which the sun had difficulty penetrating, he found the address he sought.

He knocked quietly at first, feeling disturbed at the thought of being here. There was no answer, and the temptation was strong to turn and walk away. *It would be better, perhaps,* he thought, *to let ghosts of the past lie undisturbed.* The moment of weakness left him, and he knocked again, louder this time, until he heard shuffling feet in the hall beyond. The door inched open, widening slowly to reveal a dark box-like opening of bare floorboards. An old woman's face peered out at him, the eyes squinting at his unfamiliar face. She couldn't see him too well stood out there among the shadows. Bubbles looked at the stooped figure, noting how old she had become.

"It's Jay," he said, his voice sounding loud in the closed alleyway. She had not moved.

"Jay Sudswell. I've come to see Sheena." Bubbles stood quite still; his words had not brought any reaction.

"Don't you remember me? You have been getting the money, haven't you?" At last, a flicker of recognition crossed her lined face.

"Didn't expect to see you again," her cracked voice had only the slightest trace of emotion. She had been shocked to see him standing there, not expected, after three years with no word from him.

The bent old woman turned, shuffled down the passage, and half-turned to stop and wait for him. Bubbles closed the door behind him; the hall went into darkness as he did so. An internal door opened and he heard a crackling flame as a piece of coal settled in the hearth. Inside the small room with threadbare carpet, the fire's light spreading its glow along the walls, a child sat amongst a pile of plastic toys, crayons and paper.

"Hello Sheena." Bubbles advanced to the centre of the room but stopped as the fair-haired girl of five stood up and backed away in wide-eyed suspicion. "It's Daddy. Don't you remember me? Come to Daddy." The outstretched arms could not lure the little girl from her corner. She had not spoken, afraid to talk to this stranger, this tall man who smiled at her.

"We didn't tell her about you. Didn't think we would see you again. Best for her not to know, poor little mite." The old woman stumbled across the room to rest a protective arm around the girl's shoulders. An outstretched figure of a man stirred in his deep armchair beside the fire.

Bubbles had seen the white-haired form slumped there.

"How are you feeling, Grandpa?" Bubbles waited for his answer, but only a few snorts and grunts came from the aged throat. The woman bade him to sit down and shuffled away to the kitchen. Presently, the sound of clinking cups reached them.

"She's made a new life for herself, Grandpa." Bubbles thought for a moment of the woman who had left him for the excitement she craved, deserting her own child at the same time. He felt no bitterness and no anger, not after three years, but somehow it had left him empty. He had not provided enough to make her stay. Painful as the realisation had been, there was nothing he could do to make matters right except send her grandparents what was needed to care for this abandoned child. Maybe his fault, and maybe not, but it was not the child's fault either. He could not bring himself to love her, nonetheless. Perhaps he was incapable of that emotion, he sometimes thought. No point in dwelling upon it in his situation.

The child came up to him beside the chair, holding out a battered teddy bear with one eye missing for him to admire.

"This is Floppy," she said, looking at him with big round eyes. The child didn't know him, but her family accepted him, and so would she. He would provide a new audience for her parade of toys until he left. Bubbles spent a long time looking at the long blonde hair, at the fresh pinkness of her skin, seeing the likeness and the shape of the mother who had gone. He decided that he would not stay. Could not stay with this painful reminder. He had been wrong and should not have come. She didn't know him, didn't need him. It was time for him to go back to sea. It was what he knew.

John Bishop strode along the platform, well behind the crushing throng of would-be travellers. He looked through the compartment windows to see how quickly the seats were being filled. If he didn't do something quickly, there would be none left.

"Stand well clear of the doors. Move right back there, please." John threw his chest out and strutted along, allowing his voice to carry across the heads of the milling people. Most of them stopped, some moved back and a lot of heads turned in his direction.

"Front two carriages are being disconnected. Move right back there, please," John's voice sounded very deep, full of authority as he strode along the platform edge, wedging a barrier with his body between the ranks of travellers and the train.

"The train will be shunting backwards and forwards during the disconnecting. We don't want anyone hurt. Move right back there." John was thoroughly enjoying himself, shouting orders at the bewildered faces. A man's voice challenged John.

"You're not in uniform. Are you an official?" John dropped the holdall, brought his arms up and, very importantly, tucked both thumbs behind his jacket lapels, hands closing around them to lend dignity to his reply.

"I am," he said, rocking gently backwards and forwards on his heels, the voice rising as though defying anyone else to challenge him.

"I am the track and carriage inspector for Northern Region of British Railways." John kept his head thrust back, looking haughtily over the heads of the shuffling crowd.

"Keep right away from the edge there." John's arm had shot out to point up the platform, stooping to retrieve the bag with his other hand, and continued to saunter arrogantly. A door lay opened back on its stops. John came up to it, stepped up into the carriage, faced outward and leaned up towards one end.

"Carry on driver." The scrawny wrist stopped pointing, grabbed the door firmly and shut it. John was two carriages down, by the time people started fighting to board the train.

"Excuse me, Inspector." A large woman in a sprawling green hat stopped John on his way to the buffet car. She had recognised him as the man giving instructions.

"When do we get to Oxford.?" The woman was finding it a strain to look up from her seat in the aisle at the tall figure carrying a brown bag.

"Eight hours, Madam." John swiftly glanced at his watch.

"Precisely fourteen hundred hours." He was gone before the gasp of astonishment had fully developed. *Silly old cow, she's on the wrong train,* he thought, using the bag held before him like a battering ram.

The barman continued to polish a glass, ignoring the influx of tardy passengers who couldn't find a seat. A lean chap with the holdall was looking at him, comfortably seated at the end of the counter. "Ah-hem." John cleared his throat to attract the steward's attention. That white-jacketed individual took no notice, continuing to polish his glass.

"Pale ale for me and one for yourself," John's voice carried across the car, enough to make a lot of heads turn. There were angry glances from the dozen shoulder-crushing bodies, all trying to be served first.

"Right, you are, sir." The steward took his time, ignoring everyone except John, who was now treated to a full minute's conversation while the drinks were poured. The journey passed quickly and pleasantly. The bar steward was talkative, quite happy to pass the time away with an amiable fellow like John. The glares of the other men faded as soon as they realised that it had no effect.

John sat quite relaxed, not a care in the world. He told the steward a few jokes and listened to the man's stupid life history with a nod and a smile, making a suitable comment here and there. Getting an order of drinks presented no problem. The steward kept his eye open for John's glass to empty when he would come straight across, no matter how long the others had been waiting. "Liverpool in five minutes, got time for another." The barman winked at John. John had bought two drinks for the man, and here he was trying to get another.

"No, I don't think I will, thanks." John was all smiles but turned away before the man's face dropped.

On his way through the dining car, one of the occupants addressed him. "Aren't you the official chappie who held us all up at London?" John noted that the man was well dressed, middle-aged and looked like a company rep., probably having an expense account lunch. John looked casually at the man, who scowled at the delay in answering and then at the man's bottle of wine. John had done some quick calculating.

"Afraid you are in error. I am with the Inland Revenue. Do I look like a railway porter?" John's voice had geared itself into a high, snooty tone. The businessman's face blanched visibly at the words 'Inland Revenue', a feeling of guilt flooding in upon him. By the time he had recovered composure enough to speak, John had disappeared.

The mid-day rush on Lime Street Station threatened to sweep away all the frail and unwary passengers who alighted from the London train. John waited for the flow to pass, bringing up the rear. There was a long hold-up at the narrow ticket barrier as a milling crowd pushed their way into the gap. The ticket collector could see nothing but the sea of faces around him and could not know that one of them had slipped the net, having jumped the barrier further down.

People dashed past, competing for the taxis. John sauntered by and out of the station, past the long queues for already crowded buses, but one of the girls caught his eye. She wouldn't have known him, so he didn't bother to introduce himself, not yet anyway. They had met at a party the last time he had been here, probably about nine months ago. No, she wouldn't remember him, but he certainly recognised her. John saw all the shopping bags she had, and it didn't look as though she would manage to get on a bus with that lot. He noted the names of dress and other local shops' names on the side of the bags. She had been on a shopping spree and was obviously trying to get home, but her timing was bad, coinciding with this mid-day rush.

John walked on, crossed the road and headed down a side street until he reached the garage. A man in oil-stained overalls was bent beneath a car's bonnet. Two customers stood about, hopping silently from one foot to another in agitation at the delay. "Hello Eric, is my motor ready?" John slapped the overalled figure on the back. The man withdrew himself, annoyed at the interruption.

"I've not had time, John. I got your phone message, but I've just not had time."

Eric looked troubled; he was worried about what the boss would say when he came back and saw all these customers not being attended to. The man wiped his hands on an oily rag and then stopped as he saw the fiver in John's hand. His mouth widened in a slow smile spread. "The boss will be back in half an hour, John."

"I haven't got half an hour, Eric, got somebody waiting for me." The five-pound note disappeared as John thrust it into the man's top pocket. John strolled over to the waiting customers, rubbing his hands together as though pleased to be of service.

"What can I do for you, gentlemen? Would you like to step into the office?" Without waiting for a reply, John led the way past the showroom cars and into the office. He wrote the first man's complaint on a scrap of paper, propped it up against the telephone, assured him it would be attended to immediately and turned to sort out the next problem.

The engine spluttered, hiccoughed, and purred into life. Eric sat at the controls, monitoring its performance. John picked up the 'trade licence plates' and dismissed the next customer, telling him the shop manager would be along directly. "I'll borrow these for a couple of days, Eric." John started to hang the red number plates from his bumpers.

"For God's sake, don't let the boss see those!" Eric climbed out and let John get in. With a clanging shuffle of gears, the neglected vehicle fought its way out onto the main road and pulled up at the bus stop, regardless of people and traffic alike. John climbed out, left the engine running, and went across to the girl.

"Hello, Deidre. I was just driving past thinking of you, and I saw you standing there with all your shopping; what a coincidence. How are you keeping? Haven't seen you for ages." John was smiling, putting on the charm, sweeping the girl off her feet.

She was flustered and flattered at the same time. She vaguely remembered him from somewhere, but it had been a long time ago. "Waiting for a bus, Deidre? I don't think you'll get one with all this, my dear. I've got the car just there." John picked up two of her bags, pointed at the car and started to shepherd her towards it.

"I'll give you a lift home, my love. Still, Meredith Road, is it? It's no trouble; I'm going past your place."

With gentle persuasion, a charming smile and conciliatory gestures, John persuaded her that it was in her own best interests. Buses trying to pull in at the bus shelter tooted angrily at the car. John took not the slightest bit of notice, quite unhurried in his actions of carefully placing the girl's parcels in the back seat, talking easily as though to an old friend all the time. By the time John had ushered her into the passenger seat, she felt as though she had known him for years. *He is good-looking,* she thought, *how lucky that he had come along just then.* I wonder how he noticed me amongst all those people, she thought. John was keeping up the gentle persuasion as he put the car in gear and edged his way into the traffic stream.

Able Seaman Blinveld took a taxi to Heathrow, paid the cab off outside the terminal, and sauntered towards the building. The glass-paned doors opened to his light tread upon the pressure plate and shut with a minute swoosh of air behind him as he confidently strode along. People sat or stood by luggage, waiting for someone; something to happen, or an event to be announced from the ceiling-level speakers.

Queues were forming at some of the airline desks, the uniformed staff of various airlines courteous and smiling behind them. Blinveld strolled amongst the people, looking at the airline titles for the one which would suit his purposes. The desk was not busy; a dark girl with a severe hairstyle smiled at his approach. Already, Blinveld's hand had reached into the inside pocket and withdrawn the wallet.

"I would like a return flight to Paris, going out on the next flight, first class." The girl smiled warmly and consulted her schedule.

"12:05 would suit you, Monsieur?" there was only a trace of accent.

"Any chance of a cancellation earlier than that?" Binny glanced at the terminal clock in the centre of the hall; it read ten past nine.

"The flight for ten thirty is fully booked, Monsieur, but if you leave your name, I will notify you if there is a cancellation." Binny produced his passport for the girl to note his name in pencil on the passenger manifest.

"It will be about thirty, maybe forty minutes before I will know Monsieur Blinveld." The girl was slightly apologetic to the impressive-looking gentleman with the oh-so-English style of clothes.

Binny occupied his time with a glance along the paperback shelves. One book caught his eye amongst the display. He picked it up, passed it to the check-out and paid for it. The woman at the cash register gave him a disbelieving look as she glanced at the title. The cafeteria held an assorted group of different nationalities, carrying their many coloured airline shoulder bags and other hand luggage. He found a glass-topped table unoccupied and uncluttered with the usual cups and crushed wrappers. He seated himself with his own translucent plastic cup of airport coffee and began to read the cowboy saga.

"Will Mister Conrad Blinveld report to the Air France desk immediately?" the loudspeaker announcement was repeated. Binny had become engrossed in Sudden's duel with the Meskellero Kid and had lost track of the passage of time. He made his way down the stairs to the long hall.

"There is a cancellation for the next flight, Monsieur Blinveld." *The dark blue uniform suits her,* thought Blinveld, watching as the pen poised to enter his name for the flight. "Oh yes, certainly. Put me down for that. Splendid. I don't know yet when I shall want to return but I will pay for both flights now."

The chequebook lay open on the desk; the silver pen began to scribble out the name and, after a brief pause, the figures when she had consulted the current fare list. "No luggage, Monsieur?" The girl was surprised at his lack of even an overnight bag.

"I'll do a spot of shopping when I get there." Binny was confidential in his manner.

*The English are mad,* she thought; *surely, he must know what the prices are in France today; he must be rich.* An announcement for another passenger interrupted her thoughts. "Have a good trip, Monsieur." She handed him the flight card, cabin card, and his passport. She gave him a brief, dazzling smile of farewell. He made his way directly to the departure lounge. There would be no time now to change currency. Soon the flight would be announced. Binny made a long casting look, as most passengers did, out of the wide viewing windows to the tarmacadamed runways, always with three or four aeroplanes idle, waiting for cargo.

His gin and tonic came. The waiter accepted a tip and, having done so, gave a brief salute and turned on his heel, bearing away the empty glasses. "Ding-dong." The two-toned sound filled the lounge to attract attention to the announcer. "Flight AF212 for Paris departure time 10:30. Will passengers for flight AF212 for Paris make their way to boarding gate three, thank you." The same two-tone sound and the announcement came again in French. Binny sighted the designated departure gate, watched the queue form, and noted that the cabin steward had not arrived yet. He stayed where he was, legs crossed, umbrella dangling from the crook of his arm, and waited. Several people glanced at the neat figure in the homburg hat, seeing how impassively English he was. A few managed to read the title of the book he was so diligently reading, and the image of the archetypal Englishman was shattered.

An air steward and pilot had arrived at the head of the crowding people. They smiled in plastic greeting to each tiny group while inspecting the cards and allowing each to pass. Blinveld flicked imaginary dust from the trousers, uncrossed his legs and, taking a new purchase on his rolled umbrella, advanced upon the dwindling numbers. "Jolly good weather for it." He beamed at the stewardess, who politely smiled at the aristocratic-looking gentleman.

"I hope you will enjoy your flight with Air France, Monsieur." She took his cabin card. Blinveld walked down the sloping aisle alone. *Company rules, I expect,* he thought, *for the crew to address passengers as madame and monsieur, never sir.* Probably thought the English liked it, a touch of romance and all that. The French passengers were chattering, filling the aeroplane's small aisle between the seats. They waved each other to different seats, uttering streams of sentences rapidly, all trying to sort each other out.

"I say, excuse me. Thank you. Er, excuse me." Blinveld made his presence known, squeezing past bodies at the rear of the plane. A stewardess settled them as quickly as possible, and almost immediately, the 'no smoking' light winked on. Propellers turned, and engines started to hum.

"Good morning. Captain Pierre Pasteur welcomes you aboard flight two one two for Paris. Our flying time will be one hour and thirty minutes." The girl stood just outside the pilot's cabin, imparting this information by intercom, and then instructed them on the usual safety precautions. Monsieur Blinveld continued to read the cowboy book. A powerful roar of engines denoted their imminent departure, accentuated by extreme vibration prior to the brakes being released. The runway flashed past as they gathered speed, giving a smooth lift-off, noted by the passengers' temporary loss of equilibrium and a dull gnawing sensation in the stomach pit. The wing tip dipped and fluttered in oscillating compensation until the pilot had the feel of his controls. The plane banked, giving them a glimpse of the ground and airport buildings they had so recently left behind. The vision was gone in a smooth levelling process. In almost no time at all, the trolley was wheeled to the centre, loaded with miniature drinks of many varieties.

"Good show. I'll have a gin and tonic." Binny looked up at the girl. She smiled at the English preference for gin and tonic and sorted through her tray for them.

"Better make it two, save you another trip." *After all,* Binny thought, *this is a short trip and before long, they must start the long descent.* The French coast came into view in a broad contour of white-rimmed land. From the cabin, the Tannoy announced the obvious fact.

"La belle France." The pilot sounded enthusiastic. Glad to be going home; end of a tour of duty, no doubt. The thoughts flicked across Blinveld's mind while he sipped the cold drink. He wondered what the pilot was going home to, whether he too had an over-doting mother who delighted in the company of only the 'best' people.

For the first time today, Blinveld thought about his life, the one he had made for himself, so different to the one that had been prepared for him. Oh yes, he was indeed pleased with himself. The other passengers close by wondered at the Englishman far away in thought, who suddenly laughed out loud at some thought that tickled him. It was quite unsettling. His mother would be flabbergasted if she knew who his paymasters were and towards what end he worked. Blinveld amused himself with the thought of the horrified expression on his mother's face if only she knew. To be honest, he could not quite comprehend his reasons for this outlandish behaviour and his attitude to his own class. Why he should be this way was a mystery in itself, but it gave him grim satisfaction to be so amused at how ludicrous it all was, the sham of respectability and self-regard his mother and friends all showed to the world at large. He meant to take them down. Show them up, ridicule them all. What satisfaction he would gain from it. He smiled to himself, enjoyed his other drink, settled back in his comfortable seat, and relaxed, feeling a little smug at his expected prize.

This time, Blinveld would give her a real shock. She would expect him to be arriving by cab up the long tree-lined driveway about now. How many times had she told him to telephone first so that Charles the chauffeur would come for him in the 'Rolls'? It wasn't that he didn't like the regal trappings of his family's wealth, but he could not abide the style his mother employed or the people she chose to entertain. I shouldn't think any single one of them had ever washed their own knickers, let alone knew what the real world was like. Binny detested them all and everything they stood for. He had made it his life's work to end all that, to banish it forever.

The plane was coming in to land. His thoughts had been so busy that the warning lights had flashed on without him noticing. A gentle skidding screech of rubber in short braking jabs slowed them to below flying speed. The engine pitch increased, expanding the flimsy frame in halting vibration, and the monster stopped its careering slide. The plane taxied at a ridiculously slow pace compared with its previous speed. Already, the passengers reached above their heads to retrieve belongings from the rack.

Lights blazed from the buildings of Orly airport as though it were night. The long, slow procession began its trickling crawl along the long hallways. The customs thought it strange that he travelled without even hand luggage, but they merely shrugged their shoulders when they heard his accent. They were a little more dubious when, in answer to the question, he replied that he did not yet know how long he would be staying. One whispered to the other, hand held over the ear. The two officials agreed it was not normal, but for the English, well... they shrugged their shoulders and let him pass. His papers were in order, and they held the completed questionnaire, which was compulsory for all visitors.

"Metropole International?" Binny held the telephone close to his ear and waited for the affirmative reply.

"Conrad Blinveld here, send a car for me to Orly airport, will you? There's a good chap." He listened to the reply.

"Yes, I telexed a reservation from London." There was a short pause. Apparently, his name had not been appended to the register.

"I booked a suite. If you don't want my business, old man, I'll go elsewhere." The hotel car arrived at the entrance. The driver waited for a few minutes, but no one answered to the name he had called.

"Monsieur Blinveld, please report to the Air France desk," the announcement reached the cocktail bar. Binny found his way down, made himself known at the desk, and did not allow the driver to carry his umbrella.

"Look, old chap." Blinveld had signed his name to the reception register. "Telephone round a few of the better men's outfitters and tell them to bring a selection of casual and evening wear around, will you?" The receptionist twiddled his waxed moustache in slight discomfort. The English could be so difficult.

"Certainly Monsieur. I will telephone your suite when I have the time of their arrival." The man cocked his head a little on one side as he bowed in a little stiff movement. Blinveld telephoned the operator from his suite.

"Get me a connection through to London, will you." He gave the operator his number and the number he wanted.

"Yes, I will be here, thank you." *Good, I've got time for a bath,* Blinveld thought and then spent an hour in the tub, answering the call from his reclined position.

"Hello, mater. Awfully nice to hear you," the voice at the other end of the line was concerned.

"No, Paris, actually. Thought I would stop over for a few days. Jolly nice weather," his mother's voice sounded alarmed.

"Just have to tell them I was unavoidably detained, my dear. Can't possibly get there for your masquerade ball. Terribly sorry, old thing." There was a long pause at the other end of the line. His mother didn't, for once, seem to know what to say.

"Look, just give me a tinkle," Blinveld told her the hotel number.

"Yes, when they've all gone. I'll come home and we can have a nice long chat alone. Jolly good. Toodle pip mater." Blinveld hung up and sank deeper into the luxury of his bath.

The acting was over; now the cold and calculating real self could emerge. Soon, it would be time to immerse himself in the realities of the world. He had taken a decisive step in freeing himself from the overwhelming smother of the way of life that he hated and he was going to make quite sure that he was never again caught up in it. Blinveld had found a new sport in life. He would use the education and money that was forced upon him to embarrass them and turn the tables on them by making a caricature of the type of man he was expected to be, then use that caricature to bring down their world.

Blinveld was going to enjoy this, devising new ways of ridiculing his own class. Joining up as a common seaman had been an absolute topper. They still couldn't get over it; they didn't even know the depth of his deception. Blinveld laughed uproariously to himself, allowed himself another measure of hot water into the tub, and waited for the outfitters to arrive. He glanced at his watch. As soon as the outfitters had gone, he must make contact. There was business to be seen to. He really was enjoying this new sport. Spying was indeed great fun.

The outfitter was confused by the Englishman. Patently, he had expensive tastes. He wanted a lounge suite and evening dress. It was expected, of course, that such a gentleman of leisure would also require less formal wear but to actually ask for this sort of thing. They did not, after all, cater to the working classes.

As Blinveld expected, the rendezvous was to be in a back-street cafe. His contact would know him by the clothes he wore. Indeed, he would be conspicuous by the cut of his suit. Andre, the student, was suspicious of the fine quality of the clothes at first, but the Englishman's credentials were in order, and besides, he had brought a gift. They could certainly use the documents and especially the pay books. Andre would see to the clothes. He could certainly not attend the meeting looking like this. Apart from the fact that the students would not accept him, the gendarmes were everywhere. No, it would not do. They made a second appointment.

The streets were dark and narrow. Many of the window shutters were still open. It was the French way, Blinveld knew. Few of them showed lights. Not many would be behind those grimy windows at this time of the evening and in this derelict quarter. The tall lamps of the street gave only a chill glow, but he found the cellar.

The place was seamy and packed, as Andre had told him it would be. Little attention was paid to his arrival. The red-haired youth leaned away from the wall and inspected his identity paper. He was not to know it had been provided only that evening.

Out of the midst of the crowd came his contact, who drew him too into it. There was a table, already crowded, but room had been made for him. Blinveld felt out of place in this environment, but the cool, calculating side of himself came out to assert itself.

They were talking of planned riots. This youthful rabble made plans to challenge the authority of the administration. They claimed proudly that the ministry of the newly elected President Pompidou would soon fall. Communism would take a step forward.

Danny, the red-haired youth, came over to their table. His eyes burned with enthusiasm and hatred. He, it was, that initiated the huge street riots in Paris. This was a large cell, a militant cell; they would accomplish great things. They had well-connected financial backers, even if foreign, with an agenda to suit their political purpose. It mattered little to this group. In only a few months, Algeria would be independent of France. Another blow had been struck for freedom. Soon, the great General De Gaulle would fall. The confidence of the people in democracy would fail. A larger slice of influence would come to the Party. There would be a new president, perhaps a fifth republic of France. It would come to pass, and swiftly, they were sure of their soon-to-be success.

Blinveld was unaccustomed to dealing with fanatics of this calibre, but he listened. They fought for the same cause. These French students were so wrapped up in their own internal struggle that they did not seem to be aware of the greater issue. Blinveld told them of the great things happening outside. Rhodesia would soon be divided. Already, the African people were being formed into a cohesive action force and were being trained and armed. The people's fight would take away the riches and power of the corrupt whites and Afrikaans especially. As he talked, Blinveld held a vision of his own home, of his mother and her class. The great Soviet people, he told them, would march across the Pacific to take a foothold in the homes of the people of Cuba. The capitalists would shrink back in fear. Thoughts of his mother's horrified face came to Blinveld. *If only she knew,* he thought. If only she knew he was part of the downfall of the West.

# Chapter 21

*S12* lay in the dock, silent and deserted, save for one sentry who crouched inside the fin, as the tower was known, as this is what it resembled whilst diving or surfacing. He was reading his book, able to see out at any approaching figure. The dock was empty, devoid of all life. The sentry felt a creeping shudder run through him, probably the cold of night, but maybe a fleeting feeling of being so alone.

The crew were accommodated in the forbidding brick buildings, ugly, tall, and so exactly alike that it was necessary to count the number of buildings stretching along the wide avenue of the barracks to make sure of entering the right one. Inside, a double row of angled metal bunks stretched, side by side, with a few feet of individual space between, from the single door entrance to the far end wall. The dormitory was barren of any decoration and had multipaned high windows, with no outlook but the roof and upper walls of the buildings, so near on either side.

A pot-bellied stove, dwarfed by the expanse of floor, stood in the centre of the room, its black tubular funnel rising high into the arched ceiling. Three old, tattered and much-abused armchairs filled a small space near the stove. It was rare for all three to be occupied at once, even with bunks for forty. So unpleasing was the decor of this temporary home that none of the submariners spent more time than was essential within its walls. The door opened, and a line of aggravated men streamed in from their evening meal. Lockers were opened, shirts and trousers were laid out, and men began their preparations for a shower and social get-together down the canteen. The sound of hissing water from the annexe of showers and wash basins filled the room.

"Bloody cold in this place." A man hopped from one foot to the other, naked except for a towel. Like figures darted for the use of a shower.

"Hey! Did you see that 'Jenny Wren' down the NAAFI?" Scouse lathered himself under the hissing spray, turning around constantly to let the hot flow run all over his body.

"No chance there, mate. You'll get done for cradle snatching," the voice from the next cubicle was loud, fighting against the new arrivals' chatter and churning of gushing geysers.

"They're old enough. Sixteen, aren't they?" Scouse had got the notion and wasn't about to be put off.

"They might say they are, but they are only kids, man. Don't know what it's all about yet, do they? Christ, they only joined the Navy five minutes ago." A man leant out and winked at some of the others in an attempt to get everyone going on the same theme, just to upset Scouse Peters.

"Just like two juicy watermelons, they are." Scouse was in raptures over the young girl, who had incautiously left her jacket undone whilst in the NAAFI buying sweets.

"Come on, man. They might as well be wrapped in blankets for all that uniform does for them." Someone was having a go at the ardent admirer.

"Like to get my blanket around that one, anyway." He wouldn't be put off; his visions of passion were far too vivid.

"Yea, well, don't use all the bleeding hot water while yer thinking about it." Two or three men were waiting for a cubicle to empty, feeling a bit stupid standing about naked, waiting their turn for the water.

The consensus of opinion was that they might as well have a few pints in the canteen and at least have a few females to look at, even if they were little girls. "Better than staring at these bare walls," as someone put it.

"Give us a squeeze of yer toothpaste, Nobby." One of the sailors had forgotten to bring his.

"Squeeze of me what?" The man was pouring water over his head and wasn't sure what he had heard. Whistles and cat calls filled the air with the men's good humour, joining in with horseplay in spontaneous acceptance of each other's mood of humour.

"Hey, Garth." One of the for'ard Mess had seen the giant figure of the leading stoker stepping out from a cubicle. The remark drew a lot of eyes to Hogarth, it was unusual for all the crew to be together in one big Mess.

"Garth, what's that black stuff on your chest, then? Coconut matting, is it?" The man who made the remark didn't have much in the way of chest hair or a torso so muscular as the big stoker. Garth stopped towelling his head and looked up.

"Oh, go and soak your head, man!" There was no irritation. He could take a leg pull the same as anyone else.

"Don't take any notice of him, jealous he is." The speaker jerked a thumb backwards and then turned with a broad smile to face the man.

"Can't all be, Apollo, can we?" The smile was broadening.

"It's just that we stokers has to have lots of muscles, and we has to sweat, not like you lot up for'ard." The kidding went on between rival bunches, not that there was any serious intent. The crew got themselves ready, raked loose change and a note or two into their pockets. Money was left lying about on locker tops and in lockers with doors that few bothered to shut.

"Coming for a pint, Garth?" one of the stokers was asking the big man, who just at that moment was searching through the locker.

"No, I want to write a letter home." He was busy looking for the writing pad.

"You wrote one yesterday. Come on, give yourself a treat. You don't want to stay in this dump," the voice persisted. Hogarth found what he wanted.

"I'll be down soon, in an hour or so, soon as I've written this letter. You can get me a pint in, all right?"

"Suit yourself, only don't leave it too late, or Scouse will have all the women to himself." The sailors left the Mess, laughing, taking Scouse along with them. The sound of their merry voices and the echoing steps faded along the pathway outside. The single door swung backwards and forward on creaking hinges, coming to eventual rest. Hogarth settled into the best of the armchairs, aware of the overshadowing silence which descended on the huge dormitory, and began to write, thinking of home.

The group of submariners ambled along the roadway, past the forlorn-looking Victorian blocks of masonry, towards the open space of parade ground and its surrounding cluster of hut-like shelters and buildings. The canteen's wooden frame shone its bright lights out across the surface of the square. Lumbering stragglers climbed the single platform step and jostled for entry to the warmth within. Numerous chairs were grouped in circles about empty tables. The whole floor space was taken up with them, all but for narrow access between them. Only a dozen or so men lounged about while a half dozen of the dizzy giggling wrens stood in small groups or sat watching the newcomers.

"Twenty-four pints and a packet of fags," the first one to the bar ordered to save time, but each was paying for his own or that of a small group. Tables were being filled whilst two or three passed conversational gambit at the trainee girls, some of them only having been at the barracks for a few weeks. In no time at all, the single-storey building reverberated to the throaty voices and a few shrill ones, in doubtful songs, sung by generations of sailors since times forgotten. The commotion was intense, and it became difficult to talk in a normal voice. After successive rounds of ordered pints, the submariners had so completely taken over the place by sheer weight of numbers that outsiders to the exuberant clan decided to leave. All that is, except the females. For them, this was the excitement that they had joined the service for, to meet and be with the earthy, raucous young men without the restraints of home.

"Come on, girl, drag a chair over here and have a drink." One of the sailors was leaning over the back of his chair, trying to entice some of the bashful ones to join the giant circle. The young wrens, already interspersed with the group, shouted their encouragement. The girls came across to seat themselves, embarrassed but attracted all the same.

"What will you 'ave darling?" Scouse was his normal suave self. He stood up to fetch more of the booze.

"I would like a Babycham, please," one hesitant answer, which brought some mirth from amongst the men.

"Babycham? You don't want that rubbish; I'll get you a pint." Scouse couldn't quite understand that not all people liked beer, but that was what he brought back. That was all the girls were getting, so they drank it, pretending it was nice so as not to seem silly. Later, after most of the gathering was well on the way to being drunk, somebody decided to fill his lighter. The canteen staff were bored with all the noise. It wasn't all that good a job, they thought, but a couple of hours of this rowdiness every night, and then they could go home, having helped to supplement the housekeeping.

"Petrol, dear? For your lighter, is it dear? Yes, we've got petrol. Well, we've got these tuppenny tubes, dear. Just one, is it? Thank you, dear." The woman's cigarette ash dropped on the counter as she scooped up the coins, absently put them in the till and turned to her cronies.

"Oh, my back's killing me, Edna. My Bert thinks it's lumbago, but it can't be, can it? I'm only fifty-one, too early yet for lumbago." Edna flicked her ash at the ashtray.

"Well, I can manage here, Doris. Why don't you go home to your Bert?

This lot will go soon, and we can clear up in the morning, eh?" Doris collected her Mac and handbag, tied her headscarf on, and left it all to Edna.

The crew were having fun and were not about to leave. The empty plastic tube of lighter fuel lay in the ashtray discarded, and so did somebody's cigarette, still burning. It seemed amusing when the ashtray flared up in a brief splendour of flames. The show was quickly over. A lot of the girls, not used to this quantity of beery liquid, needed to vacate the premises temporarily and often.

"Right, we'll have a bit of fun." Somebody had a brain wave and went to get some of those little plastic tubes. When one of the wrens came back, she was treated to a display as a lighted match was tossed into her pint. The vapour ignited, burning fiercely on top of the beer, and then gradually died out. Soon, they were all at it, buying the tubes, waiting for someone to go out, and playing the trick when they returned. One of the young trainees was more nervous than she wanted to admit but thought perhaps it was all harmless fun and she was being unnecessarily silly. None of the others seemed to mind.

She lifted the pint unthinkingly to take a sip. It was going to be all right; nobody had done anything while she was out. The glass came up to her lips just as somebody lit a match and flicked it into the brew. She shrieked at the burst of yellow that leapt towards her, dropping the glass, which shattered on the floor. Nobody quite understood how, but the beer separated away from the fluid, which continued to burn. The men nearest thought it uproariously funny that the girl should have reacted in this way. Meanwhile, the flames caught one of the not-quite-empty tubes littered about the floor. A lot of the fluid had been scattered around. It was still funny when a sheet of expanding flame leapt up the side of the table. The more sober, who saw what was happening, were hampered by the slow, lurching, drunken bodies and screaming females.

Edna sat knitting in her box-like corner, taking no notice. She had been hearing this commotion all evening. It wasn't her job to interfere with their fun.

The wood was dry. It had not been doused by rain for several weeks, and that itself was surprising at this time of the year. Flailing arms and colliding bodies pushed past each other, overturning tables in the close surroundings, preventing any effective chance there could have been of stifling the fire. It took hold of the wooden furniture and building in a matter of minutes. By then, the group were incapable of containing it. The only thing left to do was flee before the full weight of authority could fall.

Edna, the slow-moving NAAFI assistant, grasped her bag of knitting and stood in open-mouthed wonder on the parade ground alone, watching the sheet of flames beat upward in frenzied activity.

The barracks' emergency party wheeled out their cart and hurriedly connected all the hoses. It was obviously too late to save the canteen, but still, they plied cylinders of gas and pumped hosed water onto surrounding buildings. The fire brigade arrived to stop the spreading holocaust, retiring afterwards to leave charred splinters of smouldering remains.

By morning, a full investigation was underway. A tearful Edna explained, as best she could, how it had been caused and what she knew of the evening's customers. With bloodshot eyes, anguished wrens confessed their knowledge of the incident and its circumstances, to their questioning superiors.

The dockyard CID thoroughly investigated and questioned all the barracks' personnel during the course of the day. None of the submarine crew knew anything; they had all been ashore, except for one leading stoker who had remained alone in the Mess to write letters and one sentry onboard the submarine. The investigation took statements in writing from those who knew anything, made up dossiers, and concocted lists of names which the wrens could remember. Most of the names, of course, were useless to the team officers, being only nicknames and therefore not on any official list. It was apparent, though, that a good few submariners had been involved.

Lieutenant Graves, the newly arrived First Lieutenant, was immediately and rather obviously given a nickname of his own. 'Digger' conferred with the dockyard officers and decided that due to the serious nature of the complaint, the Captain should be informed. A telegram was sent, and the Captain returned from leave to sort the matter out.

Lieutenant Hawks listened to the evidence so far collected, and implication that his crew had been instrumental in causing the fire. He went to look at the sorry shambles of the wooden hut and walked through the damage. Secretly, he found the episode quite amusing and the seriousness with which so much time had been spent on compiling useless information. So far as he could see, the shack, and it was after all little more than that, had not been of any particular value. What concerned him more was the possible repercussions to his crew, the likelihood of Courts Martial with loss of time that would entail. No, he decided, it could serve no useful purpose.

The Captain persuaded the investigation that his submarine had vital, quite imperative missions to perform. It would be useless, he insisted, to hold an identity parade. The wrens, after all, had been intoxicated and hysterical. Besides that, the news story would be damaging to the Service. The Captain had his way, the problem was resolved. There would be no further action.

# Chapter 22

First leave party of men returned to the submarine to hear news of their opposite numbers' goings-on during their absence. It was a blow to most of them since the canteen was not going to be rebuilt, and they would take the brunt of any new animosity against submariners in general.

Lieutenant Hawks stayed on for two days in order to hold more talks with the dockyard technical staff and administration. He was assured that the boat would be ready for sea on the prescribed date. He sent in his report to London, attesting to that, assuring his superiors that he would be able to fulfil the forthcoming commitment.

Jeff Hawks had his First Lieutenant assemble the crew. Senior rates were exempted. The canteen had been no part of their territory; there had been separate facilities for them and so they were in no way involved.

He was not pleased, he told them, with the disgraceful behaviour which had brought about this sad affair. Due solely to the fact that this submarine would soon be on an important patrol, there would not be any further disciplinary action taken. The Captain pointed out, however, that there would be no repeat performance here, or anywhere else, of this appalling conduct.

The assembled crew, suitably admonished, made no comment. They understood their Commander's position. Whether he believed it or not, it was part of his job, and he had delivered the pep talk. Now, life could go on as before.

The Captain had received a report from his contact about those tests on possible metal fatigue of his torpedo restraining clamps, the ones which had apparently failed and allowed a torpedo to break free with dire consequences. His friend Edward's report concluded that there had been no metal failure. It considered the bands must have been loosened deliberately and they could not have vibrated loose. It suggested an investigation be launched to discover those probable suspects.

Second leave party, comprising the majority of married men, left for a welcome break from service tedium. Second leave was always more popular, especially for those who lived far away, since it shortened, though only by two weeks, the period between sea time and the precious moments at home.

Eventually, LRO Swingle had been persuaded to comply with Blinveld's request. At first, of course, he had refused to even consider telling the pinger anything he might learn from classified signals. The man was very persuasive and very charming in his manner, and Swingle certainly could use the money. Blinveld at least treated him in the right way, respected his position, gave him a due amount of respect. The LRO was finally convinced that it could give his career a lift. Naturally, he had been suspicious of Binny's careful overtures. Swingle appreciated, of course, that the upper classes, the landed gentry he himself admired so much, were able to maintain their position by being in possession of the most accurate and up to date facts available.

It would be a two-way thing, of course. As irrelevant as the information might seem to himself, being uninitiated into the upper circles, he was assured that together with other sources, it could be very profitable. Certainly, Blinveld had assured him that he would receive the benefit of knowing just how the information was turned into profit. A good man on the inside could expect help from the right quarter, too. Blinveld had friends in high places. Swingle knew that for sure, and his percentage of the profit would be well worth having. Blinveld made contact, and passed on the location of that Edinburgh clinic to which their recently departed First Lieutenant would be welcomed. Still, there was little success to report on the new sonar.

The dockyard had stripped and removed the offending port shaft, which had become distorted. In record time, a new one was brought in, and the dockyard worked night shifts to get everything back in its place, lined up and tested.

During the second week of the late leave, stores arrived by the dockside for loading. Extra sentries were mounted to watch them and deter any pilfering. The stores would have to remain on the dockside for one extra day until the work team had finished.

A new special sonar dome was being fitted onto the for'ard casing. It was short and squat with a white top. It came to be known as the 'Penguin'. It was administered to, and accompanied by, a very reticent team of specialists. They had worked in secret on this project for a long, long time, and they were proud of their success. Unbeknownst to the crew, this special 'Penguin' was the real reason for the extra sentries. None of the specialists could be persuaded to talk to the crew or handlers about it.

A line of sailors stretched along the deck to unload each tray of stores as the crane swung its load to a lowering halt. With just one day to spare before the rest of the crew returned, work was completed, the dock flooded, and the submarine was moved by tugs out to a basin wall.

In the early afternoon, after her full crew came aboard, *Orestes* was brought out to the middle of a basin and carried out its first trial dive. Everything functioned as it was supposed to; there were no leaks, and the inspection team were satisfied.

When submarine *Orestes* sailed out of Chatham, there were no cheering waves of farewell, no soft-spoken words of parting. On surface passage up the channel, her crew once more turned their thoughts from their short period of leisure ashore and concentrated on the business at hand. The sea was calmer now that Spring was imminently due. A Spring that they would miss the arrival of.

During the long, slow days spent traversing the length of England's waters, many of the men who were not normally required to do so volunteered for a stretch of lookout duty up on the Bridge, which then afforded them a last opportunity to see the sun and sky, and fast fading shoreline astern.

From this point on, complete radio silence had to be maintained for the whole of their nine-week trip until they could surface in British waters on completion. Once land had been lost to sight astern, there were fewer volunteers who wanted that last lungful of fresh air. So duty was resumed as normal by the seamen. Shipping became scarce and the sea became a vast, barren and far-reaching outline of gently rolling blue-green with the absence of tell-tale dots upon the skyline; officer and lookout used each other's company to fill the long hours on Watch.

Theo Brooks, the Navigator, was thinking of home, like many others. The lookout, enshrined in the square metal opening some five feet behind him, coughed in the chill salt air. Theo was reminded of the presence of another human being. The time was usually so well-filled that the gulf between officers and men was not usually crossed. In consequence, the lookout's face was well known, but virtually nothing else about him was. Here was an opportunity to correct that.

"Thinking about home, Brown?" The Navigator took one last look at the empty horizon and turned round to face the man.

"Aye, sir. I was." The man never had very much to say for himself. *He stays well behind his own barriers*, Theo thought. In our own way, we all have problems of communicating the things that matter most to us, and this man always gave the impression of wanting the world to think he preferred it that way.

"It feels strange to be travelling towards the top of the world, doesn't it?" Navigator spoke aloud his private thoughts.

"Aye, it's empty, right enough," the answer was short and terse, so typical of the man, but it showed some sense of feeling. The officer wondered just how Brown saw the world.

"Just think, the Vikings would have seen just what we are seeing now and were maybe awed by nature's vastness and power."

"More likely, they were too busy trying to find their way." Jock was not interested in what the Vikings or anyone else thought, only in what his own future held. The officer was not to be daunted from his train of thought, though. "Don't you have a sense of history? To be sailing the same waters as so many famous adventurous men, Brown?"

"They did it mostly for plunder. What they could get from somebody else." Jock couldn't see the Navvy's point of view about long-dead men.

"You have a good point there. History is always written by romantics, and usually long after the event. Don't you agree, though, that it takes men of vision to cross the oceans in open, wooden boats?" Theo Brooks was curious to know just how this man thought.

"Why they did it was only important to them. What difference does it make to us? We have to live in the world as it is. To do that, we have to earn money to live on, in any way we can. We are never going to do the things they did, so what does it matter?"

"That is a very narrow view of life, Brown," The Navigator was perplexed and slightly irritated at such short-sighted views.

"It's a very narrow existence." Jock saw that here was yet another officer who thought that no one else's way of looking at things was valid.

"If you feel like that, then why did you join the Navy?" Theo was exasperated by the man's attitude, but he still wanted to reach him if he could.

"I need the money, and it's better than the life I had before. Anyway, at age fifteen, what does anybody know? You look at the adverts and think, 'That will get me away from home and a bit of excitement.' By the time you know better, it's too late," Jock stopped talking and wondered what Navvy would say to that.

"You seem to feel bitter, Brown. Why do you stay? Weren't you a volunteer for submarines?" Theo Brooks realised as he said the words that the man would think it a criticism. *I suppose we all make traps for ourselves,* he thought, *and as time goes by, the trap is harder to escape.* His thoughts were wandering back to home and the wife who, at one time, had been everything to him.

"I'm not bitter. I've accepted that life is like that. It is just the same anywhere else; that's why I stay. What else can I do anyway, with a wife to keep?" Jock wasn't angry. He had thought about all these things before and sorted it all out to his own satisfaction.

"So why join submarines when life is harder than in general service?" Theo asked the question again, almost sure now of the answer he would get.

"Well, I didn't know that then, but at least nobody bothers about 'spit and polish' type discipline just for its own sake. What I like about it is that if you do your job properly, it's all anyone asks. They leave you alone, then. I make sure I do my job, and then nobody can tell me anything." It occurred to Jock how unusual it was for an officer to listen to all this without getting uptight about criticism of the system, and not then shutting him up.

Jock wasn't interested in any promotion. He didn't have any prospects anyway, so he could say what he liked, and it wouldn't matter. Better to let some other keen sod get ahead and break his neck trying to keep in line with the official way of looking at things.

Both of them fell silent. The officer had learnt something. The able seaman had not, except that sometimes an officer could listen. Jock Brown didn't want to talk any more. He had said far more than was normal for him anyway. Fortunately, he wouldn't have to now. A grey dot had appeared on the horizon, a ship which would keep them both occupied in watching its progress.

*Orestes* sailed on at a moderate pace towards the Norwegian Sea and Arctic Circle. Below, the boat had been made ready for diving. Above, the sky was so clear that the two men had spotted the ship at just about the maximum viewable range. She appeared to be stationary since it took another hour for them to appreciably close the gap. She was still not identifiable, but certain possibilities could be ruled out. The Navigator used his binoculars, trained them and focussed. He was fairly sure that it must be a trawler, but there was something vaguely disturbing about it. He glanced at his watch. Only another five minutes to the designated time for diving. Theo went back to his task of observing. His hand reached down in hesitation for the microphone button.

"Chart table, Bridge. Tell the Captain we have a trawler at approximately five miles. She has an unusual configuration of masts." Jeff Hawks, never far from the Control Room, heard the broadcast and was there within a minute.

"Up periscope." His hands were out, ready to grasp the handles, as the steel shaft smoothly eased upward. A flagging motion of the left arm told the hydraulics operator when to stop. The periscope rotated slowly through three hundred and sixty degrees. The horizon was quite clear but for the one grey hull bobbing in a slow-moving swell.

The Captain viewed for some two full piercing minutes, snapped the handles upward and flagged the 'scope down. A large volume of blue-bound Gray's Fighting Ships was withdrawn from its slot and carefully perused upon the chart table. The minutes ticked by while the Captain read silently. He decided it must be either an Elint or Elat spy ship. The number of antennae were definitely for wide-ranging use, so long-distance travel. Not something a conventional trawler would need. They must be monitoring *Orestes*' progress northward. The trawler was Russian but closely resembled their own trawler fleet's outline.

"On the hour, sir." The PO of the watch held his wrist out for the Captain's glance. The hour had arrived for diving. Nothing more was said; the Captain was reading and calculating in his head. Then he read their position from the chart and disappeared into his cabin. The details of his sighting went into his patrol log, which he alone recorded. No one else would see it until, finally, it would go to Whitehall for analysis.

The Captain reappeared. "Right, we'll give them a run for their money. Lookout below." The submarine commander rubbed his hands together thoughtfully. At the same moment, a pair of legs appeared from the tower. Brown took his position by the conning hatch.

"Dive! Dive! One hundred feet." Immediately, the klaxon sounded its urgent, strident warning twice. Air began to expel from the ballast tanks, hastening the rushing feet on steel rungs. The officer of the watch, face red from pumping exertion, stood in the Control Room catching his breath, then crossed to the chart table and looked at the open page of the Gray's.

The tower lid clanged shut. Water rushed over them, and the boat angled downward from the receding sound of seawater shuttling across the hull. The book page cast its photographs up at the chart table light. The Captain's finger pointed, and the Navigator read the information sheet for future reference.

"Hydrophones, twin screw, small vessel, heading towards," Sonar reported, and John Bishop's head peered into the passage from the doorway.

"Sounds like a trawler, but more powerful," he committed the thought to words in a loud voice, which carried to the chart table.

"Two hundred feet. Group up. Batteries in parallel. Full speed ahead. Steer…" A moment's hesitation while the Captain noted the present heading and altered five points to starboard.

"Steer zero four five," he completed the order.

The powerful hum of speed rocked through the hull. Faces looked at each other across the Mess. "Full speed, for diving?" someone voiced the common thought.

"Must be something up there. One of those Red spy trawlers, probably," Bubbles spoke, having thought out the implications. Nobody else spoke, all of them listening to the thrum of vibrating metal around them.

Simeon was the only one who moved. He tried to control his wide-eyed stare whilst crawling into his bunk, pulled the curtains shut, and lay there. "Going to listen to the water in the pipes, are you?" A broad grin spread across the sneering speaker's face. Too late, he saw Bubble's upraised hand trying to prevent the remark. There was no reply, no sound but the vibrating hum. The Mess dipped downward quite noticeably at this speed. Men sat still, feeling a slight increase of pressure inside their ears. A few held their nose and blew, expelling the lungs' air into the head to release ear pressure.

The motors slowed, and the vibrating pulse throb dimmed, but the Mess began to heel dramatically to port, only for a few seconds and then levelled. "Evading tactics. Definitely something up there." The Mess fell silent again.

In the Control Room, the helmsman adjusted to the new course, fighting the downward surge as the boat found deeper water, preventing the ticker-tape needle from flickering past its one-degree error. Time elapsed, and still, the helmsman tried to bring the boat head onto course. As the boat levelled, the needle swung, and the helmsman, with a sigh of relief, reported the new course heading.

"Slow together. Group down. Batteries in series. Switch off all unnecessary machinery," the Captain's voice, as always, was assured and calm. He paced the six yards to the sonar shack, its door folded open against the bulkhead.

John looked up into the Captain's face and shook his head. "Still there, weak, but he knows where we are," John continued to look into the eyes. There was no flicker of reaction. Three paces back towards the helmsman, and the sequence was repeated.

"Full speed both engines. Group up. Batteries in parallel." The thrumming sound filled the space inside the hull once more.

The Captain was timing the run; ten, fifteen minutes crept by, twenty and now twenty-five minutes of full power given from his batteries. If he could act and close down the sub's machinery quickly enough, he could perhaps save having to use another draining burst of power.

"Stop together. Four hundred feet. Ultra-quiet routine," immediately after the words were spoken, silent figures moved around the deck space, switching off all but essential lighting, fans and machinery. Anything that made a noise and which was not vital was closed down. Another seven minutes passed before the clicking sound of oil controls diminished into a sporadic, even pattern of flow. No one moved unless they had to, and then it was done quietly, some actually holding their breath as though the action might be detected by the craft above with its listening equipment. *Orestes* floated at neutral buoyancy in its cradle of deep, undisturbed waters. The air within grew warm and heavy until even the remaining lights appeared to become dimmer. An hour must have passed before the sonar operator reported.

"She is sweeping in an arc, sir. I think she has lost us," John's voice was quiet, though the words were carried in the stillness.

"Right. We'll stay like this for another hour. Keep reporting, Sonar." The Captain went into his cabin, made his notation in the log and read again the latest intelligence report, which had come by special messenger just before sailing. He noted the pick-up point and calculated the new time of arrival. There was no way he could get a message to them about this delay. It was vital to throw off the chase before rendezvous. *The enemy's network was too good by half,* he thought.

The hour seemed much longer than sixty slow ticking minutes of silence, to the Control Room crew. All pullovers and jackets had been removed. The men sat, sweating in rolled-up sleeves, and some just in string vests. There was very little talk, and then only murmured. It was as if talking might give away their position to the Tracker. Also, it seemed that if they all keened their ears to listen, they might hear it coming. Nothing happened, and they heard nothing but the harsh breathing of men and the click-clack of hydraulic controls.

"Contact very weak, sweeping in larger circles, heading away," John made his soft-voiced report and handed the headphones into the outstretched hand of his commander. The Captain listened, could hear nothing and was satisfied.

"Maintain quiet routine. Slow ahead together. Course three five zero. Group down, in series." The submarine crept at low propeller revolutions out of her silent niche, heading into the closer regions of the Arctic Circle. Her Captain intended that they should, for the moment at least, maintain depth and rose into denser water. It was not certain that the sonar scan from above would not follow them. The batteries had been used prematurely, bringing forward the time when they must be recharged. In order to do this, the blanket of night and cover of land must be sought.

*Orestes* skirted closer to land and managed to elude the trawler as day turned into night. Sonar remained on full alert, as always when dived, but particularly so in these northern latitudes. There was always the danger of floating pack ice, and now that the Spring brought warmer weather to the surface seas, the ice would begin its break away from land packs to commence a drift southward.

Throughout the boat, the topic of conversation was their brush with the intelligence-gathering trawler. "Do you reckon they've given up the search then, Spider?" Harman was not familiar with this sort of thing, and was eager to tap the experience of those who were.

"Don't think they were bothered all that much, mate. They know where we are going, don't they?" Spider, his usual ruddy-complexioned self, was quite jolly about it. He wasn't the worrying sort.

"Already radioed to Moscow by now, you can bet." Scouse Peters was always the eternal optimist.

"I don't see why they would need to bother. Reckon they knew we were coming before we did." Spider's remark brought a few smiles at the thought that any intelligence organisation could be that good.

"Anyway." A new thought had struck the ruddy-faced electrician whilst scraping the last vestiges of honey from its jar onto his ration of one slice of bread. "They watch all the boats. They know that when one comes back, another one goes. They know the numbers, the names and how long each one is going for. It doesn't change anything. Everybody plays the same game, just that nobody wants to let anyone else know, that's all."

"Well, what happens if one side catches the other side at it then?" Harman hadn't yet been with them long enough to know what it was all about.

"Ah, well, that's the thing, Sunshine. We don't know. Probably nothing, 'cos nobody wants to risk an international incident, do they? But," Spider paused to scrape a few shreds of the honey off his shirt with the knife, and then continued, "if one side catches the other in its territory, red-handed, so to speak, they can do what they like, provided no one else finds out."

Quite a few of them, despite the seriousness of the topic, were amused not only by the 'red-handed' pun but also the cheerful, sloppy way Spider conducted himself. "No use worrying about it, Sunshine. Just live for today. That's what it's all about." Spider, not in the slightest bit concerned with his appearance, ran a sticky hand through his mop of tousled hair and smartly whisked the teapot up to his cup. He seemed to do very well out of the for'ard Mess victuals, considering he was only a visitor, but nobody minded.

Captain gave his orders, and the crewmen on watch, surprised but dutiful, turned the boat south, making course for the Faroes. The run south was uneventful. Virtually no shipping plied its trade through these waters; the shipping lanes were further east and west. This corridor was ideal for the submarine's purpose.

Already a day late, Lieutenant Hawks was concerned. Even in spring, this was no latitude for men to linger in the shifting icy winds blowing from the north. Alone on the surface, somewhere out in the night, were four men. The submarine commander knew what one extra day could do to them. He had no medical staff onboard. The Coxswain had limited medical supplies. He hoped the two he was here to pick up were safe.

The Control Room was still; red lights blurred the faces of the waiting men. A strange feeling of living in limbo gripped them, just waiting, the motors dead, the boat silent in sixty feet of cold water. The only sounds were those of breathing and the occasional click of the planesmen's controls in keeping the submarine level. The appointed time grew near.

"Up periscope." The Commander assumed his normal stance, seemingly draped like some lumbering animal across the periscope handles, the rubber eye shield pressed tight, obscuring his face. The white polo-neck sweater glazed pink in the subdued lighting. It took time for his eyes to grow used to this dark before the white crosswire became clear against the sky. His hand manipulated the grip and the sight lowered to the lapping sea. A slow sweep revealed nothing but the break between heaven and sea of dark rock outline. The periscope followed the outline of an island. Nothing stirred, not birds nor seals. The Captain knew that somewhere ashore, there was life, human life.

The islands belonged to Denmark. On them somewhere lived a tiny group of government-sanctioned researchers. It had been thought prudent not to advise their government for fear of security leaks. His men were out on the sea. It was unlikely they would have landed except in an emergency.

The Captain's mind flicked back across recent events, his eyes still watchful for the tell-tale light. There had been a whole welter of security leaks lately. Some of them were plugged, but a spy network still operated. Vassall had been caught. The admiralty offices would be purged since then. Robert Soblen, sentenced in America, was still active in Jordan but the news had broken. *How many more?* he wondered.

A dim flicker reached out and died. The night was blacker because of it. Jeff Hawks knew then that his small commando party were there in flimsy boats waiting. Intuitively, he guessed at the distance from that one fraction of a second glimpse.

"Surface!" the command rang out. A momentary pause before startled response. The upper black outline broke surface in a sea cleft of white foam.

Joe Bolton played his torch directly at the hull two hundred yards distant. The numbing cold was forgotten. "Thank God," the New England voice came in exultation behind him. Together, they dipped their paddles, one either side, in a swathing stroke. The second canoe drew abreast. Joe looked across to see the grinning commando faces. In front of them lay warmth and comfort, however brief.

"Welcome aboard." The submarine Commander shook all four men by the hand as each appeared from the black circle of the tower. The butcher and the steward draped blankets unceremoniously around the figures and hustled all four down to the Wardroom. The ship's officers accepted the intrusion without qualms, unprecedented, though it was to allow this from the lower ranks. Lieutenant Digger Graves poured a tot of brandy for each in silence. Curly, the chef was already ladling steaming quantities of soup into plates, despite chivvying Randy Sandy's caustic comments outside his Galley.

So eager were the torpedo crew and detailed members of the Casing party to get below again that they very nearly lowered both commando canoes through the torpedo loading hatch. Shane arrived in time to prevent it. Within ten minutes, two of the commandos would be leaving, he informed them. The crew was buzzing with this turn of events. They had received no inkling of their arrival. This was quite out of the ordinary, and they realised that this trip was going to be very different.

The American lieutenant remained billeted in the Wardroom. He would talk about anything except his mission. The officers were glad to have this diversion from the monotony which these trips usually brought. Joe, the marine sergeant, once more moved into the chiefs' and petty officers' Mess. He wandered freely around the boat and joined in the games. The crew had been warned not to ask his purpose onboard.

During the ensuing weeks, everyone got used to seeing a strange face after visiting for'ard, just for a brief change of scene. The same was true back aft, and they always moved up to make room for a fresh outlook on life, just temporarily.

The weeks dragged by in monotonous sameness of routine. Nobody wore much more than a vest or summer shirt and shorts, with a favourite beach-worn pair of tatty yet comfortable sandals.

The Wardroom, under the Captain's direction for incentive, devised tournaments of time-honoured board games between the sailors' Messes to keep boredom at bay. A team would traipse the one hundred yards for'ard, and a return match be organised so that a team padded along one hundred yards aft, to be cursed by those who had just come off watch, wanted to sit down, and didn't want to play. Generally, the games were accepted as a jovial way of filling in time, and no one cared much, win or lose.

During this slack time, Digger Graves had read all his officers' reports on the crew. This was an excellent opportunity to go through each man's record to get to know them. It was apparent that this time could be well used to the benefit of his part-three submariners. Duly, the consistent failures were informed to stand by for their examination. To assist him, Lieutenant Graves asked Shane to accompany. The examination, as expected, took over two hours. The two part-three men felt drained after this ordeal. Once again, they both failed. It was pointed out to them by both officers that here, during this extended period away, was the ideal opportunity to make good their deficiencies of knowledge.

Simeon, quite frankly, did not care. He could not, no matter how much he tried, overcome the fears which engulfed him, shutting out all rational thought and attempts to concentrate. Harman, on the other hand, had no qualms about this way of life. Like all of them he was at times afraid, but probably through their influence, never let it get the better of him. He quite simply was no good at exams, either written or oral, becoming tongue-tied even when he knew the answers.

Bubbles decided that it was time to give Harman a helping hand. The man was apparently keen to stay, and one more failure would jeopardise his chances of becoming qualified, which would then entail a return to general service. A bleak prospect for any submariner. Bubbles figured that the only way to overcome Harman's incapacity was to drill him to such an extent that the knowledge would become second nature. The man was willing to give up his free time to be personally coached. The trip went that little bit quicker for the two of them because of it.

Amongst the deserted regions of the Arctic Ocean, *Orestes* took a constant toll on her batteries in powering twin motors during each day of long-dived reconnaissance. For very limited periods only, during daylight, the submarine came to periscope depth, took her bearings, inducted fresh air and went deep to continue the voyage.

At night, according to circumstance and at minimal risk of detection, the boat would come to sixty feet, thrust her induction mast to just clear the wave tops, and, keeping vigilant sight by periscope, run her main engines, recharging her batteries as she went. Eventually, after several weeks, it became necessary to snort air in transit whilst in the darkest phase of night. These periods meant less activity, a more pronounced relaxation for sonar crews, and conversely required greater concentrations on the Engine Room and Control Room teams.

Men off watch for four hours caught up on their sleep, before the next tour of duty. Exhaustion enabled them to ignore the alterations of pressure and vagaries of the inducted, unwelcome arctic cold. Men asleep, the same as men awake, dressed in the warmest windproof clothes they possessed during night sessions, so close to the surface.

A slip by one of the planesmen, too long delayed in correcting, could allow a steeply inclining hydroplane to carry them under depth and temporarily, in dipping the snort tube, create a vacuum unpleasant to the delicate balance of the human ear. The men got used to the occasional sight of ear wax adorning their pillow when they woke, drawn out during sleep.

The protracted trip made for a number of items becoming in short supply, and primary amongst them was water. Everyone got used to the day-long stink of foul air, the all-pervading smell of oil and dirt which needed to remain in clothes. The distillers operating at maximum could not supply more than drinking water and sometimes, but rarely if the snorting period was extended, provide a little more for washing. Each man conserved water to the extent that no one bathed unless he could manage to do everything in a quarter of a gallon of that precious fluid. Even that was too exorbitant a price to pay if any indulged more than once a week. The water in their tanks had to last through the remainder of this extended trip away from base, there was no alternative and no possibility of replenishment at sea.

Through long practice in the art of living rough, the crew became used to the idea and no one bothered very much. There was absolutely no point in complaining about a neighbour's feet when one's own were just as bad. Snorting main engines was sleep disturbing, sometimes causing a painful ear drum splitting experience. It was delightful, however, to contemplate getting new air inducted even though the cold was horrendous. It was a promise of sweet, fresh air to cleanse the lungs and clear the head of sickly, contaminated fumes.

As men do under intense, constraining conditions, extending for long periods, many held a maudlin interest in the fateful conditions which could occur when things went wrong.

The boat had just dipped beneath her snorting depth of fifty-six feet. The snort mast did not clear the wave tops, and water forced the valve on top of the mast shut, and so violently shutting off the airflow. The air inside the boat was being drawn by the engines while the engineers stood ready for the order to shut down. A vacuum was being created inside the hull because the engines sucked the air from it. The men sat around, trying a variety of methods to clear throbbing eardrums and release pressure inside.

This was a time of constant headaches and streaming nose colds for many and for the for'ard crew, especially. The aft crew suffered less; they lived far behind the engines most of the off-watch time.

Slowly, the boat raised to its correct depth, the snort valve opened and air began to flow, filling the partial vacuum. The for'ard Mess members were thinking about this all-too-common occurrence. "So, what would happen if we didn't get up fast enough?" Harman was being inquisitive.

"Well, the officer of the watch would be watching the inclinometer bubble to see which way it was going and make a judgement accordingly." Ginger Bates answered the question.

"What if he was too slow or doing something else at the time?" someone else was following the line Harman had started.

"That's his job, so he wouldn't be doing something else, but in any case, he would feel it the same as the rest of us, in the ears." Ginger was patient, but really, it seemed so obvious.

"Yes, but…" the question was cut off by Ginger.

"I know what you're going to say. At the same time, the Engine Room chief is watching the vacuum gauge, and if it goes to six pounds per square inch, he doesn't wait for orders; he shuts down anyway."

"And if he isn't quick enough, we would all know about it," Bubbles finished the explanation.

"Just think, though," Scouse interrupted, "if he suddenly suffered a heart attack or something, those engines would suck every drop of oxygen out of the boat, and we would all be dead."

"They reckon it's a painless way to go." Spider was attempting to offset the maudlin element in the previous statement.

"And quick," he added as an afterthought. "Since nobody has lived to tell the tale, how can anyone know that?" Harman sounded sarcastic, which wasn't like him. He thought the other men were dressing it up for his benefit.

"Asphyxiation, Sunshine." Spider carried on fixing his bunk light as he uttered the words.

"The brain is starved of oxygen and blacks out. It's just like shutting the brain down for sleep, except that it doesn't wake up. Four minutes later, it has deteriorated beyond use, and brain cells can't reproduce, even if it did get oxygen after that," Bubbles was matter-of-factly discussing the details as an amplification of Spider's brief comment.

"How long would it take for all this to happen once the vacuum went below six pounds, then?" somebody else was curious to know the worst.

"Nobody knows that, but probably not more than one or two minutes," John offered his accessary to the pool of knowledge and then added, "they reckon it would happen at twelve pounds per square inch. By then, everyone would be dead."

"So, if we dipped, and nothing was done quick enough, there would be no warning; we would all just quietly fold up and die." Harman's voice was incredulous.

"Yes, and the engines would still be running with nobody left to stop them. All the air would be sucked into the intakes, and when the last drop had gone, they would shut down themselves." Ginger went quiet, and so did they all for just a moment. It was one of those rare silences while men think.

"And no one would hear them stop."

Harman had the last word, having finally got the answer, and wished for a moment that he had not.

"Well, I dare say we have got time for a last cigarette and a game of Uckers unless you reckon it's going to happen in the next five minutes, that is, Sunshine." Spider, his usual cheery self, had broken the spell. Everyone overreacted in exuberant bustling, retrieving the game board and setting out the pieces. The moment had passed. The Sword of Damocles still hung by a thread. The crew were not despondent. Life went on, cramped and unhealthy though it was.

There was always something to occupy time, and everyone, out of necessity, overlooked obnoxious habits or the grating words of someone who was not liked. For the common good, every man made the best of the situation, along with every other member of the crew. During the long vigil, people adapted to circumstances. They changed, each according to his inner capacity to cope. The changes were so gradual that no one noticed. Any change in mode of speech or behaviour was seen merely as an extension of that individual's personality. It was difficult to spot behaviour that became irrational and extreme.

When battery levels were high, *Orestes*, in the shroud of night, followed a bleak coastline of Zemlya in search of that grouping of lights, which gave a brief indication of their sought for thriving military habitation. *Orestes* had arrived at its destination to launch their onboard commandos into those flimsy craft and a dangerous paddle ashore on their intended, highly dangerous mission. *S12*'s periscope rotated in a slow arc across the scene, scurrying a vee shape through a foaming sea. The Control Room, illuminated in a faint red glow, witnessed an assembly of infra-red cameras to take images of those shore-bound activities. On occasions, Sonar gave warning of a fast patrol boat meandering in watchful gaze along its occupied sea zone.

Unobtrusively, they slipped away, hidden by the rolling sea and the pulse of darkness. The flicker of intrigue grew dim as the boat careered vigorously into the deeps. The business aboard *Orestes* was once more about maintaining silence, to remain undetected.

The Captain summoned Lieutenant Palmer and Sergeant Bolton to his cabin. "I'm sorry about this delay, gentlemen, but we have patrol boats to contend with." Jeff Hawks looked at their too-young, fresh faces, already filled with the look of too much experience. He knew how agonising the delay must be; he could see they were keyed up for this operation.

"How close to shore will you be able to get us, sir?" The lieutenant accepted the cigarette. He noted that his own fingers, as he took it, were calm. No nervous twitching as yet. Maybe that would come later.

The chart was placed between them so they could note the depth markings. "This depression is what amounts to an undersea bay." The Captain reached across from the desk, seeing the chart upside down, and indicated with a pencil.

"The narrowest point is too shallow, some sixty feet. This area is around seventy, maybe eighty. If we're lucky, it hasn't silted up since this chart was plotted." Both men understood. In two years, the seabed could change its contours. Much depended on the tide.

"That is your closest point to the target. Even then, it leaves you two miles to swim." The sergeant looked up, hoping he had been wrong.

"We can't use the canoes, sir. Is that what you're saying?"

"I'm afraid that is exactly it, gentlemen. I can't risk surfacing. It seems likely our presence is known." Jeff Hawks had thought long and hard about whether to tell them. In the end, he had decided that since they were risking their lives, they should know what the chances of discovery were. *These were brave young men,* the Captain thought.

There was not a flicker of doubt in their expressions. "How do we go? - through the tubes?" the marine had answered his own question. He could tell by the Commander's concern.

"It hasn't been done before, and it will be uncomfortable while we flood. You may get buffeted around a little, but it will work." The Captain paused for thought. "I would suggest waiting another day, but honestly, I don't think it would improve your chances."

"I think you're right, Captain; we will go in tonight. What time do you think, sir?" The lieutenant did not need to ask the sergeant, but he could see he agreed anyway. The Captain laughed.

"I have to find this inlet first. We should be ready for you by midnight. How much time do you need?" There was no need for the two men to deliberate. They had lived every second of the mission for weeks, over and over in their waking thoughts and more than once in sleep. Fear they could accept; it was natural.

"If we can't do it in six hours, we can't do it at all, sir. Midnight will be fine." The sergeant, however, had an afterthought. He grinned broadly.

"If you can give us an extra hour, it might help."

"I wish you luck." The Captain stood and shook hands with each and then came to the fore-ends himself to hear what his Torpedo Officer and Torpedo Instructor had to say. Charlie was not happy about the idea.

"The shock could kill them, sir. They'll take a hell of a hammering when she floods, and as for equalising!" Charlie was shaking his head at the very thought of it.

"We have no choice, TI," Captain could not be swayed, "the aft tubes are smaller. We could flood and get them out faster." Shane was not sure his suggestion was an improvement, but they had to explore the possibilities.

"Too small. That Joe has got big shoulders, and with their bulky diving equipment, I don't think so. Could easily get stuck, and we couldn't help them." Charlie knew he was right about this. The Captain agreed.

"It would be too long without air. It will have to be the front tubes. It will give them room for air bottles. Besides, I don't want them near the screws. I may have to get *Orestes* out in a hurry." The implication of the Captain's last statement had not been lost on them. The submarine could be vulnerable in shallow water.

Jeff Hawks was considering how tricky it would be if a patrol boat detected them; he wouldn't be able to manoeuvre. In order to get these two in as close as possible to the radar installation, he had to nose his boat into what amounted to a narrow undersea lagoon. For the moment, his problem was how to get them out and back. "We will use the top two then." Shane sorted out the final details with Charlie.

"Yes, sir. Less pressure for them when equalising. With luck, their eardrums won't perforate. I will give them a last-minute warning on what to expect, sir." Shane knew perfectly well that the boat commander had other concerns. He couldn't spend too much time on this one.

*Orestes* cruised warily into the shallows. Her echo sounder traced an outline of the sea bed. The Navigator was busy translating the depth readings into a recognisable chart overlay. They had to know within a few feet just where they were on their charts. The Navigator's brow was beaded in sweat. The Captain and First officer appeared unperturbed.

# Chapter 23

Blinveld, outwardly calm, apparently jovial as usual, seethed in a rage of uncertainty. He knew now, when it was too late, exactly why the submarine was here. Seeing the two commandos prepare their equipment had put it all together for him. Ever since the trawler had attempted to track them, he had racked his brains for a method of contacting them. He felt cut off and isolated. He had thought of writing out a long and explicit message, sending it out with the gash. He knew it was impossible. Only infrequently did the bags get jettisoned during a patrol. Each one was carefully weighted and checked, before being allowed into their air pressure gun designed and built into the hull for it. There was no chance of those bags being retrieved by another ship. Often, he had watched this operation without drawing attention to the fact, but he could see no chance for it to succeed. No possibility either of sending a short signal by patch link as this needed the boat to be close to the surface. Also, the risk of detection by other crew operators near the radio shack was too great at this time. Blinveld was helpless; he would just have to wait it out.

*S12* slipped into the shallow sea bunker cautiously. Her propellers were still. Under the propulsion inertia, she slid further in, slowing. The Captain watched the flicking trace of the sonar. He had only feet to spare.

Joe nodded at Shane, understanding and acknowledging his instruction. Easing straps around his shoulders, he took the full weight of twin cylinders on his back. Bubbles passed concertina-like air hoses over his head to dangle its attached mouthpiece on Joe's chest. Jock Brown assisted the American lieutenant. A ladder had been rigged temporarily and somewhat precariously against the centre tube rear doors. With the unaccustomed weight of the air bottles tending to tilt them backwards, the two men were wary of tearing their wet suits. All around were metal projections, any of which, in one moment of carelessness, could severely limit their chances of survival in the searing cold outside. Inching their way forward, face down, the smell of rubber paint and dank sea water deposits enveloped them, in the embracing twenty-one-inch cylinders.

"Are you ready?" Shane stood directly behind each tube to ask the all-important question, going quickly from one to the other. By pre-arranged signal, a foot was raised and lowered several times to indicate their readiness. The torpedo crew shut the heavy steel doors, racked the outer ring clockwise to lock it, and securely bolted down the Thetis clip. There was no turning back now. No sound, frantic or otherwise, could come through that steel wall.

Joe lay in the pitch darkness, breathing from the cylinders, which felt like a ton weight on his back. His arms lay stretched before him. He tried to bring them more comfortably down to ease the ache in his shoulders. Quickly, he discovered the smooth curved walls would not allow it. Along with the sound of his harsh rasping suck of air, he could hear the gurgling rush of air coming up the pipe beneath him. As soon as the noise stopped, he knew the air would be replaced by cold, all-encompassing water seeping from the tank below. In a flicker of doubt, he wondered if his companion not four feet away in a similar attitude was all right. The experience could be more frightening for him. It was like a tomb. They were so close and yet totally isolated.

"Easy, easy," Charlie coaxed the airflow valve open, talking himself into controlling the flicking gauge pointer to crawl upward. The needle crept towards the inscribed line, indicating fifteen pounds of pressure per square inch. Charlie dared not exceed it. Bubbles exhibited similar caution upon the other tube flow. The water spluttered and hissed, gathering in a widening pool around the pit of Joe's stomach, spreading to surround his body. The first touch on his hands was like a knife thrust. The pain of cold sucked the warmth from his body. The waiting was intolerable, and the sheer weight of his own body pressed it, especially his knees and shins, into the narrow strips of upraised metal on the tube floor.

Charlie cracked the valve wider, willing the water to flow in smoothly. Joe felt the numbness of his hands; pins and needles began in his arms. Soon, very soon, the water would engulf him and ease the burden on his back. Again, he tried to ease his hands downward towards his face. He wished now that he had donned his goggles before entering. Water came up to his neck so slowly that it seeped in. There was no way he could get his hands there to ease the seal tighter around his neck. The pressure eased under his body, lifting the nagging ache away from his muscles. The tube was half filled, and the turbulence began. Pockets of compressed air raced up the flooding tube and lathered the water into thrashing life. Joe felt himself buffeted in the close confines. His cylinders clanged in terrifying loudness against the roof. Seconds passed in a torrent of bubbling, turgid wash, each seeming like a minute to the submerged marine commando.

The great relief of buoyancy came, and at last, the rush slowed in searching out the last air pockets in the tube. The ringing valve spindles mellowed, indicating to the torpedo crew that the flow was easing. The flow valves were carefully clamped, and the flooding valves shut. The air vents were gushing a continuous bubbleless stream. They shut down.

A silence pervaded the torpedo room. There was no way to know if all was well. The two commandos were beyond assistance. Shane gave the order. Joe lay in his cocoon, hearing the new creaking of harsh metal rollers grind across their tracks. The sea met the internal phalanx of water as the bow cap came off its seating and compressed it. Joe felt himself lurch backwards, and his feet made contact with the steel support of the rear door. Some mechanism inside his ear popped, and the last seconds of the grinding, creaking metal sound ended. The bow cap door clanged in finality back against its stop. Joe flipped his feet gently and, inch by inch, elbowed his way along to the dim twenty-one-inch diameter circle before him. The air bubbles streamed in line ahead of him with each blow from his lungs into his mouthpiece. The bubbles chased each other along the roof and out, curving upward and away. Free at last, Joe was able to don his goggles, and the pressure on his eyes eased.

The lieutenant also floated free, and they swam upward, breaking surface. Waves lapped gently over their heads and subsided to leave a clear view of the not-so-distant headland. Together, they swam close to the surface towards it, the dim red light on the shallow box strapped to Joe's arm flickering first to one side and then the other.

John Bishop sat, relaxed and warm, his foot jammed against the sonar shack door sill. The door was firmly bolted and he was alone with the circular screen before him. The double line of blips rippled sinuously across it, died away and then pulsed anew. Below, the box flickered from one red light to another and alongside each a luminous display of the frequency count. John's delicate control of fingers adjusted the fine tune knob and watched the frequency count change, clicking gradually upward to hesitate and stop. The count space between the two beams was now accurate. John was satisfied for the moment. He judged the two divers to be about halfway to the installation outcrop. *At least one of the divers was,* John thought. Presumably, the other was with him.

Waves lapped nonchalantly on the pebbles of the shore, sucking some of them in a slithering rattle back towards the sea. The two men rose, half crouched and peered into the gloom. The sky was heavy with brooding clouds. No ray of moon filtered through. They dropped to the beach as the sound of gravel, heavily trodden, paced nearer to them. A guard passed by in ignorance; his wide-lapelled, double-breasted coat fluttered and flapped against his boots in the drab grey of night. A red metal star glinted briefly on his fur hat. A black latticework of girders rose to a pyramid behind the next hill dune. In the hollow, sheltered for a momentary rest, the lieutenant prepared his equipment. Joe unfolded the map from its plastic container and spread it wide upon a boulder. Raising themselves into the biting force of the wind, they keened their ears to listen. No one approached, but far away came the churning thrum of a patrol boat's engines.

John Bishop monitored the patrol crafts progress on his earphones and, from long experience, jotted down his assessment of its bearing and projected course on his knee pad. At the instant his pencil finished its scrawl, the red lights flickered and went out. The frequency count remained steady. John pressed the intercom button.

"Sonar. Party have landed. Patrol boat is sweeping the area." The button clicked off, followed immediately by a double click from the Control Room in acknowledgement. With a final check on the control box lock, John tucked the key inside his shirt to fall on its chain around his neck. Shane was waiting as he unbolted the door, swivelling it back. It was intolerably close in the small shack. He was glad of the faint stream of cooler air filtering in. Shane eyed the pad with its revealing notation and leant forward, crushing himself against the door frame. He wished Blinveld would hurry himself in passing along the narrow passageway.

"Terribly sorry. Do excuse me, sir. Frightful squeeze along here." Blinveld noticed the lack of any response; hesitated as long as he felt prudent, scanning in rapid eye movement to try and read instruments within the shack, but to no avail. Shanes body blocked his view and so he sauntered on through the Control Room.

Captain's door slid back on its nylon rollers in faint protest. Shane turned, glimpsed the look of enquiry.

"Torpedo tubes drained down, sir. The fore-peak should have lifted by now." Shane noted the peremptory nod. His Commander was preoccupied with thoughts for the safety of the boat. Lieutenant Hawks paced his way to the Control Room, deep in thought. He was concerned at not knowing precisely how the tides ran in this coastal estuary. All the indications were that the tide ebb would be negligible. However, with only a few feet of cover, he could not take the risk of staying in this vulnerable position.

"Sonar, Captain. Inform me when HE contacts are at the furthest sweep path."

"Sonar, Roger. Approximately fifteen minutes to go, sir." John heard the double click in response to his information.

The crew went about their business, unaware that the bow had settled into a soft patch of clinging shale and mud. The Captain consulted his watch, the fifteen minutes were up. At that moment, the Sonar Room gave its report. "Twenty-second burst on main. Blow one, two, six and seven, chief," The blowing panel chief directed his assistant to manipulate the lower two valves. A hiss of air, channelling under great force into its main ballast tanks, filled the Control Room. Almost as soon as their ears had identified and grown used to the intrusion, it ceased. The hull began to creak in protest, and the stern raised up just enough to cause an uncomfortable angle in the boat.

"Captain speaking. We are lifting from the bottom now. There may be some disturbance and awkward angles. Stay prepared. That is all." The Tannoy buzz faded, and the sound of the hull scraping against the shale predominated. The crew kept silent, waiting.

"Slow astern both. Revolutions five zero." The helmsman set his indicators as ordered and made ready to chase the lubber's line of the ticker-tape compass.

"Sonar, three HE contacts, two patrol craft, one destroyer approaching. Approximately six thousand yards." John readjusted the headset, attempting to settle it more tightly around his ears. The water disturbance had prevented him from picking them up sooner, and he was annoyed with himself.

"Stop both." The Captain and everyone else remained still. The thrum of two shafts straining against the boat's weight stopped, but the hull continued to tremble. In a great lurch, the decks tilting level, the bows sprang free. Crockery jumped and began to slide. Men were flung off balance. The submarine slid backwards and started to dive by the stern.

"Blow seven," the Captain ordered. Immediately, a hiss of rushing air filled the space and drowned out the intercom voice. John waited, releasing the button on hearing that first piercing scream of releasing air. He was flung back into his seat as the shafts rotated, flinging them out backwards into deeper water.

"Cavitation. High speed. Patrol craft approaching head-on." John quickly switched off, and closed his hands tight either side of his head, pressing downward on the foam pads.

"Full astern together. Revolutions two zero zero." The Navigator and Captain both watched the echo sounder trace indicating deeper water.

"Eight feet, ten feet, fifteen feet," the Navigator was calling out aloud.

"Half ahead port. Half astern starboard." The boat lurched, torsion setting into the metal surrounding them. The propellers bit deep into the water, causing great masses of bubbling turbulence that sprang upward, breaking the surface in a giant spur of seething foam.

"Full ahead both. Batteries in parallel. Group up. Revolutions three five zero. Wheel amidships." The helmsmen relinquished control of the steering bar. Took his hands away from it, resting them in his lap. The tape pulsed in clacking crescendo, wavered and settled to an infrequent notch amidst the heightening thrum of the motor's increasing speed. The hum of vibrating steel enshrouded them. The men closely bunched in the for'ard Mess held down the rattling cups, arms pressing them down on the tables, as the bows pitched and thrust through the sea.

"Sonar attack team close up. Emergency stations." The submarine commander flicked the switch upward and off.

"Depth hundred feet. One degree of bubble." The planesman grasped the hydroplane hands tight, knowing that the slightest pressure too much downward, held for a second too long, would send them plummeting at this speed.

"Easy, easy. Don't fight it," the Captain's voice, directly behind his shoulder, was calming, soothing away the anxiety which showed in the planesman's knuckles. The depth needle flickered towards the hundred-foot marker.

"Stop both. Ships head?" The helmsman cranked the engine telegraph handles towards each other furiously to bring their pointers to zero.

"Ships head at one hundred fifty degrees, sir."

The helmsman was fascinated by the tape clicking to the left, holding for a second and then tripping to the right of the three central numerals. He had forgotten for the moment to repeat the Captain's order to stop engines, though he had complied. No mouthed note of censure assaulted the back of his head. He kept very still, waiting for the next command.

"Starboard twenty. Port telegraph slow ahead. Group down. Batteries in series. Depth two hundred feet." Slowly, the boat started a gradual corkscrew motion, cleaving her way downward to deeper water.

"Sonar attack team closed up. Three contacts. Closing. Should pass over in two minutes. Destroyer lagging."

"Roger." The Control Room button lifted.

"Both ahead slow. Three zero revolutions. Steer three three zero." Without prompting, the petty officer of the watch crossed from the chart table and wound down the revolution order indicator, allowing the helmsman to concentrate on keeping the course.

The pulsing throb of propellers hovered for an instant and were gone, diminishing with the distance. "Half ahead. Revolution one hundred. Three hundred feet. Steer two seven zero." The Captain took the three paces necessary and consulted his charts.

"Sonar. Two contacts returning, crossing to port. One destroyer. One patrol boat."

Two men strode casually through the Control Room, heading aft for their last leg of the Uckers tournament. "Do you hear there? Lieutenant Graves speaking. No passage through the Control Room until further notice. That is all." The intercom whine had hardly faded when a new alteration of course was ordered.

"Steer due east." Slowly, the boat clawed its way in a tight circle, still descending.

"Stream both bathygraphs." The petty officer of the watch turned the handle, releasing the instruments and cranking slowly until satisfied they were clear of upper casing obstructions.

Very few of the off-watch crew slept. They sat idly playing cards, showing more interest in each new dip or turn of the vessel than in what they were doing. From time to time, they could just discern the sound of passing screws churning the waterway above. It had been an hour and a half since moving out of the mud.

The Captain felt more confident after this lapse of time, but he knew that, if not already, then soon, a tight sonar screen of surface ships would be attempting to box him from one end of the Barents Sea to the other. Fortunately, the initiative was still with him. He had plenty of sea room to manoeuvre in. Hopefully, his adversary would expect him to use it to make a run for it out of the area. He had pondered the advisability of doing just that. Playing a home game like this, the other side could call on vast resources. Intelligence briefing before sailing had made him well aware of the number of ships available at Kronstadt and Riga. Fortunately, they were several days away. Arkhangelsk was, however, an unknown quantity. He felt quite sure that the vessels searching for him now were on regular patrol out of Arkhangelsk. Reinforcements would be called in from there, only a few hours away.

The Captain pondered the difficulties of his situation. In four hours, he wanted to be within five miles of Murmansk to pick up his other commando team. In four hours, that could well be impossible if all available ships were brought into this area to track his submarine. *Perhaps,* he thought, *they could be drawn off.* Could he make them believe that he was after something else? *Yes,* he thought. *Possibly, Zemlya Island might do.* The distance was staggering, but in this vast, empty, arctic expanse of ocean, if he could lead them in a straight line towards it, what else could they suppose he would be interested in? They could not know that he'd already had all the necessary photographs of military radar and other installations taken two weeks ago, transmitted to him.

"Steer zero eight zero." The Captain had determined to lay a trail to the east, hopefully a cautious one.

"Relax from emergency stations. Able Seaman Harman and Able Seaman Simeon report to the First Lieutenant." Digger Graves waited for the two men who had been foolish enough to cross the Control Room sometime earlier whilst *S12* evaded the surface vessel's search.

At three o'clock in the morning, *Orestes* came up to snorting depth, heading due east for the island, which lay some seven hundred miles away, the biggest island land mass at this latitude. "Group up, revolutions two zero zero. Let's give them a good view." The Captain knew well that at speed, his protruding induction mast would leave a long streaking vee-shaped foam trail in the sea. The trick now was to know when an aircraft had sighted him. He could afford one hour only on this track. The Navigator was already laying off a predicted course for the run back, calculating from their expected turning point.

First Lieutenant was in consultation with Captain, along with the Torpedo Officer. There was very little room left in the Control Room to move about in. The officer of the watch continued his monotonous and continuous rotation of the aft periscope, his eyes glued to the horizon in search of approaching aircraft. So far, the search was fruitless. The Captain wondered momentarily if he had tricked them too well already. He could not really believe that he had shaken them off so easily. Shane was convinced the torpedo idea would work.

"How long will it take to fit the head for self-destruct? We don't want to make a gift of an intact 'homer'." The Captain allowed himself a smile to ease the tension which seemed to have considerably built up amongst his officers and crew in the preceding few hours.

"Probably half an hour. Fifteen minutes to load and fifteen minutes for flooding and preps." Shane knew, as he gave the answer, what the next order would be. Charlie the TI shook himself awake from a brief cat nap, rubbed sleep from his eyes and got the torpedo crew together.

John Bishop was warned that his services would soon be required and that he should take the next hour off. There was no point, he knew, in trying to sleep. A couple of cups of coffee and a wash would stand him in better readiness. The steward's coffee pot was nearest, the quality of its aromatic contents much superior to the for'ard Mess rations.

With ten minutes to spare, the single gleaming silver aluminium torpedo was ready. At five minutes to the hour, a single reconnaissance plane appeared scanning the sea. "Stop snorting. one hundred feet," the officer of the watch gave the command from his periscope position. He felt sure the aircraft had spotted their wake and had duly reported it to its commander.

"Fire One." The aluminium shell churned its way out, took up its ordered depth and continued the submarine's course, levelling down in speed to simulate the submarine's ten knots.

Once clear, *Orestes* began her corkscrew evasion, her Captain hoping the aircraft sonar buoys would not be dropped on the first pass. Luck was with them; the Russian pilot on routine reconnaissance was not expecting to find a snorting submarine. He had overshot before his responses allowed him to order the detection device drop. Sweeping in majestic splendour to the west, he made another pass, straddling the still visible track with sonar pick-ups. Quickly, he checked the submarine displacement chart. No, he was sure now. None of their own submarines were operating in this area. The pilot radioed base and settled to the chase, linked to his detector buoys transmitting the reflected propeller noises heading east.

*Orestes* headed west at breakneck speed, pacing against the clock in an effort to reach Murmansk before dawn. At midnight, she came up to sixty feet to begin her usual one-hour snort. Ten minutes before the allocated snort period ended, a message patched through marked 'Urgent'. Jeff Hawks read the signal. 'The Murmansk raid party successfully recovered by submarine at 2300. Radar components were retrieved intact. Resume your other patrol orders.'

Joe pulled the fur-lined jacket closer around his shoulders, raised the binoculars once more to his tired eyes and scanned an expanse of sea. He saw yet another warship, the fifth to arrive, cruise in unhurried progress to comb the depths.

A man groaned close by and began to struggle against the nylon cord which bound him. The other two had not stirred. Joe decided it would be unnecessary to inflict further pain upon the sentries held hostage. In desperation, they had perhaps been too severe on first taking over the radar platform. The borrowed jacket slipped along his rubber-sheathed shoulder. He considered whether to put it on properly, decided against it, and turned to see the lieutenant struggling with the last of the bolts. For a precious few seconds, the American rubbed his hands together, chafing what warmth he could into the unbending fingers. "Here, I'll finish it." Joe dropped the glasses into the man's lap, took the spanner and ferociously attacked the last restraining chassis links. The umbilical cords came away easily. Each of the three equipment modules went into one rubber sack. Hand over hand, Joe lowered the sack through the gaping hatchway into a void below, careful not to knock against the steel latticework. The lieutenant helped. Their arms ached with the considerable muscular effort required to lower the stolen components safely to the soil.

Night was disrupted by a repetitive series of flashes coming across the sea. "Quickly, down," the lieutenant ordered. He took a brief look around the observation platform, making sure the men were helpless to hinder them. In dismay, he saw a launch being lowered from the nearest ship. The Aldis lantern continued to flash out its message to this unresponsive radar installation high on the headland. He dared not stay longer to count the number of men in the launch. Without any doubt, there would be enough.

Tying the rope to what was left of the cubicles, he edged himself over the lip of the square edifice and slithered down the rope. His hands were warming with the friction, and in an effort to slow his descent, he attempted to trap the rope between his feet. The most imminent threat now lay in the possibility of ripping his suit. Lieutenant Palmer landed on something soft, recognising it as the discarded jacket, and located his fleeing companion by the sound of his scraping sack. In the dim first light of morning, he could just detect the crouching figure of the other diver in his loping, muscle-rending run towards the sea. The sound of rubber scraping along the hard-impacted earth sounded eerie. A new sound of scraping wood reached his ears and he knew instinctively that the launch had beached. The crunch of booted feet on shale confirmed his suspicion.

The American ran, his heart pounding. He could feel the sweat writhing inside its rubber wetsuit sheath. His eyes stung with salt beads running in rivulets now into his eyes. Momentary panic seized him at the thought of his own wild running; he knew not where. He tried to clear his head of the dreamy mists of tiredness. They were heading for the sea. Once in the water, they would be safe from those nearing pursuers. A cacophony of stuttering impacting thuds rang hollow from somewhere behind. The lieutenant's mind was grappling with the meaning of it when a spark of searing pain plunged into his shoulder. A scarlet pad of light screamed before his eyes, blotting out the silver tinge of early morning starlight on shimmering waves. The crumpled thud of rifle bullets halted. The sound echoes died, and the splash of broken water came to his ears from somewhere up ahead. He hoped it was Joe, his sergeant, getting away into the sea. His own legs seemed to have become leaden at the ankles and yet rubbery where his knees struggled to articulate him forward to the beckoning promise of the waves.

Joe forgot the wrenching ache of pain in his arm, furious in his crab-like run. He knew the rubber bag he dragged must be shredding away on the rocky soil to near-nothingness, but the urgency of rifle shots demanded that he ignore all pain and focus all his energies on a flight with the precious cargo.

His steps grew lighter, the sound muffled by saturated shale. The sea rushed up at him, eased the wrenching load from his arm and enveloped him. The chill embrace shook the rigid tiredness away, refreshed him, gave him new strength and replaced the old danger with a new one. In complete disorientation, Joe floundered downward; the weight of purloined property took charge and spun him, spiralling down. He guessed that he had sunk ten feet. His experience of the sea gave him an instinctive feel for the depth, but he knew that instincts could easily deceive. He was becoming weightless, the spiral downward decreasing until, at last, he could maintain a static position in the dark.

Now he fumbled for the mouthpiece strapped tight against the left side of his chest, close up to his arm. The seconds ticked away in his watery sarcophagus. The moments of life left to him would be few if he could not soon displace the strap. In an agonising slowing of time, the buckle released. Joe felt slight relief, enough at least to allow himself to expel some of the long-held air from aching lungs. The pain in his chest eased. He sensed that the impression of being held weightless in this one spot was false, that he slid unnoticeably downward. He knew that the air in his lungs would compress and would last him that fraction of time longer with the increase in depth.

The foul taste of salted rubber stung at his teeth and tongue. The familiar need to gag and retch came over him, but as always, it was transitory, and he resisted. The left hand churned its wrist in a flicking motion against the valve spindle. Not for the first time, Joe wondered if the cylinder at his lip would contain the life-giving compressed air that he now needed desperately. He knew it would be there; it always was, but he always had this momentary fear. After so many years of this work, he still retained the knowledge of how vulnerable his situation was. It had never left him. The cold pressure of air washed away the acid taste of rubber, and in final relief, Joe expelled the remaining stale, used-up and long-held gas from his lungs. In the same instant of breathing one great lungful of the clean pulsing flow, he could feel himself imperceptibly rise, noted by the incessant pull of the weight dangling from his right wrist. His own immediate danger over, now, for the first time, he could allow himself a moment's thought on the fate of his partner.

Slowly, Joe began to swim in a tight circle, his left arm brought across his body while he tried to tune in the box strapped to it. The red lights on it flickered unceasingly from one to the other. He continued the swimming turn and noted the steadying flicker of just one dim red pool of light from his strapped-on box. Another gyration of his body through a complete circle would give him his direction, he knew. Somewhere out there, between the two unseen sonic beams, the submarine lay, being its focus and provider. Without it, Joe knew he would be dead in less than an hour. Joe lowered his legs in a frog-like thrust towards the surface. He had maybe twenty minutes of life-supporting air in the six-inch cylinder, he must conserve it as much as possible. He would have given a lot to have the reassuring bulk of the standard twin cylinders strapped to his back, but they were lost somewhere out on the headland. Joe had no doubt that the Russian landing party would have found them by now, two sets probably.

Where was Lieutenant Palmer? Joe wondered. He was on his own now; they both were. He knew really that the lieutenant's chances were negligible without him and the direction finder. If he had made it to the sea, he could only flounder for some short time and then die alone in an empty wilderness. Joe pushed the thoughts away from him and gulped in the chill, surface air. He could see a stark outline of the headland, perhaps a mile away. He had been lucky; the tide was ebbing, carrying him out and away to safety, beyond immediate reach.

A cold wind stung his unprotected cheeks. It felt like sand pebbles being blasted into his face, and his eyes streamed from his tear ducts. His vision was clouded and the sea horizon was empty in the shafts of morning light. He turned and back paddled for a while, riding the gentle lulling thrust of waves, facing the headland. Bright pin flashes of torch beams rode in one small patch of the shore. Further away behind them reached the stark latticework of the radar mast, forlorn and forbidding against the sky. With the wind behind his head, Joe's eyes cleared. He was growing used to the half-light and now, far away to his left, beyond the headland, he could discern the tiny red and green lights on a low outline. He thought he saw another ship silhouette beyond that, and then he was sure. There was another, this one moving fast if he could judge correctly.

Without seeming thought, he knew why. It was heading straight out to sea, this low-lying destroyer with the gently curving forepeak. Joe turned in the water, sought the direction of the submarine, consulted the flickering beam indicators, and felt completely helpless to intercede. The submarine was there somewhere and approaching. The surface ships were waiting, and the destroyer was going in to attack. Joe began to swim, his precious haul dangling inert from his belt. Occasionally, one of his thrusting legs would catch a scraping blow against it, but he would endure, correct his direction and continue onward until his strength was gone. This was his mission, and he was alone. This is what they had trained for, and, for the moment at least, he held the valued prize in his rubber sack.

Lieutenant Hawks glanced at his watch, still listening to his Electrical Officer's report. The batteries were low. He had used them unsparingly in the frantic dash back to Murmansk. He had very little reserve for what he knew must come. "Steer one six zero degrees. Group down," he ordered. The helmsman pushed the steering bar down, reached sideways and altered the battery order indicator, repeating the command. Jeff Hawks glanced at his watch again in worry. The luminous dial stared back; the second hand swept inexorably onward. The submarine commander knew that the time for flight was now, possibly the last chance to slip the inevitable pursuit. Sonar confirmed the trap. His resources of power were dwindling. Time was against him, and the light of a new day was spreading to aid his enemy. He saw little, if any, chance of retrieving his two commandos.

"Sonar contact. Twin screw cavitation approaching fast. Possible destroyer." The intercom faded and immediately crackled once more into life.

"Swimmer contact, carrier with asdic beams reflecting. He is sending his position, sonar device transponding. Estimate the swimmer at three miles Red four zero," John Bishop finished his broadcast and nodded at his co-operator, who was anxious to give his report.

"Destroyer intercept course at Red six zero. Range ten thousand yards." In turn, the third operator of the submarine attack team was given the signal to make his broadcast. Around them, the steel hull began to vibrate.

"Stop both engines. Maintain sixty feet. All unnecessary machinery to be switched off. Ultra-quiet routine," the Captain stopped speaking. His brow furrowed into deep lines. It went completely against his instincts to shut down all his machinery, to make himself, his boat and his crew so vulnerable. And his enemy knew exactly where he was. The Control Room Watch stared in disbelief, numbed by their commander's decision, but each was glad the decision was not his.

The thundering slew of propeller blades came nearer, filling their ears, and passed on overhead. Only one minute later, the double-triangle pattern of depth charges thudded into the sea and sank. The deafening roar of splintering metal thudded its raging thrust at the vessel. The hull lifted momentarily and shuddered. The steering bar jerked violently left and right, breaking the helmsman's wrist. His arm dropped into the man's lap; an agonising pain swept through his arm and shoulder. The deafening roar passed away, and the boat settled.

"Belay all damage report. Fore-ends only report," the Captain's voice thundered through the intercom, drowning out the falling dishes, straining wood and creaking metal.

"Fore-ends secure, sir. No damage," the words were hurried crisp, and then the intercom went still.

"Fore-ends open all bow-caps," again, the Control Room crew were dismayed at the Captain's order.

"Ahead full. Ship's head?" The Captain looked towards the helmsman, exasperated by the momentary delay, and saw only the left arm going upward in response, saw the bowed head and pale, grimacing face. The Captain's finger shot out towards the petty officer on watch. Within an instant, the man darted in, relayed the telegraph order and virtually lifted the helmsman out of his seat. The helmsman lolled against the control console and grabbed at the Perspex plotting chart nearby for support. By now the petty officer was behind the wheel.

"Ship's head one four zero, sir." The new helmsman steadied the ship's head, manipulating the bar and willing the boat to slow its bucking progress.

"Sonar! Report swimmer." John was momentarily cowed by the raucous bellow from the speaker.

"One mile, closing. Dead ahead." The double click signalled acceptance of the message.

"Stop both engines. Fore-ends report." The Captain waited impatiently, and in the ten or so endless seconds he waited for a reply, he mentally stilled the racing of his own heart. He knew the destroyer was turning, about to commence another run over them.

"All tubes flooded. Bow caps open. Fore-ends, over."

The Control Room crew could hear the harsh gasping breath coming over the intercom as Captain forgot to release the button. Jeff Hawks took mental note, saw the faces around him, and knew that it was imperative to assume the cool, assertive face that his position demanded to mask his true feelings.

"Thank you, fore-ends. We can expect our swimmers on board at any time now. All fore-ends crew to the fore-ends. Listen for swimmers' signals. Carry on," the slow, deep, measured voice, unhurried and calming, reassured them all. They had confidence once more in their commander.

The second depth charge burst hit them immediately and shook the submarine from stem to stern. Several men were shuttled into bulkheads and metal obstructions. The cloudy, persistent hiss of escaping high-pressure air syphoned out along the Control Room from the Wardroom passage. The intercom crackled abominably. The words lost and finally shut off. The outside ERA dashed through the Control Room from the Engine Room, slammed into the bulkhead of the Wardroom passage, clawed his way around the corner and, reaching upward, shut down the offending leak on the number four bottle group. The scalding hiss of air died away.

All the torpedo crew stood by the torpedo rear doors waiting, keening their ears for the sound of any kind of banging inside the tubes.

"Swimmers range zero. No contact," John reported and waited, not knowing what would happen next. In the torpedo compartment, all was quiet. No one spoke and Bubbles held his breath. He felt that he heard something thud into a bow cap or a tube. He couldn't be sure, but looking at the other's expectant concentrating faces, he knew that the other three had not heard. He waved a finger at Charlie the TI. Still, no one spoke, but Charlie cocked his head to one side, his ear close to the tube. After a minute, he shook his head slowly from side to side.

They all heard the destroyer coming back. Would this one be a direct straddle of charges, they wondered. So far, they had been lucky; the pattern of charges had been irregular. They hoped their luck would hold and the pattern would not drop evenly around the slender hull.

The third barrage lifted the whole submarine five feet and then dropped it. Practically everyone was flung to the floor, pressed hard against the steel deck plates. Water sprang from hull glands, spraying from sheared bolts, worming its way in increasing torrents past disrupted seals. Sporadic damage reports were voiced to the Control Room. "Fore-ends shut all bow caps and drain down," as the Captain's orders faded away, they heard the second ship coming in.

"Fore-ends report," the voice was tense, urgent.

"Bow caps shut. Have commenced draining down," the torpedoman panted from the frantic dash to reach the intercom.

"Dive! Two hundred feet. Full ahead together." As men picked themselves up, tried to ignore bruises, and peered around, hoping not to see signs of severe damage, they breathed sighs of relief. At least now they were moving. They stood a chance while they could still manoeuvre. In the midst of this imminent disaster, the crew's spirits lifted. They had a good Captain, and the boat was moving away.

The torpedo tube's rear door swung open, the vestiges of draining seawater poured over the lip and down to form a spreading pool on the floor.

"Good God!" Charlie uttered the words in disbelief at sight of the prone, cramped, black-clad figure inside number one tube.

"Give us a hand." Charlie beckoned Bubbles to help him drag the diver to the tube edge. He was virtually a dead weight, being apparently unconscious. The mouthpiece was still clenched firmly between closed teeth. The eerie rasping suck of air sounded loud in the compartment. As there became room, the other torpedoman lent a hand to carry Joe out to a space in the middle of the compartment. Blood oozed still hot in a coagulated ribbon from eyes, ears and nose.

"Quick, hold his jaws." Charlie virtually ripped the attached hose and mouthpiece out, watching in helpless stupefaction as blood trickled out of the gaping mouth. Somehow, Joe was managing to breathe past all that.

"Lay him face down, gently does it." Charlie managed to get the man onto his side. The thin ribbon of crimson fluid mingled with the water and spread its shallow pool on the dull silver aluminium deck plates.

"Control Room. Fore-ends. One diver retrieved. Coxswain with medical kit required in the fore-ends, over." There was no response. Another attack was commencing. Everyone could hear the propellers coming closer but far, far above them. Muffled explosions shook the boat.

"They've got their depth charge settings too shallow. Thank God!" Bubbles spoke to no one in particular.

"The next one won't be," somebody remarked.

The boat increased in speed, heavy vibration started up along the hull, and the boat tilted sharply to port. The Coxswain struggled to keep from falling over; the deck angle had increased so much while he tried to force himself through the hatch and maintain a footing to reach the stricken marine sergeant. One close look was enough to tell him, just from the places the blood emanated from, that the injuries were bad. With luck, his internal vital organs would survive the shock waves. Maybe he had a chance if he could get him to hospital soon.

Jock Brown sighted and found the scarred rubber sack, crawled up the tube after it and dragged it out, needing a hand in the final stage. "Get number one tube rear door shut; we're still under attack." All tube rear doors were locked shut. Charlie stood, knowing there was nothing more to be done for the moment to help the sergeant. They had no doctor. The Coxswain would do what he could, but there were no medical aids, no surgery, and limited oxygen, and they were far, far from home. The American lieutenant had not even got this far. His fate could only be guessed at.

The Captain evaded yet another attack and was now hopeful of making deep water and the open sea. He could expect help from dense water layers soon. It was a big sea to get lost in. He had a few moments now to spare for an assessment of the mission. The truth, he had to admit to himself, was that he did not know. He had got them in and had tried to get them out, risking the safety of his ship and crew. It had been made clear to him by Captain SM at the patrol briefing that it was absolutely imperative to get the commando team out with their information. It looked to Jeff Hawks as though he had failed. One diver is missing, and one is probably dying. The importance of the three captured radar modules was not known. Only the experts in Portsmouth would be able to determine that. It seemed so futile, but he knew that was just a human emotional evaluation. They would not have been sent out if it had been unimportant. This is what they trained for.

"Two frigates approaching Red ten and Green forty. Contact one at twenty knots, range eight thousand yards. Contact two at thirty knots, range twelve thousand yards." Jeff Hawks acknowledged and set himself to the task at hand. He watched the flickering ink trace of the depth recorder. It took five hours to finally extricate the submarine out of the box formed by the searching ships. The submarine maintained her maximum depth and crawled slowly out of danger. They had been extremely lucky and had suffered no major damage. The Engine Room crew had worked constantly through every attack to repair damage. All systems so far were intact and operating. *S12's* batteries were nearly exhausted. It must get to snorting depth soon if they were to survive. They needed dusk to arrive quickly.

The Captain heard the Coxswain's report of the sergeant's condition. How long could he keep him going? The Coxswain considered there was enough oxygen to sustain life for maybe an hour or two.

Jeff Hawks sent his signal asking if there was an aircraft carrier with hospital facilities within a hundred miles. If there was, he'd get a helicopter sent for Joe Bolton. Is it possible? Maybe. Soon, they will know. No certainty as yet, but the Captain was hopeful that the commando would survive.

# Chapter 24

*S12* made her way south, having completed the third phase of her patrol, managing to avoid any further contact with the Soviet ships. She transited through the night to the final phase.

The crew sloughed off morose forebodings of the silent deep. The atmosphere lightened with a sense of relief and then humour. One more week, one more sector to cover in this mission, and again, they would filter their way south into the sunlight.

All the fresh food, vegetables in particular, had long since been used. The at first droll and amusing cover employed by the two cooks to hide this deficiency grew weak. The salads, with no salad but with names of eastern promise, no longer rewarded the weary men with a fixed period of time to look forward to. The highlight of the day became a shabby replica of all other days. Men drank more coffee, smoked more and ate less. The eating habit deteriorated from a fixed sequence to a nibbling habit, replenished through the day with accessory foods from filched packets retrieved from hiding places.

Leading Mechanical Engineer Owen Hogarth tucked what was left of the dry biscuits under his bunk, turned again to the long table and took another sip of hot watered meat extract. He glanced at his watch, careful not to nudge another's elbow, all so tightly packed alongside.

"Time to go on watch," he said, more as a direct instruction to force himself into the necessary mood than as a communicative comment to the after Mess. He stood, picked up his cup and waited for the man next to him to move out, allowing him to pass.

"Play this hand out, Taff, they won't mind staying on watch another minute or two," the speaker had shuffled while he spoke and now dealt the cards as though the matter was resolved.

"No, fair-do's. I likes to relieve on time. A few minutes extra make a lot of difference at the end of a long watch." There were a few words of agreement at Taff's remark from around the table. Every one of them knew how minor irritation at such things seemed to grow out of all proportion during a long trip.

Big Garth left the Mess, climbed through a hatch into the Motor Room and noted the weary, bored expression of the electrician at his panel. "Cheer up, boyo. You'll soon be off watch." Taffy smiled in passing and retrieved his wheel spanner from behind an overhead water pipe, sticking it into his overall pocket.

"Trouble is, I've only just come ON bloody watch," the electrician's dejected voice followed him down the short passage and into the Engine Room. Taff noticed, as he walked down the aluminium centre plates, how the killick stoker at the far end had visibly perked up at the sight of his arrival. The man had, for the umpteenth time, consulted the dial of his watch, almost willing the minute hand to brush closer to the hour. He felt happier on seeing his relief approach.

"Right, Taff. We're going up to snort in another hour. Main bilge is getting a bit overfull; we need to pump out when we go up. Hub oil is playing up a bit; pressure is low. The chief says we got to keep an eye on it." The man was rushing through the turnover report.

"Slow down, boyo. It's not that desperate, is it? How about the tank dips? Taken the readings yet, have you?" Taff saw the man's involuntary shudder and realised he was just about breaking his neck with a controlled effort.

"You better go now before you have an accident. I'll read the log while I wait." Taff pulled out the clipboard and began to read while the stoker leapt through the hatch in an earnest hurry. The Engine Room chief, about to make a smiling remark to Garth, saw the light come up on his order indicator from the Control Room. He turned the gnarled knob which would, in turn, indicate his acceptance reply.

"Pump to sea," the chief read the illuminated order. He shrugged his shoulder.

"They all want to improve the boats trim the minute they take over." He shrugged his shoulders in resignation. The new oncoming officer of the watch was not, of course, aware of the reaction elicited by his order. The First Lieutenant had decided that for the next snort, he would make the stern a little heavier, which should correct the tendency for the planesman to dip the bows too far. Garth went and opened up the sea valves and thereby missed the remainder of the report from the leading stoker going off watch.

The 'Stop pumping' sign came on. The chief shut down the whining thrum and shouted to Garth, who was down amongst the bilges. Almost immediately, a new order was lit up on the panel.

"Christ! Why can't he pump from for'ard to aft, through the trim line, like anybody else?" The chief was in an ill temper at this messing about.

"That has got to be Jimmy. Jimmy always knows more about trimming the boat than anyone else, so they think," he muttered to himself and then aloud.

"Hey, Garth. After sea valve – open it. We're taking some in." Garth stumbled his way down the Engine Room, under the plates, climbing with difficulty around its steel struts.

"Open," the single word was flung out from the hull bottom. He could hardly hear it himself as the cascading rush of seawater flooded through the pipes under great pressure. Garth climbed out onto the upper region. He stood waiting for the thumbs-up signal expected from the chief down at the far end.

Sonar reported approaching cavitation noises, and without further delay, the Captain ordered five hundred feet depth. The planesmen, realising that the bows would take longer to go down due to the shift of balance, rammed the control to full down. Lieutenant Graves' attention had been distracted by this sudden event, and his mind was now occupied with it.

The downward lurch vibrated an intermittent electrical contact fault into a full open circuit. The contact wire separated into two open ends, and the order light went out. The boat continued to slide down, levelling out while still descending. The depth gauge needle flicked past five hundred, five twenty, five hundred and thirty feet. They were still going down but with a bow-up attitude.

A fearful rending sound of splitting steel burst through the Engine Room level, seawater suddenly rising in turbulent swirling eddies around the steel struts. The executive officer's hand reached up, manipulated the pump order knob, but no lights came up. Men scattered everywhere in the Engine Room. The pump was not running, and the chief, in his agitated rush, had missed his footing on the edge of the deck plate, and his body flailed outward, falling. His head made contact with the port engine, knocking him unconscious.

Men were shouting, but the words were not heard above the din of rushing water. Gushing white foaming spray lifted upward, and thronging vapour stirred in motion around the upper spaces.

Garth, still at the back of the Engine Room, wracked his brain for an answer. He fought his way, even with his great strength, not an easy task against the crushing pressure, feeling his eardrums burst in a single moment of agonising pain. His legs kicked out to thrust him into the dark, battering water. By sense of touch alone, he dragged himself deeper, his muscles aching in the struggle. His hands fumbled, found the valve, and turned clockwise. His body tried to float upward. He had to hold tight to the valve, kicking downward and wrapping his legs around the twisted pipe. Numbing, cold hands fought the wheel's resistance, arms stretching in fatigue to shut the flow of water off. Pins and needles started in his chest. He needed to draw more air into his lungs, but if he went up, would he have the strength to claw his way down to the valve again? He seemed to have been down here for a long, long time. The lungs felt as though they would burst, but the water flow was diminishing. The wheel turned steadily through its last complete revolution and jammed. It would turn no more. His senses rallied enough to register that the flow had been stemmed. It had worked.

Hogarth's powerful arms clawed him to the surface to bang his head on the underside of the deck plates and knocked the last breath out of his tired lungs. The mouthful of oily water spurred him to the final effort of dragging himself clear into the heated air. His mind still functioned. On hands and knees, he crawled along the plates to the circular hatch, his vision of it wavering before his gaze. Two rough pairs of hands dragged him through to lie in a spreading puddle on the floor. He dragged himself upright with their assistance, the overalls clinging desperately to his skin.

He coughed water as he spoke. "Sea valve shut. Fractured pipe," he managed to gasp out. They stopped him going back into the Engine Room. He had been going to start the pump. The Captain knew, they all knew, that water was no longer flooding in. It had come up the engine walkway level and was lapping over the Motor Room floor. For the time being, they must remain as they were. Somewhere above, a patrol boat would be listening for submarine emanated noises. They did not dare to start the pumps to clear the flood or start the motors to bring the boat level.

They hung suspended at this bow-up angle in some six hundred feet. Time was on their side; if only they could hang on. The boat had found neutral buoyancy and no longer slipped downward. She hung there like a puppet without strings.

The men waited and held their breath. A muffled curse sounded through the hatchway. The Engine Room duty man objected to the iodine being applied to his gashed head. A few men smiled to themselves. *He was all right*, they thought, and they watched the Coxswain tending to the chief's wounds. Hogarth blinked. Water still ran down his sodden hair and into his eyes. He wiped the hair away. His lungs did not throb so much, and he was recovering his strength. Sonar reported that the boat had gone, apparently unsuspecting. Hogarth staggered back into the Engine Room, and as the order came by voice through the hatch, he started to pump the deluge out to its rightful place.

The Coxswain brought a neat tot of rum and held it out to him. The fiery liquid burned a warm glow through his chest and made him cough. He smiled at the tight-lipped figure. He was all right now, and as he sat down again, vivid pictures of his home and family came back to him.

The resulting mess was cleaned up. The electricians were all called out to remove panel covers and inspect electrical equipment for damage. One went for'ard to make good the loose connection in the Control Room. A team consisting of the engineer and his technicians climbed down into the Engine Room bilges and inspected the twisted pipe and the fractured gland. The line was effectively out of action, without any possibility of carrying out emergency repairs. It was apparent that it could take no more pressure. The whole line would need to be inspected for further flaws and a thorough test when they got back to harbour.

The Captain was informed and duly noted the latest incident and findings in his patrol log. If Big Garth had not been welcome in the for'ard Mess before, although he always had been, he certainly would have been now. It was time for another visit to the for'ard Mess for a cup of tea. They made room for him, not making a fuss about the incident but nevertheless wanting to hear the full details.

"Well, the valve was open, and water was rushing in, so I shut it, that's all." Hogarth sipped his tea. *He hadn't really done anything spectacular,* he thought. He had just been the nearest.

"How did you know it was flooding through the valve? It might have been on the hull side," one of the seamen asked him.

"I didn't have that much time to think about it, but, well, it had to be that." Hogarth was grinning.

Somebody had to ask, "Why?"

"'Cos we wouldn't be here now if it hadn't been, that's why," the casual manner in which it was stated took all notion of offence out of the remark.

"So, you would have been supping tea with Davey Jones, then." The seamen were playing up to the stoker's throw away style.

"You too boyo!" Taff took another huge gulp from the cup, but his eyes twinkled above its rim. They all smiled thoughtfully but enjoyed the fatalistic, dark sense of humour that, perversely, kept them sane.

A strange whimpering noise distracted them. Bubbles held his hand up for silence, and no one moved or spoke. The alien sound came again, and this time, they knew where from. A hand reached quietly out and drew aside the bunk curtain to reveal a reclining figure on its side, legs drawn up. The figure burbled some unintelligible words from the white-drawn mouth, and the curled figure continued to listen.

"It's Simmo," a subdued and amazed voice was silenced by the outstretched hand.

"Shush!" Bubbles looked, as they all did. Simeon had a glass, its wide, open end in contact with a water pipe. He held its base close, touching an ear. He was intently listening to the hollow sound of water residue trickling down the tube. Bubbles spoke very gently in what he hoped was a persuasive manner.

"What are you doing, Simmo?" he held both arms out for a moment to warn everyone to be silent. There was no response. The man's thoughts were completely absorbed in the self-imposed task.

Bubbles moved himself to the seat next to the bunk, sat down, leaned confidentially on the edge of the bunk, and brought his head closer to the man.

"Why are you doing that, Simmo?" He looked into the eyes as he spoke. The eyes glimmered, almost lifeless and swivelled to stare at him. All the while, his glass stayed in position.

"Can you hear me? Do you understand what I am saying?" Bubbles never allowed his gaze to shift from the man's eyes. The Mess was in total silence. Everyone watched. Simeon's eyes flickered wide in a surprising movement of alertness, and the white face stretched out an effortless smile.

"The water will be coming soon," the sound was childish, almost gurgling in a surfeit of saliva.

"I'm waiting for the water to come." The smile faded in a slow, painful withdrawal. The eyes dimmed and rotated in the direction of the glass.

"Can you hear me? Listen to me," Bubbles spoke gently but accentuated the word 'listen'. The eyes did not waver, and the ear was engaged in waiting. There was no way to reach him. The fear had taken too firm a grip and would not release the man's mind now.

Bubbles looked at the men. Surprisingly, there were no cruel taunts, no leering expressions, and even Scouse was subdued. It seemed from their faces that, at last, they understood what had happened, what had been happening to the creature they had called Simple Simon. Too late, they sensed the anguish of some deep-seated, congenital fear. They had not known, could not have known, what caused it. The man had hidden it. Had tried to fight it alone and had lost. Now that it was too late, the onlookers saw not a personal weakness but an inherent defect that any one of them could perhaps have suffered.

Bubbles went to find Coxswain, who came, thinking it was merely a question of discipline. He applied the normal brusque manner which belonged to his trade.

"Come on, Simeon, get off that bunk." There was no answer.

"Pull yourself together, man, and do as you are told." Bubbles interrupted the tirade.

"I don't think you'll get through like that 'swain. His mind's gone. He's beyond authority now." The Coxswain glowered at this veiled insult, but the truth was, he knew that it was so. Simeon stayed where he was, under sedation for the few days remaining of the patrol. The sonar crew doubled up on their watches and managed without him.

Blinveld saw yet another opportunity come his way. With Simeon now incapable of duty and the remaining sonar men working almost double shifts, it would probably create an opportunity for him to get at the new secret sonar circuits. He had pieced together the implication of this mission and was extremely sour about it. Here, he was right in the middle of the enemy espionage camp, and he had been helpless to prevent it. It was vital now, not only to gather all the information he could about this sonar but also to somehow destroy the three stolen radar consoles. He racked his brains for an answer. For the moment, he could see no way to get at them. They would stay under lock and key until they reached Faslane, he knew, and after that, a tight security net would encircle them.

*Still,* he thought. *He had other problems to resolve.* Blinveld churned the possibilities over in his mind. It might, he felt, be an advantage to volunteer as an escort to Simeon for his trip to Edinburgh. It was most likely that he would end up at the same 'funny farm' as Raging Reggie, who could now be very dangerous to the network. *It would help,* he thought, *if he, Blinveld, could get inside the medical establishment and arrange for an accident for Reggie.* Blinveld's co-operator on watch glanced briefly at the bland countenance and foppish mannerisms of his opposite number and suspected nothing of the man's sinister thoughts.

*Orestes* continued southward, commencing a long hike back to home waters. After the recent events, the crew had become melancholy at a time when their spirits would normally soar. It was time to leave all this and go back to the land of the living. To once again be among people who breathed fresh air and walked clean in the warm glow of the sun. The spring had come, given its new life, blossomed into a new ripening of seeds and then gone, replaced by summer. These men so wanted to see that last part of summer before it, too, could wilt away.

The submarine surfaced and they breathed in the fresh air. She sent her first radio signal in nine, fully encumbered weeks. She was two days from home, and as the men took their first look around them, the Elat trawler was there waiting, recording, sending its own radio signal.

# Chapter 25

Submarine *Orestes* returned to her base at Faslane amidst brilliant sunshine. The Casing party were privileged to be the first to enjoy it, while they prepared berthing ropes, gangplank and flag masts for coming alongside.

For this special occasion, not often permitted, wives and children waited in the *Maidstone* well-deck to receive them. Lieutenant Hawks, the first to step aboard the depot ship, was greeted lovingly, clasped by his ash blonde willowy and extremely attractive wife. It was difficult for her to relinquish him to the welcoming brigade of much-decorated officers, but knowing that she must, she did. For the time being, she must take second place until after the desk-laden de-brief.

Other wives, friends and relatives were more fortunate, for having welcomed their particular hero, they could hold him near in a long and uncomplicated embrace. The engineer, older perhaps than the others of the crew, more sophisticated and rather less demonstrative, met his wife without any show of emotion. Yet they touched hands, and each looked for and found the warm glow of affection and longing in the other's eyes. With arms casually held around each other, they walked away.

*S12's* Electrical Officer temporarily neglected his wife. His primary concern was with obtaining depot ship assistance in repairing damage to his department's equipment. There was not much time, a two-week break, and barely enough for replacement and repair before they sailed again. It was hoped by the inboard team that the boat's batteries could hold charge. To replace them now, mid-tour would be a major undertaking.

Lieutenant Phil Green expected no welcoming committee and received none. He cared little and knew that he was the day's duty officer long before it was mentioned formally. He was the only single and unattached officer onboard. Naturally, he could expect to be duty on the first day in. He would use this time wisely for further study, at least until he received the expected telephone call. Shane had a momentary feeling of foreboding. He knew instinctively that a telephone call would come. The peremptory and lilting Welsh voice would summon him to another unwelcome interview.

Much of the welcome gathering had dispersed. A few small groups, some intimate in their privacy, isolated from all happenings around them, formed into enclaves. Theo, the Navigator, climbed the accommodation ladder and had no need to look back. He knew that she would not be there. For the first time since he had loved and married the girl, he felt no sense of loss in her absence. It had come hard to him, and after a long struggle within himself, he realised he no longer needed her. Deborah had humiliated him for the last time. Theo looked neither right nor left and stepped down the long, sloping gangplank to dry land, his footsteps firm, decisive.

Officers, crew and their friends had gone their separate ways. The well deck was deserted. It had become again no more than bare wooden boards in long straight lines from for'ard to aft, caulked between with black pitch.

Harman was going on leave. He was spending it with his parents. Moira was already with them, helping with the celebratory party preparations. He waited for his fellow traveller, standing by the ladder top, aware of the silence of the well deck and the long black outline tied to it below. He, the new submariner, had arrived. He could not help it. He just had to examine again the new gleaming gold braided submarine badge on his sleeve. The cocktail sausage, they had called it, and a few had laughed at him for sewing it on his cuff. It was true; no one else would wear it. *Truly,* he thought, *it does look like a sausage on a stick, but it meant something to him.* He had worked so hard for it. Well, he would wear it proudly until he got home, let Moira and his parents bask in their pride, and then, when he returned, would cut it off to be like the others. He had passed the exam, held only yesterday. Bubbles had worked hard for him, insisting to Jimmy that he, Harman, was ready. Surprisingly, the First Lieutenant had conducted a special verbal exam just for him. *Yes,* he thought, *he had arrived.* He was now truly a submariner.

A white-coated figure clambered awkwardly, as though not used to it, on deck. He held something that looked like a hypodermic needle in his hand. A second figure arrived and then a third, Bubbles this time. All three hauled on the rope and a stretcher slowly appeared after jerky movements of the rope. Two more men came on deck, one of them also in a white cotton jacket. An encircled red cross was emblazoned on his arm. This tight group of men lifted the red canvas and bamboo stretcher with its dormant occupant and commenced the slow struggle upward, pausing at every third step or so. A sharp left bend at the top of the ladder, and the cortege passed him by. Harman looked down at the peacefully sedated, sleeping face of Simeon, so recently his confederate in adventure. Beside the prone figure strode Blinveld just as jauntily as ever. The normal bland exterior betraying no feeling or remorse. *The man was a rock of strength,* Harman thought.

Those of the crew who could go on leave did. The pace of evening life alongside the depot ship slowed almost to nothingness.

Bubbles read his latest letter, waiting for his feelings to crystallise and become subdued before doing so. He knew what it was and more or less what the message would be. For the moment, he didn't want to think about it. He recognised the beautiful curving strokes of her pen. She was very artistic and seemed to take so much care about everything she did. *Nothing could be changed,* he thought. He could not go back. He had already cut himself off from her life, well, almost.

Shane viewed Brown's request to go home. He did not have authority to grant it under the circumstances, he explained. Privately, he was not so sure that it would be a good idea. He had a strong suspicion that Brown would not come back. Here he was, under open arrest and therefore confined to the boat, and yet he had the nerve to apply for leave. Shane thought about the man's predicament, and all due to an insult which had produced a charge of contempt. *What I think about it must be overruled,* he thought. It was not his function to judge, and despite the open animosity the man displayed, he somehow had a sneaking admiration for the way he defended himself. The man would not be intimidated and showed a blatant disregard for authority. It seemed that Brown could not in any way reconcile himself to the thought of authority over him. Only days before the submarine's return, he had disobeyed and showed extreme discourtesy to the Coxswain, thereby earning himself this awarded punishment.

The telephone rang, and the Captain answered. *Good, he is at home,* Shane thought and commenced his discussion about Brown. Later that night, the Captain came all the way back to the ship to see Brown and, after a long talk, eventually allowed him the one day's leave he asked for. The punishment warrant had not yet been returned from the flag officer's discipline office. Brown's fate hadn't yet been decided. The Captain did not, of course, tell Brown, but he personally had recommended a suspended sentence of twenty-eight days in detention quarters. It was his fervent hope that the threat would be enough to make Brown see the error of his ways, and he didn't want to lose him. He was a good submariner. Brown was warned that any further disciplinary breach would aggravate the offence and would undoubtedly earn him the full sentence.

The Captain and Torpedo Officer sat alone in the Wardroom, the first opportunity for some time. "I want you to accompany those radar units to Portsmouth. Apparently, our mission is considered a success, having acquired them." The Captain paused, then poured them both a glass of wine and watched the younger officer's face.

"This could well be the turning point, the breakthrough we needed, sir." Shane sipped his drink.

"I certainly hope so, but we may never know the answer to that directly. It is, of course, top secret." The Captain's face spread into a vague grin.

"You may know more about that than me." Shane did not see the humour in this situation.

The Control Room telephone began its incessant ringing. Shane wished that he could ignore it. He felt tired, drained after the long trip north. He wanted only a quiet evening's duty, with no necessity for deep thought.

"Do you expect me to return immediately, sir, or remain in Portsmouth?" Shane wanted very much for the telephone to stop ringing, but the thought was useless. He stood up, ready to go.

"That decision will be made elsewhere, but I think it likely you will be seconded to the scientific team, but probably only for one week. I will see what I can find out tomorrow." The grin spread wider.

"You had better answer your contact, Lieutenant Green." Shane noticed that the smile did not reach his Captain's eyes. Reluctantly, he went.

*Orestes* resumed a full but inactive life alongside. During the first week, a team of technicians arrived to endorse the engineer's report and confirm his convictions. Work began on the steel piping in the Engine Room. A few days later, another team, this time electrical, came aboard and carried out their requested work. The Electrical Officer remained very much in attendance, to the detriment of his home life. His submarine batteries appeared to be in good order.

Storing ship fell to the second leave party on the last day before they, too, could hand over to their sad-eyed returning comrades and catch up on those missing weeks of summer. All too soon, the brief one-week leave was gone. Everyone assembled to hear the modified programme and adjusted sailing duties. The Mess was crowded as they waited for the broadcast.

"What did you get, Jock?" The second leave party had missed the punishment warrant reading.

"Twenty-eight suspended." Jock was not unhappy with the verdict, but he didn't show it. Any pronouncement would have been greeted with the same stoic expression which was habitually his. He just didn't give a damn about authority.

"Good-oh! Lucky for you. Have to watch it with the Jimmy, I expect." Spider was grinning.

The loudspeakers crackled. The hubbub of voices stopped and they listened to know what new controlling factors would alter their lives. The announcement lasted a full ten minutes, during which time there were many attentive and thoughtful faces. The broadcast by their new First Lieutenant informed them that Lieutenant Grimes had managed to take his own life whilst confined in the mental hospital at Edinburgh for tests. None of the crew had liked their late First Lieutenant. Few had even thought of him as a human being; he had merely been a symbol of authority. Now that he was dead, it bore thinking about. He had, after all, been mortal flesh like the rest of them and, for this alone, was owed some small consideration.

His relative had asked for a military funeral at sea. Naturally, it was explained the request would be complied with. Bubbles was surprised that it had even been admitted officially that an officer had committed suicide, let alone receive this final military tribute, despite it. Not for the first time did he wonder just what Raging Reggie had been involved in. Thoughts came back at him through the sculptured writing of the dark-haired girl, Alicia, in Glasgow. Her letters had been full of a suspicious, secretive meeting that had taken place at the back of the shop, which she had silently observed. This involved the lieutenant's girlfriend Sophie, who frequently visited, ostensibly as the shop's book buyer. It appeared she conducted other meetings of a clandestine nature there also on occasion. Bubbles had dismissed most of it simply as the imaginative creation of a bored and romantic creature.

However, the characters she described were familiar somehow, and some of the coincidences were too strong. Bubbles regretted, in that instant, that there would be no chance to pursue it. There was never any going back, but he should go up to Glasgow one last time and explain himself, his reasons, fully. He had thought the delicate dark-haired girl had understood last time they spoke of these things. A picture of the way she looked came up before his eyes and the sorrow he had felt at their parting words. He thought at the time that he had been right to end it for her sake rather than his own. He owed it to her to give her a chance to retaliate if she wanted to. *He had not been good for her,* he thought. He would wait until his leave and spend a day with her, let her vent outrage at him perhaps. He owed her that, at least.

Within the hour, the lieutenant's coffin was brought onboard and placed on the for'ard casing. The stark wood was draped with a White Ensign, weighted at each corner to defy the wind's attempt at ripping it away. The dark-clad and veiled grey-haired figure of Lady Grimes held tight to their Captain's arm as he escorted her down the depot ship's companion ladder and onto the submarine casing. She was helped to the decks below in the dying fluted whisper of the bosun's pipe salute.

Before the boat sailed, a few adjustments were made to re-arrange the duties of her crew. Several old timers had left for various reasons. For some, their contract for submarine service was up, and they would return to general service.

"To get a quieter life with blokes who are sane," as someone put it. Others had completed a long stint with this boat and were now going to pick up another boat, perhaps running from some other base. A few of the chiefs and POs went back to the submarine training school to teach a new influx of recruits. This last marked a personal change for Ginger Bates. He was formally confirmed in the job of Second Coxswain, and since the crew were one short on full complement of senior staff, he was promoted. Ginger had waited for three long years since passing his professional exam, and the great day had dawned. Everyone knew and pretended not to notice when he came back to the for'ard Mess from the Captain's table, face wreathed in smiles.

"Yeah, I'll have another cup of tea." Spider set the mood of nonchalance as the new petty officer swung the passageway door open.

"Cup of tea for you, Ginger?" Spider had his back to the door, as he winked at the Mess in general. His tone of voice was casual, confidential. Someone leant towards the electrician and said, in an actor's stage aside so everyone could hear.

"You can't call him that. It's 'sir' now, you know."

Ginger strolled casually to his locker, taking no notice of the quip, very slowly opened it and took out a carefully sealed polythene bag. Undoing the taped fastening, he withdrew the brand-new peaked cap with its shiny, bright badge. In a nonchalantly rehearsed manner, he donned it, flinging the old battered round one into the gash bin. Everyone was smiling, sharing the big moment with him. Nobody knew just how long he had kept the hat sealed away from sight.

"Like your 'at Ginger. Get it off a milkman, did yer?" The speaker was chortling.

"Wait till you see the rest of it." Ginger was enjoying the gentle ribbing game.

"Got the uniform from a bus clippie, said she was fed up and going to pack it in." The mood was very light. The men always reacted to someone's promotion this way unless, of course, they couldn't stand him, in which case he would be ignored. With someone they liked, it was okay to be flippant, although some turned nasty; if the authority went straight to the head. It happened. Give authority to some people and they went mad with it, especially those with a low intellect. Ginger was all right; no trouble there.

Several new faces arrived onboard, and one came to the for'ard Mess as a replacement for the unfortunate sonar man, Simmo. "What's your handle, then mate?" Scouse was about to conduct an initiation ceremony.

"Tideway. I've just come up from *Dolphin*," the man's answer was casual easy-going. He didn't look as though much would bother him.

"Right, what's yer first handle then? What do yer mates call yer?" Scouse thought this an opportunity to increase his own importance with the new arrival.

"Tiddles, or Bob. I don't mind which." The man was unpacking his bag, not that he had brought much. The first thing he had learnt in training was that there wouldn't be much room, so he had given or thrown most of his kit away.

"Right, well, I'll call you 'Tide-way-out', then." Scouse laughed out loud, thinking his intended pun hilarious."

"I see you've got a Mess comedian anyway." Tideway wasn't annoyed; he had come across idiots before. He was just giving a gentle warning that he wouldn't be messed about.

"We've got several in this Mess, me included. I'm Bubbles; if there's anything you need to know, ask me." The hand was thrown and grasped in a firm once-up and once-down shake. *He would fit in quickly,* Bubbles thought, used to weighing people up. *You could tell a lot from a man's handshake,* he thought, *particularly if he looked you in the eye.* Bubbles introduced them all, picking the names out quickly. Nobody ever listened to a long list of names. This is John Bishop; he's the sonar boss, and that's Binny Blinveld, sonar number two.

"Delighted! I'll just finish orf this letter and show you abayt if you wish."

"It's okay, he's not taking the Mickey. That's the way he is." Bubbles pressed the man's shoulder down, pushing him back into the seat. *I hope he isn't going to be touchy,* Bubbles thought. Already, he could sense friction between the two, but it might smooth out.

# Chapter 26

The crew started to function again as a cohesive force. Only teamwork could sail the boat out and down the loch.

The deliberately light-hearted mood had evaporated once the Casing party had needed to change into their best suits. The impending funeral touched them all now, yet they resented it. The Casing party lined up alongside the coffin, the gleaming new nylon ropes ready to hand. In silence, they listened to the sea being cleft and scattered along the buoyancy tanks in its strange continuing swish from bow to stern. It streamed out in an ever-widening vee astern. The small fishing craft moored along the coastline rocked, nodding their masts in mock salute with each spreading wash of sea. The faces stared out to sea, backs straight, eyes on the horizon.

The ropes glistened with salt water, impervious to the straining, sweat-filled faces above. The coffin slid along the curving tanks, reluctant to embrace the sea. Finally, it rested there, unrestrained by ropes. Gently, it floated away from the ship. First, the cap, then the sword and finally, the wreath of red slid off and sailed into the foam. Still, the casket floated, askew, reluctant to trim lower in the water.

A comforting braided arm encased the mother's shoulder, led her away and down to the warm comfort of a brandy in the Wardroom. Ginger Bates alone, did not soil his new petty officer suit with verdigris, slime and oil as he ordered sailors onto the tanks. Sweating faces cursed oily stains on hands and cuffs. Even the rough cast iron sinkers lashed unceremoniously to the wooden coffin shell would not make it go down. Shane looked down from the Bridge tower, perceiving the struggle, the useless task being enacted below. He, too, was anxious to curtail this charade in a biting cold wind. Without further deliberation, he ordered the men back onto the casing, shouted down his engine orders along the hollow mouthpiece, and waited for the engine throb to increase and propel them forward. All eyes except Shanes stared out to the horizon, but all heard the splintering thud of shaped submarine steel on wood. The act was over.

On their return, albeit brief, visit to harbour to land their single passenger, Shane would need to explain his additional engine orders and manoeuvres to his commanding officer, at present otherwise engaged in solace. It would be understood as a practical solution to a coffin reluctant to sink. Shane was not dismayed; rather, his mind turned to consider the latest news from his intelligence contact. The lilting voice taunted him still. One of them onboard the submarine was a Soviet agent. Shane's task, his most imperative duty, was to determine which amongst the sixty-eight crew he was.

*Brilliant sunshine would be with them all the way, hopefully,* the crew thought, *and certainly when they got into the Med.,* but first Lorient. "So, where's Lorient, then?" Quite a few of the less travelled ones didn't know.

"France." John, wanting to read his book, flung the word out, hoping it would be enough to silence the chatter. It wasn't.

"Whereabouts in France?" the voice was persisting. The owner wanted to know for his letter home. "The coast."

John was in an uncommunicative mood. "Just down from Bridlington, turn left at Hilderthorpe, take a sharp right…" The flow was interrupted by a flying sandal, which just missed his head and crashed against the bulkhead.

"Bay of Biscay, south coast of Morbihan, district of Brittany," John told them, just to keep the peace.

"Listen to smarty, up there." The troublemaker pointed at the reclining pinger.

"If you could read, you might learn something too, one day." John had not moved, but he didn't need to in order to make his words sting. After that, he was left alone. It was an unwise man who tackled John on his own battlefield.

The day wore on, the sea calm and blue. A mood of tranquillity on deck. Sunbathers were allowed onto the for'ard casing during a calm passage. Out came sun hats and lotion. It was more like a holiday than an official trip. Those who had seen it all before slept or read a book.

It didn't seem unusual to begin with, but a few remarked on the number of letters and amount of hours that Blinveld spent writing them. It was no cause for concern. *Binny was obviously a literary type; had to be, with his education,* they thought. Binny considered the new scheme he had devised to get John Bishop out of the way, and the pen rattled across his paper at great speed.

Surprisingly, there were no incidents at all on the way over, not even rough weather, which some of them had expected when approaching the notorious Biscay Bay. Even the Captain managed, on this occasion, to get a full measure of sleep during the long nights at sea.

The invitation was declined. *Orestes* would not need the assistance of tugs, but for the sake of courtesy, the channel pilot was welcome to come aboard. The French sailors stood about on the quayside, miniaturised against the monstrous concrete submarine pens, and watched the English boat, ensign blowing in the wind, turn neatly alongside. For once, the Coxswain relaxed his tight hold on the stores' purse strings and ordered a whole wagonload of fresh milk. It disappeared into hidden cupboards and other places of concealment. The majority failed to reach its designated storeroom. The loading party, of course, knew nothing about it, but no one dared to say aloud that it could perhaps have evaporated in the hot top-side sun.

Uniforms had to be worn in a foreign port, particularly a foreign naval fortress. Even the bus parties wore uniform for the laid-on trips provided by the French tourist organisation at the town's expense. John decided to flex his cultural muscles and go with them. The buses pulled out and away on the day-long haul across the mountain vistas.

By arrangement, the two cooks also had a holiday. The crew would walk the mile-long road to the French barracks and share their company and food.

Petters, the Pet Hulk, only made one faux pas, and that without noticing. A table became vacant, the previous occupants having removed the used utensils. The four Englishmen carried their plates to the one empty table and sat down. A long, slender-necked bottle decorated the otherwise empty top. Pet Hulk grasped it firmly, thumb covering most of the opening, and showered its contents, vinegar shaker style, in some heavy-handed profusion around the plate. The three companions looked on in amazement. The vigorous shaking and slopping motion of the thin liquid went on for considerable enough time to draw many confused heads.

"Sacré bleu," was muttered from a nearby table. Possibly a quarter of the contents found its way from glass to porcelain before an animal-like contented look spread across Hulk's face.

"Like vinegar, do you?" one of the three was cautious in the tone he adopted.

"Great!" Pet Hulk shovelled knife and fork into the morass in gulping bites.

"Why's dem froggies so interested?" Pet Hulk fitted the question between delicious mouthfuls.

"Intrigued by English table manners, I 'spec." The jibe went unnoticed. The three looked at each other and at the bottle. It clearly said 'Red Wine' in French.

In the evening, the buses returned and disgorged their passengers. John was not with them, having been left behind up in the mountains somewhere. Nobody was particularly concerned about him. Probably, the normal sense of responsibility and human concern had been eroded by the quantities of wine which floated around their veins. Very much later, around two o'clock in the morning, a taxi arrived at the gangway. A somewhat angry and harassed-looking John stumbled up onto the boat and, without a word to the trot sentry, clambered down to the Mess.

A few were still awake, finishing their drunken and verbal ramble, acquainting the sleeping Mess with their exploits ashore. John barged in and apologetically rounded up all their spare cash to pay the taxi driver. Bubbles was the first to be roused from his sleep, immediately throwing his legs over the edge of the bunk and not yet able to focus his eyes. He thought it must be time to go on watch and that to be shaken so vigorously, he must surely have overslept.

"Are we dived or on passage routine?" the thick, sleepy voice intoned at the hazy outline.

"I'm a bit short of cash, Bubbles. The taxi is waiting, and I owe him thirty quid." Bubbles' tired mind fought to assimilate John's words. He needed some money, that was all he could register at the moment. His mind refused to wake him fully since it had accepted that he did not have to get up.

"There's some under my bunk; help yourself, John. Sort it out in the morning." Bubbles rolled over and drifted quickly into dream state. He had time for a last thought. If anyone else had wanted money, he would have needed to think out the implications of lending it. If John said he wanted it, then he knew it was an emergency.

John paid the driver and relaxed. For once, his charm and wits had not worked. He didn't actually remember quite what happened, except that they had all made too many stops in hotels and cafes. None of them had been used to the wine, and having indulged too much, it seemed to affect their memory.

The French police arrived with screeching sirens the next morning parked their cars in unseemly haste upon the quay. Blue lights flashed as the officers waited on deck for the ship's officer to arrive.

John's uniform cap, name stencilled inside, was firm evidence to indicate his involvement in the bank robbery. Such was the attitude of the French police. The Captain interviewed a still disorientated, fuzzy-headed sailor and was convinced that his number one Sonar operator knew nothing of the incident. John's cap had been removed by some souvenir hunter in one of the cafes in town. Policemen are hard men to convince when they hold such explicit evidence. They thought it quite feasible for an English sailor to hold up and rob a bank then, in a hurry, accidentally drop his hat on the bank floor, so conveniently with his name inside.

After a prolonged and sometimes heated discussion, it was decided that John could be interrogated in town, but only if one of the submarine's officers was present and if John was returned to the ship afterwards. The interrogating team tired more quickly than John, now in full possession of his wits. Grudgingly, they admitted in whispered conference after a considerable time, that it was unlikely that a quick-witted man such as this would be so stupid as to implicate himself. On the other hand, they decided he was the only suspect and the case could, on paper, be solved.

Shane, whom John had insisted on having as his accompanying officer, reminded them that John was not to be held in French custody. Eventually, he was brought to the boat and handed over formally to the First Lieutenant. The Captain took over and assured them that the offender would be held in custody. Those were the only terms that the French officers would accept in exchange for them relinquishing him. The police inspector ceremoniously received the Captain's signature and made it clear that enquiries would continue. Also, the release must be considered only temporary. If the French authorities decided it was necessary, the offender would be detained in France when the submarine sailed.

Jeff Hawks talked with John for some time and persuaded him that he had nothing to worry about. Unfortunately, it would be necessary for him to remain within the dock area and fortress. John, seeing a hidden advantage to it, declared that if there should be some agent of the police inside the complex who saw him, perhaps up at the barracks, it could be embarrassing officially. The Captain agreed, pleased to see such a responsible attitude. Curly and Ernie cooked meals for themselves behind closed doors in any case, preferring their own cooking to the long walk and French military cuisine. Now, there was a third to cook for, but he was good company.

The 'jolly' had not been so successful, but when the French sailors had finished exploring around the boat, the men could relax, and in turn, they learnt something of the French naval authority's tactics. An American youth inducted into the French submarine service told them that all foreign nationals were conscripted at the age of eighteen if domiciled in France, with service being for three years. His father was the managing director of an American firm operating from Paris.

"Yes," he said. "I do speak reasonably good French now and German, but not at all when I was conscripted. We had only been in Paris six months."

The English sailors found this hard to believe, and still more so that the French navy used interned U-boats left over from the war. It seemed even more incredible that the machinery onboard the U-boats still had the original German identification plates mounted. The English sailors were not impressed with French naval efficiency.

The appointed day for sailing from Lorient came, and with it, the arrival of two police cars. With much polite regret and shrugging of shoulders, it was necessary for the English bank robber suspect to be detained on French soil. Sailing was delayed for two hours, but even the hurried arrival and intervention of the British Consul could not dissuade the officials. John Bishop was marched over the gangplank and into a car. The Consul waited long enough for an agitated Shane to quickly gather a holdall full of effects, and the car whisked them both into the town centre. The Torpedo Officer had been hastily assigned to remain in Lorient and effect John's release as soon as humanly possible. Submarine *Orestes* left Lorient well impressed with the welcome extended to the crew during those five days. The warmth and affection shown to them were due in part to the RAF's bombing of the German U-boat pens established at Lorient; towards ending the war. The one-thousand-pound bombs had scored direct hits on the reinforced concrete silos. It was slightly unfortunate that the bombs bounced off straight into the town. The townspeople remembered their friends of the war years, for bringing them this thriving tourist trade to view the still-standing pens. True, the obliterated part of the town had been rebuilt, but the townspeople had long memories.

"Entente cordiale!" one small shrill voice lifted across the harbour from the otherwise empty quayside as the submarine moved away.

*Orestes* sailed across the bay and onwards down towards the Straits of Gibraltar, the waters still relatively calm and the sun beating stronger upon them. Within two days, they sighted land and approached closer to the Spanish cape. With the promise of a brief, late summer, the crew bundled up their issue of foul-weather clothing and found out-of-the-way niches for its stowage. Everyone was making room for the presents they would buy in Gibraltar. Many of the crew spent their time in writing home. It seemed strange to Bubbles that Blinveld, prolific letter writer that he was, should now suddenly shun the Mess. Here was a man who could concentrate amidst any amount of noise and confusion around him, and yet, in the last few days, apparently, his habits had changed. Now, writing case in hand, he retired to the seclusion of the sonar shack to write his letters home two or even three times a day. It just wasn't like him. Try hard as he might, Bubbles could not make any connection to this unaccustomed behaviour. No one else expressed any interest, and eventually, he let it drop from his mind.

After a long, slow weekend at sea and the showing of many old movies, the crew were eager for a sight of Gibraltar. One more day brought them to the long, narrow straits, reputedly the ancient pillars of Hercules. The dusk lights of Tangier passed to starboard, the town indistinguishable but for its fading pinpricks of light passing far astern. Now, so close to the opening, there was much to see with Algeciras to the left and Ceuta, the northernmost town of Morocco, glimpsed in an arcing swing upon the other side as the boat turned in towards the beckoning red flash of light. They entered into the portals of the Mediterranean Sea, taking navigation bearing from the morse flash from the Rock's tall radio mast. A repetitive message of two letter flashes announced to all onlookers and neighbours that the white sheer-faced promontory remained British.

*Orestes* slipped along the breakwater, turning parallel to the long outer jetty wall and berthed on its far reach, assisted by tugs to counteract the fresh crosswind. With so many ships in, and for the new arrival, the British colony of Spanish flavour kept its street of shops open late. In preparation, extra staff appeared in the open-fronted one-room pubs bearing American and English names emblazoned across their door heads, intent on enticing the sailors in. The bars were crowded with the thirsty crews of warships and tankers, added to now by the thirsty crew of a submarine. The colonists stayed aloof, protecting their patch of land against the new invaders. Profits could be counted when they had gone.

Sore heads and depleted pockets found cruising cabs to hustle them back in a long line of similar company to the various silent hulks that lay in the dockyard. On the second day, fewer were inclined to face the long, steep walk into the shopping area. The men rested and wrote their letters home, and some wrote letters of a different nature.

Blinveld's head bent to the task, ignoring all around him. The pen scratched its way through a multitude of paper sheets, the ink flowing in scrawling lines. Unknown to anyone else, Blinveld's letters could not be transmitted via the normal mail route. His incoming mail always supplied him with the name of a friendly ship and a contact on it. This would be his letterbox. The arrangement worked well and avoided any risk of interception. At last, Blinveld had achieved success. His reports could be lengthy and detailed. To be safe, he would despatch his material in separate containers.

A very tired Shane and hardly less haggard John Bishop arrived at the dockside, whisked directly from the Rock airport only an hour before. The results of a lengthy discourse between official departments in France and England eventually negotiated John's release. The wrangle had been interminable and apparently at a deadlock until political persuasion and several veiled threats of trade sanctions had prevailed. Even the parties and departments involved were surprised at the unprecedented pressure being applied on behalf of someone so insignificant in affairs of state. Unseen influences had been manipulated adroitly. The matter was resolved. The case was closed. Blinveld returned the all-important Asdic shack equipment key to John's custody. Now, of course, he already knew its secrets and had copy keys for his own furtive use.

Charlie, the fore-ends boss, knocked lightly on the door, viewed through the glass square and entered, a sheet of paper in hand. "Excuse me, lads, I need a few volunteers." He grinned, expecting the flurried reaction of groans and protests.

"Never volunteer for anything," the voice, unidentified, was shielded by a bunk cushion. Charlie eyed the ever-present pot of tea upon its table.

"Sit down, Charlie. Cup of tea?" The raised inflexion was responded to with a nod and word of acceptance. Charlie sat.

"No, seriously. The Med. Sports competitions are coming up, and we want to enter a few teams, that's all." Charlie passed the list, and heads gathered around it.

"Have they got a rifle shoot, and are we the only submarine competing?" Bubbles couldn't see the list of sports events, which was passing from group to group.

"Yes, do you want in?" The PO's pencil was poised to enter the name.

"We got one of the greenies and a taffy for shooting. Three events. Submachine gun, pistol and 303." Bubbles had a look at the names and got his appended.

"I'd better start cleaning our gear up. When is it?" he asked. Charlie checked the date on his pad.

"Two weeks."

"No need to take our own. St. Angelo is supplying the weapons. We can collect from their armoury in the morning before we go up."

A new interest swept through the boat. A competitive spirit was aroused in enthusiastic support. *Orestes* put a team in for every event on the agenda. Even the steward, Randy Sandy, who was probably the least energetic man they knew, entered for the swashbuckling sword fighting. That was how he viewed it anyway, but it was actually the Epee fencing, and besides, he might draw one of the officers for an opponent. Steward was indulging in private glee at this prospect.

The submarine cruised through the warm blue sea enroute to Malta to engage in trials for the new guided torpedo. In the protected sea of summer, the men were allowed, in spates of a few hours, to offer up their sickly pallid bodies to the healing rays of the sun. Skins healed and darkened under the solar influence in nonchalant idleness upon deck.

An impromptu competition was organised with the Captain's approval. Submachine guns and rifles appeared on deck, and various assorted cans were rescued from the gash. The boat stopped, prepared to lose a few hours in target practice. The diversion proved popular despite the constant ringing sound, which loitered for long afterwards in the ears of the participants.

The boat continued its passage, and plans were made for a pistol shoot on the following day. News came over the radio of a launch arriving somewhere in the Tyrrhenian Sea. A signal, relayed from Gibraltar, ordered *Orestes* to intercept it. It was strongly suspected that she carried illegal cargo to a trouble spot in Libya.

The lounging off-watch sailors scuttled below at a bellowed order from the Bridge. Speed increased, and the submarine altered course to North East. Bubbles waylaid his two torpedomen. He needed assistance to clean out and oil hand weapons for the boarding party. This unforeseen turn of events put him in the position of not having enough small arms ready. He could have let them go out as they were, having been used for the 'shoot-em-up' but as regulations dictated, he wanted to put them back into first-class order. He only needed ten Lanchesters, two rifles, and a pistol, but no one knew at the moment just where the launch was and, therefore, how much time was available.

A short communiqué informed them of suspected gun-running activities and that a launch of French construction had run into Livorno in Italy, loaded at night and sailed before first light. An Italian coastal patrol boat was already searching the area, but other warships in the vicinity were being called for assistance. There was a vast amount of sea miles in which to run. *Orestes* made speed towards Sardinia and hoped that a definite sighting report would be relayed before a decision needed to be made about which side of the island to pass. The weapons were ready in one hour and laid out on the steward's bunk for best proximity to the Control Room. The pistol went to the Wardroom into the temporary possession of the nominated boarding officer, Shane.

Shades of night closed, and still no word came. Lieutenant Hawks perused the charts and decided to lie in wait off the south coast of Sardinia. It seemed pointless, without definite information, to take the chance of missing an intercept during the night. *His craft was not suited to the high-speed chase, and therefore,* he thought, *let the patrol boats find her and flush her out. Orestes* lay at Cape Spartivento and sent her signal announcing the intention.

The crew went about their normal business. Supper arrived in the Mess, the boarding party encumbered by full working dress, boots and gaiters. "Looks like a 'Crushers' dance in here." One of the more fortunate tee-shirted figures observed.

"May I have the pleasure of this Regulation Two-step?" Another flippant character grabbed the booted Tideway and proceeded to do a dance shuffle in the limited space between tables.

"You'll get a regulation size nine up your backside in a minute," the retort was not angry, but the man had not yet got used to their peculiar humour.

"Ooh, you soldiers are so strong," the cavorting figure affected an effeminate voice, which brought chuckles from the others.

The Tannoy crackled. "Attention! Boarding Party muster in the Control Room. For information, the launch has been sighted and identified and is now some twenty miles away," the voice was hurried, the switch quickly thrown off after this statement. The men assembled for the briefing, not eager to be going out there in the dark. Electricians scampered around the conning tower, pacing out the cables for searchlights upon the Bridge. Bubbles struggled with the weight of the Bren gun and shouted to one of the boarding-party to give him a hand, interrupting Jimmy's instructions to the men. Bubbles took no notice. It was his fault for not deciding earlier that Bren gun cover would be necessary. Ginger Bates trailed a rope through the passageway, gathering it in looping coils as he went.

"Right, Bubbles, I'll climb up with this. Give us a shout when it's tied on." Ginger tucked the coils over his shoulder and called to the helmsman.

"Permission for PO Bates to the Bridge," the message was relayed, and Ginger felt his way up the ladder, rung by rung in the dark. The radar tracked the suspect launch, just as a speck on his screen, the operator sure now that this was the offender. Carried by radar's reports, *Orestes* gave chase, not yet seeing her quarry. The distance shortened. The opposition did not apparently keep a good lookout and did not seem to realise they were being intercepted.

Nine men huddled in among the steel struts of the tower, hands clasped around burning red specks of diminishing cigarettes. The tenth figure clambered down from the Bridge. Petty Officer Bates squeezed in with his men. Bubbles shipped the heavy black machine gun onto its metal pivot trained it for'ard and aft, checking a clear sweep for its arc of fire from the tower top back between the lowered periscopes.

"Excuse me, sir," Bubbles hurled the words against the wind from his perch in lookout's position.

"Will you tell the Control Room to get a move on with that ammunition?" Within minutes of the order, a bulging canvas bag, draped by looping handles from a shoulder, made the steep ascent to the Bridge. Jock Brown manhandled the ammunition through the crawling gap and dumped it by Bubbles' feet.

"How many did you bring?" Bubbles ducked his head beneath the metal casing so the words would not be lost.

"Ten. Do you want me to stay up here?" Jock's face was hidden in the huddled space next to the periscope trunking.

"Three hundred rounds. Won't use that much," Bubbles was talking to himself and then to Jock.

"Stay up if you want to, but there might be bullets flying. We don't know who we're dealing with yet." The officer of the watch heard him and imparted the latest news.

"Corsicans, most likely. They have managed to trace ownership. It comes from Ajaccio." Pictures of all the Mafia films with George Raft-like faces crossed Bubbles' mind.

"They're the worst kind," he shouted back, not knowing if he was right and hoping that it would not actually come to violent action.

Shane crouched by the upper conning tower lid, peered out through the open crack of the tower door and checked his pistol. *Safety lever on,* he thought, thumbed it forward and re-holstered the gun, buttoning the canvas flap down. He looked at the ten faces and decided that he, too, would have a cigarette. His hand went into the uniform reefer pocket. Someone saw the brief look in his eye and tapped his arm, a familiar gesture not usually extended to an officer, and offered a cigarette from the pack in his hand.

*Orestes* drew nearer; her navigation lights must surely be seen by now. As if by telepathy, the launch veered dramatically away and powered her engines to full throttle. The crew must have been half asleep to suddenly realise another vessel had crept so stealthily upon them. The officer of the watch reached for the megaphone thought better of it, knowing the sound would not carry audibly so far.

"Fire a quick burst, but for Christ's sake, make sure it's wide." Bubbles heard, slamming the cocking lever forward and back in the same instant. A piercing splutter of shattering sound and stabbing flashes cut out across the sea, causing momentary blindness. Bubbles released the trigger, and the cascade stopped. Traces of white spume spattered up from the surface of the sea.

The launch raced away. *Not close enough,* Bubbles thought, and swung the barrel a little closer. In the time it took to press and release the trigger, thought and reaction time jarred by the ringing chatter, three rounds had gone. Bubbles marked the narrowed gap between shell and hull, swung inward a mere fraction and hammered out a short burst of fire, maybe five or six shots. A gushing spume rose higher up the hull. *God, I've hit it!* Bubbles shuddered mentally at the thought. The spray fell away as the engine note of the quarry cut and died away. The hull was still there intact, not a mark on it. He couldn't have gotten any closer than that.

"Boarding Party out on the casing," the order rang out louder than it need have been in adrenalin-pumped agitation at the sickening hammer from the Bren gun so close behind the officer's head, the last of its empty brass shell casings falling around his shoulders to land at his feet. The Captain's head and shoulders loomed from the square depth and rose to the Bridge platform. The launch engines stopped and it wallowed in a shallow swell. Steering control was lost with the absence of moving water on the rudder and she veered broadside on. Shane, Ginger and nine men stood nearby, paced out along the deck, guns unslung, butts into the waist and barrels pointed at the sky just above the intercepted launch.

"All your crew on deck. Hands on your head. Your captain to stand on top of the Bridge," the tinny voice funnelled out from Shane's megaphone.

"Stop both. Come to port five degrees Coxswain," the words echoed down the voice pipe and were answered. The bows swung slowly in, pointed at the vessel. One by one, men clambered out onto the gently heaving deck and made their way forward into the open.

"Where is your captain?" the metallic sound broached the narrowing distance. There was no answer. Shane nodded to Ginger and told him,

"Quick burst over the Bridge." Ginger aimed high, very high. He wasn't confident of his own ability or the untried weapon's accuracy. Another stabbing clattering sound of cartridges sang into the air. The moment its resounding cacophony ceased, one more figure appeared from the narrow conning doorway, arms waving in apparent surrender. The launch captain should have realised that had he taken the initiative earlier before the shooting started, his craft could have easily outrun the submarine. The efficiency and seeming violence of its approach had stunned him and all his crew. Of course, not really professionals and more used to clandestine, uninterrupted trips. Too late now; they were caught.

"Slow ahead together," the order to the Coxswain was promptly obeyed and hardly had the submarine began to edge closer than the engines were ordered to stop and reverse, breaking the lunge forward. There was no need for the megaphone now. Ropes were thrown and secured from the submarine. The five men hauled the swaying launch in by hand, sweating with the gruelling activity, hand over hand, until the launch bumped against the ballast tanks while their leader, powerless to argue, watched from the rooftop.

Six of the boarding party, machine guns slung from their shoulders crossed over, watching the launch crew warily, keeping well out of the line of fire of their comrades. At an order from Shane, the two riflemen took widespread positions. One stood for'ard by the flag mast and the other by the fin. He was taking no chances.

The five-man crew of the launch crossed onto *Orestes'* narrow deck ledge and, in wavering acceptance, again placed hands on heads. Ginger searched each thoroughly and found an assortment of knives but no other weapons. They were bundled below to stand in sullen silence, surrounded by unfamiliar dials and controls. News of the capture and the ensuing finding of a contraband cargo of machine guns and miscellaneous arms went out by signal. Some of the boarding party were recalled and brought with them the launch captain.

Lieutenant Digger Graves took his first command, and six selected ratings for crew released the lines tethering the launch to the submarine and headed for Malta. Four of the sailors commenced a search for contraband whilst in transit.

The submariner tiffies were not pleased to be ejected from 'Sleepy Hollow', their own six-man bunk space, but the decision had been made. This was to be the temporary quarters and prison for the captured fugitives. The only reasonable place to incarcerate them. Obviously, there was no possible escape for them, but if allowed to wander unrestricted, they might conceivably decide to do some damage. The chance was too great, the boat too vulnerable, and so they were closely guarded.

The submarine resumed her course to Malta, now only one day from its capital's harbour. With abruptly concluded plans, the captives became bored, feelings accentuated by the extreme limitations upon their movement. Their temporary quarters were no more than the length of a bunk, with three of them stacked at two-foot intervals upon either side of a passageway two feet wide.

The volatile nature of all six turned into agitation towards each other. There was no room to sit straight or stand for more than two at a time. A sentry lounged outside the door, hearing the scathing, bitter remarks. Without understanding the tongue, the tone was enough to make their discontent understood.

Tension disappeared quickly amongst the crew. The action was over, and nerves eased once more. After some hours, the captives were allowed for'ard two at a time, under constant surveillance, for an hour or two's respite. Strange though they found the whole experience, hemmed in on all sides by British seamen, they were able to smile and make their thanks known for the small mercy of a cigarette and a drink. There were no recriminations by glance or attitude from the seamen. There were no political or moral judges here. They were simply accepted as men with common needs among men from different nations. This was a time of relaxation, with a small measure of human understanding, before the captured seamen's trial ashore began.

*Orestes* approached cautiously into Grand Harbour, small in her trim black shape against the towering white walls of ancient defences. She moved towards Parliamentario Wharf and secured alongside. The smell of human existence closed around them wafted from the windows of dwellings around the water.

Six stern-faced captives lined in sullen attitude along the deck, the odd packet of English cigarettes fingered in pockets gave a small comfort against the harrowing time to come. Maltese officials arrived in black vans to take them away; an official receipt was given as acceptance of the prisoners. Shane went with them to represent British interests, a report already compiled on the contraband. Vans screeched away along dusty streets, a high-blown dust trail rising into the air above the town enroute to the capital.

Across the bay, just discernible from the submarine's deck, the men picked out the low outline of the captive launch tied up at Custom House steps.

More and more of the crew assembled on the narrow walkway, at leisure to take a breath of air and hear the lapping sounds of canoe-like boats with high curving prows and stern post. "*Dgħajsa*, Johnny, *dgħajsa?*" The ragged-clothed, sunburnt men looked upward, beseeching the onlookers to hire him for a ride across the harbour.

"No, not yet, mate," an answer must be thrown down, or the small fleet of one-man-operated boats would bob in close attendance, voices cajoling forever. The crew was tired of the constant harassment and went below to supper.

"Going ashore? Come on, get your rags on." The more curious and the pleasure seekers persuaded others to join them for a run ashore in downtown Valletta.

"Canteen for me. Damn sight cheaper than going over there." A lot of them had sampled the polyglot flavour of this island before on many occasions. This being the chief Mediterranean stronghold of the British Navy, and so oft-times visited.

Duty watch had the boat to themselves, with room to spread elbows wide, write a letter in peace, take out favourite photographs, and even have the leisure of an uninterrupted shower.

A wide swathe of concrete and stone led the gathered party up the steep climb on the inner edges of the dockyard, upward, always upward, to the long, deep building on a hill.

"Have you been here before, Bob?" Bubbles had fallen into a loose step beside Simeon's replacement, Tideway.

"No, I only had two ships before Sub training. One in the West Indies, and the other in fishery protection." The man thought an explanation was due. To admit to not having been here was tantamount almost to saying that you only just joined the Navy.

"Well, it's up to you, but I would go easy on the Red Biddy if I were you. It's potent stuff!" Bubbles always tried to give helpful tips to the unsuspecting. There were always dangers of different kinds everywhere. The climb, though not particularly stiff, was winding enough for men not used to the exercise of stretching their legs; to give them an appreciative thirst.

The Corradino canteen, with a wide porticoed entrance which echoed their voices, gathered them into its large hall. At tuppence a shot for red rum and gin, and thruppence for whisky or brandy, the temptation was never resisted, and soon tables were filled with trebles and even coke bottles full of the stuff. In no time at all, the quiet, slow evening air was filled with a long pent-up release of laughter and an ever more raucous and vibrant, if untuneful, comradely song.

Bubbles felt sick, and he wished he'd heeded his own warnings. The air was warm and stifling; his head was dizzy. The singing voices seemed to trail away to distant places and rush back towards him in amplified chaos. He pushed the sticky red liquid further away from his place at the table. Its sickly, pungent smell quivered at his nose and throat. He looked around;

they all filled a private vacuum with an imitation of happiness, so intent on achieving it that none really saw his neighbour. The shipmates caroused together, all of the same experience, all of the same situation.

*No one of the shore-side crew would miss him,* he thought, and he stumbled out to the porticoed pillars, the fresh scented air clearing the swirling mists away. A few deep lungful's of it and the tinkling sound of water lapping on stone gave him the sense of aloneness and peace he needed. Moments of eternity, while the head cleared, and the foreign sounds of a distant, far-from-home place filled the night, giving a feel of timelessness. Bubbles walked down the hill to the water's edge, seeing not the moment but the past, the history of the Middle Ages and back further to the influences which had worked here.

"Dgħajsa Johnny? You want to go other side? Sixpence for you, Johnny." Bubbles stepped into the dgħajsa, holding the fluted, finely carved head post, to steady himself against the rolling motion. Wizened brown hands pushed the boat out expertly, bare toes spreading his weight on the floorboards. A single long-handled oar sculled the carved and ornate wood through the water in customary ease of motion, yet powerful and efficient. The low level of sheeted water lapped in rippling waves across the gap to twinkling lights and a broad expanse of low white steps.

"Is the Barrakka lift working?" Bubbles offered a cigarette as he lit his own. The cigarette disappeared behind an ear with hardly an interruption in the sculling flow.

"Yes, Johnny, lift open." Stained teeth, some capped in gold, grinned. Bubbles pointed to the landing stage. Two quick paddles on the left side, and the prow veered to the steps along the roadway. In darting gossamer light steps, the boatman was on the jetty holding the upright bowpost steady for him to alight.

"That's a shilling, Johnny." The face puckered to a grin

"I got family, six children, Johnny, I need shilling." Bubbles gave sixpence. *They never learn,* he thought. He would have given a shilling if he had said nothing, merely waited for the normal sixpence fare. Still, he admitted to himself, few sailors would bother. Sixpence was a pittance for that work and he put the second coin into the extended palm. At least no screeching, abuse-filled, foreign tongue would follow his progress down the road. He evaded the haranguing horse and carriage drivers and travelled upward in the caged lift, paid his tuppence and stepped through into the surrounding potted garden atop. For a minute or two, Bubbles stood in the garden, with its bench seats empty at this time of evening, and stared over the wall at the harbour and its toy ships laid out below.

Out into the streets, brightly lit narrow cobbled roads and gaping shop fronts of Valletta, the capital town, or was it city? He didn't know. The size of a small town back home, but it had a cathedral; there were sixteen around the tiny island, so he believed. Immense riches within them and the people in rags, he noticed. If that is their priority, then it is their affair. He could think no more about it. He hadn't come to be depressed.

Uniforms filled the streets, sauntering in casual ease from one bar to the next. A taxi took him out of town, the driver flailing the machine through clouds of dust as though demented. *Tyres must be very cheap here,* he thought but said nothing. It was just their way. For heart-fluttering moments of careering seconds, the driver averted his face from the road to duck and peer in angelic fervour at each and every church with accompanying two rigid fingers crossing the forehead. Miraculously, the cars never seemed to hit each other. Always they cleared by at least six inches.

"Ten bob, Johnny." The taxi stopped beside the nightclub. A quiet and well-ordered, single-storey building on the outskirts of Sliema. Bubbles was dressed for the occasion in an old corduroy jacket, which had seen better days, and otherwise what he always wore. This club, open to all the public except servicemen in uniform, catered naturally to the few who had money to spare for such comforts. He liked it for its Italian mood and, if they were the same musicians, Italian light-hearted music. *Strange,* he thought, *that it should have an English name after Britain's wartime statesman.* Not so strange, he supposed, if it had been built after the war years when colonial patriotism had still run high.

Inside it was as he remembered, peaceful and suave, genteel compared to what he had recently left behind. In the hall a study of photographic studio stills depicted the billed entertainers.

Only one he saw. The poised, outstretched stance, beautifully proportioned face and figure of a dancer. *Too perfect,* he thought. The finely sculptured face of brittle expression and lovely eyes of pure hardness.

At a table and with a drink, properly iced and more acceptable to a more refined palate, the lilting music floated around him. In subdued, unnoticeable steps, other tables filled around the room. Lights dimmed, replaced by a vague glow from beneath an elliptical sector of glass flooring at the centre, uncluttered by any obstruction. Music filtered into haunting eastern tones inviting, calling to someone at the edges of the shadow.

A fragile figure danced into the light, hesitating on the sceptre of shadows; white swirling films of sheer material floated in arcs across her body as she moved. The perfectly proportioned limbs undulated in swaying rhythm and entered to the centre of attention. A beautiful smile enticed them, drifting in lulling strides to rhythmic time.

The girl dominated the room with her graceful turns and gyrating body, drawing all eyes to her form. Her eyes lanced in a new direction in smiling invitation, long black hair trailing in covering mists to tantalisingly hide and then reveal the charm. In frenzied tide of changing pace to the strands and pounding sound, she oscillated the bare midriff with its trailing chiffon. The faces of onlookers gleamed, enchanted, focussed in animal concentration.

She floated, dwelt at the perimeter of each group for an individual moment of torment, drew their desire and stepped lightly in whirling stretch of muscles into new forms of grace and beauty. She came to him with a smiling taunt to draw man's need. Captivated by her siren's look and the urgent need in her eye to draw a man's lust, he held her eyes with his own and laughed at her intent. He had seen the despair and hatred but also the need for admiring glances. His eyes smiled, too, and laughed at her tricks. Try as she might with ravishing magic, she could not entice his look downwards from her face. He would not stare in lurid yearning at her body.

She flitted on, each bare footstep delightfully in time to every single beat, lost in the transport of every living, moving part of her body, transforming those eager faces to mires of sweat. The tinkling sounds of rapturous music faded, the magic dispersing. On the dying note, she vanished into shadow.

Lights grew bright; the faces modulated to a semblance of order and masculine show of restraint. Some chosen clown for this performance still haunted himself with the memory, a single chiffon shawl draped about his neck as though he were the victor. Bubbles felt amused by the insight as sophistication slipped from the faces, but he was himself lost. The girl came in normal dress and invited herself to join him.

"Jay," he told her, "but they call me Bubbles."

"Melody, and yes, it is my real name. My mother was a romantic. That's why she married a sailor who deserted to be with her." Many resentful glances came his way, but he ignored them. He was in captivating company until her ageing agent decided to protect his interest. The false bonhomie fooled no one but, in his sophisticated circles, was accepted as the normal way of behaving. Bubbles entered a different world, trying to create his own inside its complexities and falsehoods. Afterwards, he walked the long, lonely streets towards the capital. It gave him time to think.

The duty officer turned on the lights and roused the Mess in the normal morning procedure. Half-empty Coke bottles littered the tables. Bubbles roused himself and the men, who fought for a few minutes more of rambling solitude. He sniffed at the bottles, knowing full well what they contained. There were two major causes of trouble on a boat. One was women; the other was booze. He had one problem, and he didn't want two.

"I don't know who brought this stuff down here and I don't want to, but let's get this clear. No booze in the Mess, okay?" Bubbles, never a disciplinarian, still had the responsibility for what happened in this Mess, and they all knew his views and how he interpreted the regulations. They knew better than this, and that was why he was angry.

"The next one to bring booze down and leave it lying about can standby to get trooped." They all listened in awe. It wasn't often Bubbles lost his rag, but when he did, they took notice.

"What you keep in your bunk or locker, I don't want to know about. If I, or anyone else, gets implicated over this stuff, somebody is for it, okay?"

A lot of them, the ones who didn't know better, thought he was soft because he didn't rant and rave like some others. That's why, when there was cause, he had to make a real show. Personally, he couldn't have cared less as long as it didn't affect efficiency and smooth running, but the rules stated no booze ever, apart from issue. His job was to see that the rules were not infringed.

"Pep-talk over," he said smiling now. "Come on, let's get this lot cleaned up." In the afternoon, various teams went away to use barracks facilities in practice for the sports tournament soon to be held. There wasn't a great deal of time to prepare or brush up on neglected talents. Service work took precedence during the day.

The Maltese naval authorities, accompanied by civilian police, arrived at the dockside where the captured launch lay. In consultation with the Flag Officer's staff, it was decided that a courtesy invitation of Lieutenant Green and three British naval ratings would be allowed onboard during the launch search.

Shane had to admit to himself that the joint endeavour was thorough. It was clear to him, however, that the Maltese were interested only in smuggling activities. He wondered if they were privy to the information, he had managed to glean via intelligence sources. This launch, it transpired, had been used on several occasions during the past year by a rarely encountered, criminal organisation that more usually operated from Turkey. It was significant that the organisation that held the launch hire contract, were a quasi-permanent Soviet trade delegation.

Shane continued to watch the search, directing his own men to delve into rather smaller possible hiding places that the Maltese showed little or no interest in. Eventually, the whole party were satisfied and returned to naval headquarters in town with the few extracted articles. Only one item interested Shane. With great misgivings, he watched the package being opened. A reel of film lay on the table. The small dark policemen immediately closed around it, jabbering an interest.

"This is the property of British Naval Intelligence gentlemen. I cannot allow you to examine it." Lieutenant Green surprised even himself at the outburst from his own lips, but the heads had lifted, the footsteps ceased and this gave him his chance to close his hand tight around the small canister. There would ensue an argument; he knew it, but Shane was determined. This film would not leave his possession. He was, after all, in a foreign land. Without knowing how or why, he simply sensed that the film was of vital importance. The voices became raised in discussion.

There was time now and then, during the forthcoming evenings in harbour to go and see Melody, but Bubbles, more often than not, didn't get to see her alone. He had to contend with the fact that she was constantly ogled.

Men of all types and descriptions gloated at the sight of her wriggling tummy and undulating hips. At first, he thought that he suffered a mere attack of jealousy, but that didn't bother him. What was there to be jealous of amongst them? No, there was something else. He realised that she was intrigued by his attitude and mildly perhaps found him attractive. He could see that she was not interested in him as a man. It was that fact, once he had established it, that galled him. He wouldn't fight it. Life had taught him not to. There was no real connection; he could see that.

Charlie came down the fore-ends with Shane to tell the torpedomen about their new trials. A special trip was laid on, and all five went by bus on the bone-shaking ride into the hill settlement, where scientists and technicians ministered to a new gleaming metal monster. The intricacies of the tin fish were explained and the new loading arrangements. Care must be taken at all times, they said, pointing out various delicate mechanisms. It was all very hush-hush. Top secret, they were told.

In the morning, a covered trailer arrived amidst special security arrangements. Each fish, carefully lowered by dockyard crane, was ensconced in its individual shroud. A once familiar, from long ago, pattern emerged.

The boat went out early in the morning, carried out several test firings, monitored by special electronic test equipment and then, late in the afternoon, back into harbour to load with a new consignment, ready for the next day. For a full ten days, the torpedomen were back in the limelight and consequently suffered great restrictions on their spare time. The rest of the crew had other diversions. There were few commitments for the sonar men during this period. It became common practice to leave inboard a limited number of crew, a dozen perhaps, to amuse themselves ashore and re-join the boat for the next trip and allow someone else to have a day off.

John Bishop discovered a nurses' colony somewhere on the island. English nurses, at that. Quite a few of the men knew about it. It was common knowledge, and even where the hospital and quarters were. John, more enterprising than they were, found the private haunts of this select clutch of females and proceeded to introduce himself. John never passed on this kind of information.

"John will be getting engaged again shortly, I suppose," someone in the Mess remarked during one of the subject's long absences.

"It will be as short-lived as the others if he does. John's meat is barmaids, really. Reckons it's a good way to get free beer." None of them minded John or were jealous of his activities. His kind were appreciated and understood by all men. There was nothing pretentious about him. The charm he used was natural, not manufactured; it was just that he could turn it on or off at will.

"Charm a snake he could," sneaking admiration came with this remark. It was well known that John would not waste his talents in that direction.

# Chapter 27

Squadron sports took precedence in the crew's minds. The participants were hard-at-it, polishing up their techniques. The shooting team collected weapons from St. Angelo's barracks armoury and brought them back to the boat. Now, it was just a question of waiting for transport inland. Bubbles drew the ammunition locker key from the Wardroom, and selected a quantity sufficient for practice. For want of something better, they used an old canvas grip, which had been utilised from one end of the world to the other on many forms of transport and for many purposes.

The three of them sat on deck waiting, using the interval for checking the Arms and loading ammunition into the cartridge cases. "Just look at this!" The chief artificer, Joel Skilly, held up his Stirling machine gun and worked the mechanism several times.

"I don't know how they expect us to win anything with gear like this."

"Look at the state of this rifle. It must have seen service in the Boer war, judging by its condition." Bubbles suspected the rifle barrel was worn if the evidence on its stock was anything to go by. They wouldn't know just how accurate the weapons were until they had used them, but with only one day to practice, it would be too late to change them if necessary.

"Guarantee you that St. Angelo's been raided by other ships' teams. That's why we've got this rubbish." Spider's cheeky face peered down the pistol barrel. It was severely scratched and obviously much used. Bubbles took a long look at it. In his opinion, it was unlikely to be accurate.

"I'll nip down and get you one of ours, if I can persuade the Wardroom that is."

Bubbles was surprised that the Jimmy agreed and allowed him to take one. The honour of the submarine was at stake so far as he was concerned. Bubbles said nothing, listening to a remonstration that it must be looked after. Bubbles listened, expression impassive, and decided he needed to be magnanimous because this man didn't yet know his crew well. If he had, he would not have found it necessary to state the obvious to people, he should have known, had sense enough to work things like that out for themselves.

A utility van arrived for the team, who piled the equipment in and clambered in after it.

"Right, mate." Spider gave the driver a cheerful grin and a pat on the shoulder. The Maltese driver grinned back and ferociously let the clutch out to spin the van off towards the dockyard gate.

"You got any trips lined up after this, cock?" Spider's mind was definitely working out some plan, the other two observed. The driver had another trip, but not for two hours.

"Well, it's like this, matey. We want to go up the range, but not just yet. Know what I mean?" The driver understood Spider perfectly. Bubbles and the 'Tiffy' looked at each other.

"Hang on, Spider. We can't go traipsing round bars with this lot, and we can't let them out of our sight."

Tiffy 'Silky' had something to add, "I don't think it's a good idea to go boozing anyway."

"No, you got me wrong. We'll go up to my place. Quiet snack, cup of tea and my missus can come with us up the range." Spider's eyes twinkled, and they agreed. A few of the crew had brought their wives out for a very brief holiday, hiring apartments for a week or two, depending on what they could afford. With the submarine commitments, it wouldn't be much of a holiday for them.

They couldn't begrudge Spider this chance to have a little more time with her. "We're all going shooting, lovey." Spider dropped the grip and bundled her up in an enormous hug.

"This is Bubbles and that's Silky. Right, lads, plonk yourselves down. I'll go and help Maisie." The two men knew by his look that he would be a hindrance rather than a help in getting the tea.

They heard the giggles from the kitchen and felt a bit embarrassed to be invading their privacy. Spider's head appeared even more tousled if that was possible.

"Only be a minute, lads. Tea's coming up." The cheeky frame disappeared. The intruders had more leisure to check their weapons and set the sights up. Bubbles plucked two hairs from his head and carefully aligned them as crosswire on the back sight, holding them in place with a lick of hardened grease. He sighted down the barrel, which was filthy. It hadn't been cleaned, certainly not for several months.

"I think we can forget this tournament," Silky agreed with him, but at least they would have a go. Bubbles was still sighting down the barrel, but this time from the breech, directing it towards the light from a window.

A terrific scream and flow of gabbling squawks broke out from a balcony nearby. A fat woman in middle age, her hair in a tight bun and with arms flapping in concern, was waddling as fast as she could go. Her loose shawl and flowing dress in some black shiny material flapped its alarm around her.

"I've just upset one of your Maltese neighbours. She must think we are a bunch of bandits." Spider had rushed in at the sound of the fearful outburst. He flung the windows wide.

"All right, Missus, it's only a couple of friends," his voice checked her retreat. She stood her ground, legs firmly braced, arms waving, and a stream of what they supposed must be abuse coming from the angry circle of her mouth.

"And you missus!" Spider shut the window.

"I'll go and sort it out with her old man later. We get the same performance if a pigeon drops its card on her balcony. Right, sup-up lads, dig-in."

They were all ready when the 'tilly' van honked its arrival at them from the dusty street. Miles were burned away in billowing clouds of dust to choke a few pedestrians on the lonely roads. The long winding track shook the passengers and equipment up and down like so many dried peas in an empty can.

"Here, you have got another couple of gears on this monster, mate, slow down!" Spider had his arm around Maisie to cushion some of the effects. She grimaced quietly to herself. Bubbles noticed how alike they were. They had the same ruddy complexion and tousled hair, except that hers was a bit longer, and even had the same splotch of freckles around their noses. They also shared the same casual manner.

The tilly van screeched to a halt, and they gratefully climbed out. Silky arranged the time for the driver to return. Crowds of people, mostly sailors from various ships, aligned in assorted groups to await instructions. The four of them ambled along, two in shabby working dress with shirt buttons undone in the fierce heat and two in just as disreputable shirts and jeans. Spider and his wife carried their open cargo of ammunition and arms between them, a handle apiece. They sauntered from range pit to range pit.

All of them occupied by white-hatted and booted figures with all the correct padding.

"So, this is our practice day, is it? Where's the range allocated to us?" The small group were agitated and disappointed. Some PO and a gunnery instructor, from his badges, seemed to take exception to their presence and non-military bearing.

"Where, may I ask, are you a-going of?" The ramrod figure, immaculate in shiny boots and 'blancoed' ankle gaiters, addressed them and inspected their attire in a withering glance. Silky pulled his battered, oil-stained cap from its hiding place beneath the guns and jammed it on his head in an untidy fashion.

"*Orestes*, and we booked the range for today. How come this lot is on it, GI?" Silky's manner was easy-going, but his words were not. He had seen the look of officious meanness in the PO's eye and had now forestalled his intention by wearing his chief's cap.

"Submarines, that explains it. I don't know about the range being booked. My team booked it solid for a fortnight," his tone was extremely hostile, and the man was again looking them up and down.

"Why aren't you correctly dressed, and why is a woman with you?" He glared at them. Spider edged forward, the light of anger spreading into his face. Bubbles held an arm out to restrain him.

"Look, GI, the armoury hadn't got any decent gear to give us. Some other teams got here two weeks ahead of us. This, by the way," Bubbles made the direction of his glance understood, "this is the gunnery officer's wife, so I wouldn't be hasty about ordering her off."

The combination of Silky's cap badge and Bubbles' explanation seemed to make a difference to the man. Bubbles followed up his advantage. "The tournament is tomorrow, and we are our boat's official team. We haven't had any practice at all yet, and we don't even know if our weapons are any good. When can we use these facilities?"

"You'll have to wait. My lads will be about two hours, after that it is all yours." The GI turned smartly on his heel and marched back to the 'Pits'.

"Shows how much he knows, ignorant basket. Oh, sorry, Mrs W!" Silky had forgotten she was there. Spider's wife smiled, her eyes gleaming in mischief.

"You haven't got a gunnery officer." Her freckles were very prominent.

"Yes, but he doesn't know that, and all GIs are afraid of gunnery officers." They all laughed at Bubbles' trick. Now, there was nothing to do but wait. It so happened that the petty officer gunnery instructor had just taken a position to fire. They stood and watched for a while.

"Well, there's your competition, mate." Spider nodded at Bubbles. The PO was scoring nothing but bullseyes. They noted that he had a brand new, lightweight, self-loading competition rifle with a telescopic sight. After several hours of drifting aimlessly from one competition stand to another, the three men and girl watched as the teams packed up their equipment and marched off to waiting transport.

Dejected or not, they were determined, and spent the rest of the day in solitary practice, calibrating the armament as best they could. The Maltese driver became insistent. They must come now. He had to be on the other side of the island in thirty minutes.

Spider and his wife walked arm-in-arm up the white stucco steps to their apartment and turned to wave as Silky and Bubbles went on their careering way back to the boat. Their arrival coincided with that of another transport, from which piled a muddy and disconsolate bunch of men in football strip. Intermingled were men of the boat's hockey team and, among them, a very pudgy Blinveld.

"Abysmal show, chaps," he greeted them with an upraised hockey stick.

"Bally awful, in fact. I'm afraid they trounced us somewhat." To hear Blinveld's merry tones, it would seem that he enjoyed his game and couldn't have cared less about the score.

They were not dejected long. As soon as they got below, the mail in bundled profusion and disarray cheered them up since it overflowed the table tops. Amongst it, there was one for Bubbles.

"Ho, ho! You're all right there, mate." Bubbles found it particularly offensive when Swingle, of all people, tried to be chummy. He knew that he wasn't all right, even if they had all smelt her characteristic perfume on the letter, and sat there grinning like Cheshire cats. He hid the letter under his bunk to be read later. He knew it was a 'Dear John', and didn't want the others to be watching when he read it.

The remaining matches of the tournament held far more fascination for the crew at this particular time. Time after time, ill-equipped and out-of-training submariners came back to report yet another failure. On each occasion that some individual managed to scrape into the next round of some sport, the focus of attention narrowed towards him. With a subsequent defeat, the supporters felt the loss more. At last, a most surprising figure came to the fore. The slight and ungainly shape of a very physically unfit steward managed to hold a place in the Fencing final.

Randy Sandy, like most, had seen all the Errol Flynn movies, had suffered no other form of preparation, and appreciated none of the subtleties of the art of fencing. He didn't even know the meaning of finesse, let alone apply it. When not drunk, which occasions he minimised to the utmost, he had a swift eye, good coordination and a supple wrist. This last, he explained to an admiring crowd, was due entirely to the constant application of tea towels to the inside of officers' wine glasses. Naturally, steward always swore when explaining about officers.

In the final match, Sandy's opponent, a foppish two-ringer from some ship, had made a grave error. He had allowed himself to be fooled by steward's plum-red nose, mangy seeding of hair and usual slovenly, docile appearance. Not for a single second, at the nominal introduction, had he suspected any tenacity or ambition from the steward. With great panache and an apparent virtuosity, he tested Sandy's skill. It was almost non-existent. The hacking and bludgeoning facsimiles of Flynn style were no contest to a master. Sandy, however, did not allow himself to be touched. He was driven back to stumble in a fallen heap. The spectators gasped at Sandy's imminent demise. Randy Sandy would not admit defeat and continued to swash-buckle from a prone position. He did what no one expected of a demoralised, unsuspecting underdog. He fought back, thrusting and parrying, taking the lieutenant by surprise at his display of determination. Steward saw the flicker of hesitation in disbelief and lunged from the horizontal, arching his back upward with animal ferocity. Spectators roared in delighted approval with arms flung wide in recognition of his strike. There was no doubt whatsoever that Randy Sandy had won. They picked him up and carried him off, shoulder-high. Sandy tittered in absolute glee. Hero of the hour, and as scruffy as a scarecrow.

Ringing sounds of gunshots still echoing in their ears, the team arrived onboard to the cheering procession and news of steward's triumph. Their personal scores from the shoot were known but not the order of merit. News would come by telephone in due course.

Practically, the whole crew celebrated in the Corradino canteen, toasting everyone and everything in an exuberant mood. The word was passed from the boat to the canteen by telephone. News of the shooting match had been delivered. An elected Blinveld, who had the poshest voice around, became the master of ceremonies.

"Ladies and Gentlemen, Sailors and Sludge-mariners," the booming microphone voice was applauded at his last word in an overwhelming crescendo of cheering.

"The pistol shoot was won outright by EM Spider Webb. Big hand for Spider, Gentlemen." Some were too enthusiastic and thought big hands meant 'slap his shoulders until dislocated'. Spider, with a cheeky grin, took it all in good fun.

"I also have the pleasure to announce an equal draw for second place in the Stirling light machine gun competition." Blinveld held his hand up so as to be heard.

"Chief Artificer Joel Skilly. Big hand for Silky!" The clapping was a little more sedate, in deference to his rank, but enthusiastic too.

"In the rifle event, Ladies and Gentlemen. In second place, but only just, and by only one point. Our very own killick of the for'ard Mess…" Anything else that Blinveld intended to say was completely removed from his thoughts by the tumultuous and spontaneous outburst.

All of the assembly had come to realise that their submarine had won the championship trophy and, in the moment of doing so, drowned him out completely. Almost everyone got decidedly drunk, except for those who left early with, if not exactly, homes to go to, then someone to go to.

The highlight of the trip was over, and they had settled into the routine of more torpedo trials. The scientists were still not satisfied with its performance. Time was short, and the programme had to be completed and a successful report sent to London at its conclusion.

The weeks rolled by in the sameness of day-running from Grand Harbour. Wives went home after a welcome interlude, even if most of each day had been spent waiting for evening shadows to fall.

By the end of September, no more wives or girlfriends came. The trip was too expensive to warrant it at this late date. The crew were growing bored with this foreign island and the monotony of their routine. The Summer was going, and it began to grow cold.

John's romances lasted from one week to three, and then another bright prospect for adventure would appear on his horizon. Bubbles grew cold with the weather. His single, all-consuming romance faded for lack of fuel.

The difference between them was too great. They wanted different things and held values too independent of the other's needs.

By the third week in October, the trials were complete. It was time for *Orestes* to leave the Mediterranean, with one last call at Gibraltar for one day. *Orestes* sailed out from the sheltering high walls of the harbour. A few girls, and also non-interested citizens who just happened to be there, waved goodbye from the Gardens of Barrakka. From this island high-point, the toy-like black hull slipped past, breaking the sea into white spumes abreast its tanks. The miniature flag flapped idly against its post, waiting for an open sea wind to set it in motion.

"It's getting near Christmas, you know. Time to think about 'rabbits' for the kids and relatives." Spirits were revitalised at the thought of going home, and they were on their way.

"I think I'll buy my Granny one of those silk kimonos with flowers down the side and a Suzy Wong slit in it." One man at least was seriously considering the list of presents he would buy.

"That's not a good rabbit for your granny, is it?" Somebody had to rise to the bait.

"No, but a good one for me, grandad." The reply brought laughter and the thought of what home meant to different people.

"Where are you going for Chrimbo, Jock?" Tideway had not yet realised that Brown was one man who never participated in frivolity.

"As long as it's off this boat, I don't care." Jock Brown did care very much where he would be for Christmas. The truth was, he didn't know, and he never did, from one year to the next. That was how his home life was, but he wasn't about to tell it to anyone.

"Right, I want some good suggestions for toys to get my kids in Gib. Any ideas?" One of the Mess had his pencil poised, waiting for the other fathers to come to his aid.

Jock didn't want to listen. He did the same as always when the conversation turned to homely things. He ducked into the torpedo compartment, found the metal polish where he always left it, and began to polish the already gleaming copper pipes. All his energy went into it in a desperate bid to shut out all disturbing thoughts.

# Chapter 28

*Orestes* reached Gibraltar and this time, there were very few ships in. The crew virtually had the run of bars and shops to themselves; just about everyone who could, went ashore. The roving band of men joked and laughed their way up the steep hills to town, intent firstly on a binge at the Military Club and then a slightly drunken shopping expedition. Bubbles remained onboard with no particular reason to indulge in either. As a favour to Jock Brown, he took over the duty. This was the best place they knew for the buying of reasonably priced presents, and it was the only chance left this year.

"I suppose John has gone up-homers, then." The duty watch had noticed that John had not gone with the main group. He never discussed his plans with the Mess, remaining very much the man of mystery.

"Even he won't trap any Parties here." It was known to the speaker and all of them that though there were plenty of girls to be seen during the day, by night-time, they had gone.

All the labour on the Rock, whether manual or clerical, was Spanish and returned across the border at La Linea each day. "All those colonial types keep their daughters locked up, I reckon." The duty man joked, but only half-heartedly. For most of the crew, there was little or no romantic interest anywhere they went.

"At boarding school in England, more like," somebody else disagreed. *This obviously was going to be the main topic of conversation,* Bubbles thought, *among the six detainees of the duty watch.*

Bubbles went into the torpedo compartment to his usual perch for privacy. He read the still-scented letter. 'Dear Jay, I feel very warmly about you and the wonderful times we had, but I have my career to think of.' Bubbles read it through and quietly folded it away. For the moment, he could still not bear to throw this last link with her away. In a few days, perhaps, he would be strong enough.

The massive group of merrymakers drank their last toast in Fundador brandy and swayed drunkenly out of tightly gripping cane chairs. The paved patio of the Military Club resounded to the clumsy footsteps of the departing group. Only three stayed amongst the empty bottles and vastness of eight tables which had been pushed together for this session. White-jacketed waiters appeared, to clear away the shambles and re-arrange chairs in informal groups around the open yard. Bob Tideway was decidedly drunk. Fumes swirled about his head. The unfamiliar brandy was taking its toll. Nobody had warned him of its extreme potency. Also, no one had warned him of its strange effects on the mind. He was about to find out.

"C'mon Bob, 'nother drinky." Scouse looked as though he could hardly stand. It was noticeable that his eyes had achieved a glassy stare.

"No." Tideway burped uncontrollably and, with difficulty, forced his way out of the chair.

"Going walkabout," he muttered, fighting his way to the arch leading onto the road. The other two were incapable and in too rosy a glow of their own to try and stop him.

"Sailing-ing in the morning-ing." Creeper Swingle's finger waved into the air at the departing back. The fumes were heavy in his head, too. Tideway stumbled along the steeply shelving narrow street with its high stone wall, having no idea at all where he was. A befuddled brain told him that if he got down to the lowest possible level, then he would be at the water. The boat could not be far away, his reason told him. The man clambered over a low wall and commenced trekking downhill among the boulders and grass-covered stones on the hillside. An eight-foot wall blocked his path downward. At that moment, as his mind attempted to overcome the problem, the full blanketing effect of the brandy swept him away. Tideway shook his head and stumbled onto the roadway. His memory had blacked out completely, and all he knew was that he had to follow the road down. Strangely, this was a double-width road and tarmacadamed with a white line along its centre. If he followed the white line, he would get there quicker. The thought consumed him. Cars whistled by, and some honked their horn while screeching away into the dark. Red flickers of weaving twin lights seemed to follow them.

The van screeched to a standstill, and two white-capped figures of the naval patrol grabbed him by the elbows and lifted him into the back.

"Where are your clothes?" one of them asked. They were trying not to laugh. Tideway looked down and saw that he wore only underpants and one sock.

"Rock ape took 'em," was all he could mumble.

"Up there." He banged his pointing finger on the metal side of his prison.

Tideway fell into sleep, to be woken at the patrol headquarters. "What is your name?" The neat man in dark civilian clothes was sat behind his desk, talking to him.

"Oh," Bob wanted time to think, and the effort was tremendous. "where am I?" he asked. The pen made a note on the white sheet.

"Patrol HQ. I'm the Provost Marshal. What is your name, rank and number?"

"John. What country is this?" Bob's head felt extremely heavy, and it lolled. The pen moved across the paper whilst the other hand indicated to one of the patrol men.

"Get some black coffee," he ordered. His attention turned to the prisoner.

"This is Gibraltar; where did you think you were?" The stern expression was relaxing to a gentle smile.

"Don't know. Thought maybe Malta." Bob sipped the coffee. He was feeling the cold now.

"Can I put me clothes on?" He looked at the man. The patrolman helped him with the shirt and trousers.

"We only found one shoe," he said.

You said your name was John, John, what?" the question was fired at him to penetrate the haze.

"John the Baptist. You want my bloody head, don't you?" Tideway's outburst was ignored. A patrolman brought in a polythene bag with the contents from his pockets. Among them was a very crumpled identity card. The provost made notes.

"What ship are you from, Tideway?" *There didn't seem to be much point in lying now,* Bob thought.

"*Sludgemarine*. I'm a sludge mariner, you know." Bob felt awful, with tight bands of pain around his head.

"Why did you take your clothes off?" The man's question seemed simple to answer, but the submariner didn't reply. The first thought that had come into his head had been. *So you bastards wouldn't see me* but somehow, he deemed that he would be in deep trouble if the words were uttered.

"So, I wouldn't tear me clothes getting over the wall." Miraculously, it seemed, his senses had cleared. *This probably was the reason,* he thought.

"Finish your coffee, and the patrol will take you back to the submarine. I warn you now, that after due consideration, a patrol report might be sent to your Captain."

The Provost had finished speaking and waited for some comment, pen poised to note it down. Tideway kept his mouth shut until he was out at the van. Now that the official part was over, the patrol sailors were prepared to be friendly, chatting and lighting a cigarette for him. "Don't worry, mate. We see a lot of people throw a wobbly here; it's the Fundador wot does it. You didn't do any damage, and they can't do you for indecency. Chances are you'll get away with it."

The van drove away, leaving him at the gangway. Extremely tired, the man stumbled down to climb into bed. The crew returned in the usual manner, in a cavalcade of taxis. Most of the men were cheerfully drunk yet tightly clutching numerous parcels. All manner of personal articles and kit were removed from lockers and thrust under bunks to make room for the brightly packaged 'rabbits'. Many of them found their way to safe niches behind pipes and in fan trunkings. The men cared little or nothing for their personal property, but family presents for Christmas, that was different.

*Orestes* sailed the next morning to battle its way into the Atlantic. The Bay was expected to be rough and would no doubt delay passage home. Armed with this knowledge, the men secured everything which could cause havoc if allowed to slide freely. "Where did you get this, John?" Already, the boat was rolling its hull through the Bay of Biscay. The trim dark hat had fallen from John's bunk. He was not about to disclose his secret.

"Hey! It's an air stewardess' cap. You crafty old man. So, you did get up homers." John apparently had achieved the impossible.

A voice muttered from the depths of a bunk, "Put him in the rotten desert, and some bird would come along and take him home.

The Tannoy screeched and gave way to the voice. "Rough weather ahead. Batten down all loose gear. We expect to be in Faslane in time for the weekend. That is all."

The announcement ended, the submarine made weigh for home.

# Chapter 29

Commander Ruskin paced the marble floors of Box Ten's communication centre and read again the new communiqué. He was pleased at this good news. He noted the puzzled expression of his aide.

"The Murmansk radar has been analysed. Also, the captured components from Zemlya." The Commander's face lit with a broad grin; the heavily ridged eyebrows lifted momentarily.

"Those Portsmouth boffins have done it again. They say here it's a major breakthrough."

The Commander's finger tapped lightly at the flimsy sheet. The younger man noted how elated his superior was. "Technical conference at 1100, sir. Is this what it's about?" The lieutenant knew already that the conference was limited to senior staff only. He could not be there himself, but if the Commander was going, it would surely mean a lot more paperwork for him.

The lieutenant glanced at his watch. "Yes. Three weapons research staff will be attending. This should really be instructive. It's not often we get ahead of the Americans in this field."

The Commander rubbed his hands together. "Surely it will be turned over to them, sir. They have the resources for development, after all."

The two men continued their pacing. "Yes. They will get it now that our chaps have done the donkey work. Quite probably, they will sell it back to us as a working weapons programme later on, too."

Commander Ruskin pulled pensively at his ear lobe, deep in thought. It aggravated him to think that the long, familiar pattern of weapons franchising to their allies would continue. Always, it seemed, at the greater cost to Britain in the long run. Unfortunately, though, this was a race against time. No doubt he thought the details for transfer to American defence departments would be issued at this forthcoming meeting. A good result against the Soviets, certainly.

The hall was now filling with the upper echelons of Box Ten, along with senior members from other intelligence services. A green light began to flicker above the conference room doors, the signal for authorised personnel to enter. Inside the doors, the figures filtered past the unusual sight of a hastily assembled security desk. Each of the visitors produced an identity card, passed his left hand over the open oblong scanner and waited until his own photograph and record of hand print came up on its tiny screen. Two white-coated figures busied themselves behind their desk, processing hand prints, logging information and, at the same time, attempting to be unobtrusive.

Within the space of time allotted, the screening process was completed, and the auditorium contained its quota. Security staff gathered up their paraphernalia and left, the huge oaken doors being locked behind them. The assembly settled, and the rustle of papers from the platform diminished.

The speaker held their attention, commencing his monologue on the technical specifications and performance of the 'New Murmansk radar', as it had been called. The speaker's pointer flicked up to rest upon a diagram, one of many pinned to a huge hardboard sheet in prominent view.

"You will notice, gentlemen, that this outer right-hand beam utilises a high-frequency band, the left outer beam operating only a few cycles per second lower." The speaker coughed, cleared his throat and continued. "The right lobe carrier frequency is in the heat sensing spectrum and is, therefore, able to detect intruders by their infrared activity. The left lobe frequency is generated not by an electronic source but by simple harmonic sound vibrations. The method, of course, is extremely complex, especially the amplification unit," the speaker's voice droned on, reciting learned details. All minds present grappled with the concepts involved.

"This then will detect pressure waves due to high-velocity movement and..." the speaker emphasised the significance of his statement by an extended pause before completing the statement, "also variations caused by course alteration. This then produces a doppler shift, which the beam can monitor and relay along its own path via a comparator unit to the tracker. This, then, is the system's defence mode controlled by two separate modules."

The pointer came down, pointing now at two sectioned replicas of the stolen chassis units, their internal organs exposed to this select group of viewers. "A third beam is incorporated..." The wooden stick wavered momentarily over the third unit before illustrating yet another diagram as the voice resumed its practised tenor, "but is non-directional. That is, it floats, so to speak, between the left and right lobes, constrained by their frequencies. This intermediate beam ranges through a predetermined sequence throughout a complete range from subsonic to ultra-radiation spectrum. The range of oscillation is timed at between ten and fifteen seconds for one complete cycle of operation. The central funnelling beam, gentlemen, is the key." The scientist accentuated the last word, turned towards his audience and administered a cursory beaming glance from one corner to the other. He was warming to his subject, noting with satisfaction the rapt attention his words produced amongst them.

"The central beam can be used in the defence mode by virtue of its ability to scan the frequency range of its target's instruments, communications and, where appropriate, carrier signal. It will identify all such frequencies and pass the information back to the tracker dish. At the same time as identifying, it will jam the signal once the aircraft or missile is within its range of operation."

A murmur of interest rippled around the room, and a few prepared as if to speak but finally thought better of it at this stage. The room became quiet as the scientist looked up from his copious notes.

"Where the radar is being used in the attack mode, which means, of course, as a guidance system, it is very similar to our own prototype Phosphor Cobalt CV6. There are, however, one or two very distinct differences. Before I go into that, I will first of all explain the floating beam principle for attack."

Once again, the papers shuffled on the desk. The scientist extracted the sheets ready for his next discourse, perused the one he was extracting the current details from and then addressed his audience. "Instead of panning through the scale, one frequency can be locked into the central beam, which now guides the missile into its target. The outer lobe beams become the vector coordinates set in the first firing sequence by the missile tracker and operator. However, the homing signal beam will, if intercepted by an outside source, automatically switch to another random frequency, continuing to home the device." The hubbub of voices around the hall distracted the speaker. Used to giving such in-depth dissertations, he realised that the time had come for his audience to consider the implications of this superior Soviet technology.

Before doing so, he knew that it was necessary for him to draw the distinctions between the two recently developed systems. "Gentlemen," the scientist had managed to draw their attention back, "you will probably be aware that our own system, CV6, has now reached the production stage. The United States Defence Department will administer this, intending to equip their surface and nuclear submarine fleets with CV6. In one essential respect, our system is, or rather will be, superior to the Murmansk Radar. Ours will have a virtually limitless range, dependent naturally on the restrictions imposed by the missile fuel."

It was becoming increasingly difficult for the professor to rivet the audience's attention on him. Many of them were leaning across to have a hurried conversation with a colleague. "The Soviet system can be operated successfully only within a relatively short range. Tests have not been carried out by us yet since this had been an extremely rushed programme. We are therefore not sure of the range, but it is our assessment that one thousand miles would probably be the accurate homing range to within fifty to one hundred yards of target."

The professor was drawing to a close. He knew the rest of what would follow was beyond his specialised knowledge. It was now a question of high diplomacy and governmental policy, as well as intelligence appraisals, which would determine what use was to be made of his discourse. The scientist gathered his papers and nodded towards the director of Box Ten.

Towards the back of the hall, a telephone light flashed its intermittent dull red warning. The nearest figure leaned over, picked it up, listened for a moment and raised his voice above the throng.

"Commander Ruskin?" the voice enquired; the telephone receiver held high above the head as an indication to whoever should answer. The grey-ridged eyebrows knitted in their customary frown, their owner rising to cross the room. His aide had thought the teletyped message vital. The Commander replaced the receiver, raised his hand in the direction of the Director of Naval Intelligence as a gesture of apology, and swiftly crossed to the huge doors.

The young lieutenant was not in the slightest abashed at his superior's thunderous look. "Just decoded from Flag Officer Malta, sir." The lieutenant handed the yellow paper over and briefly consulted the agent's report.

"Agent Foxglove's report from Havana." The outstretched hand paused and did not at first locate the unseen blue sheet. The Commander's eyes scanned rapidly, taking in the details of the discovery and retrieval of a reel of film from an intercepted Soviet hired launch in Malta. The developed film contained circuit photographs of CV6 equipment onboard submarine *Orestes*. *This was indeed serious,* he thought. Even if this one had not got through, it meant that there would inevitably be another attempt. The Soviets were certainly aware of CV6's importance. They began to walk down the corridor in the direction of Fleet Operations.

"We had better get *Orestes* out to sea again. Find out where she is, how long she is in for and what her schedule is." The lieutenant's retreating footsteps sounded loud on the marble. The commander, having considered, now had time for the second sheet. So engrossed was he in this report from Cuba, that he was not aware of Colonel Gilchrist's approach.

"Something here from one of my chaps. Should interest you, Commander." The two men stood alone in the great empty hall, the one engrossed and the other anxious to continue his own operation. The grey eyes looked up in brief greeting to the colonel.

"Morning, Harry. Influx of Russian missile technicians to Cuba. They're supervising the construction of a base." The commander was pensive.

"'Afternoon' actually, old boy. My man in Glasgow says there's a Russian agent onboard submarine *Orestes*." The Colonel's florid chin collapsed its toothy grin at the look of alarm on the other's face.

"One of the crew, you mean?" Already, the Commander was looking for the nearest telephone.

"Yes, and my agent says he is no longer a sleeper. No details yet, I'm afraid."

Colonel Harry Gilchrist had not realised until now just how much of a bombshell he had inadvertently dropped. The Commander was already on his way to a telephone, where his lieutenant saw him dialling the Northern Sector Command Centre. "Priority clearance for submarine *Orestes* to divert to home base. Yes, I will clear it with Med. and Home Command." The telephone was slammed down. The Commander was aware that the news had come at the worst possible time. It was absolutely imperative to get *Orestes* out of the way for a while. It was hardly necessary now to read the fresh-faced lieutenant's displacement order for the submarine. He had just cancelled it with one quick call.

"Dick. Get personnel security to run a Class A check on all crew of *Orestes*." The lieutenant was amazed at the Commander's use of his first name. It was most unusual and told him more than perhaps anything else could have, that something big was about to break. He also knew that he could forget his week's leave which was due.

"And Dick, I need it quickly. Three months won't do for this one." Briskly, the men went their separate ways. *The Director had better be told about this one*, the Commander thought as he again read the report from Cuba.

# Chapter 30

Sophie Wilkes rubbed her hands together in anguish, harder than was necessary to chafe warmth back into them. It was colder now that winter was approaching, sooner than anyone expected. She glanced quickly at the office calendar above the little Jewish man's head. November the fourth, she read. It hardly seemed possible, but it was not that which disturbed her.

"The submarine returns today, Isaac. We knew nothing of this. Why did we have no advance notice?" Isaac noticed, indeed could not avoid, the threat in her voice and how very cold and penetrating this young girl's eyes had become; beautiful grey eyes that now barely concealed a venomous spirit. He bowed a small nodding gesture to her before answering in calm, unhurried tones.

"Since Vassall's capture in Malta, it has been extraordinarily difficult." The man found it difficult to get his tongue around some of the words. The effect was almost comic, yet the girl nor the two men were amused.

"We have to reorganise our people to replace him. It will not be easy now. It was unexpected that the submarine *Orestes* would return so soon. We have no relevant information. Blinveld's reports are incomplete."

"Yes, we know that," the girl interrupted him, not able to control the sudden anger she felt.

Their operation was not going well. Only some of Blinveld's correspondence about CV6 had got through. The technical details were incomplete and insufficient. She could not wait for the photographs, and time was short. It was necessary to despatch immediately what she already had garnered to Moscow. The courier was ready to leave tonight.

Boris sat in silence, his brooding Siberian eyes betraying nothing while he watched her. This was her time of trial, as the Politburo had been informed by the KGB and they were not pleased. She was responsible in their view for the Zemlya raid and its consequences. She had failed to give adequate warning. Boris could detect fear behind her anger; her vitriolic words poured over the small man.

"Comrade," Isaac's voice had become like treacle, wheedling, determined to weather her verbal assault.

"Blinveld cannot be of much further use. It is likely that he is a suspect, even compromised already, yet he is too valuable to sink with the rest. We must make plans to get him out, and if possible, without destroying his credibility."

Sophie Wilkes still rubbed her hands. They were no longer cold, but it was a means of directing her nervous energy. She paced the small backroom office in agitation.

"Contact him, arrange a meeting for tonight." Deep in thought, her hand dismissed the little man from her mind. She was aware of this thickset creature watching her as though he were stalking prey, his huge shoulders hunched in concentration.

"It was a masterful play to have Castro make that announcement for a fishing fleet base, was it not?" Boris knew her mood, saw her irritation licking towards him. He was ready and would forestall it.

"Yes, it was clearly necessary to divert the attention of the American and British Intelligence. We are buying time, Comrade, that is all. How else could we explain such a heavy presence of technicians?" Her question could not be answered, she knew, but it gave her time to think in the paid for silence.

"Our operation is gathering momentum. We must make use of this missile technology lead. It will not last long, and now it becomes a question of consolidating our political strength by using it to advantage."

The girl continued to pace; her own words were bringing her comfort. Her anguish evaporated at the heady thought of triumph. Her failure to prevent Soviet radar secrets from falling into enemy hands would be overlooked in the glow of the great moment to come. "A fleet is being assembled at Vladivostok now and should be ready within the week." Boris permitted a large and alien grin to dwell on his leathery jowl.

"Your information is out of date, Comrade." The girl's face lit in haughty disdain, and for a moment, she stopped her interminable tread on creaking floorboards. She savoured the effect of her outburst, saw the grin slip away, replaced by a rigid mask of inscrutability.

"Our fleet has already sailed. Loading of missiles will continue at sea."

An icy wind buffeted through the open shop doorway for a lingering moment. The customer, chilled in the unexpected blast, experienced difficulty in pulling two-handed to make the door shut behind her. The bell above it jangled its tinny whine of protest and settled into reluctant stillness. She felt the comforting warmth of a wall heater circling in the disturbed air.

The manager's dark, lustrous hair fluttered in the fleeting draft and came to rest against her cheek. She again mused momentarily about the three shadowy silhouettes against the dimpled glass of the corner office. Allowing her thoughts to roam in pursuit of intrigue, she imagined a complicated web of espionage and treachery. The figures moved, nodded, rebuked and mouths opened, directing a stream of unheard invective. She smiled at herself, shaking herself in amusement at her own childish romantic notion. It occurred to her that she had some work to do. She glanced again at the list on the desk. Book titles stared up at her, and one held her attention. Bubbles would like that one; she knew he would and would be delighted at her gift. She consulted her watch. He would be here soon. That thought warmed her. It was her afternoon off, and they could be together for a few blissful hours. She knew the book was at the back of the store. It wasn't really eavesdropping on her colleague book buyer, and in any case, she would only be there for an instant, just long enough to pluck the book from its shelf.

The young couple sat close together in the back of his old car, alone with the faint smell of cracked leather seats and a clear sight of myriad stars against the night. Bubbles felt comfortable and relaxed, as he always did when close to her. It defied analysis, this feeling. When he was away, he forgot that it was like this. The gentle side of his nature would be driven away by the brusque, cold manner of his life, the way they all lived, the abruptness, and the very real chance of being suddenly presented with a harsh reality of imminent danger. For this moment, at least, he could ignore it. For them, here on this bleak Scottish hillside, at this moment, it ceased to exist. He could not reconcile his wanting to be near her with the fear of his futile hope of a good future for them. So his anguish simmered with this uncertainty about his feelings.

In the passing of these comforting hours, the frost settled around them, glistening in grit-bound clusters along the car's outer shell black paint. The cold crept under the doors and chilled them. Bubbles felt that this brief respite was ending. He wished it would not, but time could not stand still. She sensed his unease and coaxed the bleak story of his young failures from him. She understood now why he had been so reluctant to commit his feelings. She knew that he was afraid it could all happen again. She had no answer; there could be none from her. She trusted him and given time, he perhaps would learn to trust again.

Bubbles drove her home, back into the squalid city, which represented all that he loathed. His distaste, of course, rested on his own crowded experiences, a short lifetime of squalid places causing restless memories in only a handful of years. *Her life was secure; she was untouched and warm in her innocence,* he thought. He had no right to touch it, to change her view of the world. He had meant to end it here, to say farewell. This should have been the last time, the last kiss, but the look in her eyes unsettled his resolve.

The car drew away, and cold though it was, she waited and waved. She knew he would see her in the rear-view mirror as he drove. She wanted him to have this memory to hold on to. To know that she could wait, although the waiting was cold and bitter. The night was fresh and empty. Houses were dark, and streets uncluttered. It was a good night for thinking, for working things out. Bubbles' mind drifted back over the events of this evening, of the things they had talked about. He did not want to think about himself, about his own petty problems. He was going back along the twisting lochside road, back to the submarine, back to his own peculiar reality, and the rest must be thrust into the recesses of his mind. There was no use in dwelling upon what might be.

What had she said before they had allowed themselves to get so intense? She had been talking about the bookshop. It was her passion, one of the nice things he knew about her. She cared about her work. He had got used to the romantic excursions she indulged in. She saw things that didn't exist, but something she had said had rung somehow as possibly true. He admitted to himself a possibility of spy espionage occurring in that back room of her workplace. After all, details of what his submarine was engaged in at this time was sensitive information, to say the least. Perhaps he should report it, but to do so might well compromise this newfound trusting relationship. Did he want to risk that? He must consider the problem further; after all, it was only a hunch of hers.

The battered old car drew into the compound, the bright lights of the depot ship loomed high, blotting out that section of the sky. He remembered that she had overheard the book buyer and her conversation with three foreigners who, Alicia said, always seemed to frequent the shop but never dealt with anyone else. The name the book buyer mentioned rang a bell in his mind, but he couldn't quite place it. They had been talking about an

American lieutenant, someone by the name of Palmer.

Bubbles tucked the car into a corner, locked the door and then disconnected the battery. He didn't know how long it would be before he saw this old heap again. If he was lucky, the wheels would still be on it when he came back the next time. Palmer, Palmer. Where had he heard the name before? He had been prepared to dismiss her insistence about an exchange of prisoners as being wild fantasy. Perhaps they had been discussing the plot of some book. It seemed the most logical explanation to him, except for that specific name, Lieutenant Palmer.

Bubbles came to a sudden halt, standing just below the long gangway, and stared up at the huge round yellow lights of the depot ship. He had remembered that, just once, Joe the diver had mentioned his companion's name. Palmer had been the lieutenant who had gone on the mission. Bubbles remembered the incident well. Some of the crew, most in fact, had thought the lieutenant was English. It was difficult to say since he had kept so very much to himself, hardly ever stirring from the Wardroom. On thinking about it now, it occurred to Bubbles that perhaps avoiding the crew had been deliberate. On the only occasion that he himself had heard the officer speak, it had struck him that the accent was New England rather than anything else. It hadn't mattered to him then, but the more he thought about it, the more significance seemed to be attached to it now.

In the time it took Bubbles to cross the depot ship and descend into the familiar stale, oily smell of the submarine, he had been able to make up his mind. Someone would have to be told, and who else but Shane? Bubbles disliked the prospect, but it would have to be done.

# Chapter 31

At breakfast the following morning, the crew uncertain of the submarine's new programme waited for news. Before long they knew their First officer would make some announcement to clarify the situation. Already there was a rumour going around that their stay in harbour would only be a matter of days.

"Don't understand this at all. We dash back from Malta, exercises cancelled. No reason given. That's not like the 'pusser' at all, that isn't," the speaker aired his views between mouthfuls of Curly's offering of bacon and eggs.

"Perhaps me-lords have realised how hard they've been pushing us. Now they don't want the 3rd Submarine Squadron aces to crack up under the strain, so we are all going to get six months' holiday." No one was taking the banter of the two men as anything other than frivolous nonsense, which probably hid an underlying feeling of insecurity.

"Do you hear there?" the loudspeakers crackled into life.

"First Lieutenant here. We have received a message from Captain SM3 concerning our immediate movements. The Captain has directed that this message should be read to you now. The message begins. 'To Captain submarine *Orestes*. Due to a serious engineering fault onboard submarine Tarquin, you are ordered to take over her northern patrol scheduled for today. Due to your storing requirements and the fact that you only arrived home yesterday, your sailing is delayed until 0800 tomorrow. We very much regret the necessity of sending you but sincerely hope that your crew will understand the severe problems this squadron faces at present. We are under operational strength. You will also be aware that a crisis is looming in the Pacific, which could involve a sea presence by this squadron. Good luck. We will see you again in five weeks. Extra leave will be granted on your return. Specific orders to follow. Signed, Captain SM3.' That is all."

Men gathered in the crowded space in the for'ard Mess had listened to the broadcast in silence until near the end. They were shocked and growing restless and angry. "Christ, another bleeding sneaky peeky. What the hell are they playing at?" The man's outburst echoed only too well the feelings of the others. Bubbles was apprehensive, knowing that all the signs indicated a difficult trip ahead. They, along with some of the other more responsible ratings resented the lack of real information. It was obvious to him that much more was going on behind the scenes. At times like this, he felt that they were all just so much cannon fodder. It was necessary though, to mask his feelings. Spirits were low enough already without him fuelling their bitterness.

The loudspeaker began to crackle, heralding yet another announcement, "Do you hear there? First Lieutenant speaking. Store ship will commence in fifteen minutes. This will be an all-day operation. There will be no shore leave. Repeat; there will be no shore leave. We sail at 0800 tomorrow. The Captain will address the ship's company in five minutes. That is all." Just as the voice faded away, a wry-faced Ginger Bates knocked on the passageway door and entered, rubbing his hands together.

"Just been up top and it's bloody cold. Watch your footing lads; there are freezing patches on the casing." Ginger nodded; his flushed face grinned in acceptance of the outthrust cup of tea. His hands closed around it, crushing the warmth into his fingers.

"Won't be too bad once we can get weaving. The first load will be over shortly." The Scratcher nodded at Bubbles.

"Do you want to supervise below decks loading?" It was agreed. Those doing the first two-hour stint out in the exposed open were searching out long-unseen warm clothing.

"This is the Captain speaking." Those who could find room sat down again, squeezing in to make more room. The submarine's ultimate voice of authority was always worth listening to. Now at least, they would be given more definite information.

"You will all have heard the bad news about our going north. Well, that is what we are paid for. This is what is expected of us so we will just have to get on with it. However, I would like you all to know that our job is important. For security reasons I cannot tell you just how important, but I can assure you that the success of our last northern mission has contributed in no small measure to the security of the western world."

The calm authoritative sound came across clear and precise, holding everyone's attention. The brief pause allowed the significance of his words to penetrate. "Some of you will be aware of the trouble which has been brewing between East and West in recent years: The Cold War, the arms race, etcetera. This morning, only ten minutes ago a news bulletin was issued over the radio, reporting that the American President John F. Kennedy has announced the fact of the USSR installing guided missile bases in Cuba." Once more the crew waited during the baited pause. No one moved or spoke. The clock could be heard to tick, seeming louder than anyone could remember.

"The President will not, I can assure you, allow this situation to develop unchecked. The threat to their national security is too great. The same threat is thereby offered to the rest of the western world. There are many roles to be played by our combined armed services, in order to sustain world peace. Our allotted task is to sail north in surveillance. We will be watching those people who make threats against us at their own door. This is a vital task, and we have been chosen to see it through. We will see it through and return home to a well-deserved rest. That is all."

No one said anything but quietly donned their extra clothing and squeezed past each other in the narrow passage between tables, disconsolate and unbelieving. There was nothing to be done but get on with the immediate task. Whatever they thought would make no difference.

Despite the cold, the loading of food stores went smoothly. Towards noon, the sun made a welcome appearance, and gradually, it warmed the air. This, and the sheer effort of physical work, helped to reassert the natural boisterous spirits of the young men.

News came through by rumour that an award was to be made that day to Hogarth for his conduct on their last patrol. It had been acknowledged that his efforts had undoubtedly saved the submarine from grave damage and possibly its loss. The crew were of the opinion that if not for his action, the boat would certainly have sunk, and all of them along with it.

Under normal circumstances, he would have been summoned to London for the full panoply of an official ceremony and award of a medal. In some inexplicable way, the event had gathered dust in bureaucratic in-trays, passed from one administrative section to another, and after some short time 'for documentation purposes', passed into several out-trays as well. The shirt-sleeved hours of summer had finally given way to the full blast of central heating amidst the grey offices of winter. At last a decision was made, but due to the unusual aspect of the mission and the inadvisability of drawing news media and public attention to it, only a formal Notice of Merit could be bestowed. It had been decided on the depot ship that instead of waiting for the Admiral's visit and the full parade for Hogarth's award, it would be best to expedite the matter before *Orestes* sailed. In the late afternoon, after stores loading was complete, Leading Mechanical Engineer Owen Hogarth received his six-inch by nine-inch Certificate of Merit at the Captain's table, saluted, shook hands and went aft to change out of his number one uniform. He was interrupted by a call asking him to the for'ard Mess.

The real approval ceremony was about to begin, staged amongst the clutter of cups and carelessly thrown clothes in the seaman's Mess.

"I hereby award you the Order of the Cocoa Lid." Harman, the elected Master of Ceremonies, stood atop the table and bade Hogarth to rise. Big Garth, grinning from ear to ear, his face flushed in embarrassment, jacket undone, lanyard and collar hanging in disarray, stood for the comical play to run its course. The seamen had planned it on hearing the news, having sent someone inboard to acquire the most garish multi-coloured ribbon that could be found. Scouse had gone one better. He couldn't find anything suitable, so he brought a deckchair canvas. It was duly cut into an acceptable width of twelve inches, incorporating red, green and blue with orange seaming bands of colour through its length. Harman insisted the man should bow his head and, with lavish mock ceremony, settled the great loop with tin disc attached around his broad shoulders.

"You may be seated. The festivities will commence." Harman jumped to the floor while the tea was being poured. Garth, still grinning away in an attempt to appreciate the humour, inspected the decorated cocoa tin lid bestowed upon him; its surface was painted blue and his name unevenly punched into it by metal letter stamps, the end result looking like a row of crooked teeth. After discussing the incident and extending congratulations, the conversation lapsed into normal realms of curiosity about leave and future prospects.

Lieutenant Hawks read through the dispatch once more and noted the time of his staff briefing. He smoothed his hand over the cabin bed to remove its rumpled appearance where he had sat. *The steward wouldn't be pleased with me,* he thought and grinned to himself. He looked around the cabin. Nothing was lying about that shouldn't be. He picked up the worn executive slim-line briefcase. No doubt he would need it for the briefing papers and sealed orders. The Captain checked his appearance in the mirror, wiped away the single bead of sweat from his forehead, and switched the lights off.

As expected, the meeting had been extremely detailed, punctuated with all the latest data and the usual clutch of official papers. Handshakes all round, as was customary, ended the briefing. The night air was sharp, but he still felt the close atmosphere of the conference room. There seemed to be a fault in the depot ship's air conditioning. Jeff Hawks wiped his brow. He was pleased that he had received assurances about relief for his Torpedo Officer. It was time now to inform him of the decision.

Lieutenant Phil Green waited at the door for a moment before knocking. "Come in, sit down. I have your history sheet here, and I want you to read my assessment." The Captain sat on the bunk and watched how quickly Shane skimmed through it. He was smiling.

"Does this mean I am to take up a new appointment, sir?" Shane was sure that this was the case. The report was a good one, and at last, it meant that he could escape the past.

"I recommended you, quite forcibly, I might add, for Commanding Officer's Training School. This is your letter of appointment confirming that the posting has been agreed." The Captain shook hands in congratulation and handed the official document to Shane. The younger man was surprised that he had been selected after such a short time in submarines. It took much longer, several years longer in fact, to achieve it, normally. The Captain seemed to be reading his thoughts.

"I appended the trace records of all your attacks to my request. It is due entirely to your flair in that field, which makes you eligible. Good luck. I wish you success for the future."

Phil Green packed his few belongings ready for an early departure the next day and decided a celebration was in order before settling up his wine bill with the Wardroom. Shane was reasonably pleased with himself. He suspected that this new appointment and the bright future it offered him was not, as the Captain supposed, due solely to the duties he performed onboard *Orestes*. A mental image of the squat, unshaven Welshman flitted across his mind. It reminded him of this unfinished business with the agent and of the meeting yet to come, but he was not about to let it dampen his spirits.

The telegram arrived onboard *Orestes* to coincide with the evening meal. The Captain read it through and looked up at Brown. This man seemed to have bad luck follow him around like a dog.

"I'm very sorry about this bad news, Brown. I cannot promise, but I will try to get you away in an hour or two." Brown went for'ard and as usual said nothing to anyone while he got changed into his civilian clothes. He packed all the gear he could cram into his holdall.

"I'm going on leave. If anybody wants this stuff, help yourself." The short utterance was enough to tell them all that Jock had more personal troubles. Nobody said anything but merely sorted through the books and items of kit he bequeathed.

"You know I have never met anyone as dour as that Scotsman," Tideway said and wondered why they all looked at him that way. He hadn't been onboard very long and didn't know the man, they told him. Tideway shut up; he had been put in his place for the day.

"You'll be saying Jock's a Jonah next. Well, if he is, it is only to himself, matey." Spider was becoming a force to watch in the Mess. With such a cheerful attitude to everything and everyone, nobody could resent him for long.

"'ere did yer read this?" Scouse was reading the daily newspaper and found something of interest.

"That prophecy bloke reckons there's going to be a traumatic upheaval causing big bother in the western world."

"What does it actually say? Give us it here." Somebody took the newspaper and read it aloud, "Upheaval causing deep concern and with dive consequences. Here, that can't be right." Bubbles had a look at the paper now. Several were crowding around. Sailors were still superstitious, it seemed, or was it just idle curiosity?

"It should read 'dire' consequences, not 'dive'. It's a misprint." Bubbles pushed the paper away.

"I don't like the sound of that." Scouse had the paper again.

"It says 'ere DEEP concern and DIVE consequences. That's two words meaning underwater. I don't like it."

"Ah, belt up, you silly sod!" None of them were prepared to listen to Scouse rambling on. He reckoned it was time to get himself transferred off this boat.

"No, I'm sorry, Peters. Your request for the Physical Training School has not come through yet. See your new Divisional Officer after Christmas." Shane was slightly tipsy as he talked to Scouse Peters. He made the man see reason and then shut the door. The brother officers raised their glasses and proposed a toast.

The evening was beginning to draw a cold atmosphere down, closing it into a dense layer of chill. Frost would form on the deck tonight. The trot sentry did not relish thoughts of standing idly about, his feet on the cold steel casing while the frost bit his ears. For some reason, the duty electrician had not been able to provide any heaters up in the accommodation hatch, where the sentry usually stood. At least that would have kept his feet warm. The 'Greeny' had said something about his PO elec. taking the keys so he couldn't get into stores. Whatever the reason, he was getting damned cold up here. It looked like it would be a quiet night. The trot sentries of the other two boats alongside agreed with him. They had no intention of staying up top in this weather. There wasn't likely to be much activity. Who would be roaming about late at night if they didn't have to? They asked each other.

The trot sentry walked briskly up and down the full length of the for'ard casing. Out of boredom, he counted the steps aloud, noting the clouded haze burst away from his mouth with each word. He looked at his watch, and the luminous dial indicated it was just on nine o'clock. *Anyone who was going would have gone inboard by now,* he thought. It so happened that he had paused right beside the sonar dome. He had a sudden brilliant idea – *the Penguin could be made use of.* There it was, rigidly bolted onto the edge of the casing, close to the accommodation hatch. A little short for a man perhaps, but from a distance, unlikely to draw undue attention if it was done properly. With a furtive look round to see that no one observed, the sentry darted below and rummaged around for a spare watch coat. He found one a little shorter than the others. Anyone going on watch up top always picked the biggest one they could. The extra weight of heavy serge material was well worth the full draped protection it gave to the legs. If one could be found to extend to the ankles, then all the better.

People were used to seeing the trot sentry like that, with his collar turned right up around the ears so that only the hat could be seen above. *Excellent,* he thought, *and nobody will suspect.* Carefully noting all the accesses along the depot ship's deck for signs of star-gazing officers, the sentry fitted the spare watch coat around the penguin. He even found a piece of wood to fit inside across the shoulders.

Petters, the biggest bloke in the Mess, was asleep, so it was quite safe to use his monstrously outsized cap to perch atop the silent dome. Just for a little extra realism, a nice thick white towel went around the neck, peeking out below the upturned collar. The trot sentry was very pleased with the effect. *Now,* he thought, *should he do something with the arms?* Maybe he could rig up a newspaper or something to occupy the empty sockets. On reflection, it didn't seem such a good idea. It might draw unwelcome attention. They weren't supposed to read on watch, or smoke, eat or even drink. Of course, everyone did, but soon hid the fact if anyone approached. No, he would just stick the armless cuffs into pockets. That was better; it looked more natural. The sentry moved away to observe his handy work. *Just the job,* he thought. It was perfect, and no one would suspect.

Usually, only a boat going on patrol had this particular sonar dome fitted. The equipment was too expensive to fit on every boat. It just so happened that theirs had stayed after the last patrol. *What luck,* he thought. It looked quite natural since the other two boats didn't have one. A half-hour later, the sentry was convinced it was safe to sneak below. Actually, he meant to go up again, but he got involved in the Mess conversation and forgot about it.

The Wardroom was in high spirits, enjoying much laughter in each other's company. At the moment, they were discussing the crew and their peculiar antics. Although not at the time, it now seemed amusing that on the last three consecutive days in port at Malta, one of the crew and sometimes two had stumbled past the Wardroom door, having just returned from shore. It was well understood, of course, that the ordinary sailor was apt to complain at everything and anything. It was believed, in fact, that a sailor was not happy unless he could drip about something.

The Wardroom, full of goodwill at this moment, decided that on seeing the door open, the men must have thought it a golden opportunity. Obviously, they would not have dared ordinarily to so forcefully make their feelings known. Even the abusive way in which each had made his complaint, could be laughed about now.

Reading one's horoscope was the expression currently in favour, they believed. One of the officers had a thought. Supposing, he conjectured, that someone should decide to follow the recent pattern and read another Wardroom horoscope tonight. That was not likely, Shane informed them. Most of the crew apparently were onboard tonight. What a marvellous opportunity to strike back. Hoist them on their own petard, so to speak.

Shane volunteered to administer the required reprimand. They all found it highly amusing when he had some difficulty in getting up from the table. Shane made his way for'ard, assisting himself along the way with numerous handholds.

"I am leaving the submarine tomorrow and I wanted to say how much I have enjoyed serving with you." Shane stood on uncertain legs in the centre of the Mess. They all sat stunned at his sudden appearance in their midst, without announcing his arrival or according the courtesy of knocking. They would have to excuse him as he was obviously in high spirits.

"Before I go, I thought I would return the compliment and read a f-few horoscopes." Shane was beaming to all and sundry.

Now that he stood here, he realised, looking at their faces, that they weren't at all a bad bunch. Still, now that he had started, he must go on quickly.

"You," he said, looking at John Bishop.

"You've got brains, too many to be wasting your time on the lower deck. If you applied yourself, you could go far. Your severest fault is that you don't care about anything. You use people to get what you want." Shane turned quickly to the next before John's sharp wit got to work. John merely stared at the weaving officer. He thought it would be a waste of breath, and in any case, there was no point in trying to win an argument with an officer.

"You walk about like a rag merchant." The attention had fallen on Spider. The cheeky grin spread even wider.

"You might smile, but appearances matter if you are ever to achieve anything." Shane glanced at the next, which was Hogarth, who still held the cup of tea.

"You are too easy-going. People like you, and that means you can't be efficient. You have no drive, no ambition." Hogarth's face was turning red. It was difficult to know if in embarrassment or anger.

Shane began to wish he had not started this, but it had seemed a good idea to retaliate. Swingle looked up when addressed. "You have got the right idea. Mix with the right people, but that is no good unless you are first class at your job. You don't try hard enough," Swingle replied with an ingratiating smile, which began on hearing the first words and had then frozen permanently. Bubbles stared back and had already made up his mind that he would not answer. He didn't like this man, but at the same time, he knew that he was going to go far, being so perceptive. Shane fought past the penetrating, knowing look.

"You isolate yourself too much," Shane said, allowing himself a second to crystallise the exact words he wanted.

"You defeat yourself every time by considering all aspects, even if they are not relevant. You know better than I can tell you, but think about it. Direct yourself in some positive direction, or you will always be a loser."

Shane's head was clearing, and he was starting to feel guilty about pressing his unwanted thoughts upon them. He would finish quickly and retreat before something happened.

"As for you, steward. It's a pity you don't direct yourself in any direction at all." Shane went as quickly as he had come. He had done what he had set out to do, but it didn't seem so funny anymore. He was glad to be leaving tomorrow. He thought about what he had just done and felt he had been right not to include Blinveld. He was a curious type. One who rejected his own background, and yet he was the only one close to the Wardroom mentality. He undoubtedly would have replied and would almost certainly have mentioned the word superiority. Shane lurched back to the Wardroom passageway. *Perhaps he had learnt something about himself as well,* he thought.

The Mess was shaken. Several started to get annoyed, but belatedly. Their reactions were not really fast enough to cope with this unexpected outburst, and they all, with one exception perhaps, had an awe of authority. Blinveld chuckled to himself until it eventually burst out in belly laughter. Steward was disgusted. He'd had enough and was going inboard to forget about it, late as it was.

"I wonder if he knows he picked on the wrong people," Bubbles announced his thoughts, but he was not really concerned.

"Right, cards out. Let's forget it." Spider searched through the table drawers for a reasonable pack of cards. One that wasn't like a deck of blankets.

Later, Randy Sandy struggled back down the depot ship ladder to be informed by the sentry of the first boat alongside that it was not yet time for Rudolph reindeers to be about. Apparently, the man's thoughts were centred on Christmas, as yet some six weeks away. Steward was not immediately aware of the innuendo, and glanced at his watch. One o'clock, later than he had thought. He changed his mind, deciding it was time for bed. He weaved his way across narrow gangplanks and then at the next one, made a sharp left and fumbled towards the hatch. He was really not bothered when he received no reply from the squat, unmoving figure, as he remarked how bleeding cold it was.

Steward only missed two of the vertical ladder steps this time and caught his finger. Not bad, considering that occasionally he had managed to miss the lot. *It was just as well*; he thought *that there was a thick piled mat at the bottom.* He was very weary now. It had been a long day for him, especially staying late to serve drinks for the impromptu Wardroom party. He had soon made his feelings known about that. *Sod them,* he thought, *sod them all.* Here, what was this? Steward straightened up after climbing through the circular hatch. Who was that spread-eagled on his bunk?

Shane lay face down, one arm and a leg flung out from the bottom bunk, as his extremities flopped out onto the floor. Sandy scratched his head, pondering. "Sleeping Beauty. Well, you ain't sleeping in my pit, me old fruit," Steward was mumbling again, bent and grasped an ankle and heaved.

The body violently slewed around until the other ankle was within reach. The prostrate Shane groaned in sleepy anguish. Randy Sandy had both ankles in a firm grip and tugged at the somnolent corpse. Sandy was manoeuvring for more room, but the passageway was narrow. With an almighty wallop, the body came out of the shallow bunk and landed with a thud on the floor, the nose taking its full impact.

"Nobody sleeping in my bleeding bunk." Steward dragged his load and somehow managed to turn in the passage, uncaring of its contortions. Sandy had to shuffle backwards, keeping a firm grasp on those ankles. The relaxed muscled, dragging body followed every hump and irregularity in the floor surface. Protruding bolts tried to restrict movement, but another masculine tug from steward released the tenuous hold. He managed to get around the corner, the body seeming like rubber, as Shane slept on in a stupor. One hand, unfeeling, trailed behind him. Steward fumbled unseeing for the Wardroom door latch. He found it and slid it back. The door sill made another hummock for the nose to grind over. In the centre of the carpeted floor, steward dropped the ankles.

"One of yours, I believe." Sandy gritted his teeth and slammed the door behind him. The figure lay still on the floor. All the brother officers shuffled in their sleep at the rude interruption. In the morning, Shane roused himself from the floor. He felt awful, as though he had been dragged through a hedge backwards. *They must have all drunk quite a lot last night,* he thought and shook his head to clear the mental cobwebs.

Final preparations were made during the day for going to sea on this morning. Last-minute sea checks were carried out by the Engineering and Electrical Department. All systems were being checked. Coxswain, who had worked until the early hours to make sure his stores were complete, now turned his thoughts to leave. It was time to compile leave lists for the Christmas period. Soon, he would need to begin the whole sequence of preparation of travel warrants for the respective leave parties. Coxswain knew there would be little time left for these things on the boat's return.

The engineer, a worried frown creased into his face, knocked hurriedly on the Captain's door, a clutch of papers held like some offending thing in his hand.

The door slid open. "Excuse me, sir. My department has a problem, and I'm very much afraid we will need to delay sailing." Jeff Hawks' face contorted to a grimace at the news. He remained silent and ushered the officer into his confined space.

"Twenty-four hours should do it, sir. The port shaft packing gland is leaking. We only discovered it on checks this morning. I propose to renew the complete assembly." The frown still held the engineer's face whilst giving his report. He noted, though, the relaxation of his commander's facial muscles.

"*C'est la vie*, Michael." Jeff Hawks permitted himself a wry, tight-lipped smile.

"Keep me posted on progress. You will want to trim down for'ard. That's okay." Commander Hawks did not need an answer. He knew very well, they both knew, that the boat's stern would need to be lifted in order to carry out the repair.

It was a simple matter to lose water from the aft tanks and pump it for'ard. "Send the Jimmy along, will you?"

The First Lieutenant's news was greeted with a cheer throughout the boat. They were all glad of this all too brief respite. As a concession, afternoon shore leave was given to non-duty watches. The duty watch, however, found themselves with extra work to do. A cocktail party was being arranged for the Wardroom. Invitations naturally went out to the squadron dignitaries, together with personal attempts to lure as many unattached and attractive girls to the occasion as possible. Consequently, with the expected numbers, the Control Room floor space would be needed.

Gaily coloured bunting would need to be draped to make it all appear less austere and functional. As always, if civilians were to be onboard, the boat's depth gauges were individually covered. Steward's day was filled with numerous trips onboard the depot ship and the two boats next door in an attempt to borrow as many glasses, decanters and other suitable accoutrements for the party. Sandy was successful in borrowing what he needed. He was quite looking forward to it himself. To him, it was a free booze up at the officers' expense. Naturally, he would be required to serve. The one blight on the affair, so far as he was concerned, was the need to collect, wash and return everything at the end. This would probably be around two o'clock in the morning.

Two volunteers were asked for among the crew to attend the officers' cocktail soiree as waiters. Nobody was interested. Lieutenant Graves, therefore, ordered the two most junior ratings to perform the duty. The new Torpedo Officer, Lieutenant Charles, made his debut at the party, smartly attired in suitable evening dress. He still retained a cabin on the depot ship and therefore had room enough to keep such things. As expected, the majority of girls did not come, but soon the boat swelled with the light chatter of officers and guests. A short and customary semi-official appearance was made by the Captain of Submarines.

"I was most impressed with the duty watch efficiency last night, Jeff." The starched shirt expanded to even larger than usual proportions as the senior officer complimented Lieutenant Hawks.

"I expected that on such a cold night, the sentries would neglect their duty." The senior officer accepted a cigar and continued.

"Like to keep my finger on the pulse, you know. Stepped out for a breath of air several times during the night. Glad to see your sentry the only one to stay at his post." The officer was beaming, in an expansive good mood.

"These two." he pointed vaguely in the direction of the two boats alongside. "Received my official reprimand this morning. Well done, Jeff. Good to see you run a taut ship."

Lieutenant Hawks accepted the compliment easily and without embarrassment. He kept his thoughts very much to himself. He glanced around the smiling, carefree faces in his Control Room, noted the animation and absence of worry among his officers. The general level of conversation was becoming liquid and banal. He personally would be glad to get to sea in the morning.

"Your soda water, sir." Jeff Hawks looked at the man who proffered the silver tray. It was a surprise to him that Blinveld, of all people, should be assisting the steward. It seemed so unlike him, so out of character for him to want this duty. He noted now that one of the young seamen waiters had vanished.

"Is it too boring up forward for you, Blinveld?" The Captain stared into the man's eyes, trying to read the thoughts which lurked there.

"Jolly good party, sir. Keeps one's mind off the impending trip. No use moping in the Mess decks." Blinveld spread his generous cheeks into a wide grin, which seemed to characterise him so well. He chuckled aloud, then turned to serve the ladies. The Navigator's wife thrust her empty glass out towards him as though it were a lance.

Steward bustled around the Control Room, ministering to the guests and removing quarter-full decanters for refilling. The for'ard Mess held an impromptu drink-in on the proceeds of the steward's generosity. The members took it in turn to keep watch by the passageway door to warn of unwelcome visitors.

*She is getting drunk,* thought Lieutenant Theo Brooks as he looked at his wife starting yet another of her risqué stories. He began to wish that he had not brought her and wondered yet again if perhaps he should not have gone back to her. After that last time, he had been quite adamant with himself about ending their marriage. Having retracted his intention, he supposed he would just have to accept the situation. She had never been like this before. What, he asked himself, had caused her personality to change so much in these past few years.? She was spilling her drink all over the floor and laughing in a girlish giggle which threatened to become uncontrollable.

"We do have a long journey. I hope you will excuse us." Theo grasped her elbow and steered her around the room, making polite farewells as they went. In the passageway, she was becoming angry, not having been ready to leave.

"Glasses away. Navvy's coming." The Mess hurriedly hid their contraband liquor and waited.

"Hey! Some dolly, the Navvy's got there." A few of the men had come to peer through the square of Perspex in the door.

"That's his wife. Lucky swine, eh?" To the for'ard Mess, it appeared that her good looks and sylph-like figure were attributes to please a man. The couple strolled along the narrow passageway to the accommodation hatch. The girl had no idea that they were not alone.

"Spineless b... pimp, you are. Get your hand off me, you c... I can manage myself," the voice became strident in anger.

"I was just beginning to enjoy my f... self. What sort of a b... man are you?" She was disappearing up the ladder. The Navigator was mortified by her offensive language. He knew perfectly well that every word had been heard in the for'ard Mess. He remained tight-lipped, but now he seethed with anger himself. The couple, not speaking, strolled away into the night.

Blinveld extricated himself from the stuffy atmosphere of the Control Room. He ignored requests for every refill with a wide grin and deprecating gesture of one hand, and bore a tray full of empty glasses away to the pantry. Slowly, he washed them in the shallow sink, waited until he was alone, and then walked briskly for'ard. It was quite unlikely that his presence would be missed now. So far as he was concerned, the business was concluded. His message of the delayed sailing would get through. Now it was time for sleep; he had a busy day tomorrow.

# Chapter 32

Repair complete, and despite the excesses of the night before, everyone was up early, ready for sea. Breakfast out of the way, the Casing party were up top, singling up berthing lines, removing the boat's crest and bell for stowage.

While they worked, the men talked about the radio news at breakfast. Naturally, they were most interested in the admiralty spy Vassall being sentenced. It was a different and intriguing world to the one they knew. The Scratcher told the men to put a sock in it and get work out of the way first.

Ginger Bates directed his men in any task which might reduce the time they would all need to stay in the biting cold wind. "Get those nameplates down. We might as well stow them." Ginger cupped his hands, blew frosty breath on them and rubbed them together.

"Who was this bloke 'Orestes', anyway?" one of the sailors was reading the nameplate while passing it down to his accomplice.

"Some Greek bod. Something to do with the Trojan War," the other replied, not really very interested in Greek culture at this freezing moment.

"Oh yeah! That was Achilles and his mob, weren't it?" The man was talking to take his mind off the feeling of chill, cold wind whipping through his clothes.

"Ask Bubbles when we get below. He's all about on that stuff. C'mon, let's get this kit down before me fingers drop off." The two hurried themselves to get the boat's nameplates safely stowed.

The Captain had appeared, climbing stiff legged down the depot ship ladder. "Fall in quick." Ginger was marshalling the men.

"Straight line. Properly at ease." Ginger watched their Commander approach and gave the order for the men to come to attention. His own icy fingers stuck momentarily to the metal of the bosun's pipe and made a mess of the second note as the Captain came aboard.

"Good morning." The Captain grimaced in a mock display of displeasure at the strangled note of welcome and disappeared into the tower.

The engines thundered into life as the last lines were slipped by bored working parties of the submarine next door and quickly hauled into *Orestes*.

"Well, this is the last trip this year. Five weeks and we will be on leave, smashing." One of the men at least was happy as he worked, discussing his leave plans with his mates.

"Dare say a lot of the crew will split up, get drafted next year." Their minds reached into the likely possibilities for the following year.

Submarine *Orestes* made one curving pass around the head of the loch to observe the customary salute to the depot ship and then ploughed her way down Rhu Narrows. The sun, a dull red orb, persistently tried to break through the haze. Some of its rays sparkled on the water, to be cast upward in broken reflected pinpoints of light. A white-hatted head bobbed up and down above the metal casing. The man was busy winding on the turns of wet, icily cold rope around the hull bollards.

The submarine slipped through the water, casting white spume backwards to merge with the expanding wake. "Land ho! Port beam," a muffled voice came up from where busy hands worked close to the hull. The promontory of land slipped by. The occurrence was swiftly passed down and noted in the helmsman's log, along with the time.

Ginger crawled along the hull and made his inspection, with one man accompanying him while the rest waited in the fin. "Casing secure. Permission for Casing party below," the reply came quickly to Ginger's request and the men filed below.

Navigator stood on the Bridge, taking his fixes and making calculations. For some reason, they were making faster time than he had imagined. *Of course,* he thought. *The sea was behind them, driving them ever northward, assisting the powering drive of engines.* A towel filled the gap between duffel coat and woollen bobbled hat. He pulled the woollen hat closer around his ears. The biting wind seemed to grip them, turning them into useless lumps attached to his head. Nothing in sight, he observed. No shipping and a low-lying haze had come to obscure all but the ocean line of land.

Night was drawing in. *They were on radar surveillance now, so there was no problem there,* he thought. The quiet and vastness of the sea seemed to distort time. He glanced at his watch. Soon the new Torpedo Officer would relieve him. He calculated that, with the tide running behind them, it would be another eight hours to The Minches and another day to the diving area. Theo Brooks worked out how many Bridge watches he would have to keep until the boat dived. Next would be the First Lieutenant, to relieve the Torpedo Officer. After him, would come the Electrical Officer. The engineer would not be keeping Bridge duties, and obviously not the Captain. In this weather, it would have to be two hours apiece. Navigator worked it out swiftly in his head. Three more watches, a total of six hours. It didn't seem too bad a prospect, but he hoped the weather would not deteriorate.

*Now,* he thought, *what was he to do about his personal life?* This time, he would have to know exactly what was important to him. When they got back, he would have some changes to make. He would have to be certain, though. No evading the issue this time.

Scouse Peters was informing all and sundry about the new girl in his life. It was really a case of him cheering himself up with thoughts of how he would like things to be. Nobody else listened. Scouse filled the air around him with extravagant thoughts of his next conquest. The air encircled his own head.

The crew were in a good mood. This would only be a short trip, as sneaky peekies went. Merely a few weeks dived, then up, out and return home. Just time enough to save a couple of paydays. A useful amount, that, for Christmas. They could occupy the time by making a few toys.

On this occasion, Ernie and Curly had no difficulty at all in getting rid of old wooden crates and fish boxes. As fast as they were emptied, they were whisked away by some keen 'rabbit' maker. It certainly made their job a bit easier. No one was really irritated by the noise. It was understood that time, whilst on the surface, had to be used to its best effect. Once dived, there would be no allowance for hammering or noisy activities. All the workshops were in use. Underneath the stokers' Mess, the workbench and lathe were in full use.

"What are you making, a battleship? You're making enough row." One of the card-playing men was mildly irritated at having his concentration disturbed.

A voice came up from the chief stoker's store, "I'm making candlesticks. I hope chiefy don't want this brass. Fred over here is making a garage for his kid's dinky cars." Under the Control Room, both workspaces were occupied by various artificers and other mechanically minded types, all making something for their own children or something special for a loved one. Jovial abuse was hurled freely down and up, all in pretended anger.

The fore-ends, as the largest working space, was just as full. Men perched anywhere they could find amongst the torpedoes. Bubbles considered what he would do. In the absence of anything better to occupy his time, he would make a new bell rope for the boat's bell.

"Can I have some of your cost and gun line, Ginger?" Ginger made sure no one was watching while he sorted out a bundle of the expensive nylon line to give to Bubbles.

"If anybody asks, it came from inboard," he said, winking, before covering up the precious coils in the bottom of his store.

Blinveld, not interested in such pastimes, reclined on his bunk. Already, he was into the second of the new batch of cowboy books he had brought. The briefcase bulged more than usual. No one took any notice. It was well known that the pinger had a penchant for cowboy books and that he devoured them. No surprise then that he always brought a vast quantity. Blinveld allowed his eyes to scan the pages, but the words were obscured by a vision of his real thoughts. He considered the impact to him of the latest radio bulletin. For once, he had experienced difficulty in hiding his true emotions in the midst of his enemies. It had jolted him severely to learn of the American Naval blockade of Cuba. Blinveld felt the first brief pangs of fear. He was totally isolated and surrounded by foreign values. He continued to emptily scan the pages, flicking them over mechanically in a well-rehearsed, timed sequence which appeared to the others quite rational.

Carefully, Blinveld considered the problem of laying his charges to gain maximum effect and yet give him a chance of escaping. The briefcase should not draw unwarranted attention while he carried it through the boat. People would assume he was going aft to swap books with the Stokers. His real problem lay in the timing. Tomorrow was the twentieth, the day he would be picked up by his comrades. He had a whole day to prepare, and yet he must leave it until the last possible moment. The risk of discovery would be immense. A cold bead of sweat stood alone on Blinveld's brow. He considered his failures during the current mission and the consequences of his failure. Now, there seemed no other way to atone for it, and he must destroy this vessel before it reached Russian waters. The bead of sweat rolled very slowly down into an eyebrow. It tickled him unbearably, but he did not move to wipe it away.

"SOS signal, sir. Norwegian freighter." Swingle handed the message to the Captain and waited by the door for an answer.

"Radio Silence. No transmission, understood?" The Captain dismissed Swingle and read the ship's position. It took him only a moment to decide and walk into the Control Room.

"Alter course to three two zero. Inform the officer of the watch." The Captain had made his announcement of intent over the broadcast. They were the nearest to the distressed vessel, he explained and would render emergency assistance until another vessel arrived.

"Radar, I want to know as soon as you have another ship on a diverging course."

*Orestes* raced at the most reasonably prudent speed for the sea conditions, onward towards the sinking vessel.

"Radio supervisor, I want all the relevant wave bands monitored to intercept broadcasts. I want to know the name and nationality of any ships coming to assistance. Ignore procedures. We will maintain silence." The petty officer went immediately to the radio room to give instructions. He decided to monitor the situation himself.

Routine was disrupted. Once more, the boarding party made ready, this time without weapons. Their shoulders were heavy with ropes and torches.

*Orestes* was within one hour of its destination. The Captain was informed of two other ships coming into the area.

"Icelandic patrol vessel, sir. I estimate two hours to rendezvous. The other is a Russian fishing vessel. They did not give their name and would not announce their speed." The radio information was transferred to paper. A small group clustered around the Captain at the chart table as he perused 'Jane's Fighting Ships'. A compendium of world merchant vessels already lay open.

"It could be one and a half hours, or it could be two. Without her name, we can't decide what engine power she has," the Captain was thinking aloud.

"We could leave them to the Icelanders, sir," the new Torpedo Officer voiced his thoughts.

"That would mean another hour for the freighter; it is too long." The Captain strode to the radio shack.

"Any damage report from the Norwegian?" He knew from the PO's expression that there had been no further transmission.

"Nothing, sir. They're off the air." The operator's hands controlled the tuning frequencies. Wiping across the wave bands. A crackling whistle emanated from the set, and a Russian voice broke through. The voice faded, and immediately, a message began to be tapped out.

"The Russian says one hour, sir." All faces looked at the Captain. He was paused in thought.

"Right, we are going down," he said and stepped into the Control Room. The broadcast switch went on, and the sound carried throughout the boat.

"The freighter has necessary assistance. We are resuming original course and are diving now. Repeat, we are diving. There will be no klaxon." The lookout came down and stood by the hatch, followed quickly by a ruddy-faced officer of the watch. Air escaped from main vents, as ballast tanks filled with Atlantic sea in uncustomary silence. *Orestes* slid beneath the waves.

The Captain's announcement brought fresh beads of concentration to Blinveld's face, and his pulse quickened. He knew now that he was in grave danger since he no longer had the time margin he had allowed himself. The rescue ship was up there somewhere waiting. Every hour he delayed now would carry the submarine further away and himself away from assistance, and yet he was forced to wait until night. He had to reduce the risk of discovery to a minimum. He decided to make the attempt at ten o'clock, in two hours; by then, the senior rates bathroom should be clear and he could lay the explosives undetected.

The cold air no longer gushed through small passageways, funnelling its way into every corner. The crew retained their warm pullovers. It would be some hours yet before the temperature was comfortable without them. It was a winter sea that pressed upon the hull. Those who could, resumed their previous occupations. Now, there could be no noise of hammering. The batteries fed their current to the motors, which purred the craft along its course. Men whittled away the hours until the next meal time. Those who had nothing to do watched in fascination the others who had.

"Look at him. The ancient mariner, himself." Spider, a grin across his face, nudged his remark to Bubbles, who sat weaving the fancy rope work. Many of them sat and watched the intricate steps of his progress, and the patience which made it grow. The days and nights were already becoming confused in their minds. It was only on hearing the broadcast that a majority realised how late in the day it was.

"The skipper is starting to snort early, isn't he?" It was a question that a few of the for'ard Mess had been turning over in their minds.

"Wants to keep the battery topped up, I expect," one of them usually provided an answer to this kind of speculation.

The book's pages closed together. Blinveld tucked it under his pillow, glanced at his watch, yawned and stretched his arms out slowly in mock tiredness to flex his arm muscles. Mentally, he was keyed up, eager to start this new and final phase of the preparation. In his mind, the mission which had brought him here was over. He wanted very much to conclude it and return to his spiritual home. Standing, stretching once more in an exaggerated show of sloth, he felt under the bunk and drew out a towel. Wrapping it loosely around the neck, he grasped the briefcase and tucked it under his arm. It was heavy, and yet the weight was reassuring to him. He doubted if anyone sitting in that for'ard Mess could have guessed that it contained anything but books. Anyone aware of his movement would believe he was on his way to wash up. His orders from Russia in the last signal said he must do anything possible to destroy the submarine if he could not deliver the secret information held under lock and key within. A rescue trawler was even now in attendance for him.

Without a word to any of them and without a response, he walked unchallenged out to the passageway. A cold blast of air channelled along the narrow walkway and assaulted his face. He forced himself to walk slowly in the expected indolent manner that this crew had come to know as his.

"Bleedin' Wardroom. Coffee at this time of night!" The steward bent over the passageway sink, his hands energetically scrubbing the brown stains from a cup, muttering his oaths to himself and the large, puffy figure which approached.

"Hard luck, old chap." Blinveld broadened his grin in a display of friendliness he did not feel.

"Got any J T Edsons in there? Read all me bleedin' books, and still five weeks to go." Randy Sandy eyed the bulging briefcase.

"You can borrow the one under my pillow, old chap. Must dash. Got to do some swaps back aft." Sandy was dismayed at the swiftness with which the broad back carried away its load. *Well, he would have one book to pass the time away,* he thought.

The Control Room was in red lighting and quiet but for the clack-click of the hydroplane controls. The sound punctuated the silence, soporific in its effect. The men wished the watch would end. Another half hour would see them through, and they could slide into cold terylene sleeping bags, warm them up in their own generated body heat, and drift into numbing sleep, forgetting for a little while the boredom of a watch.

Unnoticed, Blinveld lowered himself into the lower bathroom access and felt for the steel rungs with a heel. His large, stodgy frame could only just squeeze through the access aperture. He winced mentally as the briefcase caught the thick metal edge and jarred almost out of his hold. Four more steps and he was down. The massive fridge and freezer doors were at his back, the tiny bathroom with its three stainless steel bowls was right in front of him. Blinveld was very conscious of time whilst extracting the bundles. His fingers began to tremble in agitation. Setting the detonators and electric fuses required patience and firm, delicate handling. His brain was cool, calm and calculating as it always was, but his hands could not suppress the eagerness his nervous system triggered down to them.

Footsteps passed slowly overhead, clumping along the steel floor in clumsy rubber-soled boots. The unseen passer-by was in no hurry it seemed. For one hectic moment, Blinveld had thought the man would clamber down here. The danger was gone. The matt grey plastic explosive held his thumb marks all around its edge, binding its gluey consistency firmly to the thin steel bulkhead between the bathroom and the Engine Room. The bundles were taped firmly to the unseen plumbing of each wash basin, held with black masking tape so thoughtfully provided by HM naval stores onboard.

Ten minutes to go, and the watch would change. Blinveld paused to wipe the moisture-laden bushy eyebrows. His work was nearly done. He gathered the debris of his work and the much emptier case, crossed the narrow sill and bent to the secondary task. The telemeter oil accumulators were large and smooth-walled. It would present him with a slightly more difficult task of sabotage. Blinveld consulted his watch and considered that he had five more safe minutes to work in.

In the after Mess, Hogarth got ready to go on watch. He stood up and pushed the rag doll he was making into his bunk. He stretched himself upward and banged his head quite forcefully on an unseen overhead pipe. The pain throbbed through his head; he had forgotten the damn thing was there.

"No, I'm all right, I just need a minute." Somebody had grabbed Taff's arm, thinking he would fall.

"Sit down, Taff, give it a chance." Two of his Mess mates were trying to make him sit down. Taff glanced at his watch. He was a minute overdue.

"No, I'm all right." Big Garth left the Mess. There was no way of persuading him otherwise. The pain was receding in waves, but it wasn't that he was worried about. He had been short of breath lately, and his chest pained him if he took too large a lungful of air. He had put it off too long. He didn't like to, but he would need to see a medic when they got back. Trouble was, they always thought the patients were malingering, especially if a trip was due.

Hogarth took over the snorting watch, trying to ignore the pains, while the man he was relieving gave him his turnover report. For some reason, the bang on his head had made his sense of smell more sensitive. *The bilges need clearing out,* he thought. The smell of waste oil was very strong. "Take the weight for a minute, Taff. I forgot to visit the heads before coming on watch."

Garth nodded, and the chief went to attend to his call of nature. The air seemed very close, heated down here. He hadn't realised it was this warm. Hogarth reached his arms up, crossed, with the pullover coming over his head. *Something is wrong,* he thought. The floor seemed to be sloping away, and pressure was growing in his ears. In sudden realisation of impending doom, his arms tugged ferociously to clear the cloying wool from around his face. He now knew the boat had dipped below snorting depth. Air was being dragged into the engines at an alarming rate. Garth leapt to his feet and thrust both arms upward towards the great circular wheel above. Shut down the air intake. Stop the snort. Shut off the engines. Get some recovery time for the boat to regain lift to the surface. Motor power would take over control of the boat's functions, given time.

Time was the factor needed. Pain ripped across his chest and seemed to momentarily paralyse him, and the aching thud started to live again in his head. He felt like collapsing, but he couldn't. His fingers clutched desperately at the valve wheel. Somehow, he must find the energy to turn it. The fingers flexed around it, but he couldn't breathe. Each lungful of air was seared with a gripping pain. Some instinct told him, no matter what, he must shut down that wheel. The snort valve must be shut. A thin voice somewhere in his head said to leave it. He had a vague feeling, somehow, that he had done this before.

What was it he had done? He couldn't remember. The engines!

Suddenly, through the mists of aching, he remembered the engines. The note had changed. They were slowing. He must shut the engines down before they drained the air. Hogarth fell towards the engines. A bunched fist flung outward at the red button.

The clattering of pumping pistons died away. The noise of the other diesel engine was still there. Hogarth, in a lot of pain, knew he could never reach that engine stop button. Dimly, he was aware of the sound of running feet.

Somebody was trampling over him, but he couldn't feel it. The sounds around him were going, and his senses failing him. Somebody collapsed, sprawling across him. A peaked cap rolled across the floor and teetered on the edge of the deck plates before plummeting into the bilge. His sight was going. Everything was blurred. The breath wouldn't come. The submarine angle became steeper.

The boat slid ever downward. The planesman had collapsed. Lieutenant Graves was on his knees and looked around him with fading eyes. Bodies lurched everywhere. Maybe he could reach up. He tried to stand and, for an instant, managed to reach the alarm, but his legs were buckling.

"Stop Snorting! Stop Snorting!" Lieutenant Graves bellowed into the microphone and tripped the alarm before collapsing to his knees. The effort to draw breath was overcoming him. The blowing panel chief took three bounding paces along the passage and scrambled into the Engine Room in time to see Hogarth fall. His priority had to be that engine. In haste, he stumbled over the stoker and reached for the control.

"What the hell are you up to?" The chief completely forgot his urgent need at the sight of the crouching Blinveld, who turned, a baleful glare in his eyes. One glance at the stick of white rock in those pudgy hands was enough for the chief to throw the full blow of his shoulders along that man's outstretched hand. At the moment of impact, they both felt the overwhelming restriction of breathing and heard the slowing of the second engine.

The alarm screeched in vibrating tones through the boat. Staggering bodies were unclipping doors and allowing them to swing shut under their own weight as the boat inclined down. The sudden and inexplicable withdrawal of air immediately stunned everyone. They were all dazed and couldn't think straight. It was a fight to draw breath. Those who could still think knew that this was it.

Luck was with them. The second engine was shut down just in time before it could suck every vestige of air out of the boat. Slowly, men began to recover and, with hearts pounding, dragged themselves upright, struggling against the sudden seeming immense weight of their own bodies.

"Switch that damned alarm off." The Captain held onto the forward periscope stays, as yet not capable of the necessary movement. Instead, he concentrated his energies on thought. The alarm was duly switched off by a recovering planesman. Still, the boat tried to incline its way to the depths.

"Blow one, three, five, tanks." No sooner had the order been given and air from the tanks above had been allowed into the ballast tanks than the order to stop the flow was given. The boat rocked upward momentarily and settled on an even keel. The men, hardly yet recovered from lack of breath, were once more jolted inside the steel shell. It did, however, clear their minds wonderfully.

"Depth?" The Captain expected an immediate answer to his question and received it.

"Fifty-six feet, sir," the planesman had difficulty forcing the words out of his lips. The air was very thin.

"Open snort valve. Commence snorting." Jeff Hawks brushed an elbow across his perspiring face, pleased to have survived the last few minutes' ordeal. The engineer was at his elbow. The First Lieutenant was being whispered at by the Coxswain. Two men rushed through the Control Room with a Neil Robertson stretcher. Suddenly, there was much activity around him.

"Sir, LME Hogarth has collapsed while on Snorting Watch. I'm afraid right now I can't determine his condition." The Captain looked up at the concerned grey eyes of his engineer and saw the humanity, the obvious sorrow that was in them. "Get him into the fore-ends and tell the Coxswain to get onto resuscitation."

A somewhat bruised and dishevelled Blinveld was being forcibly dragged into the centre of the Control Room. The chief, who held his arm so tight, seemed incapable of speech, the face suffused with red.

"Spit it out, chief. What is wrong?" Jeff Hawks felt the tiredness fall away in the sudden presentation of a new foreboding of trouble. The Control Room had become very crowded. There were apparently twenty men, practically a third of the crew assembled in the confined space.

"Elat class trawler approaching astern. Bearing Red one-seventy. Range eight thousand," the voice behind the search periscope was muffled, the officer's head being still firmly married up to the search eye shield.

"Clear the Control Room of all off-watch personnel. Stand fast you chief and Blinveld. Everyone stop talking." The Captain snapped upright, pointed directly at the chief who held Blinveld's arm and took the two necessary steps to reach the search periscope. In response to the tap on his shoulder, the officer of the watch vacated the seat. The Captain's right hand inched the range control of the hand grip and took a sighting of the trawler.

"Damn!" Captain had not completely recovered his composure. Events had tumbled too quickly, one upon the other.

"Sir, I must inform you. This man was sabotaging the telemotor accumulators. I did manage to detach the timing device, but the explosives are still down there." The chief was breathless. Blinveld stood limp, still winded and very aware of the firm grip on his right wrist and elbow. His mind was alive and he knew that any sudden move on his part would surely lead to a very painfully broken arm.

"What! Explosives? Where?" The Captain catapulted off the periscope seat. Without waiting for an answer, he grabbed the intercom switch and pulled it down.

"Outside ERA; Torpedo Officer; Second Coxswain, Control Room, immediately." The Captain paused, torn between two decisions. He wanted to get down, to dive away from the following trawler, but the imminent danger was of prime importance.

"Emergency Stations. Second Coxswain to the wheel. Special sea dutymen close up." The Captain did not yet know the extent of the danger, but he could not afford to take any chances. The safety of his vessel was at stake and the lives of his crew. He must get his first team to their stations quickly. The Torpedo Officer was the first to arrive, followed by the Engine Room artificer.

"Coxswain, get this man out of the way, to the fore-ends, into the Second Coxswain's store and lock him in. I want him searched first. Manacled too.

The Captain turned his attention to the chief who had intercepted Blinveld. "Chief. You and the ERA, plus another senior man, get down there. Make a thorough search. The Torpedo Officer will coordinate." The men could see their Commander was in a brisk mood with a great deal on his mind.

"Trawler closing to six thousand yards, sir." The Navigator had taken over as officer of the watch.

"Very good. Let me know at four thousand yards." Jeff Hawks could not allow himself to be distracted by the trawler until the matter in hand was resolved.

"First Lieutenant," Jeff Hawks uttered the words and turned to find Lieutenant Graves in attendance.

"All officers off watch to take an inspection team through every compartment. Search for explosives. All officers except the TO." The Captain allowed himself a wry smile at the First Lieutenant's rigid and unnecessary salute.

"Navigator, consider yourself relieved from Officer of the Watch. I will take over. You search the torpedo compartment."

The radio supervisor appeared bearing a message pad. "Another SOS, sir. The Norwegian freighter has managed to rig up a temporary transmitter and is sending from a life raft." The Captain nodded, impatient now at this further intrusion upon his concentration.

"Read it, RS." Even as he spoke, Jeff Hawks was ranging the trawler three thousand yards, he noticed.

"*SS Alfotbreen* twenty thousand tons registered Oslo, sinking. Fifteen known survivors swimming. They end with their position, sir." The man consulted his notepad.

"They are approximately forty miles from us now, sir." The man waited for orders. "Very good RS. Maintain silence. Thank you."

The Captain was anxious for his officer's reports. He wished they would hurry. Another decision would be forced upon him soon. He was considering whether to surface, but until he knew for certain, he was loathe to risk dislodging any unwelcome packages in the rough seas above. All he could do for the moment was plane the submarine a little closer to the surface.

"Maintain fifty-two feet." The for'ard planesman flicked his right wrist upward in immediate response and opened his mouth to reply.

A searing flash brightened the Galley passageway, followed instantaneously by a thunderous rip of explosive energy. The resonant blast crumpled with tearing noises and the savage grinding of metal parting. The explosion rocked through the submarine, tremors of massive vibration channelling through every metal deck plate. A choking lance of grey-blue smoke thrust upward from the access hatch and spread into the Control Room. The two planesmen were jerked lifeless three feet into the air, landing like dolls back into their seats. The debris from the radio shack began to fall, stifling momentarily the cloying dust from below.

Every section of the submarine was isolated by the nearest man to it, shut off by heavy circular blast-proof doors. Control Room men gazed in bulging-eyed horror at the crashing torrential wall of seawater thrusting its way through the shattered Engine Room wall into the bathroom below, even now bulging upward, distorting the Control Room deck in a pressurised fury.

"My God, the hull has breached," an unrecognisable voice carried their terror into speech.

"Surface! Surface!" The Commander himself staggered to obey his own order. He knew that the panel operator would be dead; killed instantly. The gaping twisted deck attested to it. A wall of water carried all of them to the ceiling and kept them there.

"Hang on, mate, hang on," Spider mouthed encouragement from the floor of the for'ard Mess to someone already beginning to pray in an abandoned, unprotected attitude next to him on the floor. The throbbing deluge denuded them of coherent thought. They heard it pounding through from the Control Room, smashing itself and anything it carried in a furious attack on the senior rates accommodation space hatch.

Those lucky few in the three remaining for'ard sections knew instinctively that all those in the other three sections were already, or very soon would be, dead. Bubbles hauled himself upright. A terrible twinge of pain shot down his side. He had landed awkwardly in the first shock and got wedged between the table and locker.

"For God's sake, Spider, separate the batteries." They all realised now that very soon the lights would go, and worse yet if the accommodation batteries were not electrically separated from the Control Room bank, they could face the horror of short circuits and a fire in their battery control panel. The stern was lurching downward at an alarming angle. Everyone was falling into everyone else. They couldn't keep their feet, let alone reach the panel.

A gasping crackle of sparks arced out of the panel and escalated into vivid blue and orange flashes.

"Evacuate! Everyone into the fore-end," Bubbles bawled out at the scrabbling mass of arms and legs. He felt stabs of pain in his legs upon trying to move. He was also temporarily blinded by the now furiously burning flashes of molten copper. The Electric Control Cabinet door was buckling. A stretcher was shoved forcefully into the opening, grabbed by willing hands on the inside. Those that could, dived in there after it. Once the fore-ends door locked shut, the rest of the crew were likely finished. Maybe a few others could escape through the centre and rear hatches, but time was against them. The seawater flooded throughout the boat.

All of them, at some time or another, had wondered about this moment. Feeling at times that it was close, but it had never come. This time was different, they knew.

"God, don't let me die. I don't want to die." Scouse was on his knees sobbing. "Give me another chance." He was grovelling on the for'ard Mess floor.

"Go like a man, you bastard." The freckles on Spider's face were blanching. He wanted to shut that snivelling whine out of his thoughts.

A muffled explosion and gushing roar of rushing water sounded from somewhere nearby in the boat. "Get in here! Get in here, all of you. Quick! Move yourselves." Bubbles was ready to shut the fore-ends door. The pain of those bursting words took his breath away. It was a constant fight to draw another breath. One of the bottle groups had exploded. There was no knowing which one, but Bubbles knew, and so did the others, that their own personal Armageddon was coming.

"Get in here! I'm going to shut the door. For God's sake, come on. Move it! Our only chance is to flood and get out." The effort of shouting at them was draining his energy. Bubbles had to wrestle with his conscience. He desperately wanted to shut that steel slab and be safe, but he knew that if he survived, he would carry the memory of their stricken faces with him until the end of his days.

Scouse Peters was writhing on the floor. Spider Webb had fallen, his arms clutched at nothing as though willing himself to reach for the door. John lay still, stretched on his bunk. He did not move, and then Bubbles heard the words and saw the lips mouthing them, "Have mercy on their souls, whoever you are, if you are out there."

The door slammed shut and cut the sound of rushing water, of leaping flames. Hull glands were starting to give way, and torrents of sea began to leak past seals. Bulkheads were running with cascades of leaking water.

*This is it,* Bubbles thought. *This is the end, and after this minute, there will be nothing.* He would flood. There was nothing else to do. *He was lucky to have lasted so long,* he thought.

Only seven of them had made it to the fore-ends. The breathing masks had been broken out of the lockers. Blinveld was amongst them, helping to get the heavy aluminium deck plates onto their supports at loading beam level. The order to get him manacled below was somehow forgotten amidst this emergency. The Navigator stood by, not knowing what to do. This was beyond his experience. They didn't need any telling anyway; Bubbles could see that. The escape trunking was already dangling. It just needed to be secured. He wondered momentarily if he should try to contact the aft-ends to see if any of the stokers were still alive. The underwater telephone could still be working, but he knew really that there was no point. Neither could help the other. Each end had to make it on their own.

The boat was going down fast. Every second counted now. They would have to make their escape within minutes.

"Flood! Start the flood!" Bubbles himself was the nearest, but he had to give them warning. Smashing the glass, he took the wheel spanner and began to turn the valve. There could be no stopping now. Ready or not, they would have to go. The pressure on his ears was unbearable, but he had to bear it. There was no other way. The sea flooded in, compressed their valuable air, reaching upward, upward towards them. Soon, the escape hatch could be opened against the sea above them. The moment had come. In the next split second would come life or eternity. Now that it was here, there was no need to be afraid.

# Chapter 33

Shane took a long, searching look at his reflection in the mirror, aware of the new gauntness of cheekbones and the depth of his eye sockets. Certainly, there was a determined set to his jaw that had not been there only one year ago. It seemed impossible as he stood, taking note of the reflection of this stranger's countenance. A single year in a submarine had changed his life dramatically. He continued with his unpacking, wishing to settle quickly into a new routine, to become a useful part of the Attack School at once. The unexpected ordeal of the afternoon's interview with Admiral Thanet was still with him. Shane was in no doubt that the admiral would never forgive him for his daughter's accident. He it was who had arranged the transfer to submarines, had got him involved with Box Ten intelligence field work, and presumably had brought him here to the Attack School. Shane knew he was being manipulated by this bitter old man. *What did he want from him?* he asked himself.

The image stared back at him, and for the first time, a flicker of remorse settled there. Perhaps he should see the girl he had confined to a wheelchair. Perhaps he could atone in some way.

More immediately, he must attend the Glasgow meeting. Until this morning, he had thought he was finished with all that cloak-and-dagger stuff, but apparently he was not. In a grudging way Shane admired the drab, dishevelled Welshman. He had come to realise that his appearance was intentional. He was meant to be dismissed as inconsequential. Behind that facade, a keen brain operated efficiently and ruthlessly. In a strange way, there was an indefinable attraction in this work for Shane.

The Hotel Astoria was as dingy as he had remembered it. An insignificant, decaying facade in an unimposing back street. "We have good news for once," the lilting voice waived him nonchalantly to a dusty chair.

"The spy cell was operating from the bookshop you told me about. Good work, that." The stubbly chin cracked when opened to an unaccustomed grin.

"The sonar operator Blinveld is the one we want now. He will be arrested the moment your submarine surfaces in the North Sea." The Welshman tipped the inevitable bottle into the inevitable glass. "Not your submarine now, of course. Congratulations, Mr Green."

The glass continued to fill in an unhurried, familiar, reassuring gesture. Shane was shocked at the news but did not show it. His mind was working furiously, putting past events into a new perspective. It all made sense to him now. A surge of anger rose sharply in his throat at the thought of the supreme supercilious coolness of the man Blinveld. He checked his anger and admitted mentally that he had to admire even this, viewing in retrospect the enormous difficulties the agent had needed to contend with.

"We have a new arrival at Box Ten. You will meet him again tomorrow." The Welshman's cold, pale eyes stared out at him with just the merest suggestion of warmth within.

"The American Lieutenant Palmer has just returned from Moscow, and by just, I mean..." the shabby raincoat rustled as the wrist twisted and elbow lifted fractionally, creating yet another beer stain on the sleeve. "just ten minutes ago. He will be alighting at Glasgow airport now. We had the devil's own job to find an exchange for him. Fortunately, we had a KGB colonel, and they wanted him back rather desperately." The wristwatch dropped back into the pool of beer, splashing the stain further along the table.

Shane was intrigued. The events of the last mission flashed through his mind. He had been aware, of course, that Lt Palmer had been captured during the Zemlya raid, but that was all. Shane considered the implications of his own, hinted at, involvement. The only reason he could think of to explain his own presence at an interview would be to do with CV6. He noted now that the Welshman stared at him in a strange way.

"Congratulations again. The promotion list will not be published for another two weeks, of course, but I can assure you your name will be on it."

The Welshman rubbed a calloused forefinger conspiratorially along the side of his bulbous nose. "We don't think the torpedoman Brown is involved in the spy cell at all, but such a secretive type must be examined. He did break ship, after all. There is the address, Lieutenant Commander." Shane saw the grubby piece of paper and the final gesture of dismissal. The glass was being slowly drained, apparently savoured.

As usual, Shane had listened, and the contact had talked. It usually turned out to be a one-way flow of information. Shane was glad to be back out in the street. At least the air was fresh. He knew now without a doubt that his appointment to the Attack School was merely a cover. His promotion proved it. It wasn't even remotely conceivable for him to remain in the Submarine Service as a Lieutenant Commander with such limited experience. Therefore, he must be working now for Box Ten, but covertly. He looked at the address on the grubby piece of paper and thought about this new minor task required of him, to find out about Brown.

# Chapter 34

Jock Brown sat in his own small front room, watching yet another strip of garish wallpaper peel away from the sodden wall. His gaze wandered around the room, seeing the crazy-paving effect cracking in the ceiling plaster and the bare wires of the single pendant light. A dull thudding noise came against a partition wall not far away. McCreedy was banging his wife's head on the wall again. Down the dark paper-strewn corridor out on their landing, he could hear the anguished cackling of the old crone from two doors along the tenement. Somewhere in the building, a cracked record was churning round on its turntable, the chanting voices of negro singers hammering out a miserable yet mesmerising tune, one he recognised from somewhere long ago but couldn't name.

The bedraggled, tired-looking woman in carpet slippers, who was his wife, slouched in from the annexe, which was called a kitchen. She handed him a cracked cup with no handle. *Even the tea looked as though it couldn't care less,* he thought. "What am I going to do with you then?" Jock looked at her standing there. The look on her face told him that she expected him to get up and hit her.

"Why the hell do you want to stay here? Listen to that. Do you want to hear that for the rest of your life?" She wasn't answering him. Her eyes told him that she refused to think about it.

Jock put the cup down on the bare floorboards, grabbed her by the scruffy old housecoat and pulled her into the tattered armchair on top of him. She didn't resist but slumped into his lap as though nothing in the world mattered at all. Her foot accidentally caught the cup and scattered its contents into a sprawling pool.

"Leave it," he told her, preventing her from completing the struggle upwards.

"Serve them right. Always playing that same dammed record." Jock put his arm around her. He could feel the tears were close to spilling. He looked down, and the pool of tea had already disappeared through the cracks in the floor. Shouting came from the floor below, but the record still went round and round.

He looked at her. No make-up, and her hair was untidy. She never bothered to get properly dressed, content to slouch about the flat in a housecoat and slippers. All his life, he had seen women drifting about aimlessly like this, waiting for some man or other to come home drunk and batter them senseless for no other reason than boredom. It was a way of life here, in this district of slums. No possessions and no hope for the future. Brown was thoroughly sick of it. He had seen a different way of life, and that was what he wanted for himself and for her. The trouble was that she didn't seem to think there was any other way of life. She didn't have any interest in anything now. Not since the child had died. He looked at the battered old cot in the corner of the room, made up of old orange boxes. Tomorrow, he would burn it. *He couldn't blame her,* he thought. He had been away to sea and had left her alone to cope in the slums with a child who was always cold and sick. Every time he gave her money, she just spent it or gave it to her mother. Sometimes, people just came and took it away from her. After a while, he had just stopped giving her any.

Then he had gone away for the first torpedo trials, and some other man had taken over. That was what happened if he went away and left her alone for too long. She lay there in his lap, not moving, curled up against the warmth of his chest and arms. *This was the only warmth he had ever known,* Jock thought. It was the only reason he kept coming back. What else was there in his life? They had been brought up in the slums. What else did they know?

A child began to cry and then shriek from some faraway corner up those long, winding iron stairs. A patch of plaster detached itself from the ceiling and fell in a crumpled scattering mess on the floor. She jumped momentarily at the sound but didn't turn to look. She still lay there curled up, waiting for his mood to change. Jock wished that he hadn't hit her so much every time something had gone wrong. They had been brought up to it. Taught by example to think violence was a natural way of life. Everyone they had ever known in the slums, or had grown up with, thought it was the only way to get what they wanted. In growing up, they had seen that a woman, naturally defenceless, just turned to any man who came along. It was either that or be at the mercy of them all.

Jock sat there with his arms around her, wondering why it had taken him all these years to see things in this way. He had always shut his eyes to it before. Had just accepted that it was a natural way of life.

After the child died, he had come home from Rothesay and battered the man senseless. It was expected, the normal way to behave. He had nearly killed him, but why shouldn't he? That was what he had thought at the time. He had blacked her eye, too, and given her a few bruises to think about.

Jock moved his arm up her back and held his hand for a moment against her head, pressing it into his neck. Somehow, it was comforting. Even the room didn't seem so bad when they were like that. She tilted her head up, and for the first time in a long, long while, they actually looked at each other, trying to see what thoughts were there. Perhaps they should talk more and try to make some sense out of all this; Jock wasn't sure how to begin. He had never told her anything that mattered. She didn't even know that he had saved some money towards a deposit for a house.

"Do you want something to eat?" her voice sounded far away, so low down on his chest. Her mouth pressed against the shirt.

"No, I want to talk," Jock said it as though it were the most difficult thing in the world to say.

"We've got to get out of here. Got to go away. Start somewhere else." Jock didn't know if she would understand what he meant. He knew they could not hold on to each other, or ever have anything good, if they stayed in the slums all their lives.

A thumping noise and the sound of breaking wood came from somewhere down the corridor. For the eightieth time, the cracked record started again.

She had not answered him. She just lay pressed against his shirt. She was thinking about the child she had just lost. He never seemed to be here when she needed him. He had got home after the first one died and again when she had this recent miscarriage, but it was always afterwards and never before when he might have been able to do something. Jock didn't know how, but in some way he sensed what was in her mind.

"I'm not going back. I'll find somewhere for us to go and I'll stay with you." She didn't believe him; he would just leave her, the same as he had always done, when there was no food, no money, or they had been fighting. Jock had told her before that he couldn't run away from the Navy. It was all he knew. He was a sailor, he had said, and couldn't do anything else. How could he get a job here? There was no work. He was trying to get something better for them, he had said, but she had always had to stay here alone. The other men in the slums didn't leave their women alone. *Only when they went drinking, but the women were brought up to expect that,* she thought.

"We'll go where they can't find us." Jock was still trying to make her believe that he would not sacrifice any chance they might have of getting a decent life just so that she would not be alone. For the first time, he had seen how afraid she was of that one thing. She could not bear to be left alone. Now that he realised it, everything that had happened seemed to have a different meaning. He could understand why there had been a long succession of men while he, Jock, had been away. He would never hit her again, he decided. It would be difficult to curb the natural instinct to strike out and obliterate the sense of having been wronged, but he would try. He could see clearly now that it would have to be the first crucial step towards a new life together.

Lieutenant Phil Green shuddered mentally at the sight of the long row of tall, dilapidated buildings. He forced himself to walk even further down the maze of littered streets. Newspapers swirled in the breeze, floating from one derelict side of the street to another. Broken glass crunched underfoot, and he paused to consult the piece of paper in his hand before finding a way between the shattered house bricks and refuse. *This, then, is the cause of all Brown's misfortunes,* he thought, looking at the broken windows and rock-scarred doors.

He had never in his life been into a slum area, and he was absolutely appalled at the dreary sight and the feeling of foreboding it gave him. Shane walked down the centre of the road to give him at least some warning if there should be lurking figures in the dark alleyways between the blocks of mouldering bricks. No vehicles would be travelling into this useless and forgotten hole. Even the tough Glasgow police didn't dare to penetrate this godless place.

It would have been fatal for him to come in uniform. He had realised it was a rough area where even the slightest hint of someone bearing authority would have come to immediate, violent grief. Shane was alone in the street, and he was glad that the casual clothes helped to make him look innocuous. Sounds came out of the buildings as he approached. Music and raised voices mostly, and a lot of other indistinguishable noises. A number hung, almost rusted away, by a single bent screw. A careless hand on it would be enough to tear it from the brick. Shane put the piece of paper with its address away in his pocket and steeled himself to enter the dark alleyway.

A moment of alarm caused him to drop to a crouch in an effort to avoid the blow that didn't come. He had made the scattering metallic noise himself, unknowing as he stumbled against the dustbin. He could smell but not see its contents on the ground. *Perhaps it had been intentionally left there to give the inmates warning of a new arrival,* he thought. Shane pressed himself in the gloom against the wall. Time enough to retain his breath and listen for skulking footsteps. The cracked record from somewhere above continued to make its hideous scraping cough, the needle distorting the unpleasant note almost every second. No rushing feet came to investigate the commotion. Shane felt his way along the wall until he could grasp the iron banister and follow its twisting course upward. *The lights which should have shown him the way on each landing must have been smashed long ago,* he thought. He wished that he had brought a torch, but the idea had not occurred to him when he set out on this crazy mission to find Brown. This was where he lived. It explained a lot about the man's behaviour.

Shane was glad now that he had seen it. A side of life he had hardly known still existed. If nothing else, this experience would broaden his outlook and give him a wider framework of experience within which to make future decisions. It would provide a better understanding of a way of life quite foreign to him.

A thin ray of light was reaching down the stairs from one of the landings. Shane cautiously stepped into it and looked for numbers. Away to his left, the sound of a breaking bottle, or maybe some other glass object, came shatteringly close. Shane moved quickly away from it, up the landing. There was only one door with a number attached to it, and by extreme good luck, it was the right one. He tapped gently on the door and then louder with his knuckle.

"Who is it?" Brown's voice shouted. "If that's welfare services, you can bugger off!" Jock had told them several times, even went into the central office to tell them not to come up, pestering his wife. He didn't want their sanctimonious help. None of them had ever done any good. A lot of useless advice about looking after yourself: take stock of the situation; make a concerted effort. They were full of talk and had no understanding.

"What do you want?" Jock Brown shouted at the door.

"Brown, open the door. This is Lieutenant Green; I want to talk to you."

The familiar voice sounded through the rotten wood and its thin plywood panels. *The paint was a disgusting mess,* Shane thought.

"I am alone. No patrol and no police; I just want to talk and try to help."

Shane did not feel safe out here on the exposed landing. The peculiar thudding noise from down the corridor had stopped, and Shane expected a door to open in curiosity at any moment. The door in front of him opened, with Brown behind the opening. He was still in his working clothes. The number eight issue shirt was open down the front, Shane noticed. "I know this is your home, but can I come and talk?" Shane could see the hostility in Brown's face, but he did let him in.

The record was grinding away directly beneath their feet. Brown moved away from the door and went to sit on the arm of a very old, torn armchair which seemed to be covered in grease stains. Brown's wife said nothing as she drifted out of the room to what he supposed was the kitchen. Brown sat, waiting for him to begin, his arms folded belligerently across his chest. Jock noticed that the man tried not to look too disgusted by the shambles of this room. He admitted to himself that Shane had shown some nerve in coming out here. *For an officer, that was a remarkable achievement in itself,* he thought.

"Look, you need help, and I have come to see what I can do. No, let me finish." Shane could see that Brown was about to stand on his foolish pride and tell him to go away, but he wanted to forestall that.

"People try to help you, and you don't listen. You were given leave to come home instead of going to sea. OK, so you went back before." Shane held his hand up as a sign that Brown must listen.

"You came home on night leave, but you didn't go back this morning. It is not going to help you solve your problems. Look, I can sort this mess out with the regulating officer."

It was obvious to Shane that Brown was not going to ask him to sit down. He didn't know if that was an insult or not, but it didn't really matter, he decided. The man was in worse trouble than he had imagined. Shane took a long, careful look around the room, at the damp running down the walls and at the way the wallpaper hung in tatters on it.

"This is not the way you want to live." Shane shook his head to emphasise the fact that he was not trying to be superior but sympathetic. He was determined to help this man if he would let him. There was no doubt that he could not make it on his own.

"I can't go back. I'm not going to leave her alone." Brown jutted a thumb backwards to indicate the kitchen annexe.

"Bring her with you, then. I will see to it that you get somewhere decent to live immediately." Shane could see a patch of plaster about to fall and decided that he must not flinch when it did, if he was to hold this man's confidence.

"I'm not going into married quarters. She couldn't take all those sniggering wives. I'm not going to leave her there with that when I have to go away." Brown glared at Shane.

"I will arrange something else. I cannot promise to get you a house, but I will try and get you a loan to buy your own." Shane glared back. It seemed to be the normal method of communication with this type of man. It must have something to do with loss of face if he allowed his eyes to drop.

"Don't you think your wife ought to hear all this?" Shane held his gaze.

"I make the decisions for both of us when I'm here." Jock was thinking how she would not understand what he was saying in any case. She did not have much equipment to think with anyway, but that was none of anyone else's business. It had nothing to do with anyone else. He would have to protect her better than he had done so far.

His wife shambled in, carrying two cups of weak looking and not very appetising tea. Both of them had cracks, Shane noticed, and only one with a handle. He thought somehow it would be a mistake to say anything in the way of thanks as she put the cups down near him. She left the room again. Shane didn't look at her. Brown seemed in some very primitive way to be possessive, even jealous, when she was in the room. Shane thought that he would not stay for much longer. The atmosphere would only become aggressive, and authority was the last thing which would work here, in the man's own territory.

"Look, you come back with me, both of you. I will find somewhere for you to stay. Then I will do what I can to find you a home, but the first thing is that you must come back before the Shore Patrol comes here for you. I will smooth it all over as best I can. After that, I will get you compassionate leave until things are better."

Shane could see the first signs of Brown actually considering what he was suggesting. "I will give you time to talk it over. There is a pub on the corner by the main road. I will wait there for one hour. After that, you are on your own." It had looked for a moment as though Brown had been going to speak, but he didn't. At least he opened the door for him.

"One hour," Shane said and began to fumble his way down the stairs as the door shut behind him.

She came into the room, and they stood looking at each other, not quite knowing what to do. Jock turned the ancient television on. He didn't want to watch it, but he could no longer listen to that cracked record from below.

"Get your things together." Jock was looking at the faded picture, waiting for the lines to settle in the tube. She had not moved, so he looked up to see what she was doing. She stood, staring at him, with eyes wide with fright. She didn't know what was happening. Jock went over and put his arm around her.

"It's all right. We will be all right. Everything will work out, you'll see." *She would have to believe him this time,* Jock thought. Something was happening on the television screen. Jock turned the sound up. A newsreader was sitting there behind the desk, and someone had just passed a piece of paper to him, interrupting the flow of his words. Jock was curious to see what would happen.

"The news has just been released that a Royal Navy submarine has been lost at sea." The news announcer's face looked up and out of the screen, directly at Jock's face, and then continued to read. "A naval spokesman reports that submarine *Orestes* has sunk off the coast of Scotland whilst engaged on a Naval exercise. A marker buoy, released by *Orestes*, has been transmitting an SOS on a special frequency."

Jock was stunned by the news and missed some of the continuing words of the news report. He could not believe it, but he knew he must listen to the rest of the information. "…Was in British waters at the time. A Soviet trawler fishing for mackerel responded to the SOS and managed to arrive in time to pick up the survivors. The names of the survivors have not yet been released, but it is understood there are seven members of the crew rescued and at present are onboard the Russian trawler."

Jock sat down to digest this news. He found it difficult to believe that all those men he had known had died so suddenly. He wondered how this could happen. It was difficult for him to concentrate, but the announcer was still talking. "…Naval minesweeper will be bringing survivors into port sometime tomorrow. Relatives have not yet been informed."

Jock looked at the cool unhurried, unflustered face of the announcer on the screen. Was it possible, he wondered, for someone to remain as calm as that? Well, of course, he didn't know them. *Who cared, anyway?* he thought. Nobody knew what they were doing, or where, or why. So why should anyone care? He had to think about his own predicament now. Time was ticking by, and he had to get changed. He hadn't even thought about still being in his working clothes. Jock wondered if this decision he had made would give the two of them a fighting chance. She came into the room and smiled. It would be all right; he felt it would be all right.

Jock was just about to take the shirt off when another sudden shock announcement came.

"We have just received a report from Washington. President Kennedy and Governor Connelly have been shot in Dallas, Texas."

Without even thinking about what he was doing, he was not capable of thinking any more. The shirt came off, and he threw it on the chair. The smell of oil, submarine diesel oil, came up to his nostrils. The smell filled the room with its pungency and lingered.

# Chapter 35

The car drew up outside the forbidding rock walls of Box Ten. Shane stepped out, noting how bleak and imposing this fortress was and yet beautiful in its way. He had only been here twice before, but it had impressed him with the bustle and urgency of its marble corridors. This was the centre of a huge trailing web of worldwide intelligence gathering. It was certainly an impressive organisation. He noted how discreet the security arrangements were. He could well imagine that no one could get within five miles without having been screened by hidden cameras. It seemed like a well-ordered security arrangement.

The corridor was vast. Uniformed figures, mostly naval, filled the place in a beehive of concentration. Huge double doors confronted him, and beside them, his liaison officer beamed a welcome. He knew too well that access to the room would not have been permitted without this staff escort.

There were only ten occupants, casually arrayed in a loose semi-circle around a central table. Alone, but for the tape recorder, a very pale and much thinner Lieutenant Palmer sat rigidly behind that table. Any casual observer would have noted at once that the American was about to face an interrogation. It all looked loose and familiar enough, very low-level and informal. Lieutenant Green was not deceived. In this place, and at this time, there was no doubt that the highest of security interrogations was about to ensue. Shane was uncertain about his own role.

At the sight of him, Lieutenant Palmer brightened visibly. The haunted look slipped from his etched face mask for a brief moment of recognition. He felt less lonely. A familiar face was welcome. There was no doubt in Shane's mind that the American had been through a harrowing experience, one that would live with him for a long time. Involuntarily, the cigarette packet had come out of his reefer pocket. He paused, looked at Commander Ruskin, saw the almost imperceptible nod and understood. He took the two necessary steps to the table and proffered the packet. The American's hand was steady, and his fear was abating. He inhaled deeply. The first contact response between the two officers was duly noted.

"Tell us about your Moscow interrogation, Lieutenant," the Commander's voice was warm, sympathetic, and apparently casual. The American relaxed visibly, and the haggard look faded noticeably. He was eager to talk this time.

"There were several interrogations, sir. After about a week, I think, was the first one," the voice still sounded hollow and uncertain.

"You were kept isolated for a week. You spoke to no one?" The Commander made it clear by the inflexion that this was a question.

"My cell was small, not uncomfortable, but the walls and ceilings were at a disconcerting angle. Permanent angles, out of true. Yes, sir, they kept me isolated." The lieutenant checked himself. He had been going to say more, much more. He felt that he needed to talk. To talk and get it all out of his system. It was difficult for him to understand just at the moment why the uniforms were British instead of American. He had expected to be flown direct to Washington. That is what the Russians had told him yesterday morning. Yesterday morning. He couldn't yet believe that he had still been in Moscow only yesterday morning. He had to wrestle his mind away from this laboured subjective rambling.

The Commander was speaking, "Tell us in your own words what happened during your internment and each of your interrogations, Lieutenant. Take your time, but we particularly want to know about the people you spoke to." The room was in silence. Everyone waited and then there was a long pause. They waited patiently for the young man to collect his thoughts.

"Well, after three or four days, I guess, another American was put in a cell just two cells along from mine." A faint rustling noise interrupted the young speaker for an instant. Cloth scraped on leather as the restricted audience sat upright, taking note of the officer's words.

"He just talked to himself at first. A sort of mumbling, really, but I knew from that that he was American. As I said he was two cells down, but across the passageway and I caught glimpses of him from time to time." The lieutenant coughed and spluttered a little. The cigarette tasted strange, unfamiliar and it bit at his throat. His throat felt dry, but he continued.

"He was a young man, I guess twenty or so, but looked younger, with a crew cut, and had a very lean, weak sort of chin. Anyway, after a while, I just wanted to talk to someone, and I asked him who he was and if he was American."

The lieutenant paused and looked around at the British officers. He knew he had their interest, even if he was making a very protracted monologue.

"He told me he was a marine lieutenant by the name of Oswald. Well, we talked now and then, sometimes just for a few minutes and maybe the next day for an hour or more. I got the feeling towards the end of the week that he wasn't levelling with me. You know, he didn't seem like a US marine officer. I pegged him around marine private. I can't say how I figured that, but he was some really mixed-up kid. Anyway, he wanted me to keep talking to him, so I did, and I called him Lee like he wanted me to, but I really couldn't get a lot of sense out of him." The lieutenant felt a lot more at ease now. All of them noticed how much colour had come back into his face.

"He knew a hell of a lot about guns, though, rifles especially; I couldn't make out what he was doing there, and he couldn't tell me. Incoherent, you might say. Then I realised that he was a stooge, 'cos he let slip his wife was Russian."

The lieutenant's speech was becoming faster, more animated now. The commander decided to slow the young man down and bring him to the specific information they wanted.

"Just concentrate on the interrogations now, if you please, Lieutenant. Were they conducted by KGB or military tribunals?" The lieutenant halted in mid-stream. He was reminded suddenly of where he was and why. It checked his confidence momentarily. The faces before him suddenly seemed less friendly. The interrogation settled into a long session. It would, they realised, take a long time to extract all the information even though it was from a willing talker.

They needed specifically to know just what the Soviets had learned about their CV6 torpedo project. Box ten had pulled a lot of political influence to get this man here.

A week after debriefing Lt Palmer, a message came in to the effect that Whitehall had decided both commandos deployed on the Zemlya mission would be mentioned in despatches both American and British. Lt Palmer would receive a gallantry award from his own country. Sergeant Bolton was to be mentioned in military papers only, since no gallantry awards could be made public. Special service personnel needed to remain incognito.

# Chapter 36

The minesweeper slowed her engines and broached her long, narrow bow through the rising waves. The men on deck were feeling the biting cold wind despite their clinging polo-necked sweaters. The sea slopped in along the wooden decks, soaking bell-bottomed trousers and penetrating the thin fabric of canvas gym shoes. Sailors clenched their knuckles tight around boat hooks, eager to be gone from the upper deck but curious at the sight that confronted them. None of them had ever seen an Elat class Russian spy trawler up this close. She bobbed silently in the water only fifty or so yards ahead while the minesweeper nosed its way cautiously nearer.

A loud hailer crackled into life from their flimsy Bridge.

"Hello there. *HMS Skerrington* approaching. What is your name and destination?" There was no immediate response from the Russian trawler. There was no sign of her crew except for the Captain and helmsman on her Bridge. The minesweeper Captain had a clear view from his high vantage point, the advantage given by the low sweeping waist to the high bow of the trawler. The occupants of her Bridge were clearly visible. The square face of her Captain jutted out of the Bridge doorway, darted back inside and mouthed a stream of words into a voice pipe.

The two craft moved closer still, nudging the waves to a rippling swell between them. A heavy steel door cracked open in the trawler's waist and widened. A dark patch exhibited behind the door. The British sailors gaped at the black void and waited. A Russian seaman stepped over the sill, out of the darkness and looked at them. Uncertainty stood out from his face. A stream of Slavic words issued from the Bridge, and immediately, a line of bedraggled, ashen-faced men tumbled out onto the curving deck.

At the sight of the dull, monotonous grey superstructure of a British minesweeper, her ensign streaming large in the wind, the stragglers raised an exuberant, if ragged, spontaneous cheer. The survivors' spirits rose. They began to jump about and wave their arms frantically, although the boat was only yards away. The Russian sailor clapped them on the back and pushed past them. Another sailor came on deck, and a third. They were all smiling, nodding their heads in appreciation of the British survivors' outburst of relief. Lines were passed from the minesweeper to bring it alongside the trawler.

A Russian sailor kept chuckling and nodding at them, throwing one arm into the air in a jagged gesture of half salute. "You come home Russia with me. Yes?" The thick white teeth grinned out of its olive-tanned face, accompanied by nodding motions of his head. The sailor appreciated his own joke and jollied the survivors into accepting it as such.

A submarine stoker laughed and his shoulders began to heave. Deep laughter issued out from somewhere inside him. Bubbles began to laugh, too. The nodding trawler crewman's head and wide white teeth were comical. The Russians had a sense of humour, a realisation of this absurdity they all acted out. Even the Navigator began to laugh. Owen did not need the stretcher now. All six of them stood, colourless drab grey blankets huddled around their shoulders and shook out the coldness from their bones, forcing it out away from them in great shuddering sobs of relief and laughter.

The British sailors grabbed the submariners one by one, grasped their arms firmly and hauled them across the leaping gap between the two craft. The six men landed safely and were whisked away below decks to a tot of rum and ribald remarks from the minesweeper crew. Bubbles hesitated for a moment and watched the two wooden ambassadors of their respective nations drift slowly apart. He felt compelled to wave just once wearily. In his mind, he waved not at the ship but at the sailor, the grinning olive-skinned sailor with a sailor's sense of humour.

"Hello, trawler. What is your name and destination?" Bubbles looked up at the Bridge, at the fresh-faced lieutenant, loud hailer in hand. He saw from the keen expression that the lieutenant really did expect to get an answer. *It goes on,* Bubbles thought, *It goes on.* The ships drifted silently away. First, the trawler engines started pulling her away to the north; then, the minesweeper engines pulled them to the south. A low outline of Scottish coast was rising from the far sea. Bubbles turned and went below.

The Navigator was quizzing a seaman on the last few days of world events. The minesweeper sailor did not have all the news; they had been at sea for two days but gave the latest known. "Khrushchev is bargaining with Kennedy. Says he will withdraw Soviet missiles from Cuba if the US withdraws Air Force bases from Turkey. No dice, I reckon." The fresh-faced sailor gave Theo Brooks a quizzical look. He didn't understand this man, having just stepped out of his predicament, firstly wanting to know what was happening out in the wide world, which made no difference one way or the other to them.

"'Scuse me, you an officer?" The fresh-faced sailor had reached a conclusion.

"Yes, Lieutenant Brooks, Navigator of submarine *Orestes*." The Navigator suddenly felt out of place amongst the other, still blanket-covered figures and the young brash sailors in the sweeper fore-peak mess.

"Not any more, mate," a barely audible remark was flung from a far corner of a bunk. Nobody laughed, but there was one barely suppressed guffaw. The Navigator felt suddenly tired and alone. He didn't have a great deal to come home to either, he reflected.

"Scotland coming up, below. Come on, helicopter's waiting to take you all home to mummy." The head disappeared from the top of the hatchway. The survivors pulled the blankets closer around them, over borrowed thick, polo-necked seaman sweaters. The Navigator looked around at the other five and wondered just for a moment where Blinveld was. Then he remembered. Blinveld, of course, would have stayed on the trawler. He hadn't even given Blinveld a thought until now. At the bottom of the gangway, an officer waited to receive them. The six men stepped onto dry land. So much had happened since they had been on Terra firma last.

"Lieutenant Brooks?" the officer addressed them, waiting for a reply.

"Yes, I'm Lieutenant Brooks." The Navigator stepped forward. The officer drew him to one side. A car waited nearby, its engine purring softly, waiting.

"Your wife has been arrested, sir. She has been associating with a known Soviet espionage network. I'm afraid that I must ask you to accompany me to an interrogation interview." The man looked brisk and yet somehow sympathetic.

Theo Brooks looked him straight in the eye. He was relieved that it was all over. He had not known about Deborah's involvement in this, and yet it did not surprise him. It meant his career was finished, he realised that. Henceforth, he would be classified as a security risk. It pleased him. Now, without shame, he could go back to his estate, to his dogs, to the land he loved.

The five men climbed into the helicopter. The door slid past them seated itself tight against its rubber seal. The blades spun faster and faster, gently lifting them off the ground. Each was alone with his thoughts. They were going home. The ordeal was over, finished with and could be forgotten. Bubbles found himself wandering back into the recent past. The events leading up to the submarine's demise came flooding back at him. The rush of air over the helicopter blades became the rush of water. The faces hung there in agonised expression before him. He saw it all, every lingering detail. He would see it again and again. The nightmares would begin.

The helicopter banked over the airfield, and the ground tilted up to the window. Bubbles looked down and saw the girl, Alicia, The New Page bookshop manager. She waited out on the field; her dark hair flowed outward in the downdraft from the rotors. She was waving, smiling. Bubbles knew that he needed her help. The Navy, for him, was finished, a thing of the past. He would start again. There was no turning back. The blanket slipped from his shoulders, and the smell of his own half-wet clothes assaulted his nostrils.

An overpowering, cloying smell of diesel wafted upward.